big
NATE

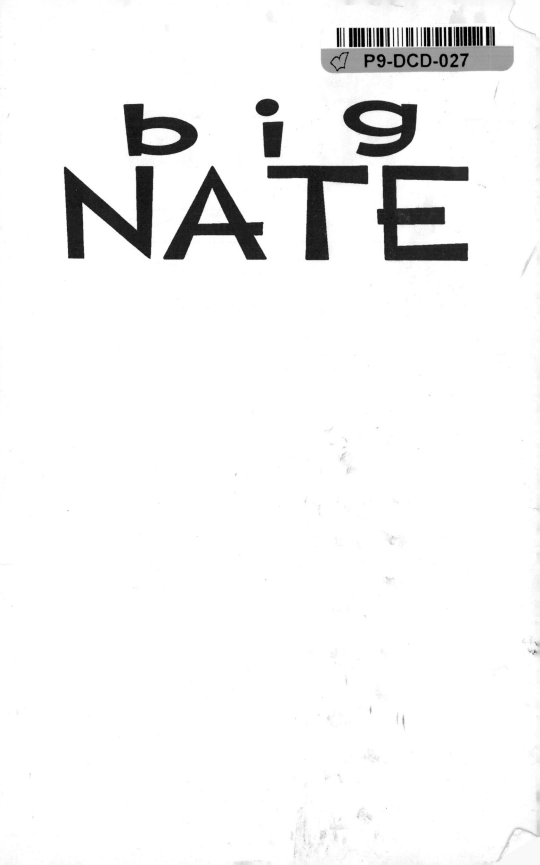

More

big NATE

adventures from

LINCOLN PEIRCE

Novels:

Big Nate: In a Class By Himself

Big Nate Strikes Again

Big Nate On a Roll

Big Nate Goes For Broke

Activity Books:

Big Nate Boredom Buster

Big Nate Fun Blaster

Comic Compilations:

Big Nate From the Top

Big Nate Out Loud

Big Nate and Friends

Big Nate: What Could Possibly Go Wrong?

Big Nate: Here Goes Nothing

Big Nate All Work and No Play

big NATE

MAKES THE GRADE

by LINCOLN PEIRCE

Andrews McMeel
Publishing, LLC

Kansas City • Sydney • London

Andrews McMeel Publishing, LLC
an Andrews McMeel Universal company
1130 Walnut Street, Kansas City, Missouri 64106

www.andrewsmcmeel.com

12 13 14 15 16 RR2 10 9 8 7 6 5 4 3 2 1

ISBN: 978-1-4494-2566-1

Library of Congress Control Number: 2012936748

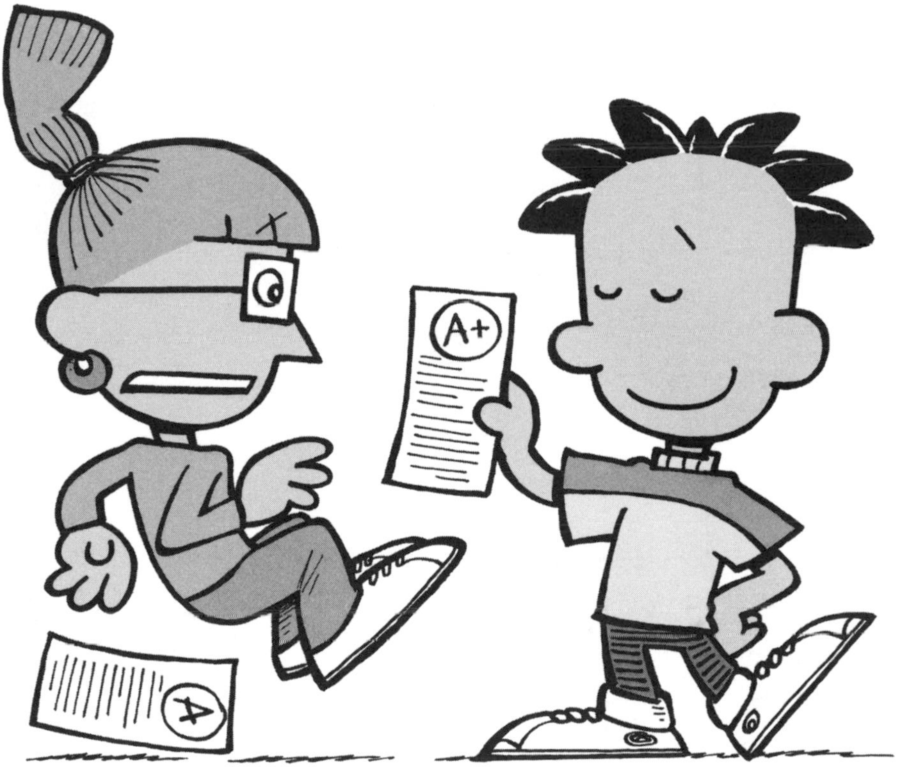
A+
A

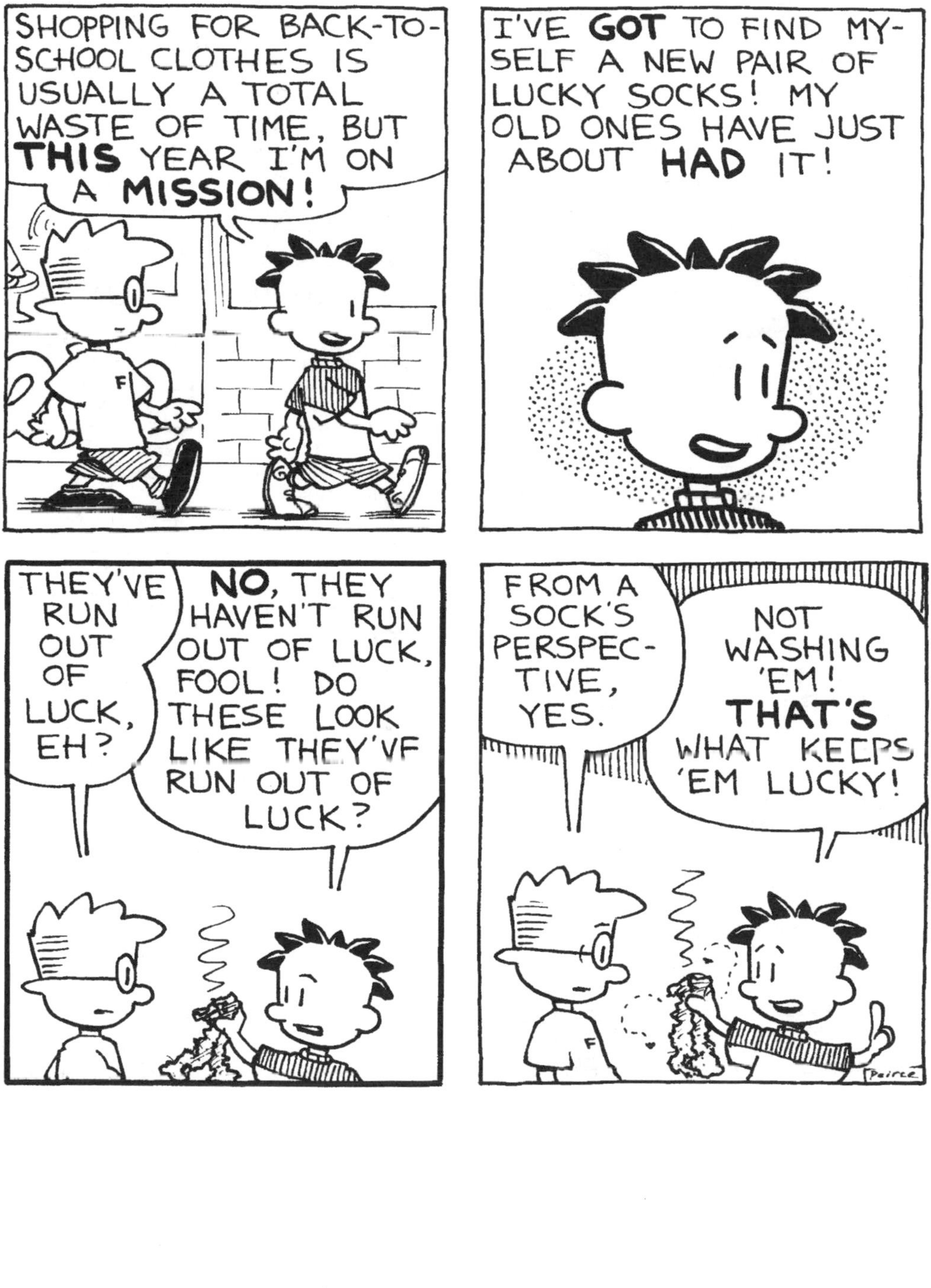
SHOPPING FOR BACK-TO-SCHOOL CLOTHES IS USUALLY A TOTAL WASTE OF TIME, BUT **THIS** YEAR I'M ON A **MISSION**!
I'VE **GOT** TO FIND MYSELF A NEW PAIR OF LUCKY SOCKS! MY OLD ONES HAVE JUST ABOUT **HAD** IT!
THEY'VE RUN OUT OF LUCK, EH?
NO, THEY HAVEN'T RUN OUT OF LUCK, FOOL! DO THESE LOOK LIKE THEY'VE RUN OUT OF LUCK?
FROM A SOCK'S PERSPECTIVE, YES.
NOT WASHING 'EM! **THAT'S** WHAT KEEPS 'EM LUCKY!
F
F
Peirce

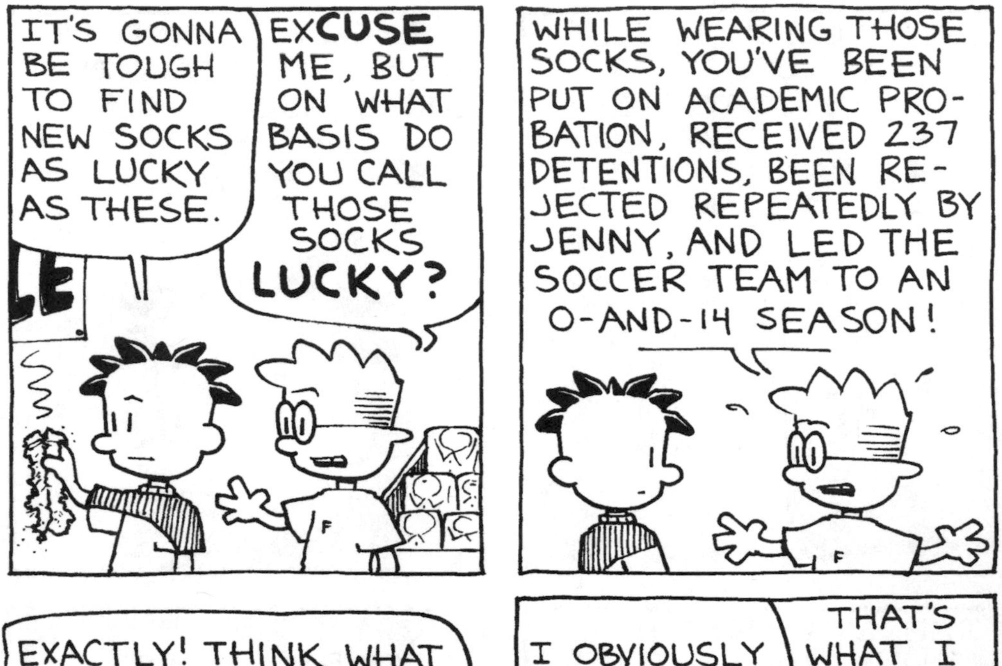
IT'S GONNA BE TOUGH TO FIND NEW SOCKS AS LUCKY AS THESE.
EXCUSE ME, BUT ON WHAT BASIS DO YOU CALL THOSE SOCKS LUCKY?
WHILE WEARING THOSE SOCKS, YOU'VE BEEN PUT ON ACADEMIC PROBATION, RECEIVED 237 DETENTIONS, BEEN REJECTED REPEATEDLY BY JENNY, AND LED THE SOCCER TEAM TO AN 0-AND-14 SEASON!
EXACTLY! THINK WHAT COULD'VE HAPPENED IF I HADN'T BEEN WEARING THESE!
I OBVIOUSLY KNOW NOTHING ABOUT LUCKY SOCKS.
THAT'S WHAT I WAS ABOUT TO SAY, BUT I FIGURED I'D SPARE YOUR FEELINGS.
Peirce

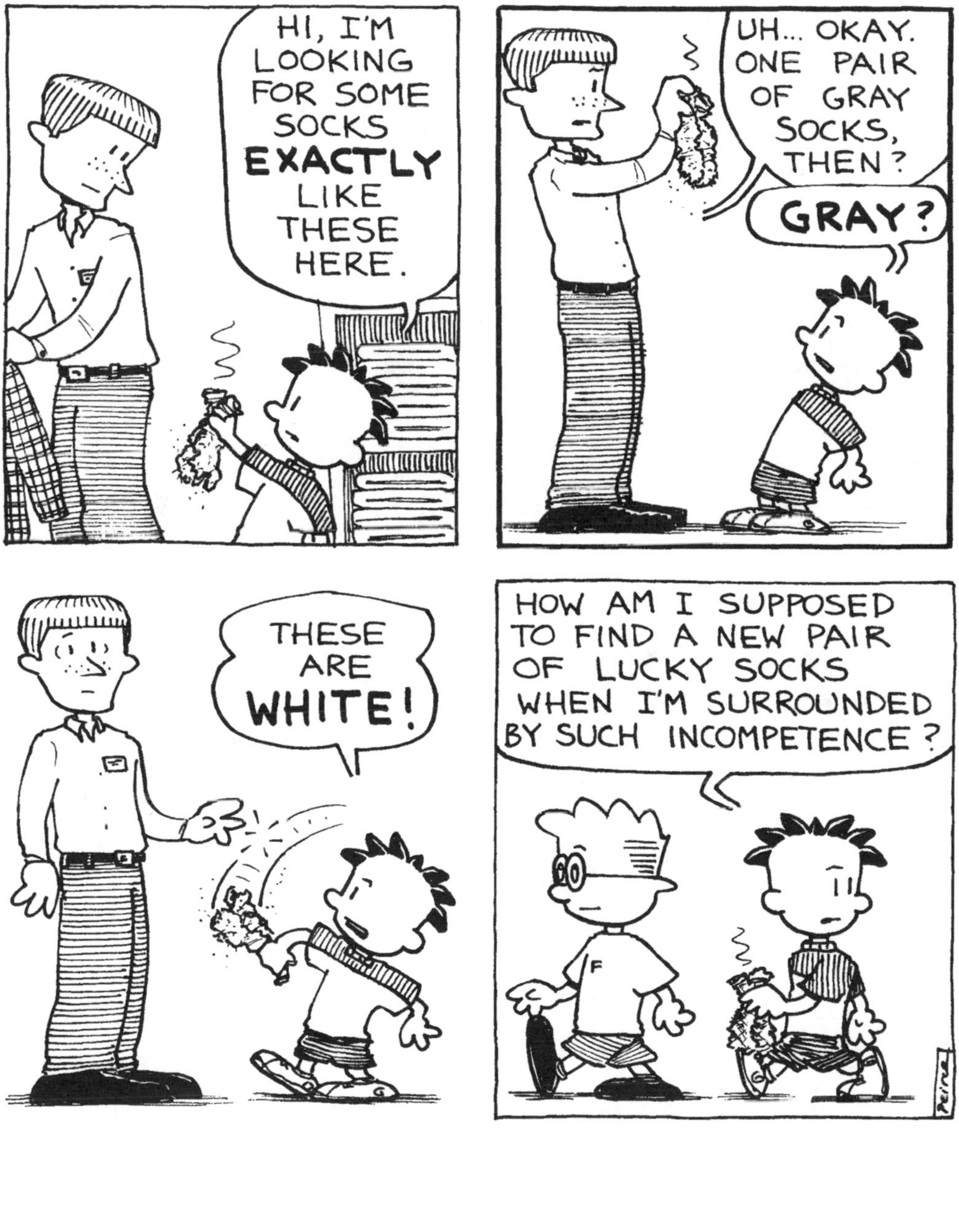
HI, I'M LOOKING FOR SOME SOCKS **EXACTLY** LIKE THESE HERE.
UH... OKAY. ONE PAIR OF GRAY SOCKS, THEN?
GRAY?
THESE ARE **WHITE!**
HOW AM I SUPPOSED TO FIND A NEW PAIR OF LUCKY SOCKS WHEN I'M SURROUNDED BY SUCH INCOMPETENCE?

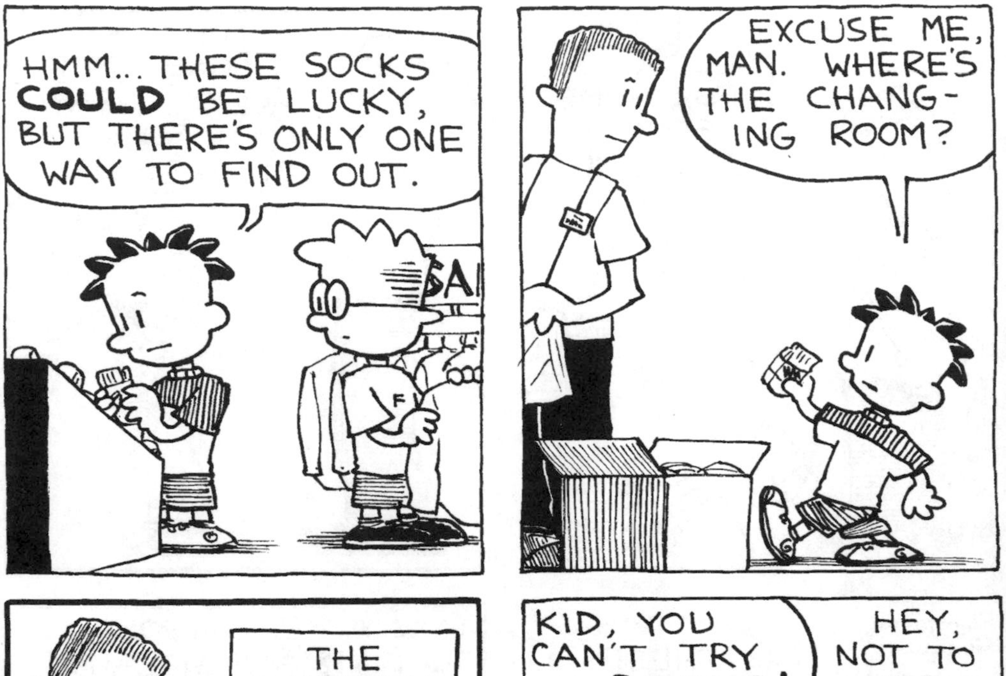
HMM... THESE SOCKS **COULD** BE LUCKY, BUT THERE'S ONLY ONE WAY TO FIND OUT.
EXCUSE ME, MAN. WHERE'S THE CHANGING ROOM?
THE CHANGING ROOM?
KID, YOU CAN'T TRY ON **SOCKS!**
HEY, NOT TO WORRY. THE ATHLETE'S FOOT HAS CLEARED UP COMPLETELY.
PEIRCE

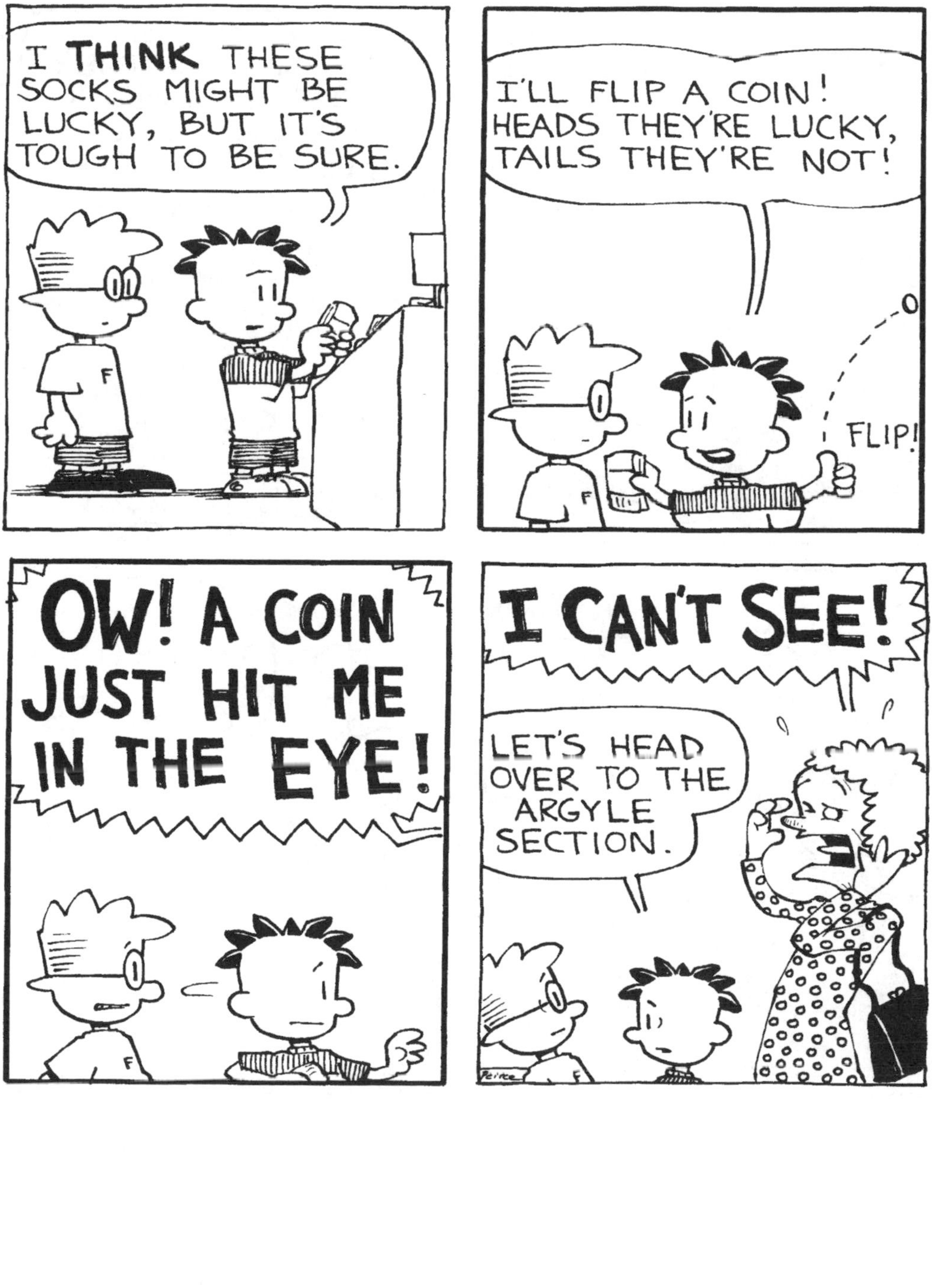
I THINK THESE SOCKS MIGHT BE LUCKY, BUT IT'S TOUGH TO BE SURE.
I'LL FLIP A COIN! HEADS THEY'RE LUCKY, TAILS THEY'RE NOT!
FLIP!
OW! A COIN JUST HIT ME IN THE EYE!
I CAN'T SEE!
LET'S HEAD OVER TO THE ARGYLE SECTION.

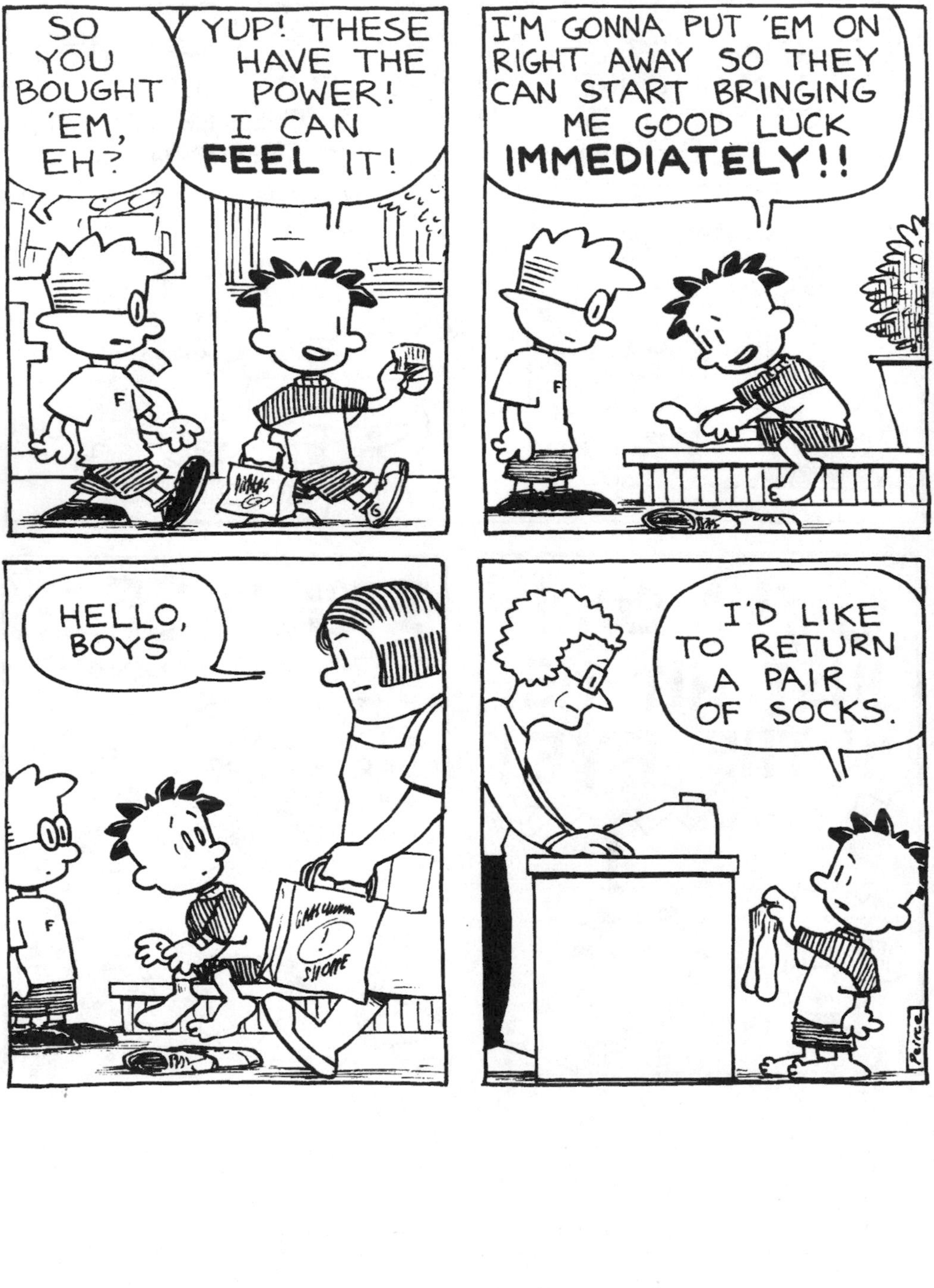
SO YOU BOUGHT 'EM, EH?
YUP! THESE HAVE THE POWER! I CAN FEEL IT!
I'M GONNA PUT 'EM ON RIGHT AWAY SO THEY CAN START BRINGING ME GOOD LUCK IMMEDIATELY!!
HELLO, BOYS
I'D LIKE TO RETURN A PAIR OF SOCKS.
Peirce

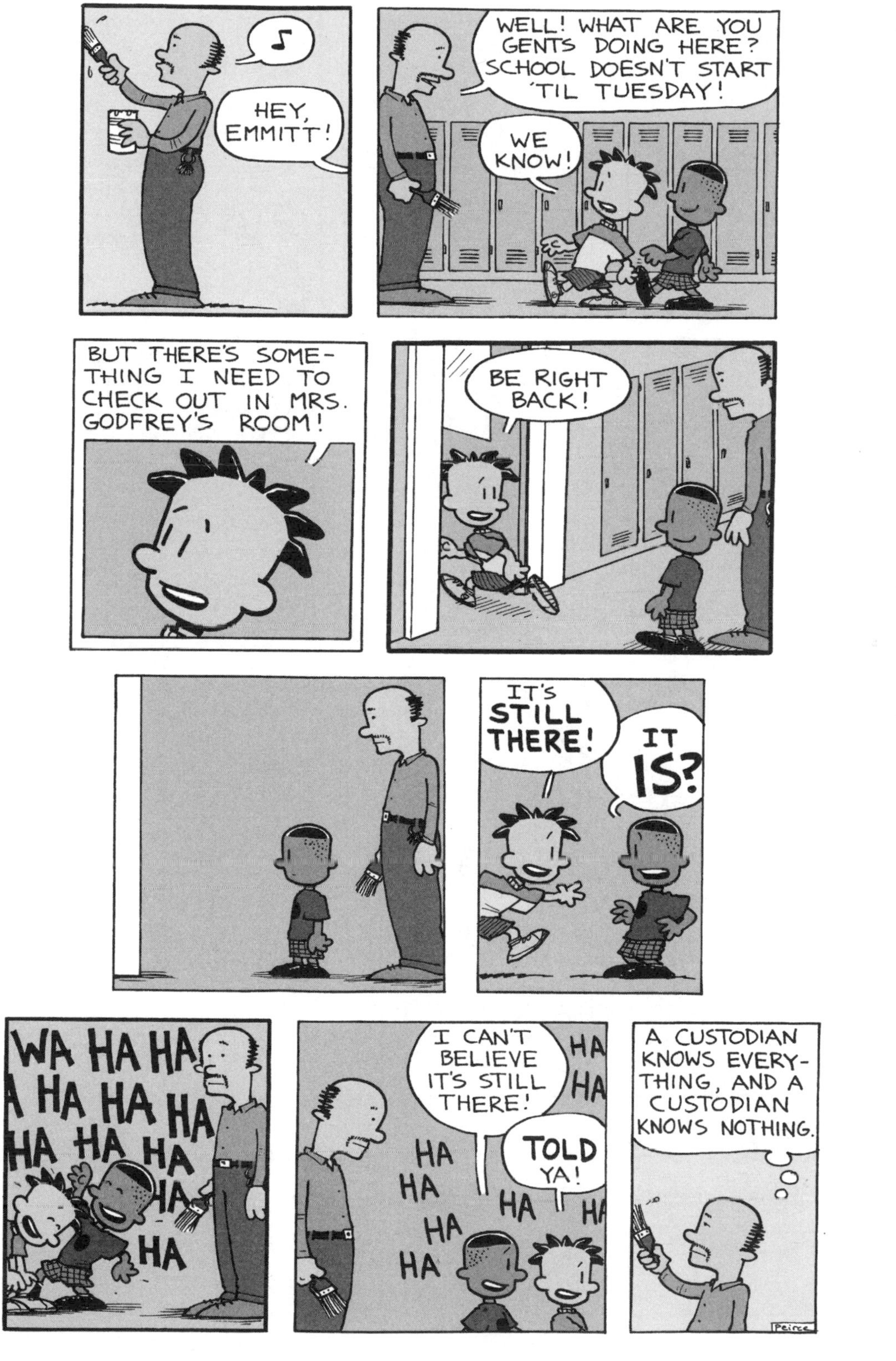
♪
HEY, EMMITT!
WELL! WHAT ARE YOU GENTS DOING HERE? SCHOOL DOESN'T START 'TIL TUESDAY!
WE KNOW!
BUT THERE'S SOMETHING I NEED TO CHECK OUT IN MRS. GODFREY'S ROOM!
BE RIGHT BACK!
IT'S STILL THERE!
IT IS?
WA HA HA HA HA HA HA HA HA HA HA HA HA
I CAN'T BELIEVE IT'S STILL THERE!
HA HA
TOLD YA!
HA HA HA HA HA HA
A CUSTODIAN KNOWS EVERYTHING, AND A CUSTODIAN KNOWS NOTHING.
Peirce

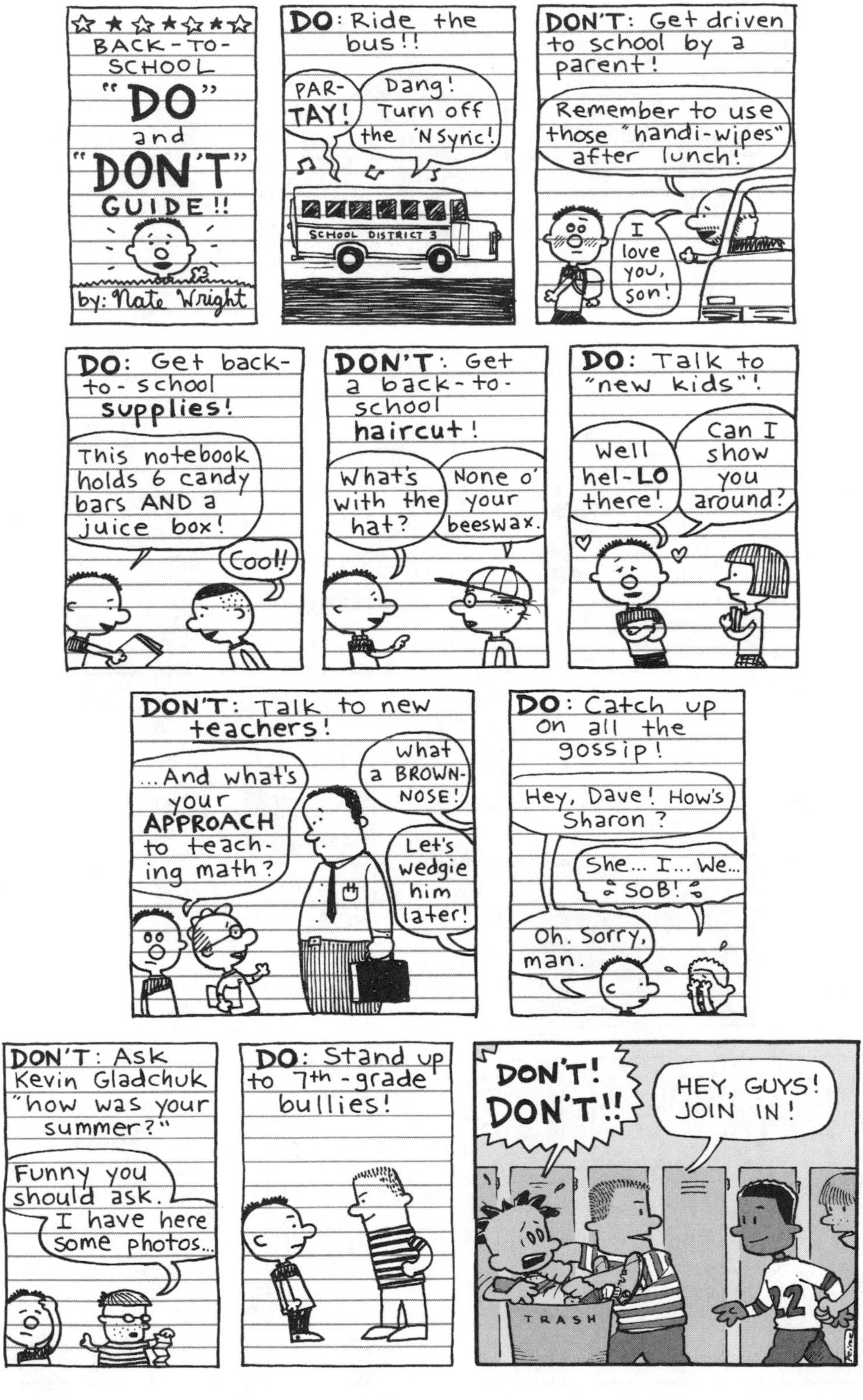
BACK-TO-SCHOOL "DO" and "DON'T" GUIDE!!
by: Nate Wright
DO: Ride the bus!!
PAR-TAY!
Dang! Turn off the 'N Sync!
SCHOOL DISTRICT 3
DON'T: Get driven to school by a parent!
Remember to use those "handi-wipes" after lunch!
I love you, son!
DO: Get back-to-school supplies!
This notebook holds 6 candy bars AND a juice box!
Cool!
DON'T: Get a back-to-school haircut!
What's with the hat?
None o' your beeswax.
DO: Talk to "new kids"!
Well hel-LO there!
Can I show you around?
DON'T: Talk to new teachers!
...And what's your APPROACH to teaching math?
What a BROWN-NOSE!
Let's wedgie him later!
DO: Catch up on all the gossip!
Hey, Dave! How's Sharon?
She... I... We... SOB!
Oh. Sorry, man.
DON'T: Ask Kevin Gladchuk "how was your summer?"
Funny you should ask.
I have here some photos...
DO: Stand up to 7th-grade bullies!
DON'T! DON'T!!
HEY, GUYS! JOIN IN!
TRASH

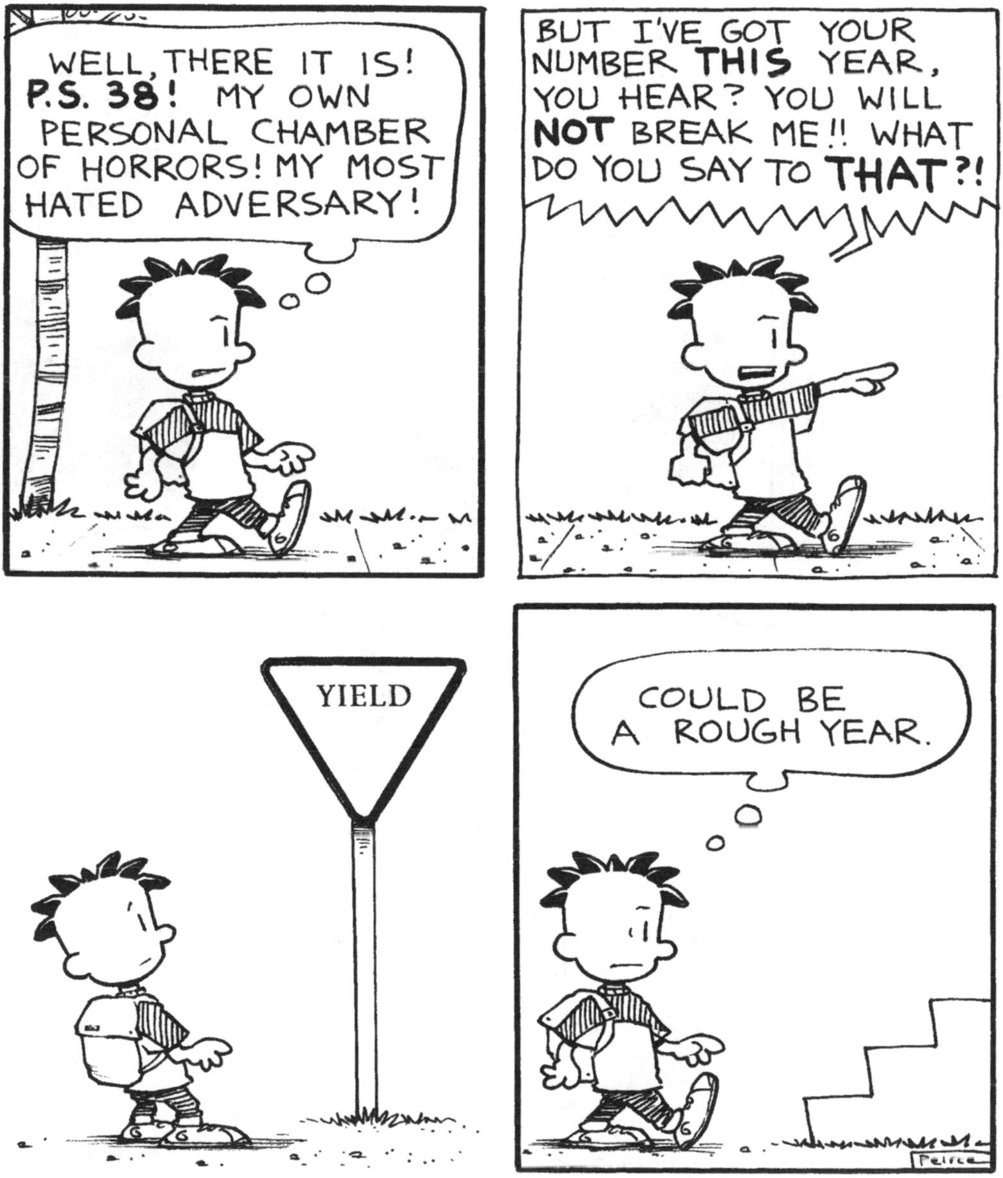
WELL, THERE IT IS! P.S. 38! MY OWN PERSONAL CHAMBER OF HORRORS! MY MOST HATED ADVERSARY!
BUT I'VE GOT YOUR NUMBER THIS YEAR, YOU HEAR? YOU WILL NOT BREAK ME!! WHAT DO YOU SAY TO THAT?!
YIELD
COULD BE A ROUGH YEAR.
Peirce

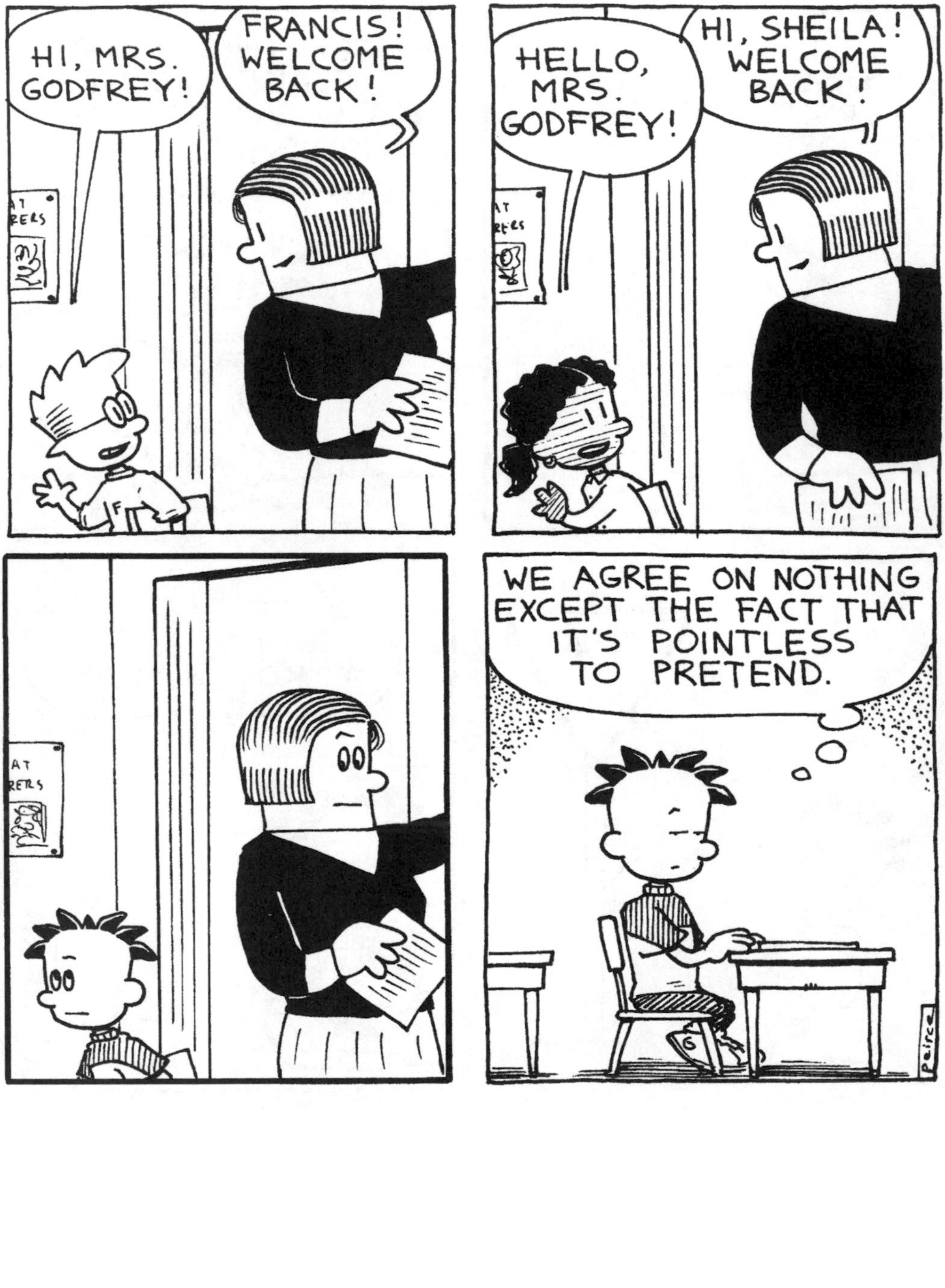
HI, MRS. GODFREY!
FRANCIS! WELCOME BACK!
HELLO, MRS. GODFREY!
HI, SHEILA! WELCOME BACK!
WE AGREE ON NOTHING EXCEPT THE FACT THAT IT'S POINTLESS TO PRETEND.
Peirce

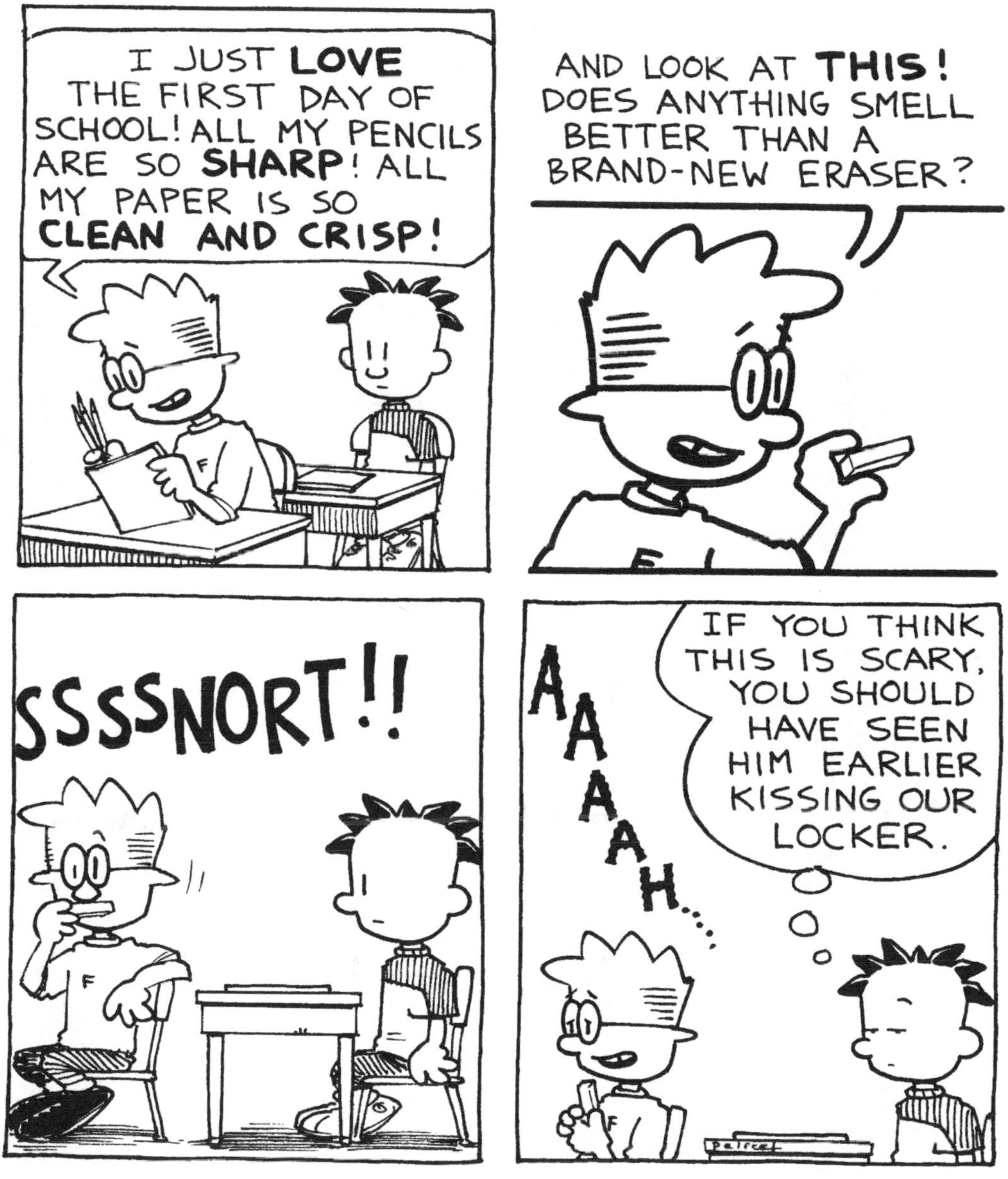
I JUST **LOVE** THE FIRST DAY OF SCHOOL! ALL MY PENCILS ARE SO **SHARP**! ALL MY PAPER IS SO **CLEAN AND CRISP**!
AND LOOK AT **THIS**! DOES ANYTHING SMELL BETTER THAN A BRAND-NEW ERASER?
SSSSNORT!!
AAAAH....
IF YOU THINK THIS IS SCARY, YOU SHOULD HAVE SEEN HIM EARLIER KISSING OUR LOCKER.

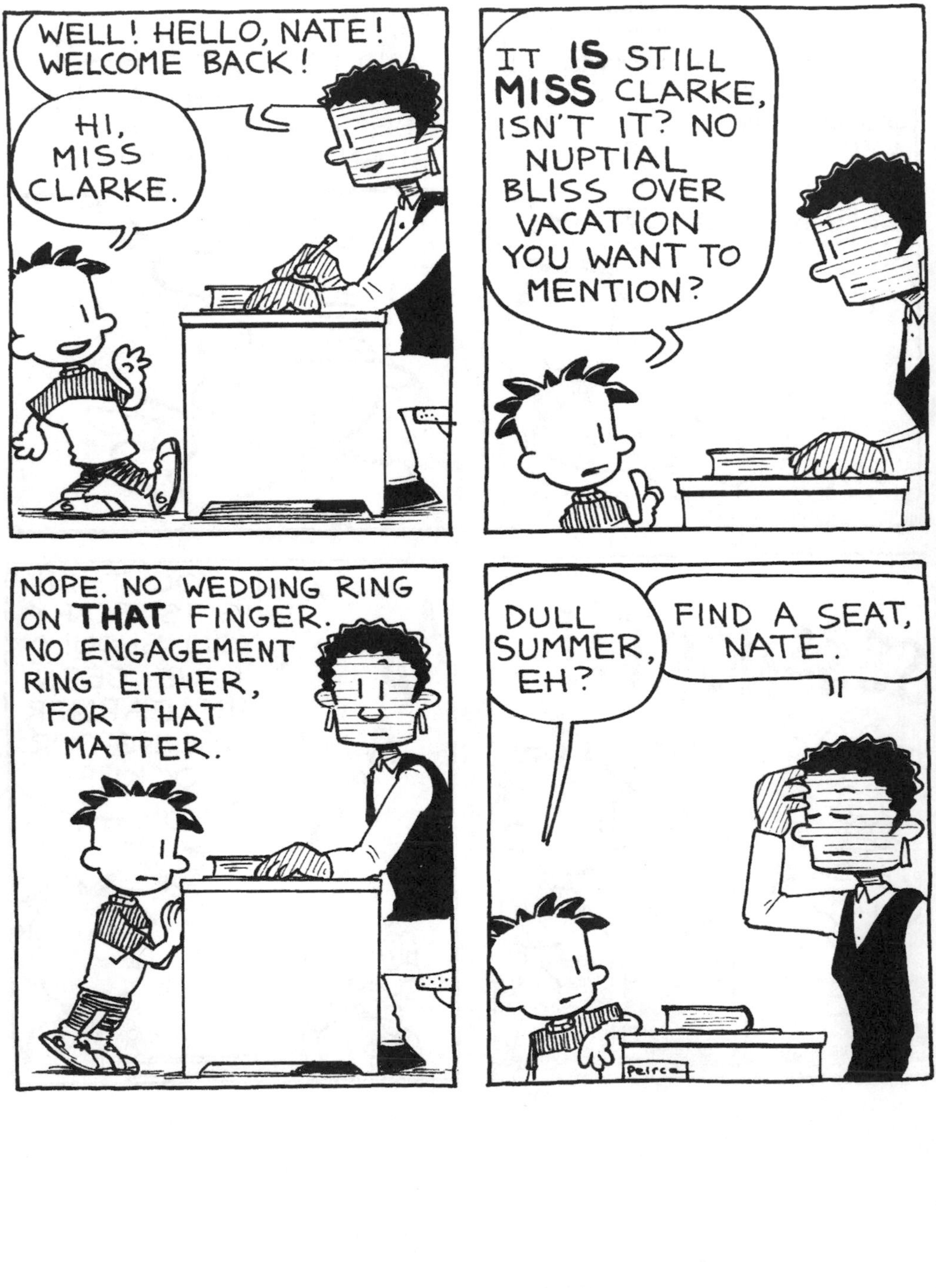
WELL! HELLO, NATE! WELCOME BACK!
HI, MISS CLARKE.
IT **IS** STILL **MISS** CLARKE, ISN'T IT? NO NUPTIAL BLISS OVER VACATION YOU WANT TO MENTION?
NOPE. NO WEDDING RING ON **THAT** FINGER. NO ENGAGEMENT RING EITHER, FOR THAT MATTER.
DULL SUMMER, EH?
FIND A SEAT, NATE.
Peirce

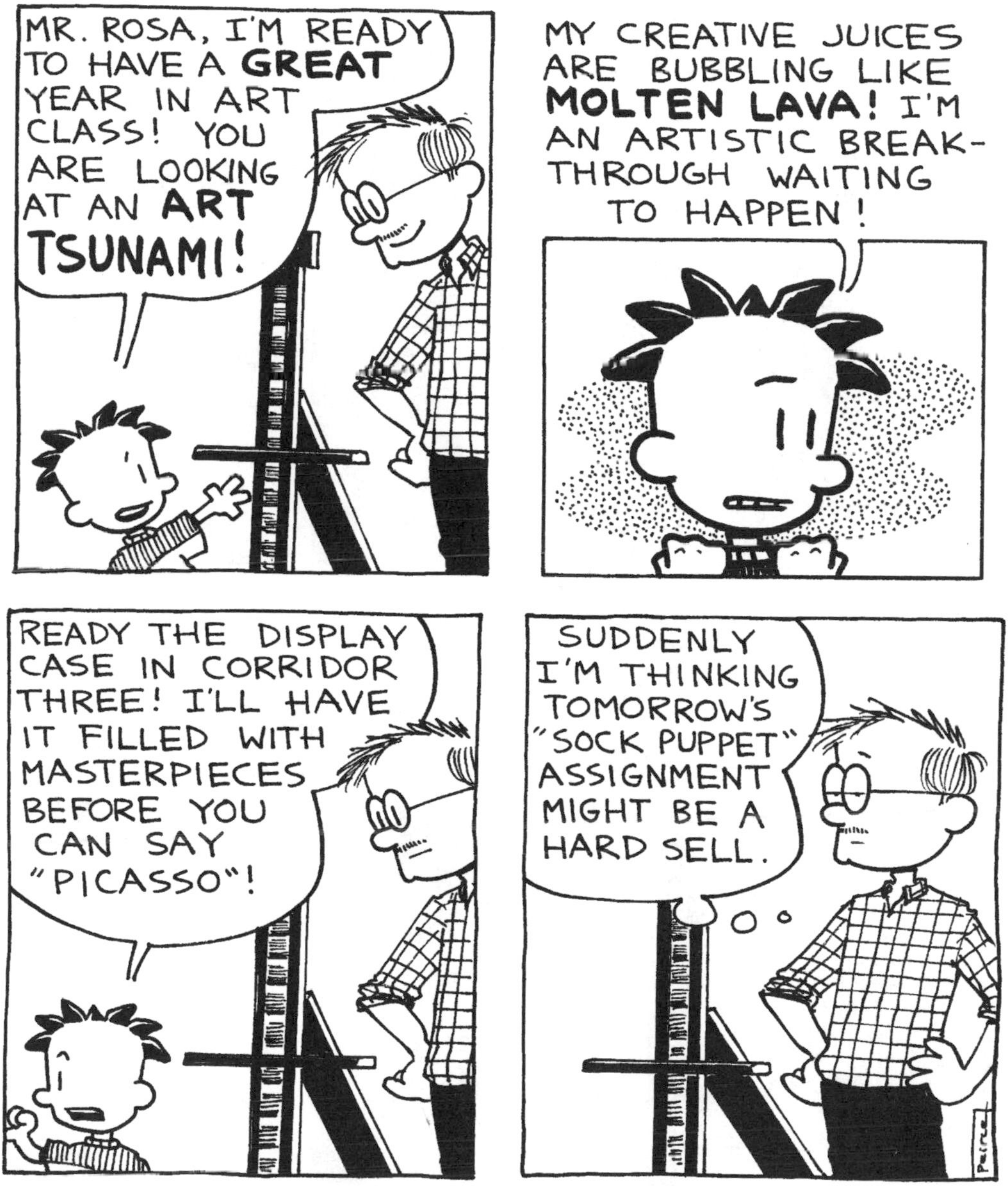
MR. ROSA, I'M READY TO HAVE A **GREAT** YEAR IN ART CLASS! YOU ARE LOOKING AT AN **ART TSUNAMI**!
MY CREATIVE JUICES ARE BUBBLING LIKE **MOLTEN LAVA**! I'M AN ARTISTIC BREAK-THROUGH WAITING TO HAPPEN!
READY THE DISPLAY CASE IN CORRIDOR THREE! I'LL HAVE IT FILLED WITH MASTERPIECES BEFORE YOU CAN SAY "PICASSO"!
SUDDENLY I'M THINKING TOMORROW'S "SOCK PUPPET" ASSIGNMENT MIGHT BE A HARD SELL.
PEIRCE

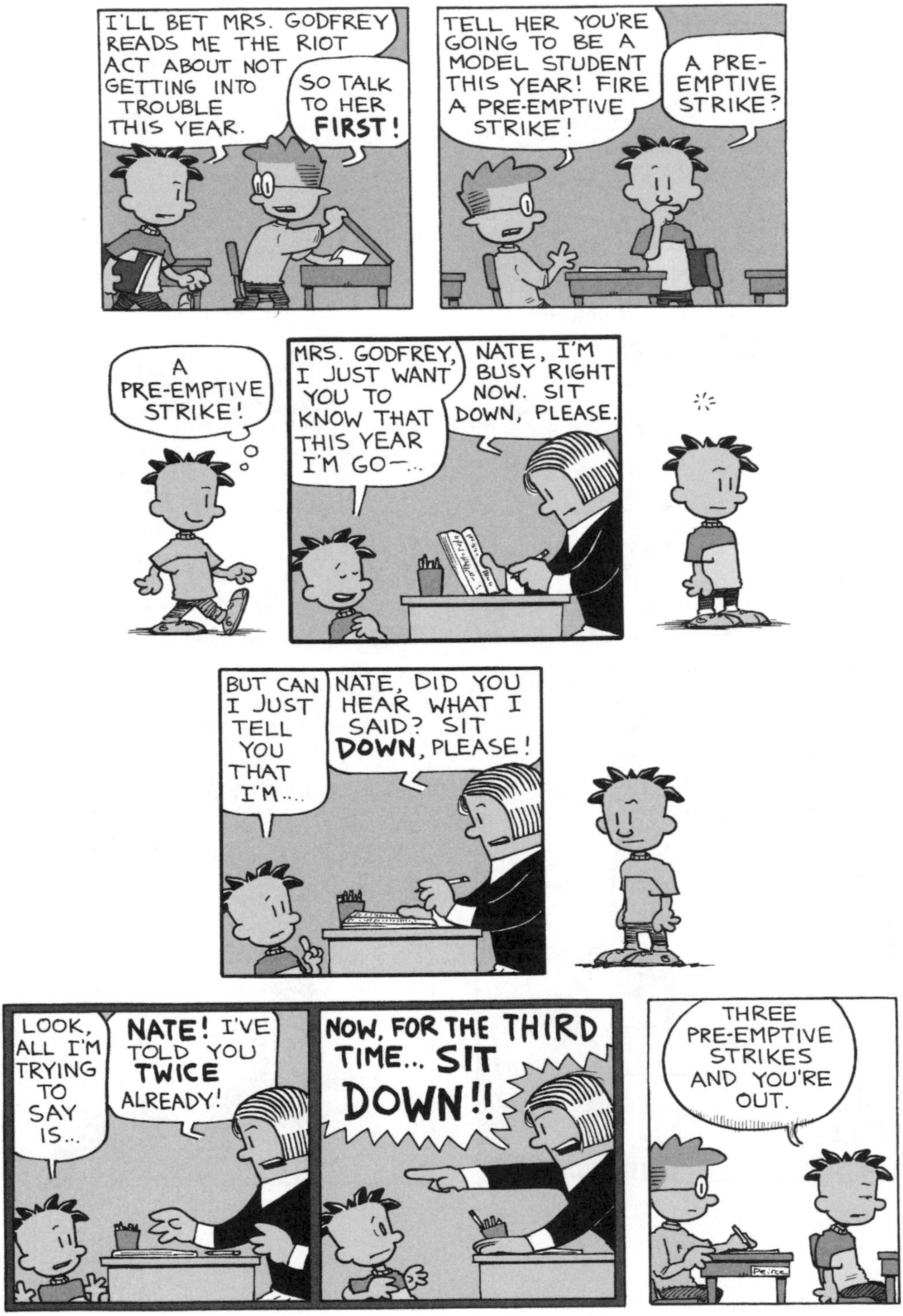
I'LL BET MRS. GODFREY READS ME THE RIOT ACT ABOUT NOT GETTING INTO TROUBLE THIS YEAR.
SO TALK TO HER FIRST!
TELL HER YOU'RE GOING TO BE A MODEL STUDENT THIS YEAR! FIRE A PRE-EMPTIVE STRIKE!
A PRE-EMPTIVE STRIKE?
A PRE-EMPTIVE STRIKE!
MRS. GODFREY, I JUST WANT YOU TO KNOW THAT THIS YEAR I'M GO—...
NATE, I'M BUSY RIGHT NOW. SIT DOWN, PLEASE.
BUT CAN I JUST TELL YOU THAT I'M...
NATE, DID YOU HEAR WHAT I SAID? SIT DOWN, PLEASE!
LOOK, ALL I'M TRYING TO SAY IS...
NATE! I'VE TOLD YOU TWICE ALREADY!
NOW, FOR THE THIRD TIME... SIT DOWN!!
THREE PRE-EMPTIVE STRIKES AND YOU'RE OUT.
Peirce

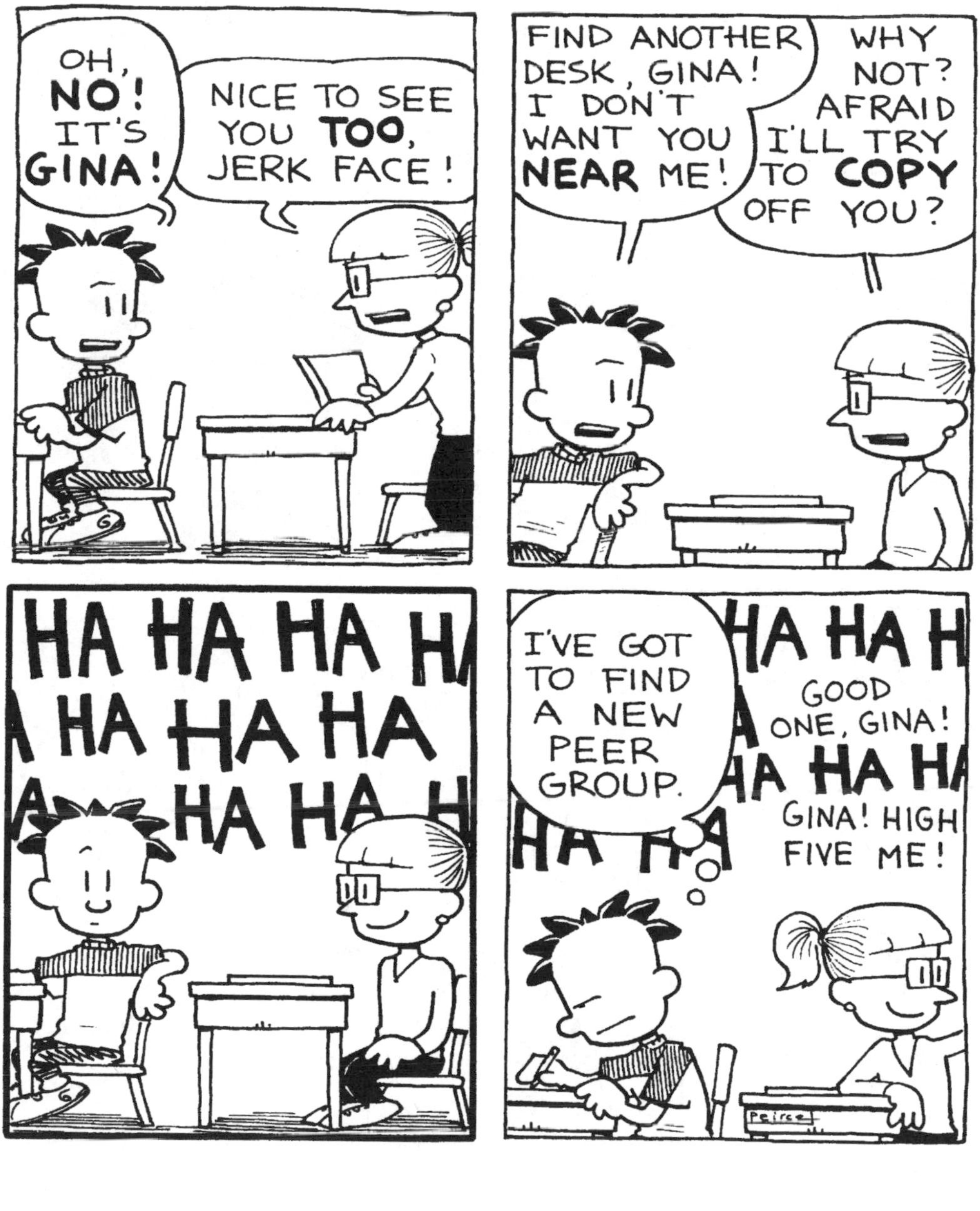
OH, NO! IT'S GINA!
NICE TO SEE YOU TOO, JERK FACE!
FIND ANOTHER DESK, GINA! I DON'T WANT YOU NEAR ME!
WHY NOT? AFRAID I'LL TRY TO COPY OFF YOU?
HA HA HA HA HA HA HA HA HA HA HA
I'VE GOT TO FIND A NEW PEER GROUP.
HA HA H
GOOD ONE, GINA!
HA HA HA
HA HA
GINA! HIGH FIVE ME!
Peirce

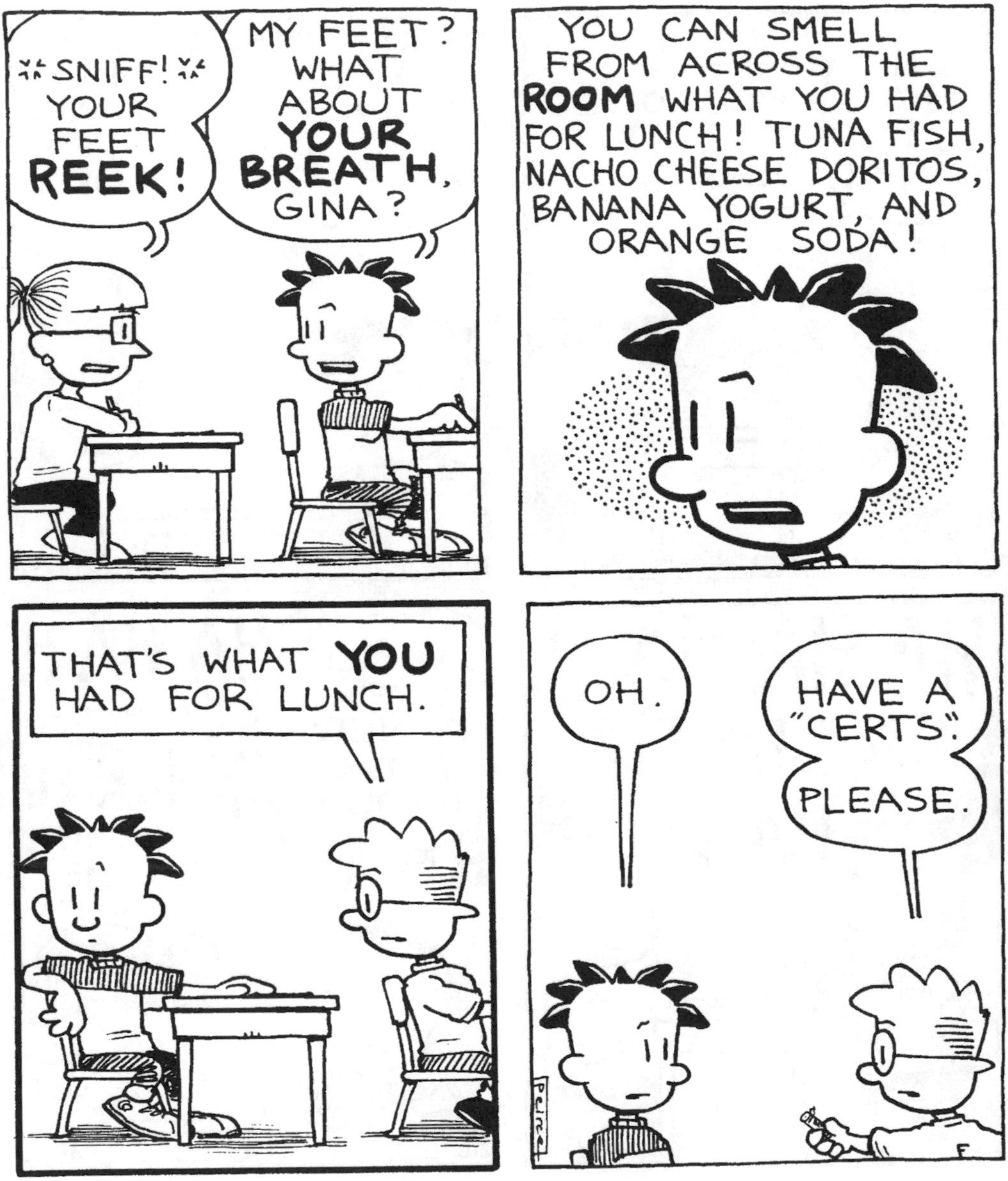
SNIFF! YOUR FEET **REEK!**
MY FEET? WHAT ABOUT **YOUR BREATH**, GINA?
YOU CAN SMELL FROM ACROSS THE **ROOM** WHAT YOU HAD FOR LUNCH! TUNA FISH, NACHO CHEESE DORITOS, BANANA YOGURT, AND ORANGE SODA!
THAT'S WHAT **YOU** HAD FOR LUNCH.
OH.
HAVE A "CERTS".
PLEASE.
Peirce

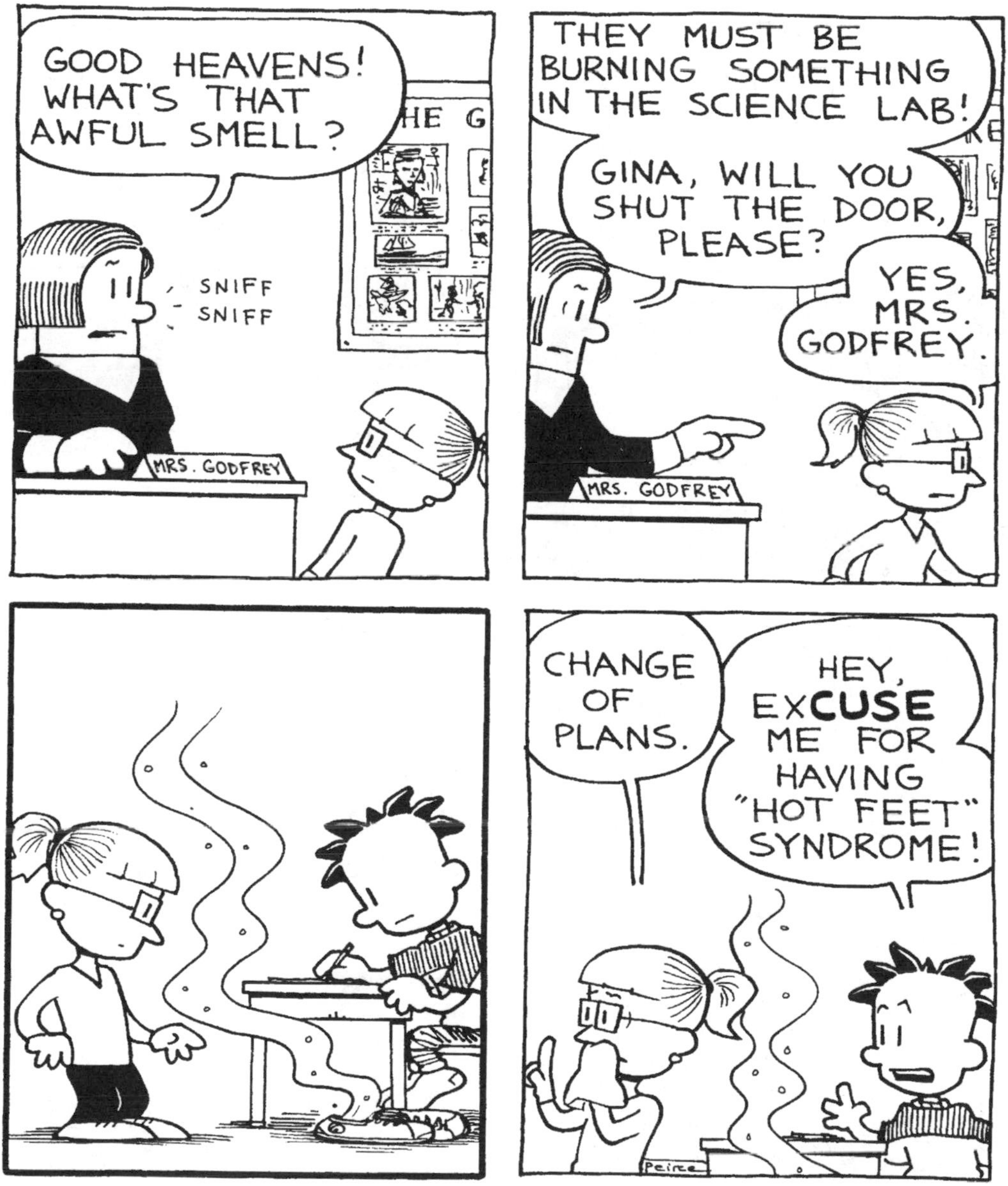
GOOD HEAVENS! WHAT'S THAT AWFUL SMELL?
SNIFF SNIFF
MRS. GODFREY
THEY MUST BE BURNING SOMETHING IN THE SCIENCE LAB!
GINA, WILL YOU SHUT THE DOOR, PLEASE?
YES, MRS. GODFREY.
MRS. GODFREY
CHANGE OF PLANS.
HEY, EXCUSE ME FOR HAVING "HOT FEET" SYNDROME!
Peirce

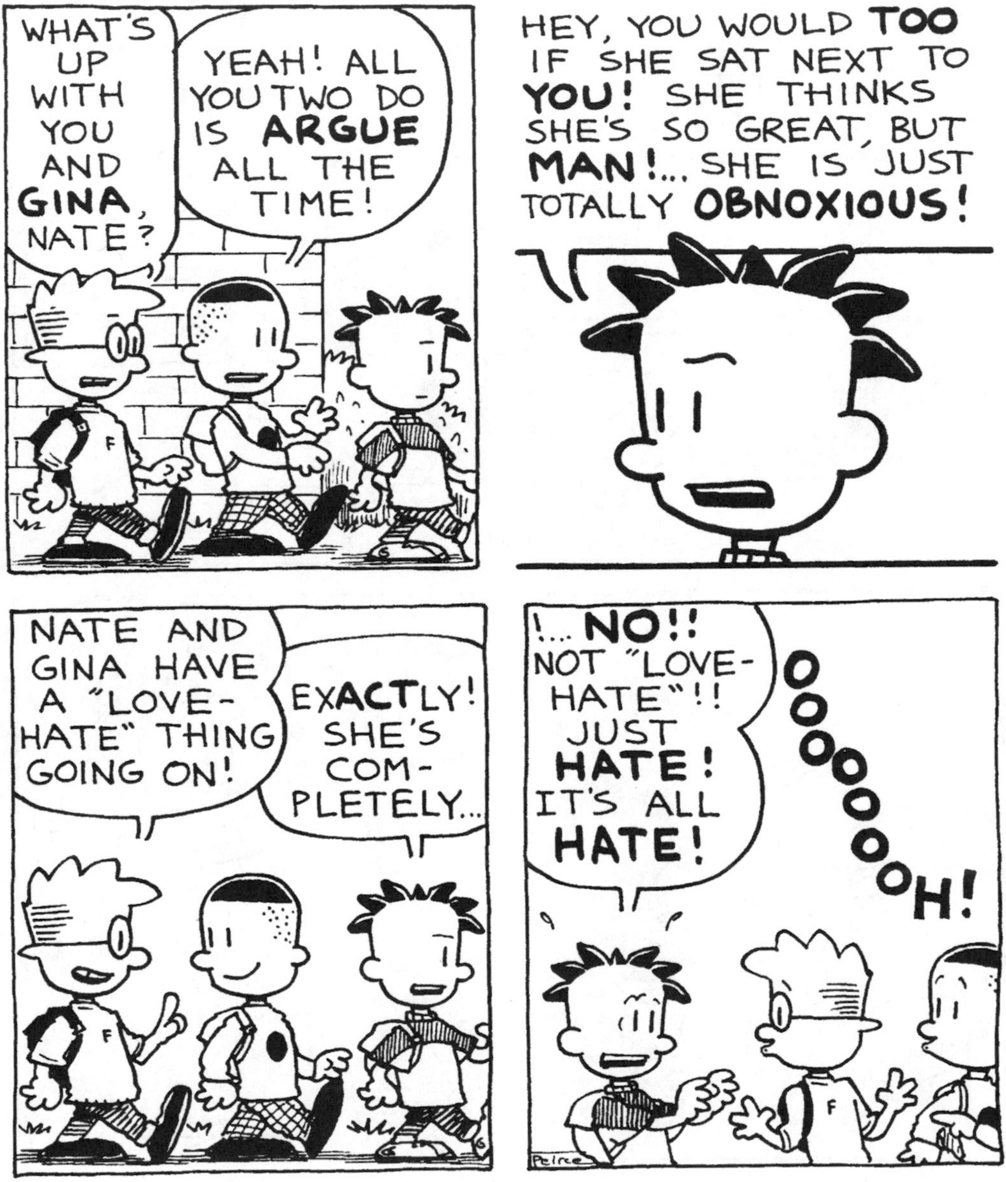
WHAT'S UP WITH YOU AND **GINA**, NATE?
YEAH! ALL YOU TWO DO IS **ARGUE** ALL THE TIME!
HEY, YOU WOULD **TOO** IF SHE SAT NEXT TO **YOU!** SHE THINKS SHE'S SO GREAT, BUT **MAN!**... SHE IS JUST TOTALLY **OBNOXIOUS!**
NATE AND GINA HAVE A "LOVE-HATE" THING GOING ON!
EX**ACT**LY! SHE'S COM-PLETELY...
!... **NO!!** NOT "LOVE-HATE"!! JUST **HATE!** IT'S ALL **HATE!**
OOOOOOOH!
Peirce

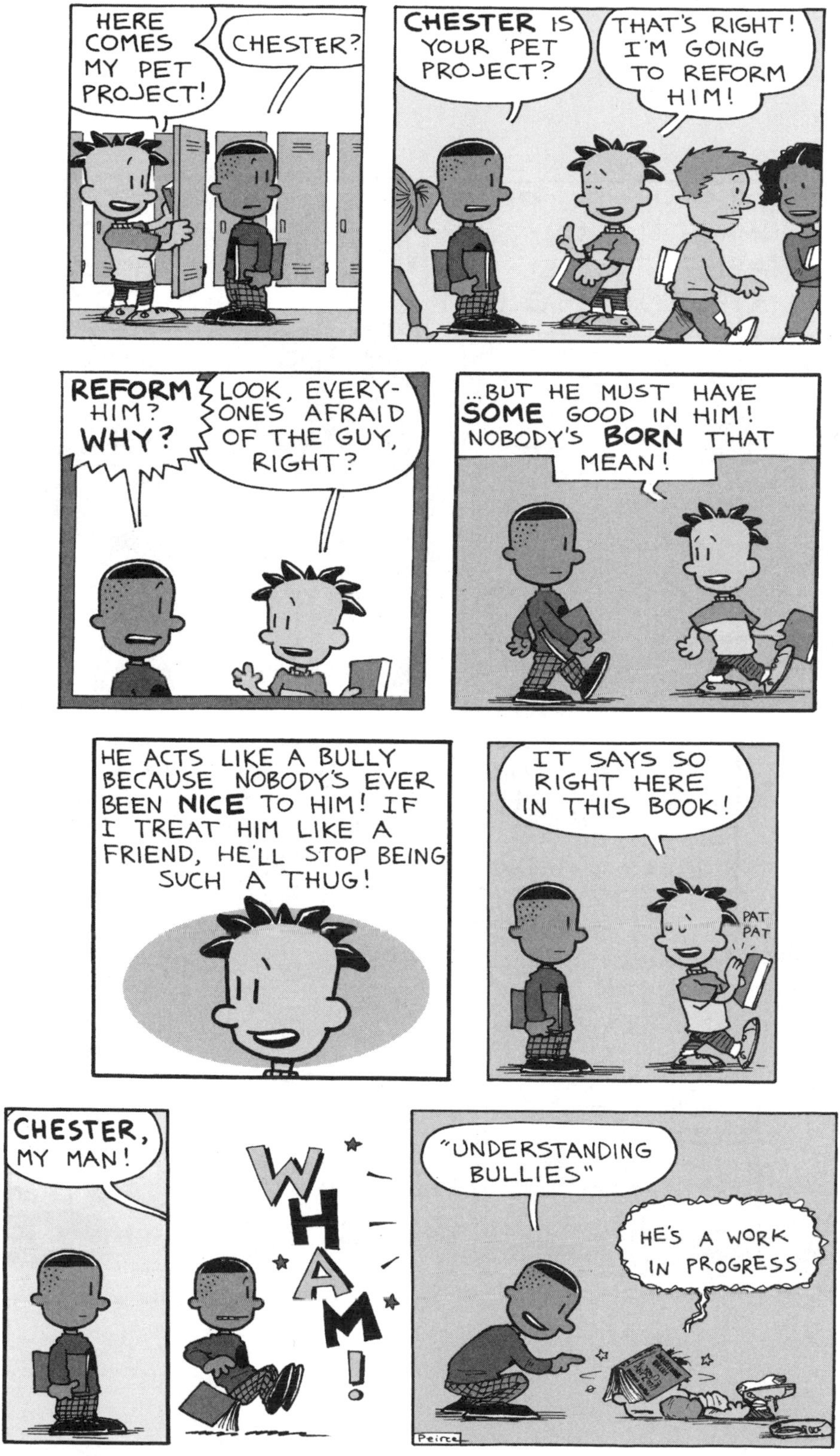
HERE COMES MY PET PROJECT!
CHESTER?
CHESTER IS YOUR PET PROJECT?
THAT'S RIGHT! I'M GOING TO REFORM HIM!
REFORM HIM? WHY?
LOOK, EVERYONE'S AFRAID OF THE GUY, RIGHT?
...BUT HE MUST HAVE SOME GOOD IN HIM! NOBODY'S BORN THAT MEAN!
HE ACTS LIKE A BULLY BECAUSE NOBODY'S EVER BEEN NICE TO HIM! IF I TREAT HIM LIKE A FRIEND, HE'LL STOP BEING SUCH A THUG!
IT SAYS SO RIGHT HERE IN THIS BOOK!
PAT PAT
CHESTER, MY MAN!
WHAM!
"UNDERSTANDING BULLIES"
HE'S A WORK IN PROGRESS.
Peirce

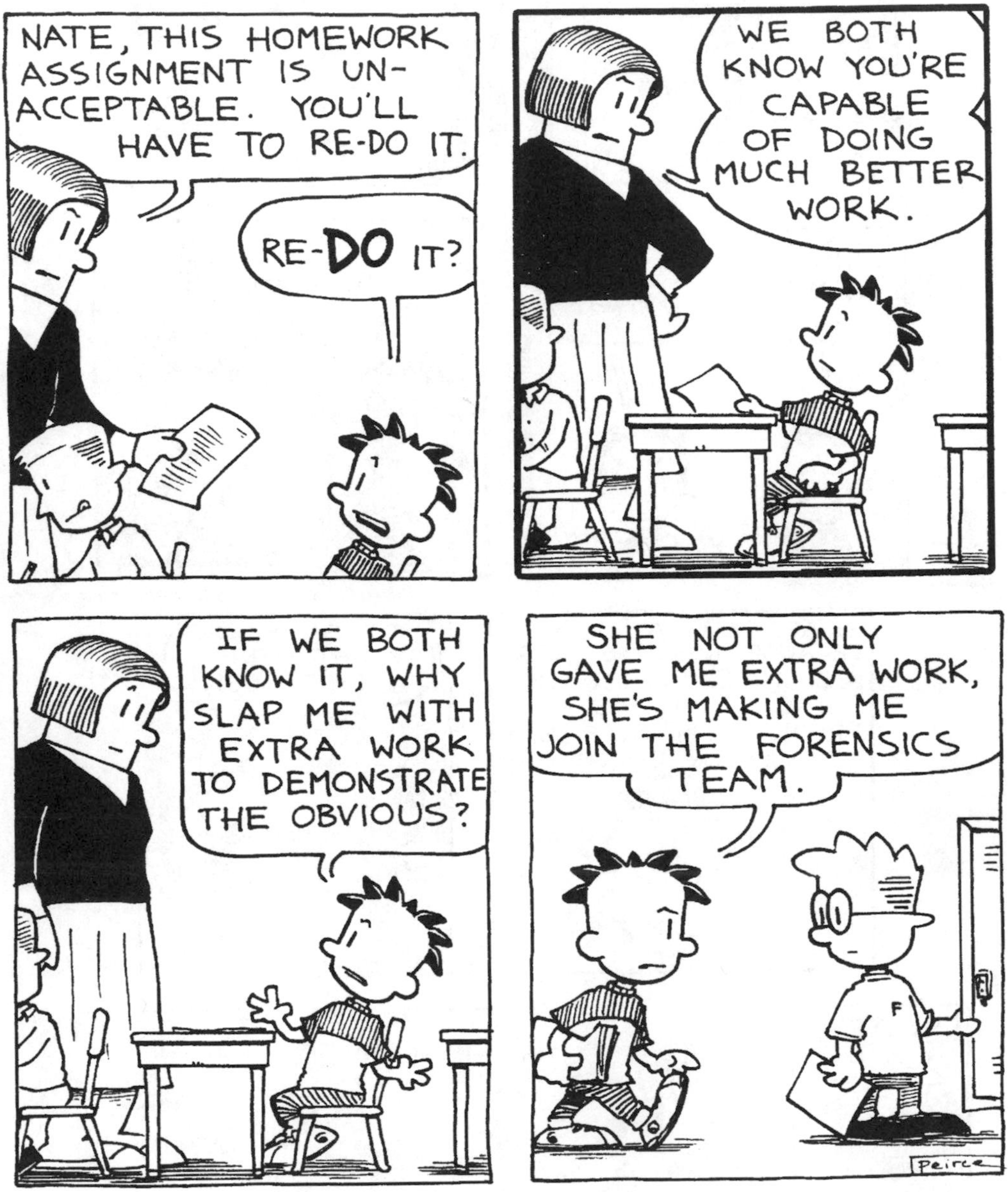
NATE, THIS HOMEWORK ASSIGNMENT IS UN-ACCEPTABLE. YOU'LL HAVE TO RE-DO IT.
RE-**DO** IT?
WE BOTH KNOW YOU'RE CAPABLE OF DOING MUCH BETTER WORK.
IF WE BOTH KNOW IT, WHY SLAP ME WITH EXTRA WORK TO DEMONSTRATE THE OBVIOUS?
SHE NOT ONLY GAVE ME EXTRA WORK, SHE'S MAKING ME JOIN THE FORENSICS TEAM.
Peirce

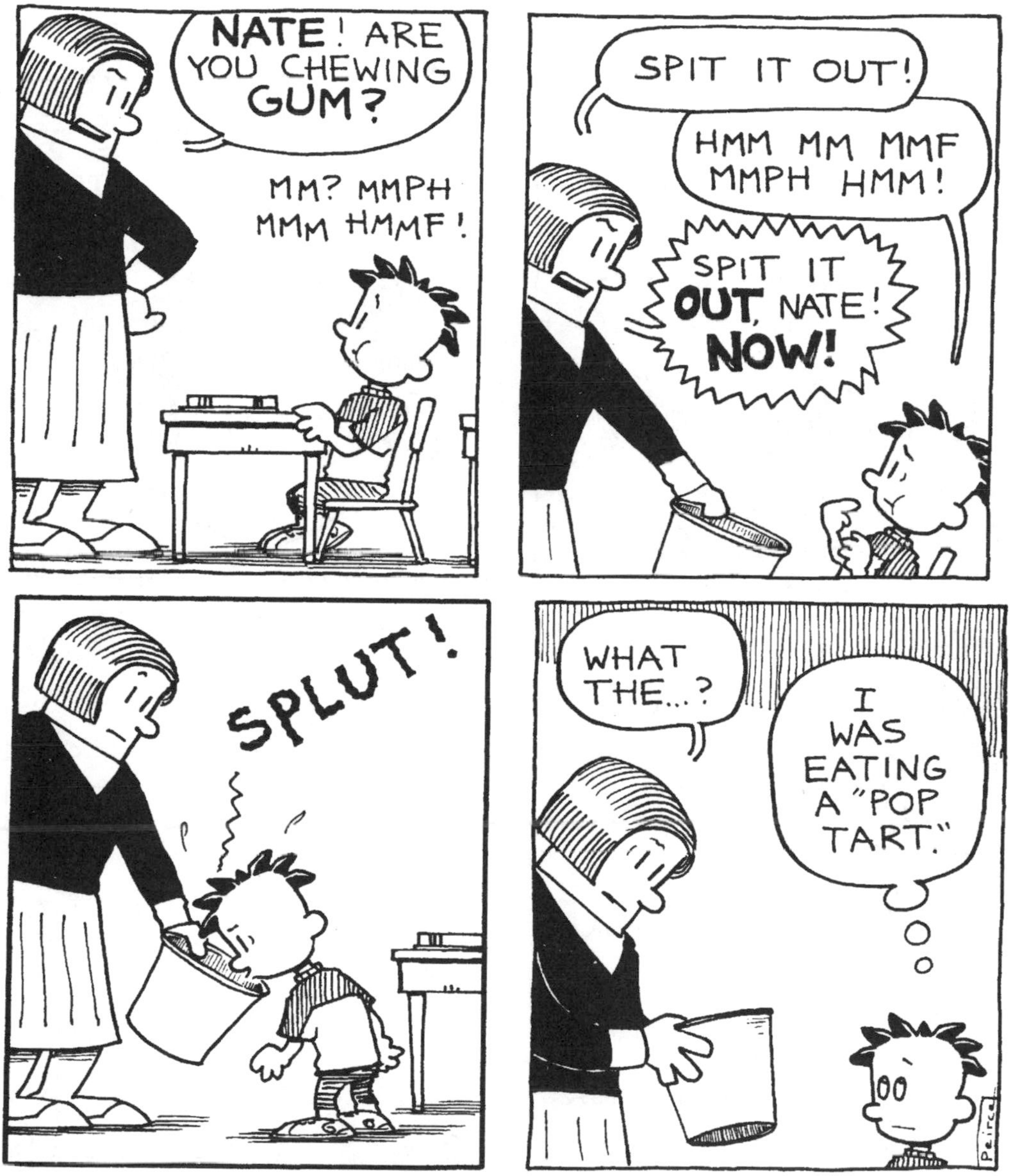
NATE! ARE YOU CHEWING GUM?
MM? MMPH MMM HMMF!
SPIT IT OUT!
HMM MM MMF MMPH HMM!
SPIT IT OUT, NATE! NOW!
SPLUT!
WHAT THE...?
I WAS EATING A "POP TART."
Peirce

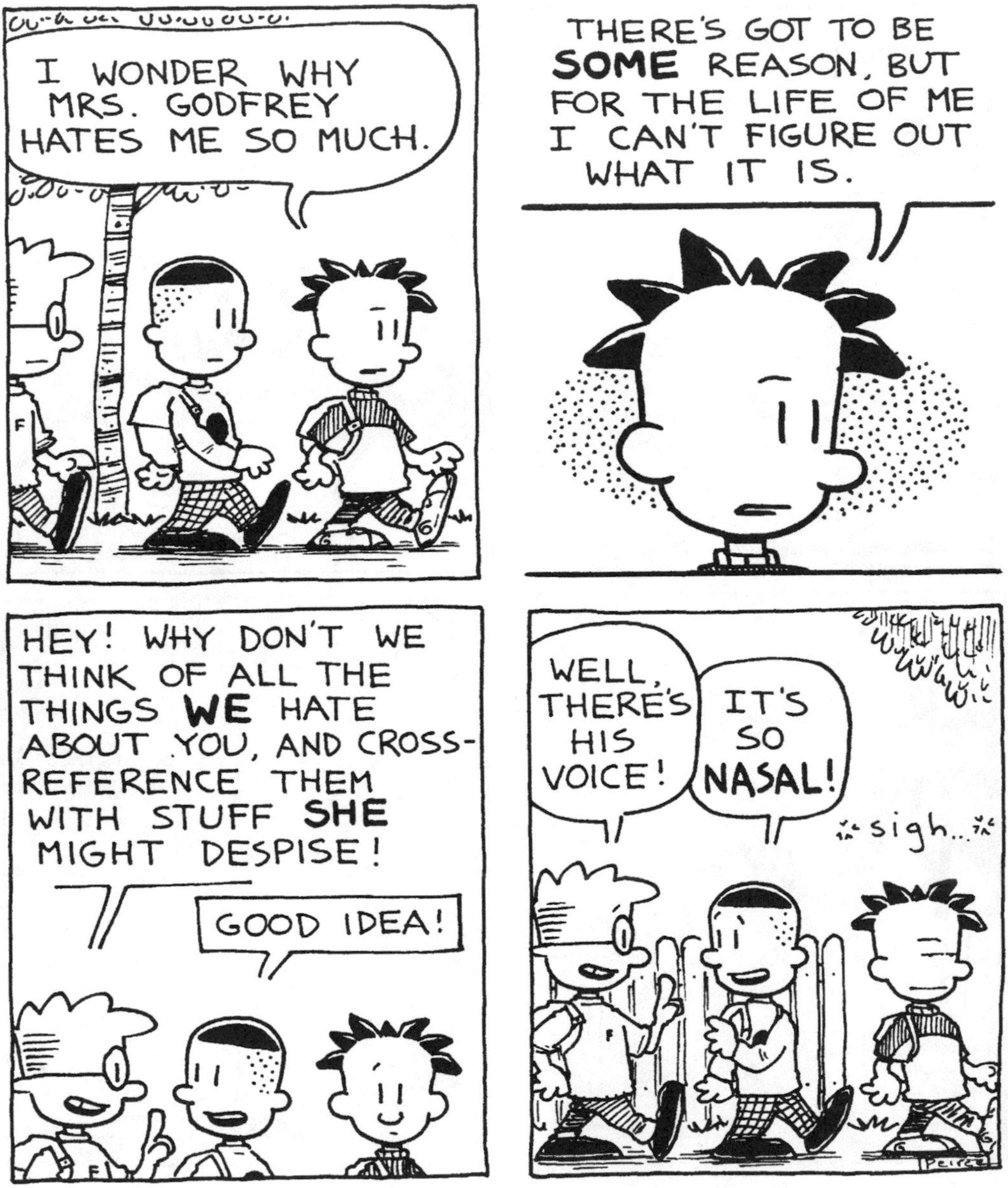

I WONDER WHY MRS. GODFREY HATES ME SO MUCH.
THERE'S GOT TO BE **SOME** REASON, BUT FOR THE LIFE OF ME I CAN'T FIGURE OUT WHAT IT IS.
HEY! WHY DON'T WE THINK OF ALL THE THINGS **WE** HATE ABOUT YOU, AND CROSS-REFERENCE THEM WITH STUFF **SHE** MIGHT DESPISE!
GOOD IDEA!
WELL, THERE'S HIS VOICE!
IT'S SO **NASAL!**
sigh...
Peirce

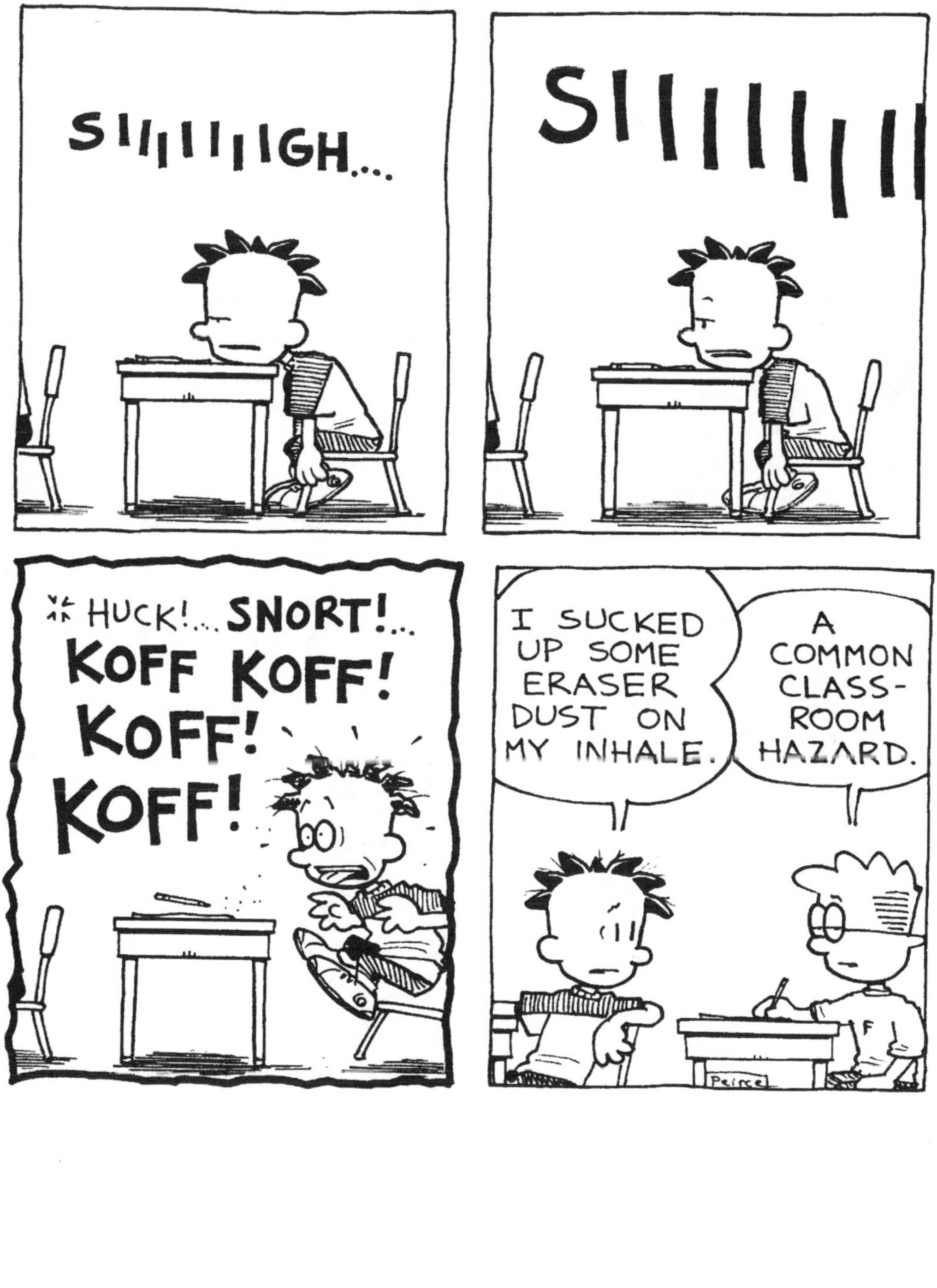
SIIIIIIIGH....
SIIIIIIII
HUCK!... SNORT!...
KOFF KOFF!
KOFF!
KOFF!
I SUCKED UP SOME ERASER DUST ON MY INHALE.
A COMMON CLASS-ROOM HAZARD.
Peirce

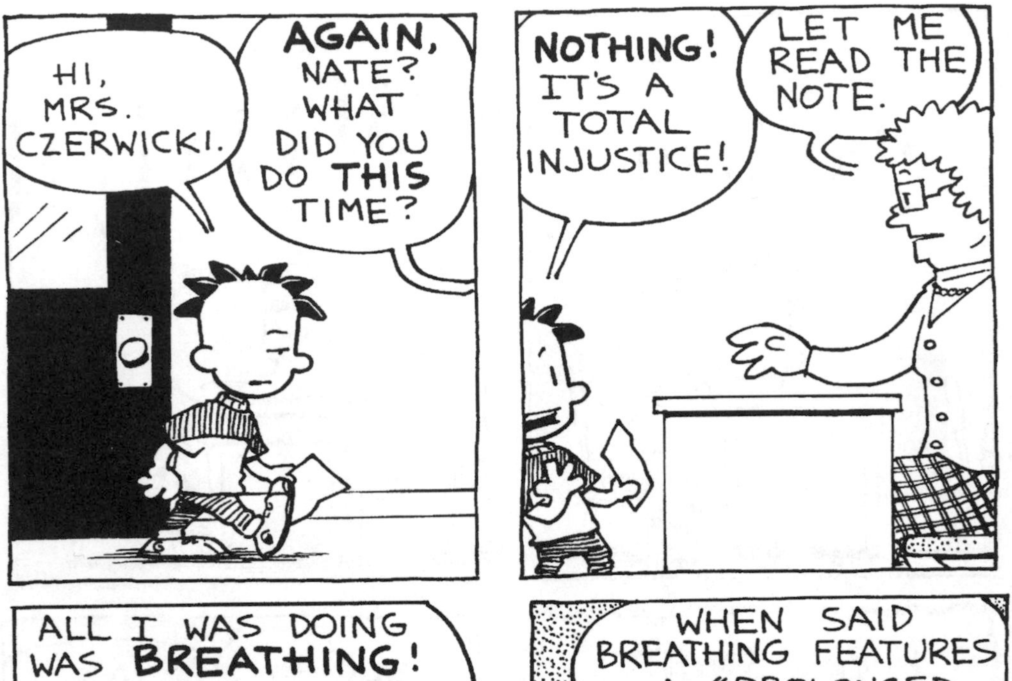
HI, MRS. CZERWICKI.
AGAIN, NATE? WHAT DID YOU DO THIS TIME?
NOTHING! IT'S A TOTAL INJUSTICE!
LET ME READ THE NOTE.
ALL I WAS DOING WAS BREATHING! THAT'S IT! SINCE WHEN DO YOU GET DETENTION FOR BREATHING?
WHEN SAID BREATHING FEATURES A "PROLONGED LIP FLAP."
I WAS AIRING OUT MY GUMS!
Peirce

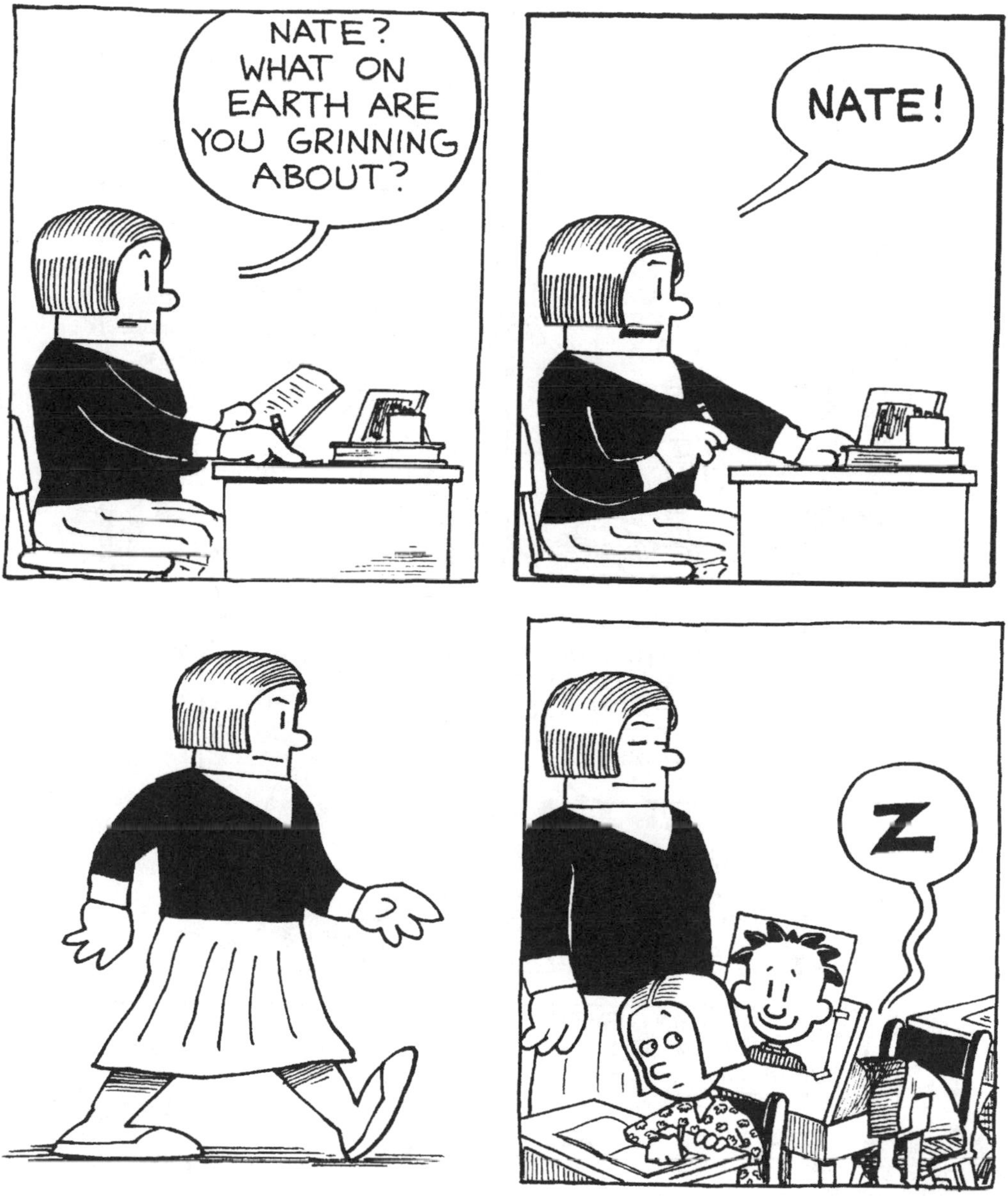
NATE? WHAT ON EARTH ARE YOU GRINNING ABOUT?
NATE!
Z

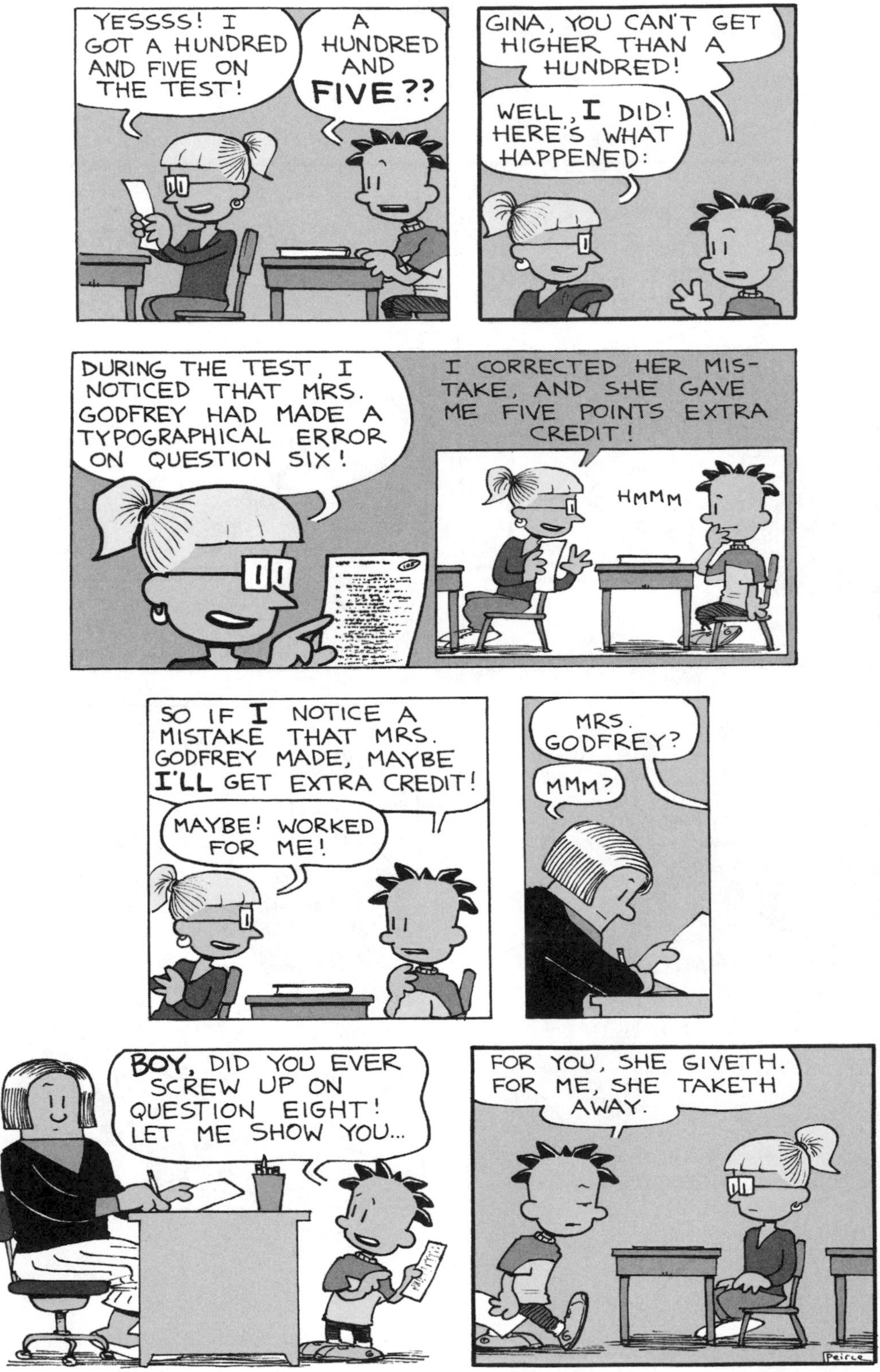
YESSSS! I GOT A HUNDRED AND FIVE ON THE TEST!
A HUNDRED AND FIVE??
GINA, YOU CAN'T GET HIGHER THAN A HUNDRED!
WELL, I DID! HERE'S WHAT HAPPENED:
DURING THE TEST, I NOTICED THAT MRS. GODFREY HAD MADE A TYPOGRAPHICAL ERROR ON QUESTION SIX!
I CORRECTED HER MISTAKE, AND SHE GAVE ME FIVE POINTS EXTRA CREDIT!
HMMM
SO IF I NOTICE A MISTAKE THAT MRS. GODFREY MADE, MAYBE I'LL GET EXTRA CREDIT!
MAYBE! WORKED FOR ME!
MRS. GODFREY?
MMM?
BOY, DID YOU EVER SCREW UP ON QUESTION EIGHT! LET ME SHOW YOU...
FOR YOU, SHE GIVETH. FOR ME, SHE TAKETH AWAY.
Peirce

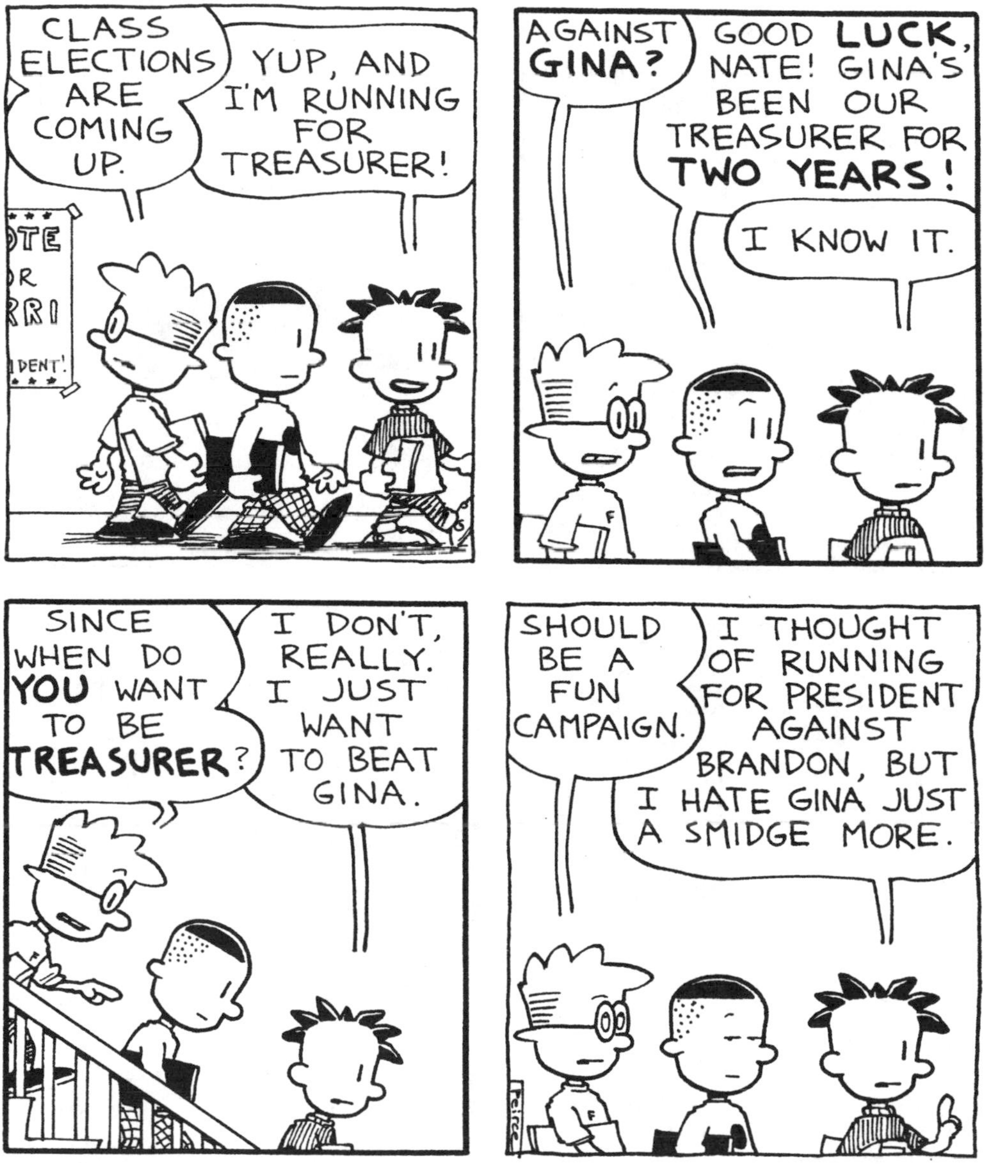
CLASS ELECTIONS ARE COMING UP.
YUP, AND I'M RUNNING FOR TREASURER!
AGAINST GINA?
GOOD LUCK, NATE! GINA'S BEEN OUR TREASURER FOR TWO YEARS!
I KNOW IT.
SINCE WHEN DO YOU WANT TO BE TREASURER?
I DON'T, REALLY. I JUST WANT TO BEAT GINA.
SHOULD BE A FUN CAMPAIGN.
I THOUGHT OF RUNNING FOR PRESIDENT AGAINST BRANDON, BUT I HATE GINA JUST A SMIDGE MORE.

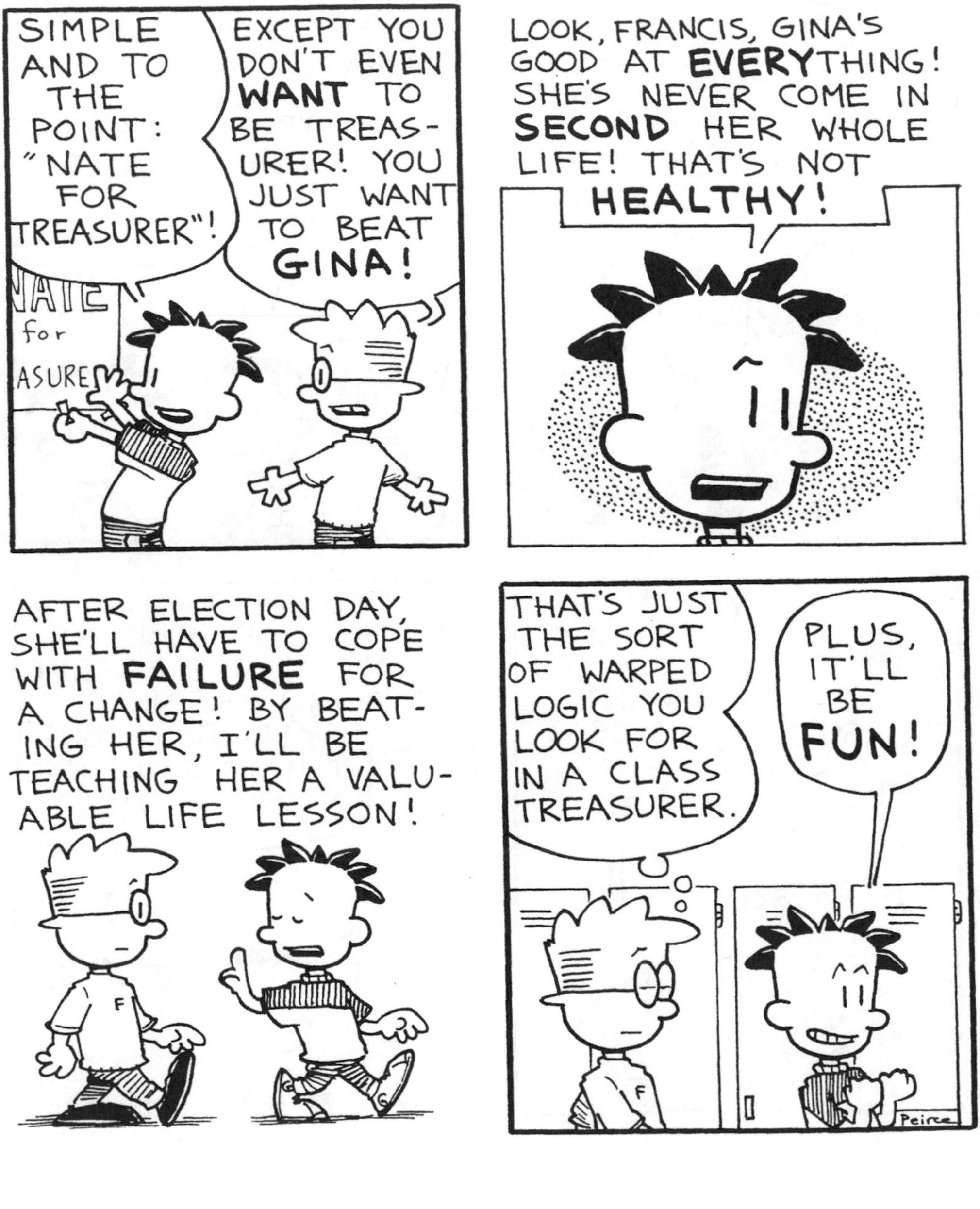
SIMPLE AND TO THE POINT: "NATE FOR TREASURER"!
EXCEPT YOU DON'T EVEN **WANT** TO BE TREASURER! YOU JUST WANT TO BEAT **GINA**!
NATE for ASURE
LOOK, FRANCIS, GINA'S GOOD AT **EVERY**THING! SHE'S NEVER COME IN **SECOND** HER WHOLE LIFE! THAT'S NOT **HEALTHY**!
AFTER ELECTION DAY, SHE'LL HAVE TO COPE WITH **FAILURE** FOR A CHANGE! BY BEATING HER, I'LL BE TEACHING HER A VALUABLE LIFE LESSON!
THAT'S JUST THE SORT OF WARPED LOGIC YOU LOOK FOR IN A CLASS TREASURER.
PLUS, IT'LL BE **FUN**!
F
F
Peirce

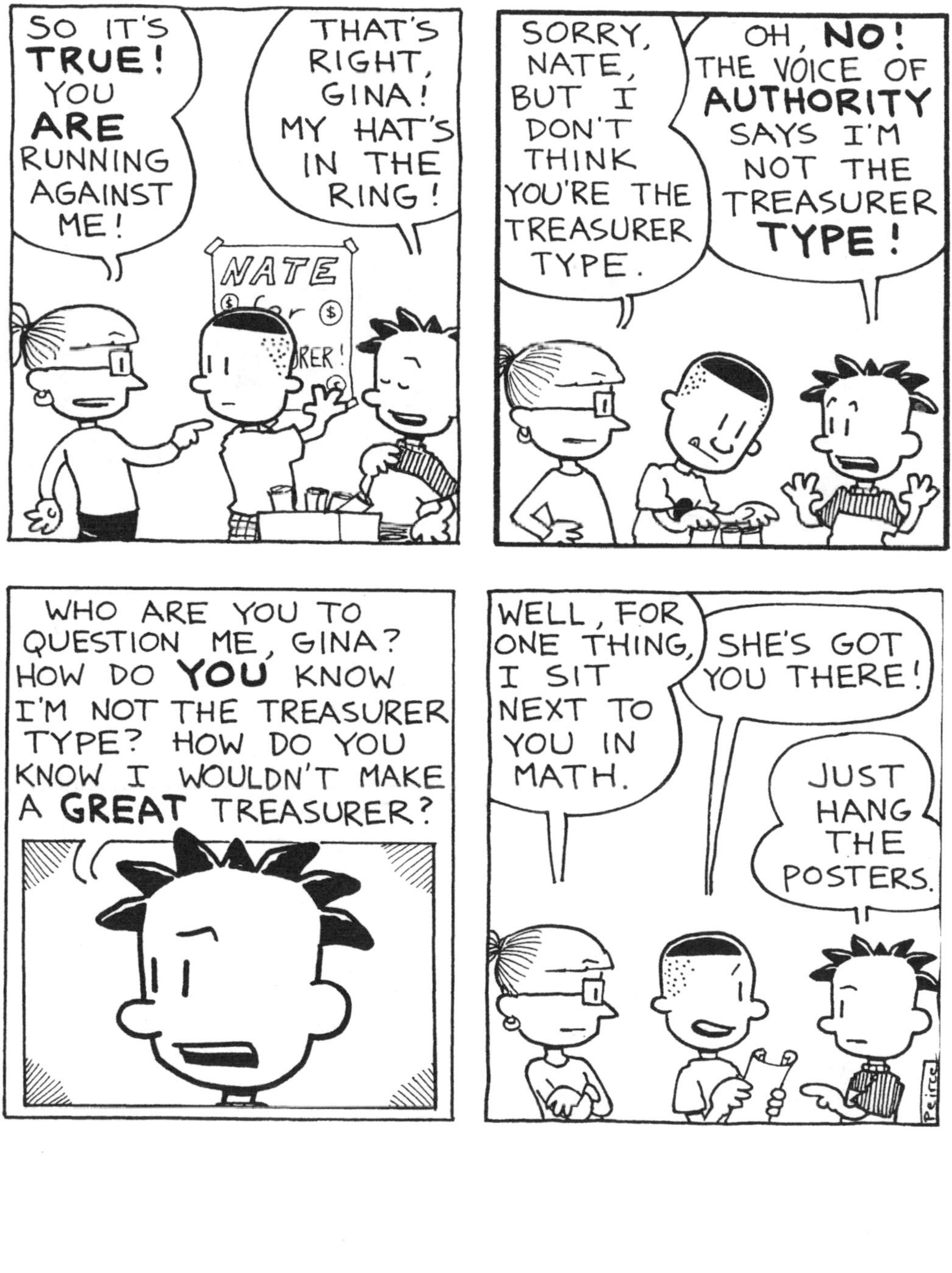
SO IT'S TRUE! YOU ARE RUNNING AGAINST ME!
THAT'S RIGHT, GINA! MY HAT'S IN THE RING!
NATE
SORRY, NATE, BUT I DON'T THINK YOU'RE THE TREASURER TYPE.
OH, NO! THE VOICE OF AUTHORITY SAYS I'M NOT THE TREASURER TYPE!
WHO ARE YOU TO QUESTION ME, GINA? HOW DO YOU KNOW I'M NOT THE TREASURER TYPE? HOW DO YOU KNOW I WOULDN'T MAKE A GREAT TREASURER?
WELL, FOR ONE THING, I SIT NEXT TO YOU IN MATH.
SHE'S GOT YOU THERE!
JUST HANG THE POSTERS.
Peirce

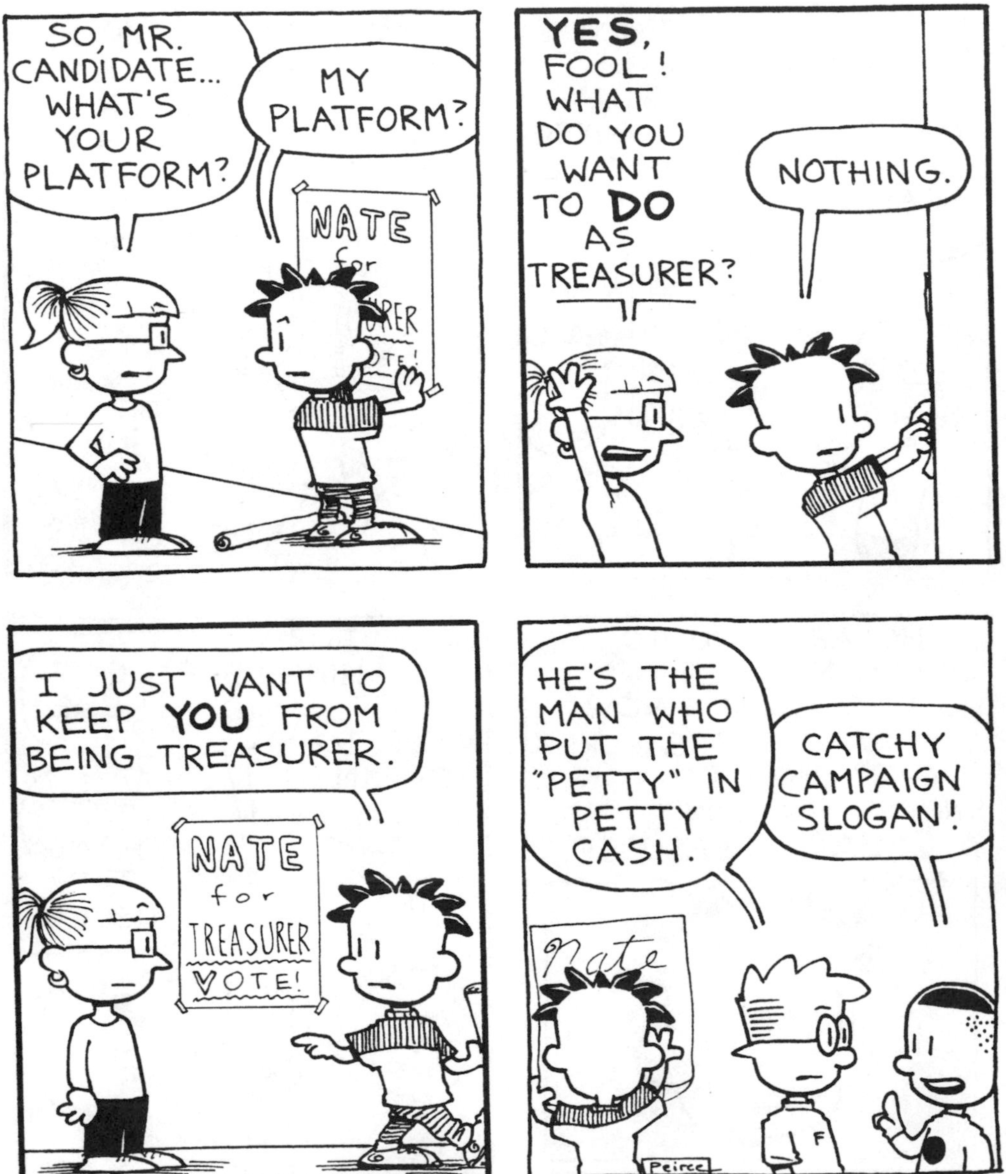
SO, MR. CANDIDATE... WHAT'S YOUR PLATFORM?
MY PLATFORM?
NATE for TREASURER VOTE!
YES, FOOL! WHAT DO YOU WANT TO DO AS TREASURER?
NOTHING.
I JUST WANT TO KEEP YOU FROM BEING TREASURER.
NATE for TREASURER VOTE!
HE'S THE MAN WHO PUT THE "PETTY" IN PETTY CASH.
CATCHY CAMPAIGN SLOGAN!
Nate
F
Peirce

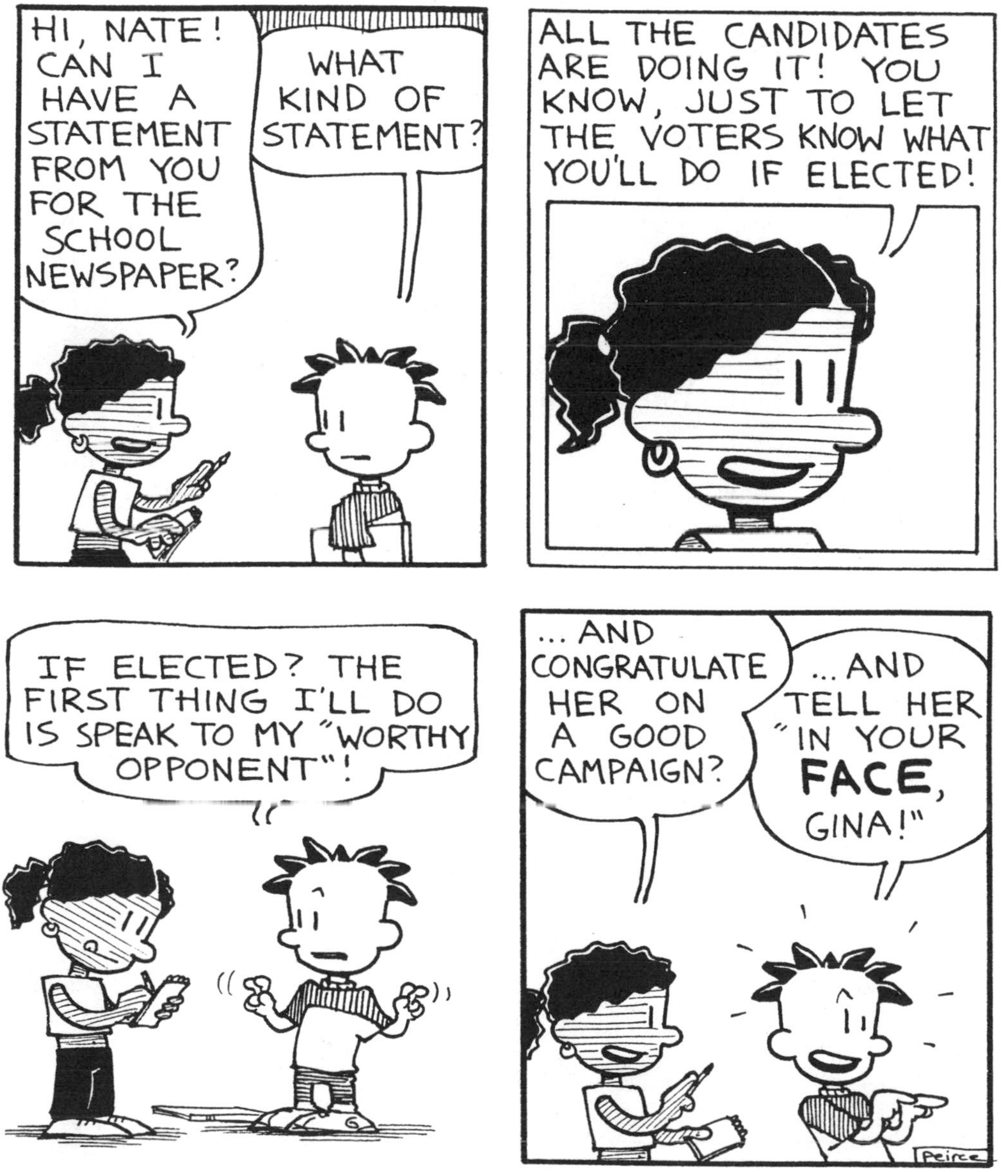
HI, NATE! CAN I HAVE A STATEMENT FROM YOU FOR THE SCHOOL NEWSPAPER?
WHAT KIND OF STATEMENT?
ALL THE CANDIDATES ARE DOING IT! YOU KNOW, JUST TO LET THE VOTERS KNOW WHAT YOU'LL DO IF ELECTED!
IF ELECTED? THE FIRST THING I'LL DO IS SPEAK TO MY "WORTHY OPPONENT"!
...AND CONGRATULATE HER ON A GOOD CAMPAIGN?
...AND TELL HER "IN YOUR FACE, GINA!"
Peirce

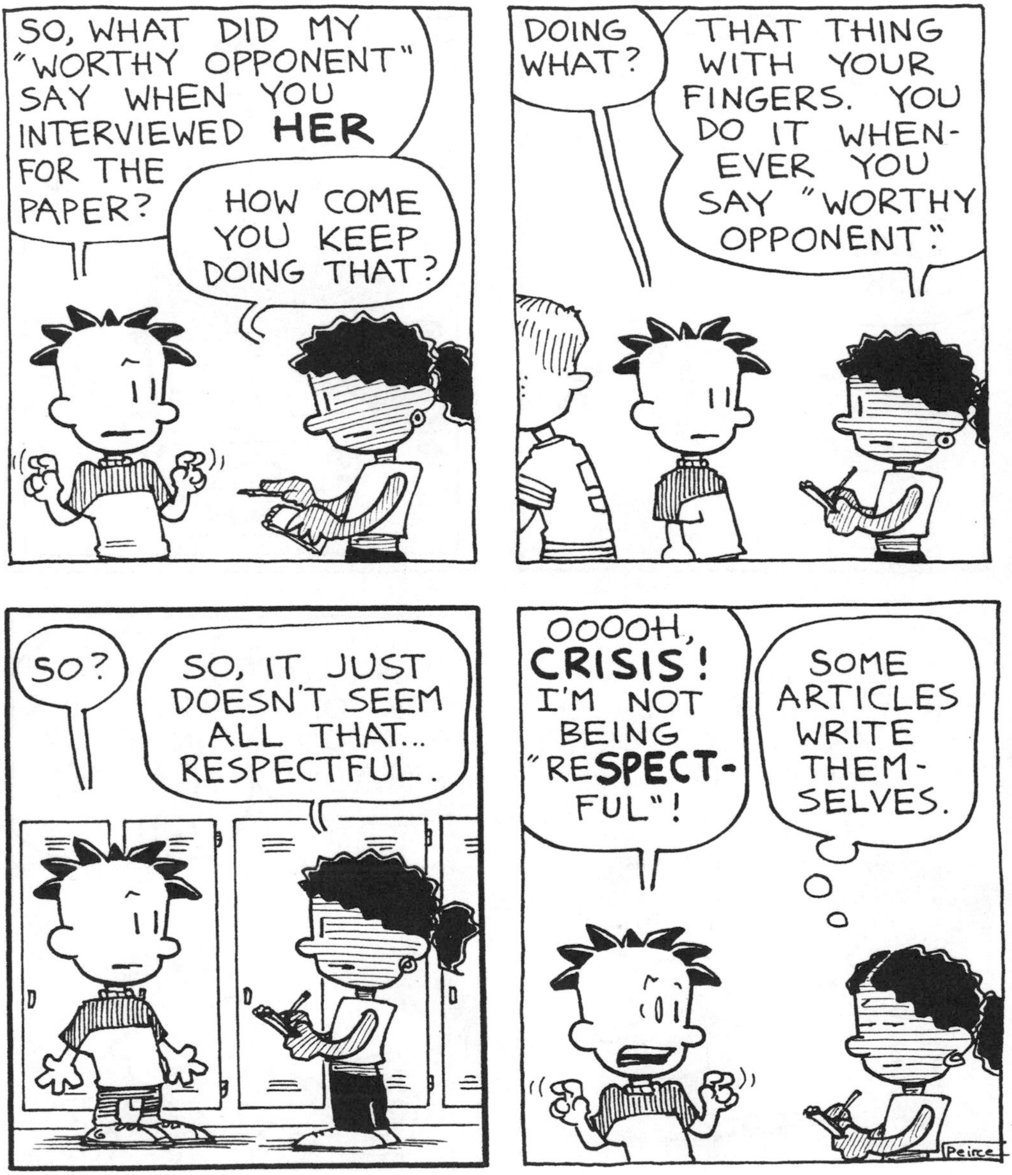
SO, WHAT DID MY "WORTHY OPPONENT" SAY WHEN YOU INTERVIEWED **HER** FOR THE PAPER?
HOW COME YOU KEEP DOING THAT?
DOING WHAT?
THAT THING WITH YOUR FINGERS. YOU DO IT WHEN-EVER YOU SAY "WORTHY OPPONENT."
SO?
SO, IT JUST DOESN'T SEEM ALL THAT... RESPECTFUL.
OOOOH, **CRISIS**! I'M NOT BEING "RE**SPECT**-FUL"!
SOME ARTICLES WRITE THEM-SELVES.
Peirce

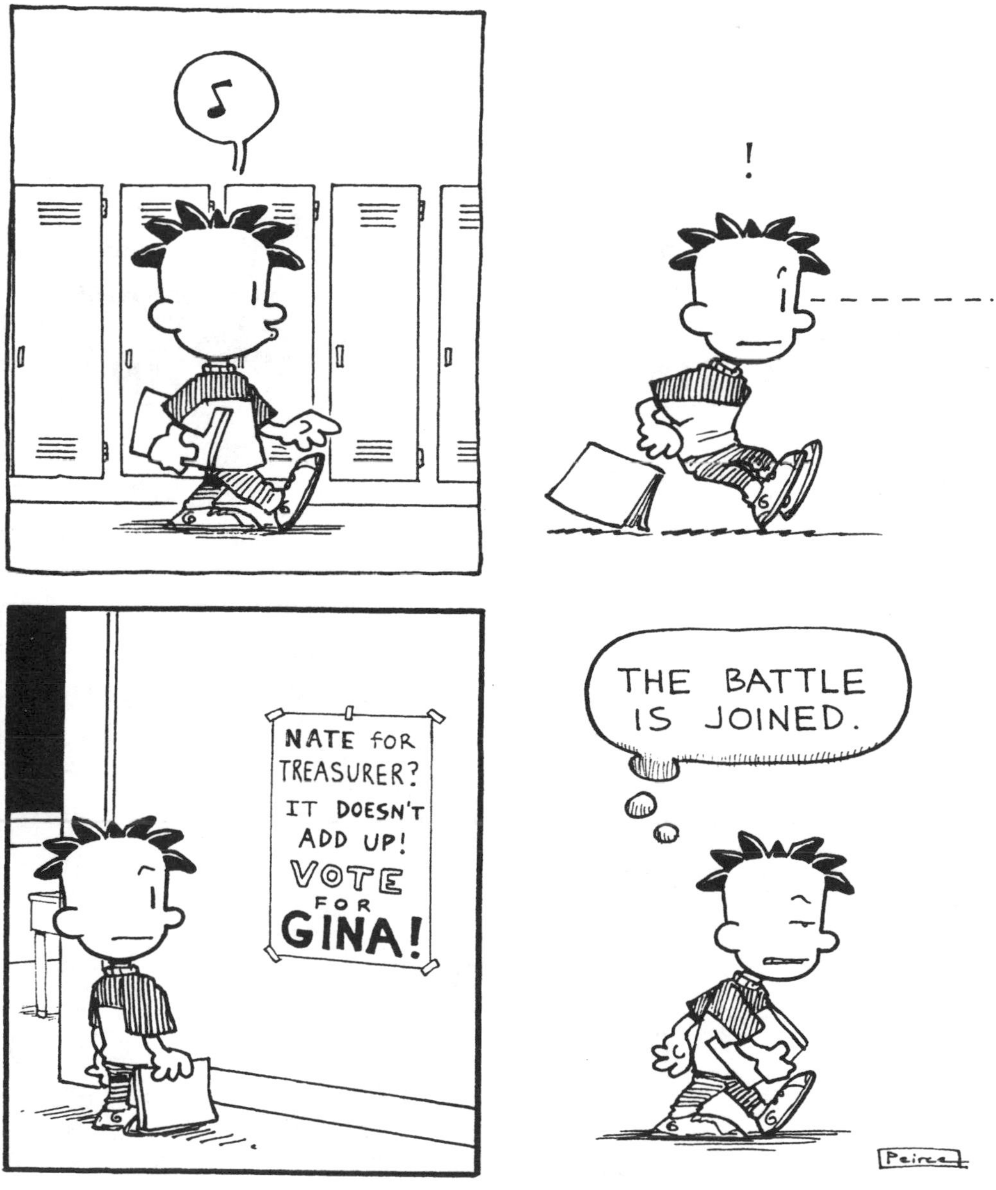
♪
!
NATE FOR TREASURER? IT DOESN'T ADD UP! VOTE FOR GINA!
THE BATTLE IS JOINED.
Peirce

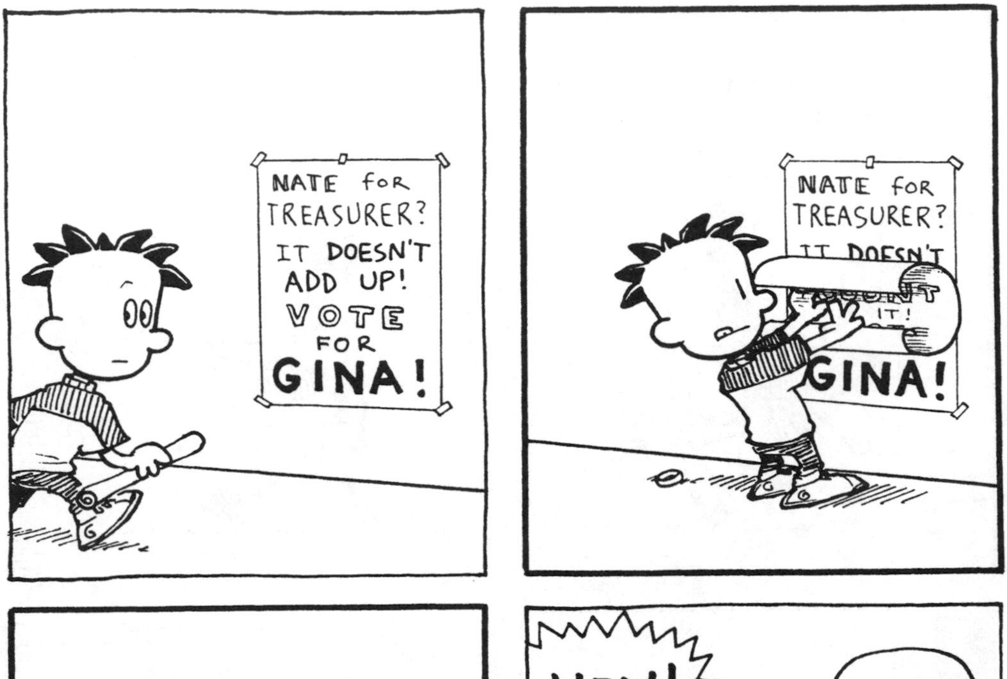
NATE for TREASURER? IT DOESN'T ADD UP! VOTE FOR GINA!
GINA!
GINA for TREASURER? DON'T COUNT ON IT! VOTE NATE!
HEY!
GAME ON.
GINA for TREASURER? DON'T COUNT ON IT! VOTE NATE!
Peirce

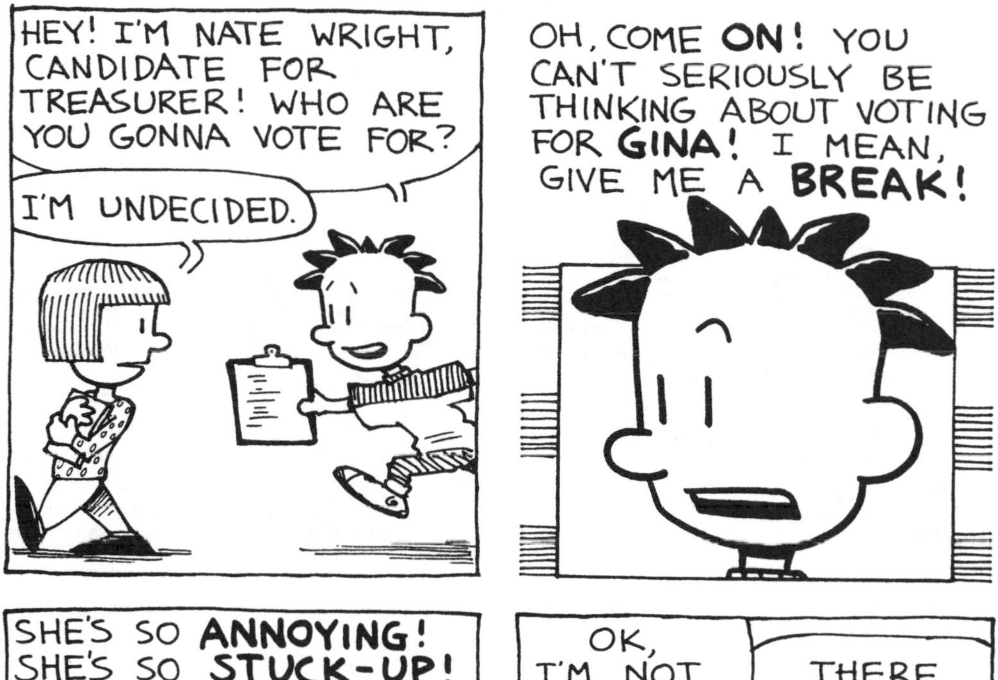
HEY! I'M NATE WRIGHT, CANDIDATE FOR TREASURER! WHO ARE YOU GONNA VOTE FOR?
I'M UNDECIDED.
OH, COME **ON**! YOU CAN'T SERIOUSLY BE THINKING ABOUT VOTING FOR **GINA**! I MEAN, GIVE ME A **BREAK**!
SHE'S SO **ANNOYING**! SHE'S SO **STUCK-UP**! IS **THAT** WHAT YOU WANT? **THINK**! THE CHOICE BETWEEN HER AND ME IS A **NO-BRAINER**!
OK, I'M NOT UNDECIDED ANYMORE.
THERE, WAS THAT SO HARD?
Peirce

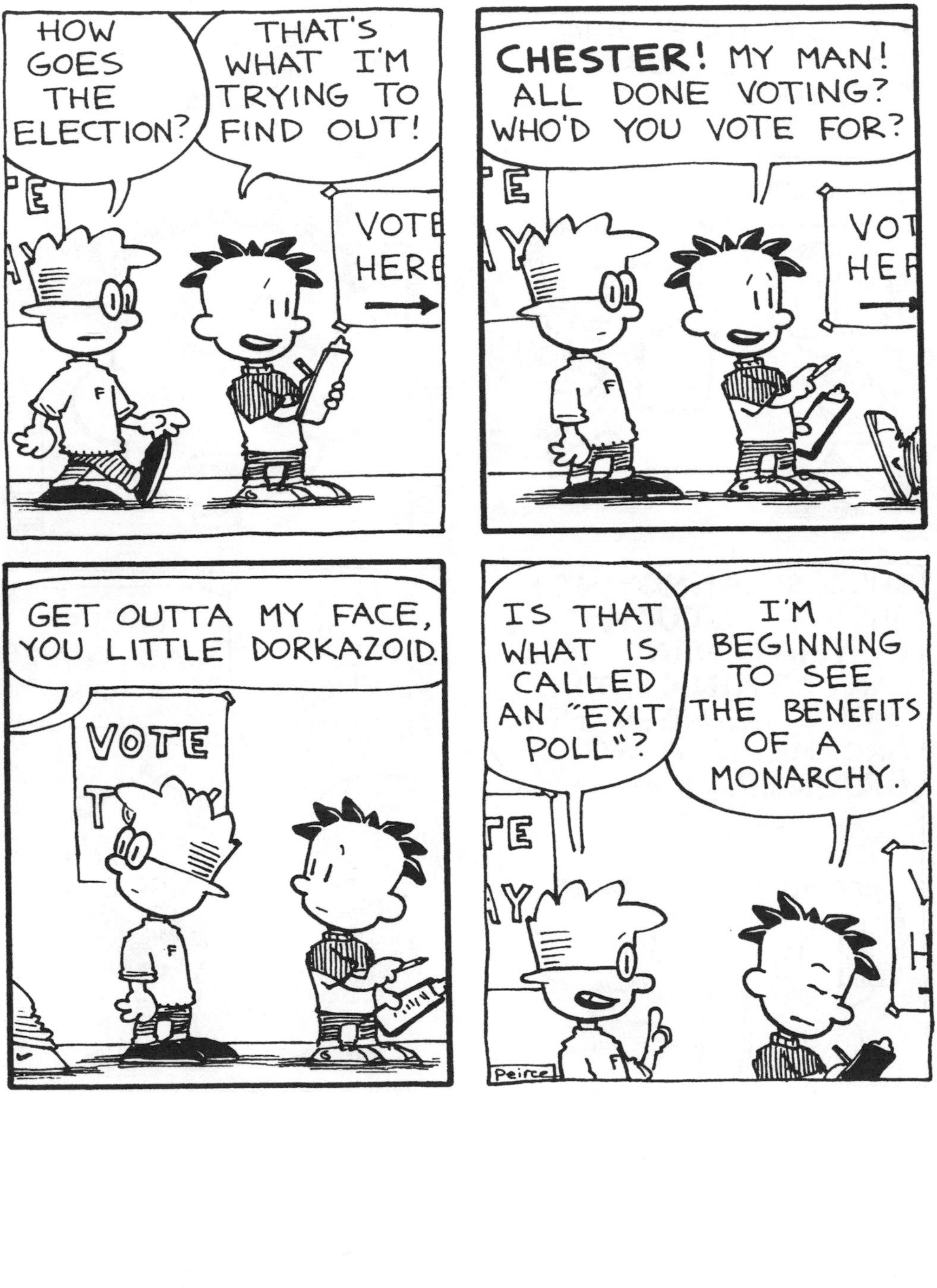
HOW GOES THE ELECTION?
THAT'S WHAT I'M TRYING TO FIND OUT!
VOTE HERE
CHESTER! MY MAN! ALL DONE VOTING? WHO'D YOU VOTE FOR?
GET OUTTA MY FACE, YOU LITTLE DORKAZOID.
VOTE
IS THAT WHAT IS CALLED AN "EXIT POLL"?
I'M BEGINNING TO SEE THE BENEFITS OF A MONARCHY.
Peirce

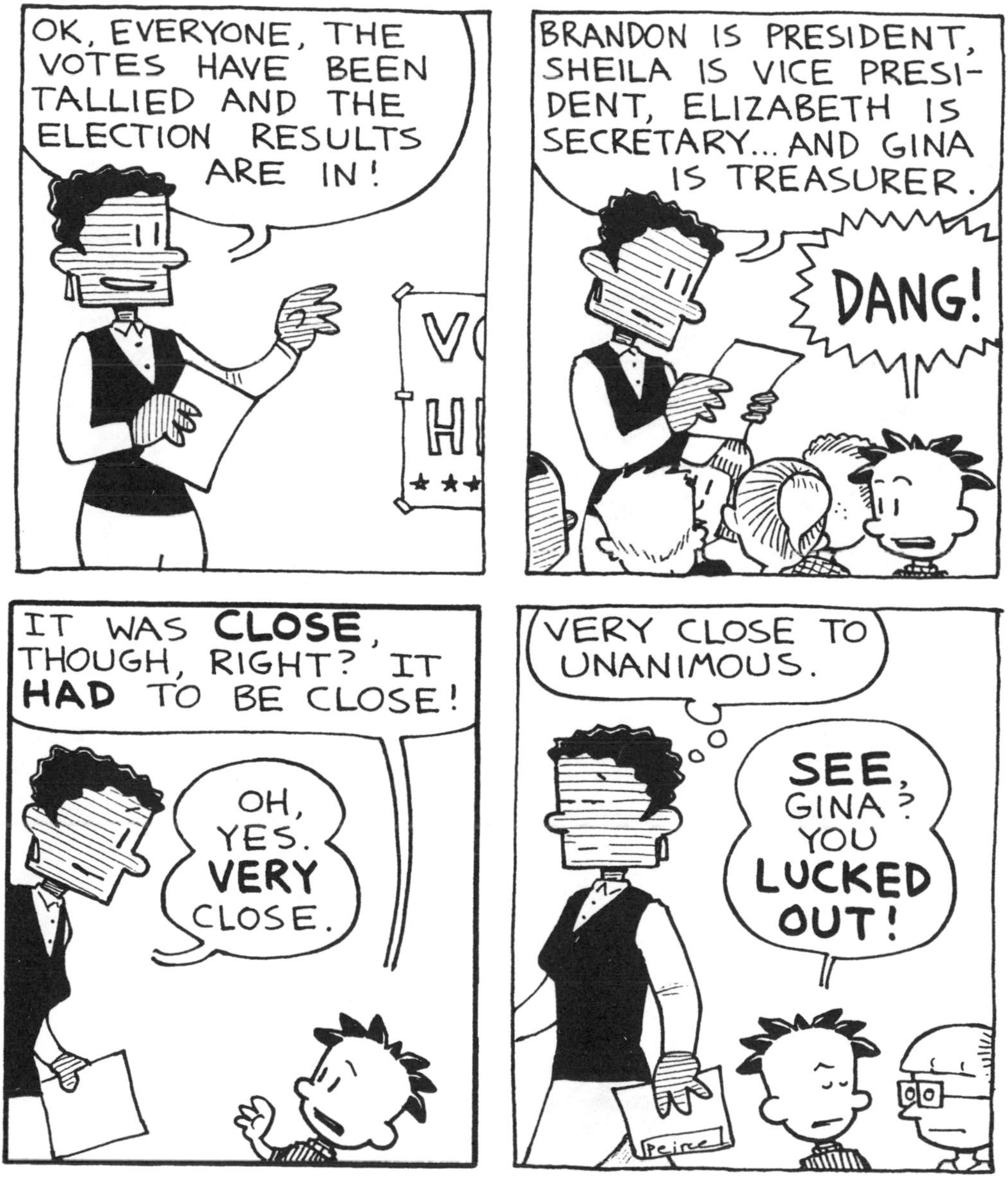
OK, EVERYONE, THE VOTES HAVE BEEN TALLIED AND THE ELECTION RESULTS ARE IN!
BRANDON IS PRESIDENT, SHEILA IS VICE PRESIDENT, ELIZABETH IS SECRETARY... AND GINA IS TREASURER.
DANG!
IT WAS **CLOSE**, THOUGH, RIGHT? IT **HAD** TO BE CLOSE!
OH, YES. **VERY** CLOSE.
VERY CLOSE TO UNANIMOUS.
SEE, GINA? YOU **LUCKED OUT**!

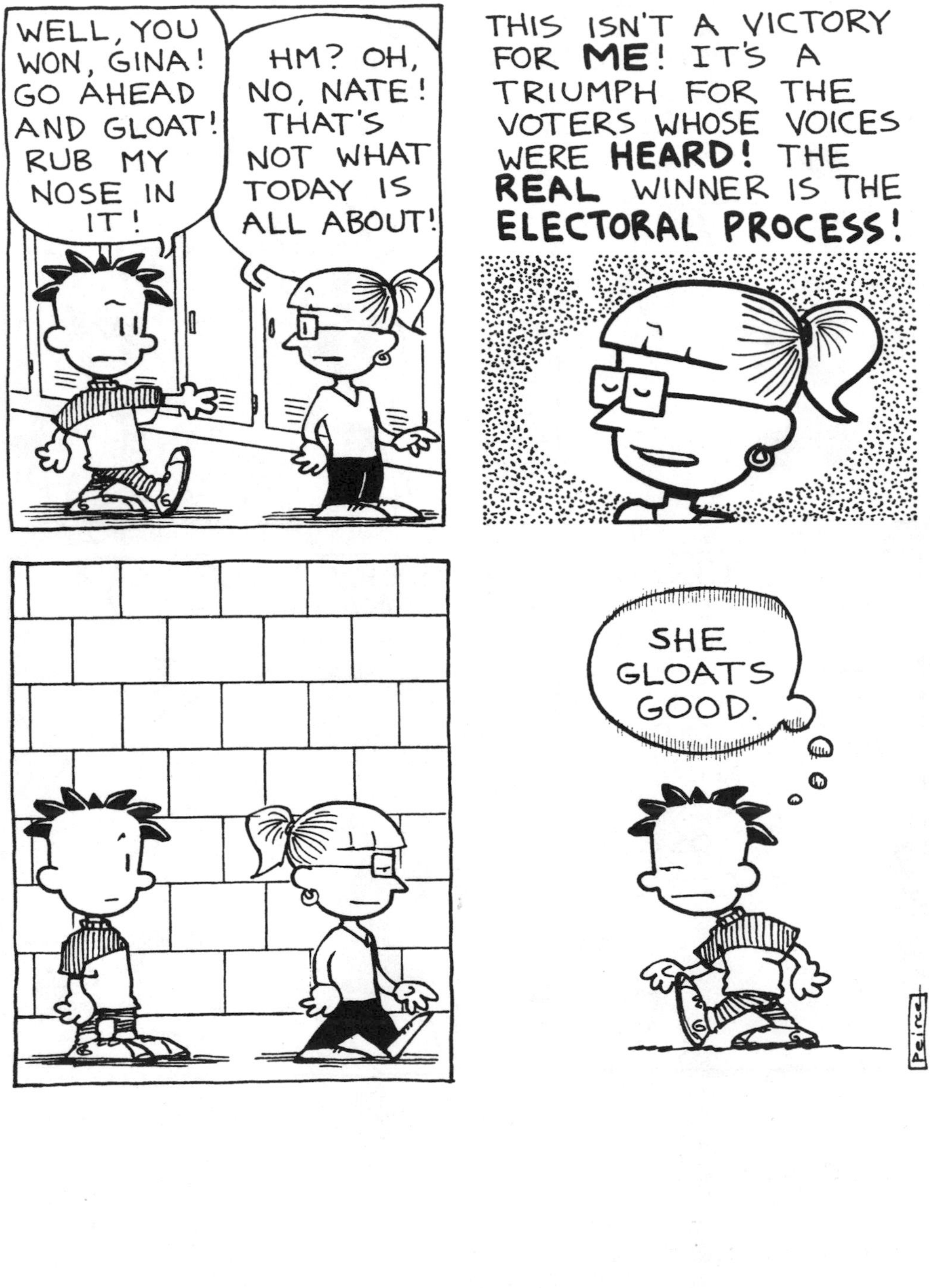

WELL, YOU WON, GINA! GO AHEAD AND GLOAT! RUB MY NOSE IN IT!
HM? OH, NO, NATE! THAT'S NOT WHAT TODAY IS ALL ABOUT!
THIS ISN'T A VICTORY FOR **ME**! IT'S A TRIUMPH FOR THE VOTERS WHOSE VOICES WERE **HEARD!** THE **REAL** WINNER IS THE **ELECTORAL PROCESS!**
SHE GLOATS GOOD.
Peirce

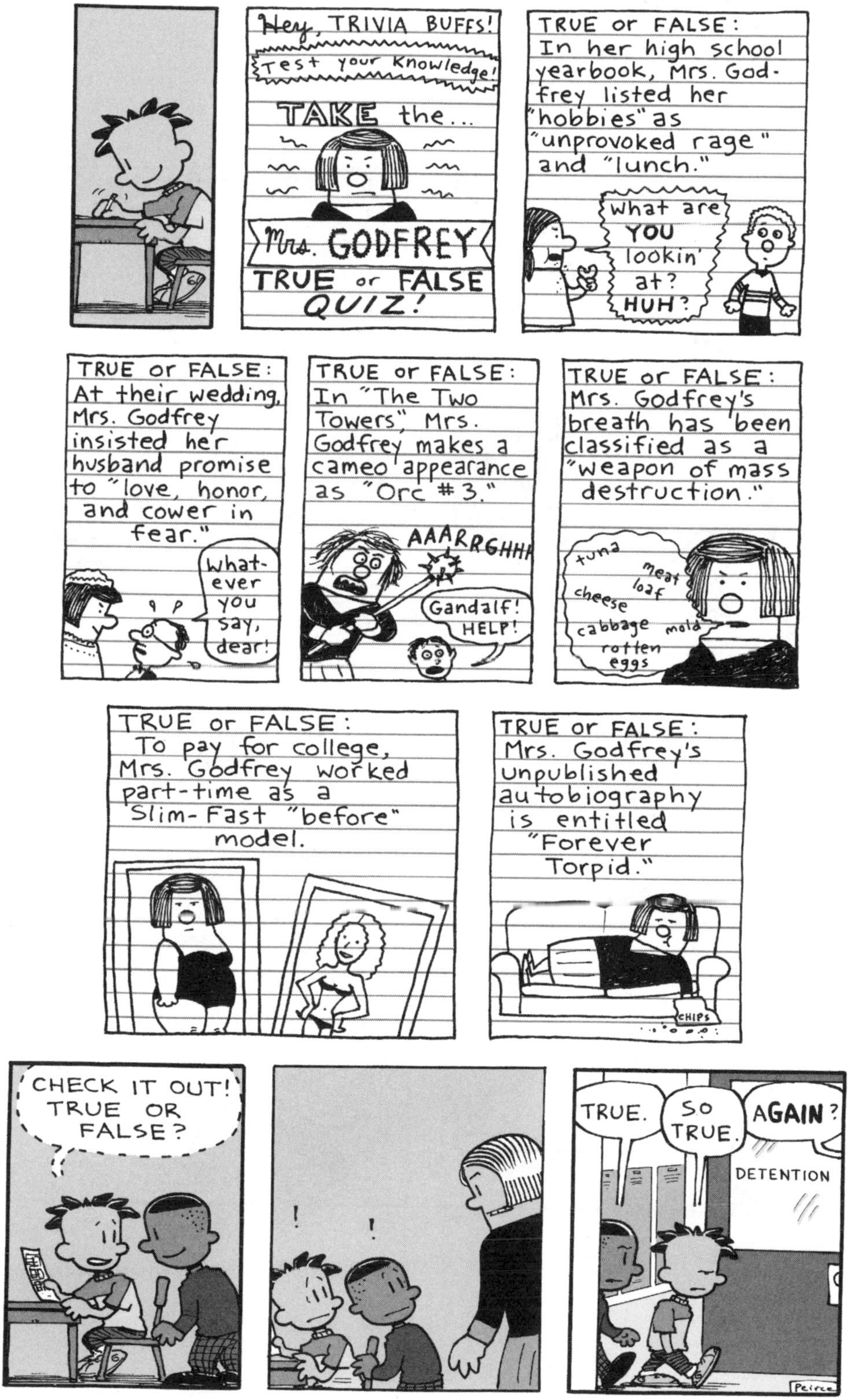
Hey, TRIVIA BUFFS!
Test your knowledge!
TAKE the...
Mrs. GODFREY
TRUE or FALSE QUIZ!
TRUE or FALSE: In her high school yearbook, Mrs. Godfrey listed her "hobbies" as "unprovoked rage" and "lunch."
What are YOU lookin' at? HUH?
TRUE or FALSE: At their wedding, Mrs. Godfrey insisted her husband promise to "love, honor, and cower in fear."
What-ever you say, dear!
TRUE or FALSE: In "The Two Towers", Mrs. Godfrey makes a cameo appearance as "Orc #3."
AAARRGHHH
Gandalf! HELP!
TRUE or FALSE: Mrs. Godfrey's breath has been classified as a "weapon of mass destruction."
tuna
meat loaf
cheese
cabbage
mold
rotten eggs
TRUE or FALSE: To pay for college, Mrs. Godfrey worked part-time as a Slim-Fast "before" model.
TRUE or FALSE: Mrs. Godfrey's unpublished autobiography is entitled "Forever Torpid."
CHIPS
CHECK IT OUT! TRUE OR FALSE?
!
!
TRUE.
SO TRUE.
AGAIN?
DETENTION
Peirce

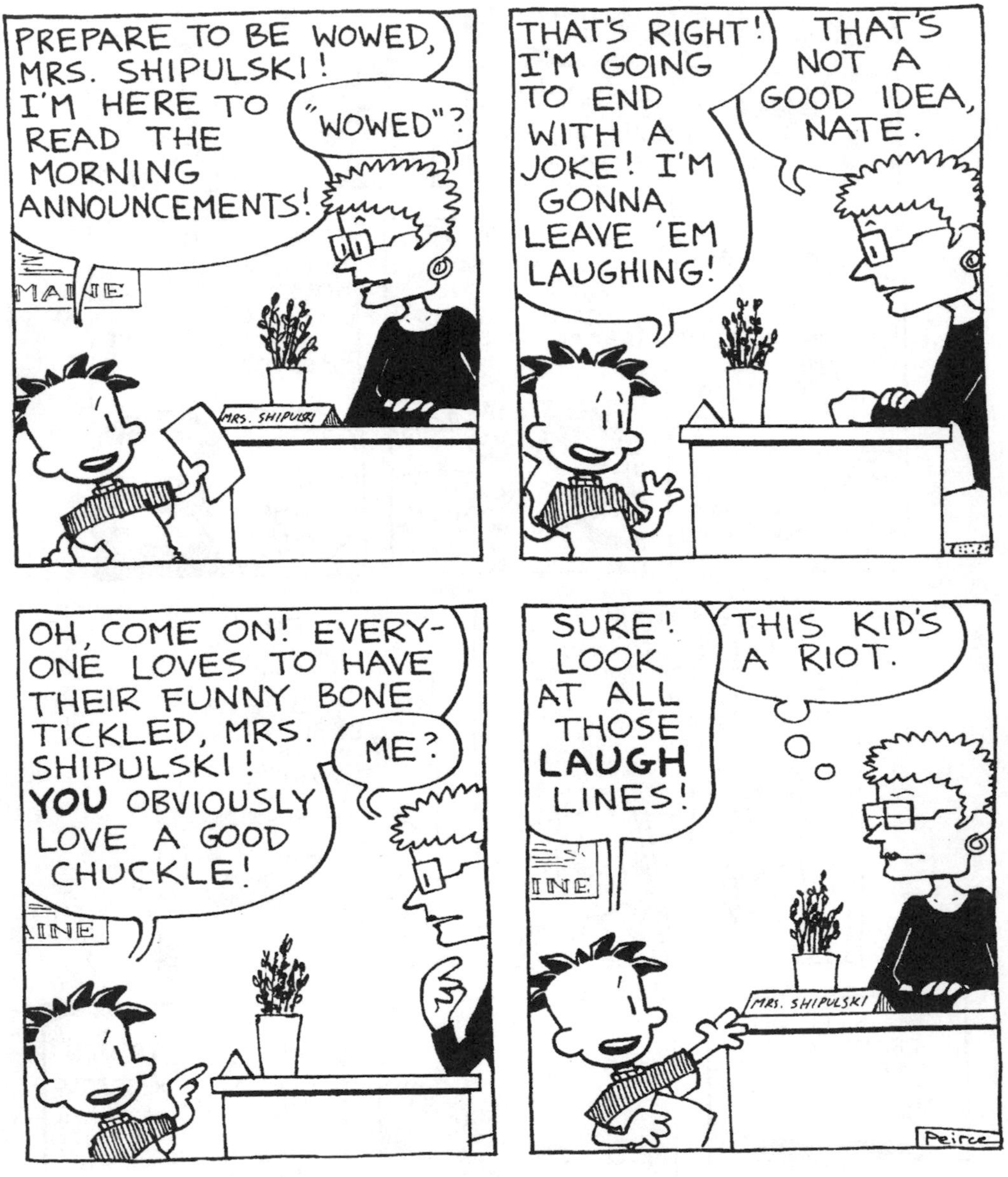
PREPARE TO BE WOWED, MRS. SHIPULSKI! I'M HERE TO READ THE MORNING ANNOUNCEMENTS!
"WOWED"?
MAINE
MRS. SHIPULSKI
THAT'S RIGHT! I'M GOING TO END WITH A JOKE! I'M GONNA LEAVE 'EM LAUGHING!
THAT'S NOT A GOOD IDEA, NATE.
OH, COME ON! EVERYONE LOVES TO HAVE THEIR FUNNY BONE TICKLED, MRS. SHIPULSKI! **YOU** OBVIOUSLY LOVE A GOOD CHUCKLE!
ME?
AINE
SURE! LOOK AT ALL THOSE **LAUGH** LINES!
THIS KID'S A RIOT.
INE
MRS. SHIPULSKI
Peirce

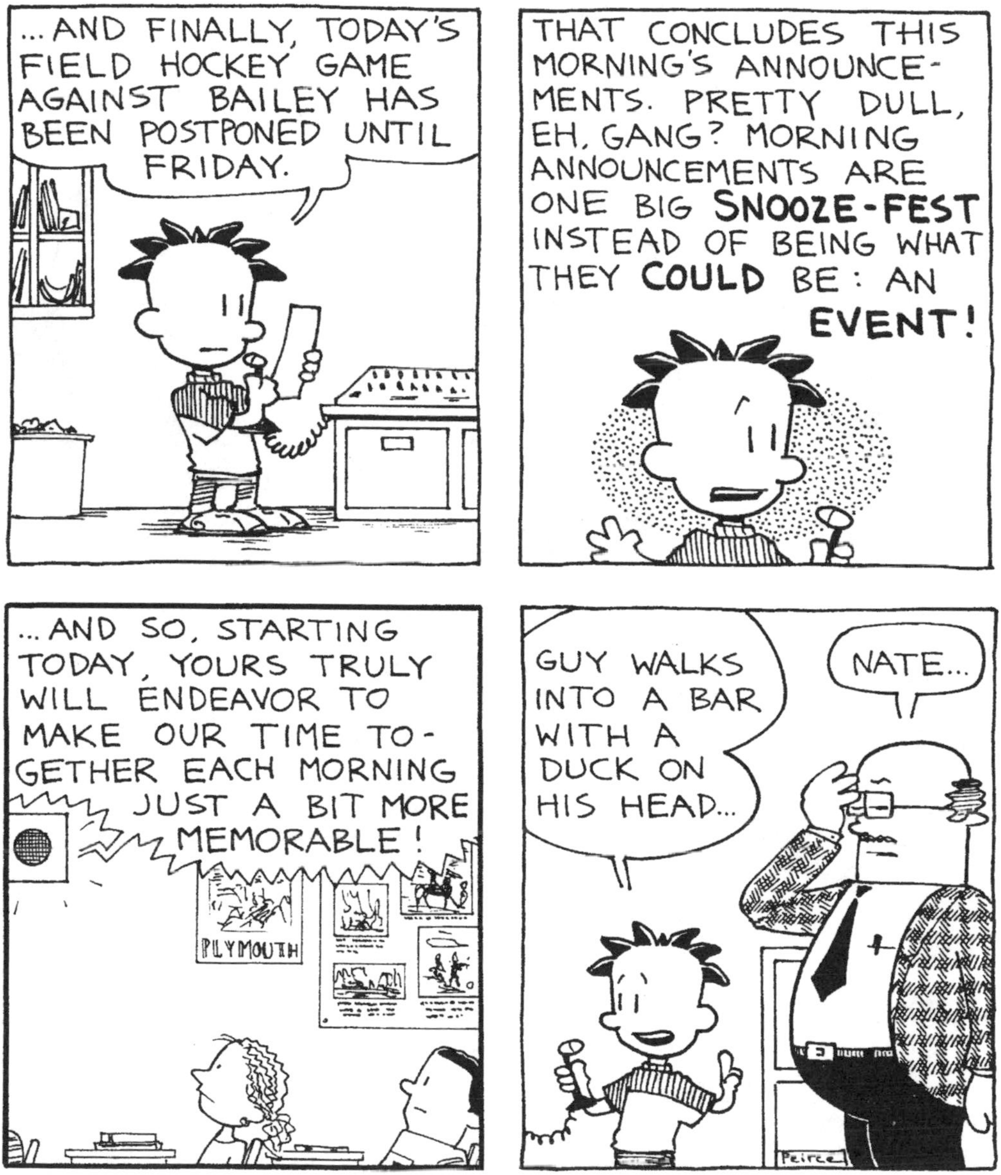
...AND FINALLY, TODAY'S FIELD HOCKEY GAME AGAINST BAILEY HAS BEEN POSTPONED UNTIL FRIDAY.
THAT CONCLUDES THIS MORNING'S ANNOUNCE-MENTS. PRETTY DULL, EH, GANG? MORNING ANNOUNCEMENTS ARE ONE BIG SNOOZE-FEST INSTEAD OF BEING WHAT THEY COULD BE: AN EVENT!
...AND SO, STARTING TODAY, YOURS TRULY WILL ENDEAVOR TO MAKE OUR TIME TO-GETHER EACH MORNING JUST A BIT MORE MEMORABLE!
PLYMOUTH
GUY WALKS INTO A BAR WITH A DUCK ON HIS HEAD...
NATE...
Peirce

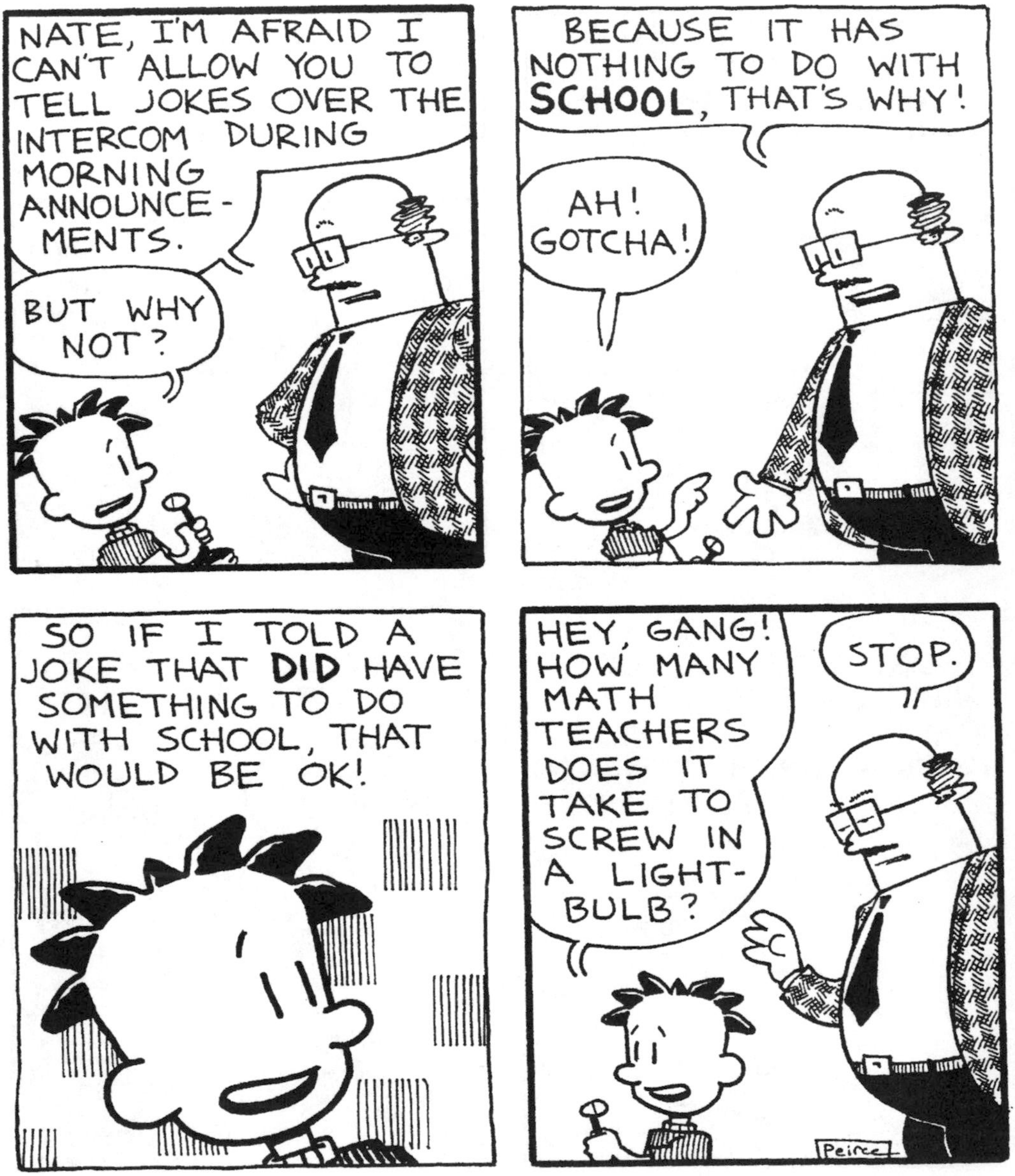
NATE, I'M AFRAID I CAN'T ALLOW YOU TO TELL JOKES OVER THE INTERCOM DURING MORNING ANNOUNCE-MENTS.
BUT WHY NOT?
BECAUSE IT HAS NOTHING TO DO WITH **SCHOOL**, THAT'S WHY!
AH! GOTCHA!
SO IF I TOLD A JOKE THAT **DID** HAVE SOMETHING TO DO WITH SCHOOL, THAT WOULD BE OK!
HEY, GANG! HOW MANY MATH TEACHERS DOES IT TAKE TO SCREW IN A LIGHT-BULB?
STOP.
Peirce

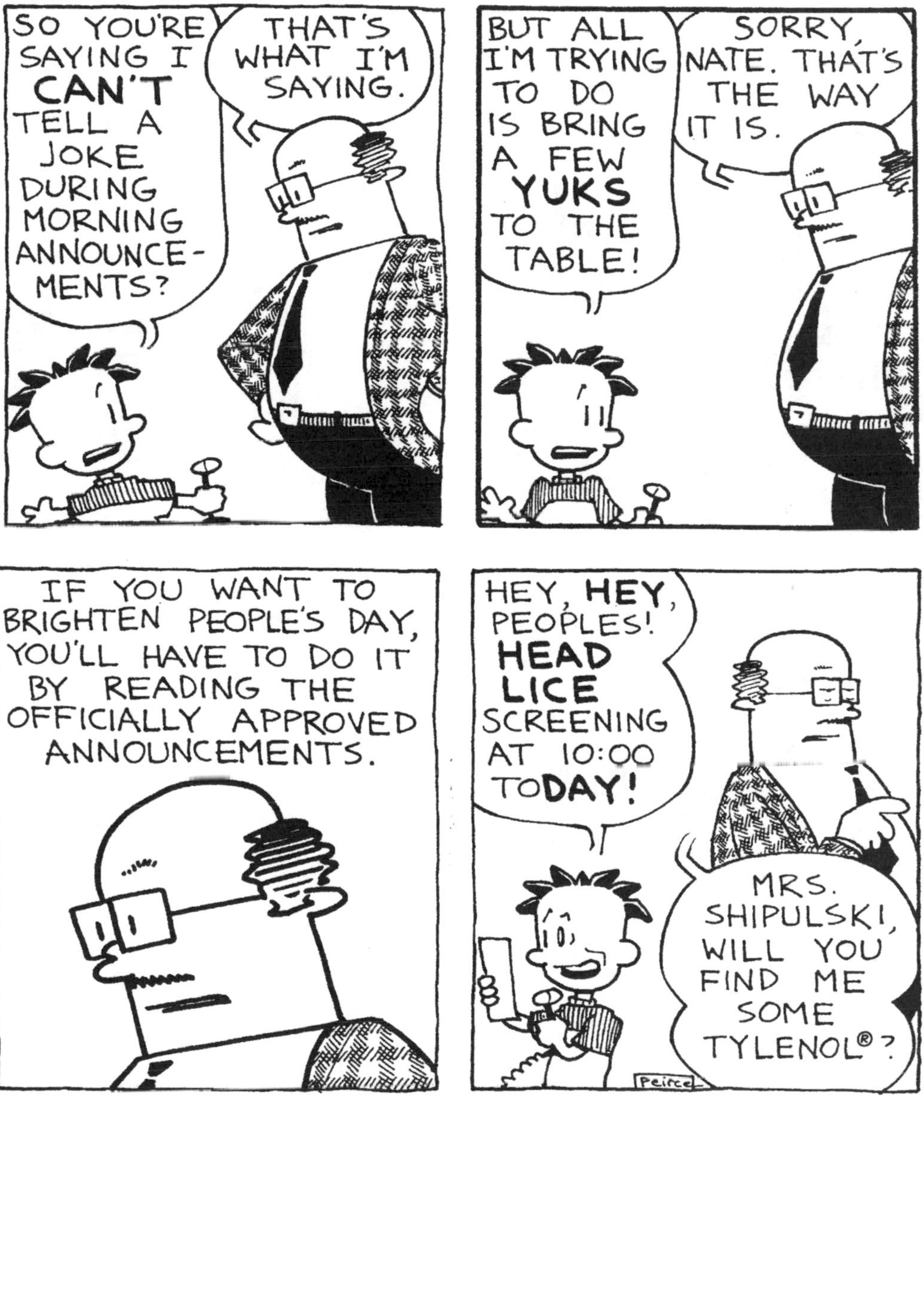
SO YOU'RE SAYING I **CAN'T** TELL A JOKE DURING MORNING ANNOUNCE-MENTS?
THAT'S WHAT I'M SAYING.
BUT ALL I'M TRYING TO DO IS BRING A FEW **YUKS** TO THE TABLE!
SORRY, NATE. THAT'S THE WAY IT IS.
IF YOU WANT TO BRIGHTEN PEOPLE'S DAY, YOU'LL HAVE TO DO IT BY READING THE OFFICIALLY APPROVED ANNOUNCEMENTS.
HEY, **HEY**, PEOPLES! **HEAD LICE** SCREENING AT 10:00 TO**DAY**!
MRS. SHIPULSKI, WILL YOU FIND ME SOME TYLENOL®?
Peirce

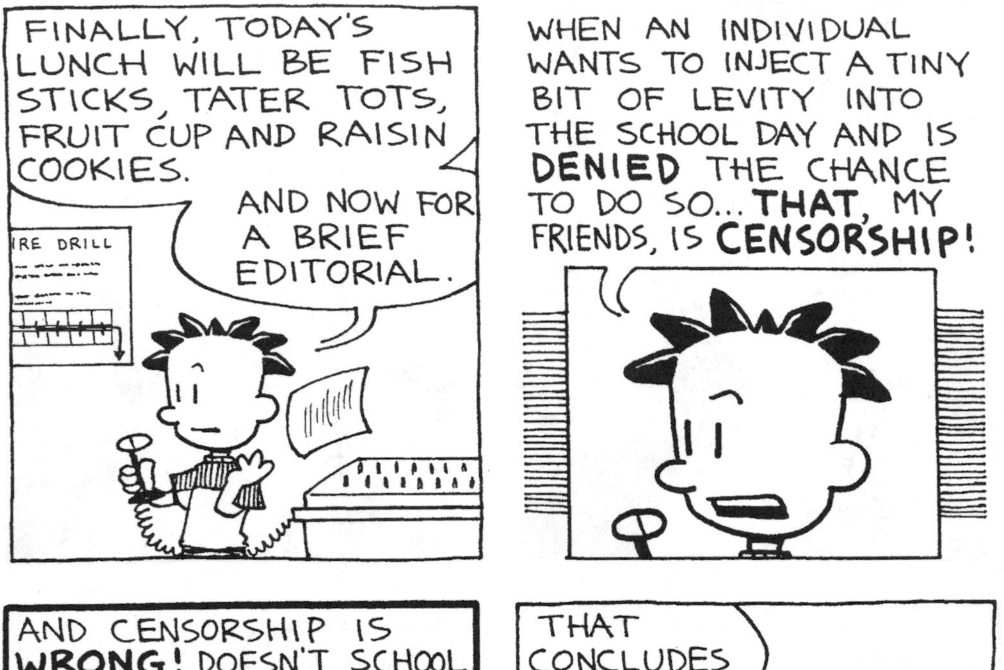

FINALLY, TODAY'S LUNCH WILL BE FISH STICKS, TATER TOTS, FRUIT CUP AND RAISIN COOKIES.
AND NOW FOR A BRIEF EDITORIAL.
RE DRILL
WHEN AN INDIVIDUAL WANTS TO INJECT A TINY BIT OF LEVITY INTO THE SCHOOL DAY AND IS DENIED THE CHANCE TO DO SO... THAT, MY FRIENDS, IS CENSORSHIP!
AND CENSORSHIP IS WRONG! DOESN'T SCHOOL TEACH US ABOUT FREE SPEECH? SHOULDN'T MORNING ANNOUNCEMENTS BE A TIME FOR OUR VOICES TO BE HEARD? I SAY YES!!
THAT CONCLUDES THIS BRIEF EDITORIAL.
Peirce

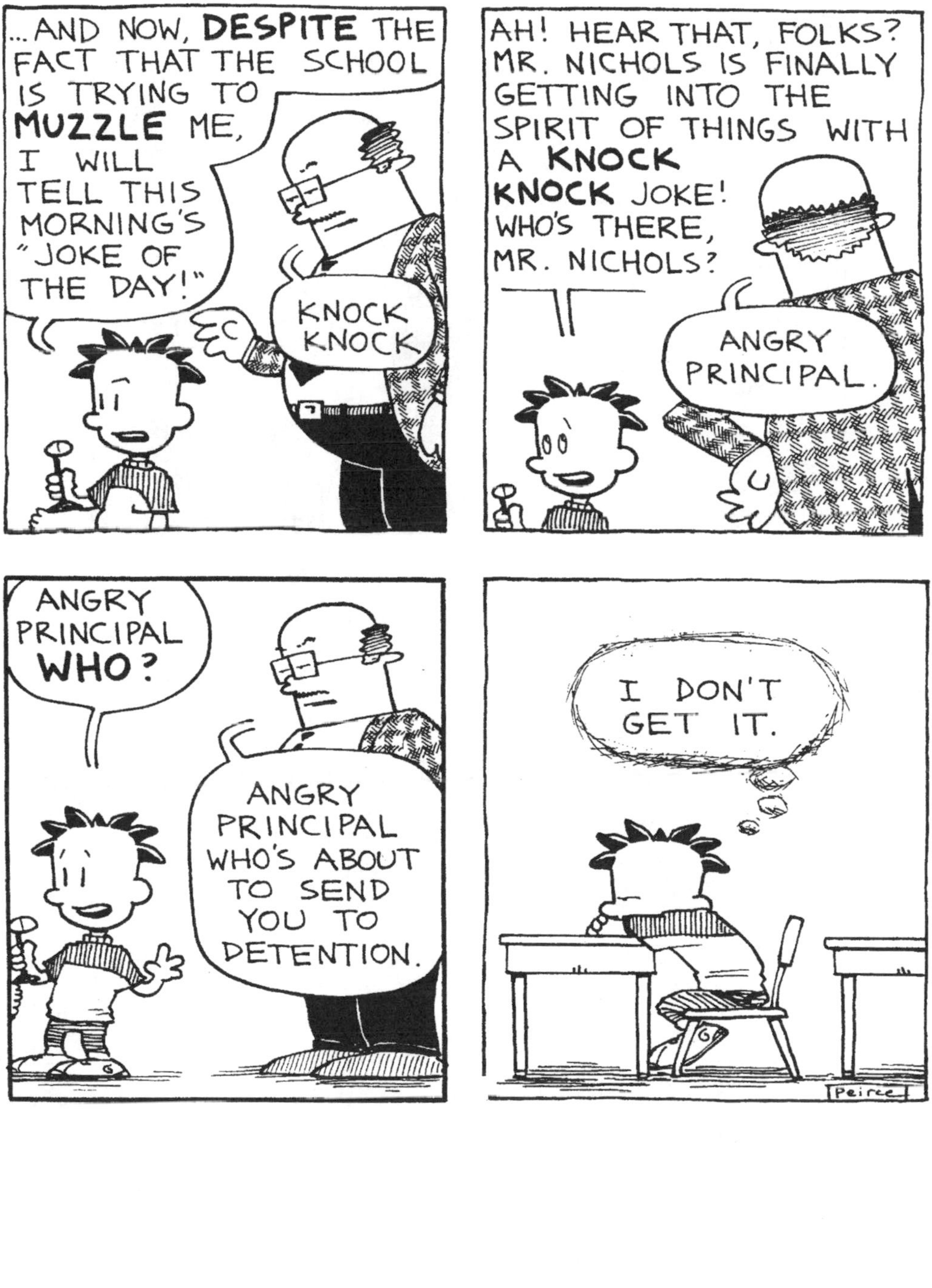
...AND NOW, DESPITE THE FACT THAT THE SCHOOL IS TRYING TO MUZZLE ME, I WILL TELL THIS MORNING'S "JOKE OF THE DAY!"
KNOCK KNOCK
AH! HEAR THAT, FOLKS? MR. NICHOLS IS FINALLY GETTING INTO THE SPIRIT OF THINGS WITH A KNOCK KNOCK JOKE! WHO'S THERE, MR. NICHOLS?
ANGRY PRINCIPAL.
ANGRY PRINCIPAL WHO?
ANGRY PRINCIPAL WHO'S ABOUT TO SEND YOU TO DETENTION.
I DON'T GET IT.
Peirce

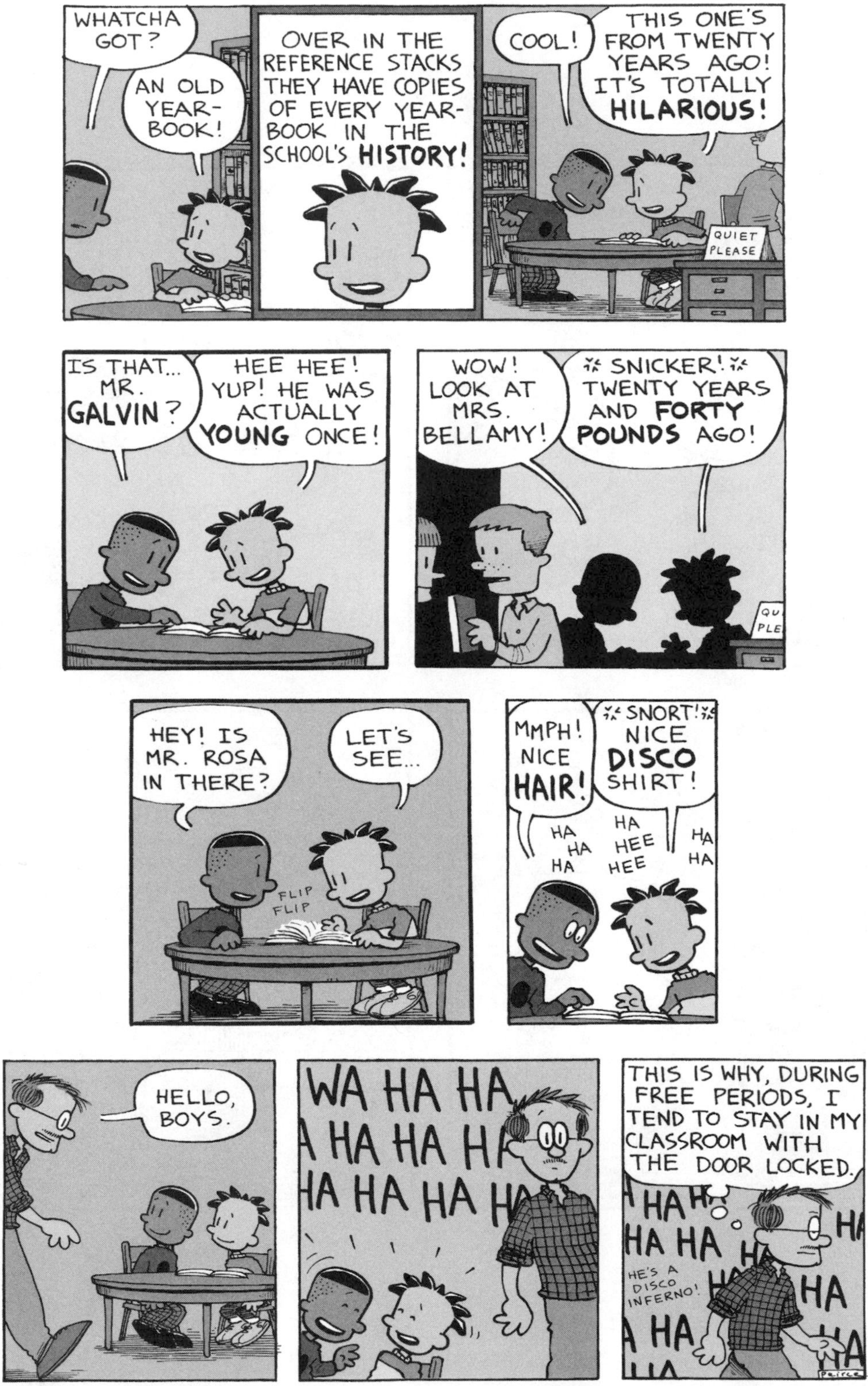
WHATCHA GOT?
AN OLD YEARBOOK!
OVER IN THE REFERENCE STACKS THEY HAVE COPIES OF EVERY YEARBOOK IN THE SCHOOL'S HISTORY!
COOL!
THIS ONE'S FROM TWENTY YEARS AGO! IT'S TOTALLY HILARIOUS!
QUIET PLEASE
IS THAT... MR. GALVIN?
HEE HEE! YUP! HE WAS ACTUALLY YOUNG ONCE!
WOW! LOOK AT MRS. BELLAMY!
SNICKER! TWENTY YEARS AND FORTY POUNDS AGO!
HEY! IS MR. ROSA IN THERE?
LET'S SEE...
FLIP FLIP
MMPH! NICE HAIR!
SNORT! NICE DISCO SHIRT!
HA HA HA
HA HEE HEE
HA HA
HELLO, BOYS.
WA HA HA
HA HA HA HA
HA HA HA HA
THIS IS WHY, DURING FREE PERIODS, I TEND TO STAY IN MY CLASSROOM WITH THE DOOR LOCKED.
HA HA
HA HA
HE'S A DISCO INFERNO!
HA
HA HA
HA

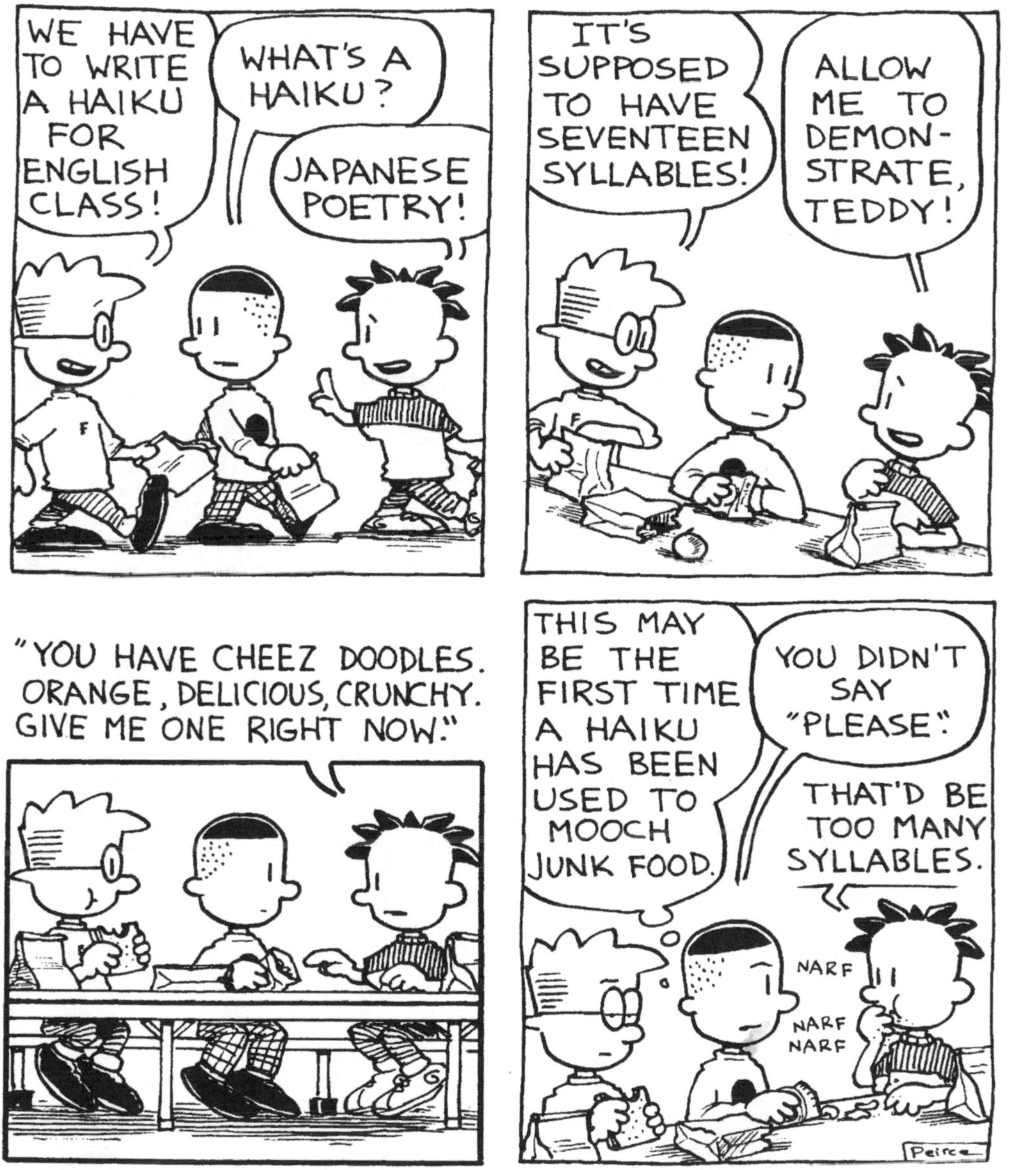
WE HAVE TO WRITE A HAIKU FOR ENGLISH CLASS!
WHAT'S A HAIKU?
JAPANESE POETRY!
IT'S SUPPOSED TO HAVE SEVENTEEN SYLLABLES!
ALLOW ME TO DEMON-STRATE, TEDDY!
"YOU HAVE CHEEZ DOODLES. ORANGE, DELICIOUS, CRUNCHY. GIVE ME ONE RIGHT NOW."
THIS MAY BE THE FIRST TIME A HAIKU HAS BEEN USED TO MOOCH JUNK FOOD.
YOU DIDN'T SAY "PLEASE."
THAT'D BE TOO MANY SYLLABLES.
NARF
NARF NARF
Peirce

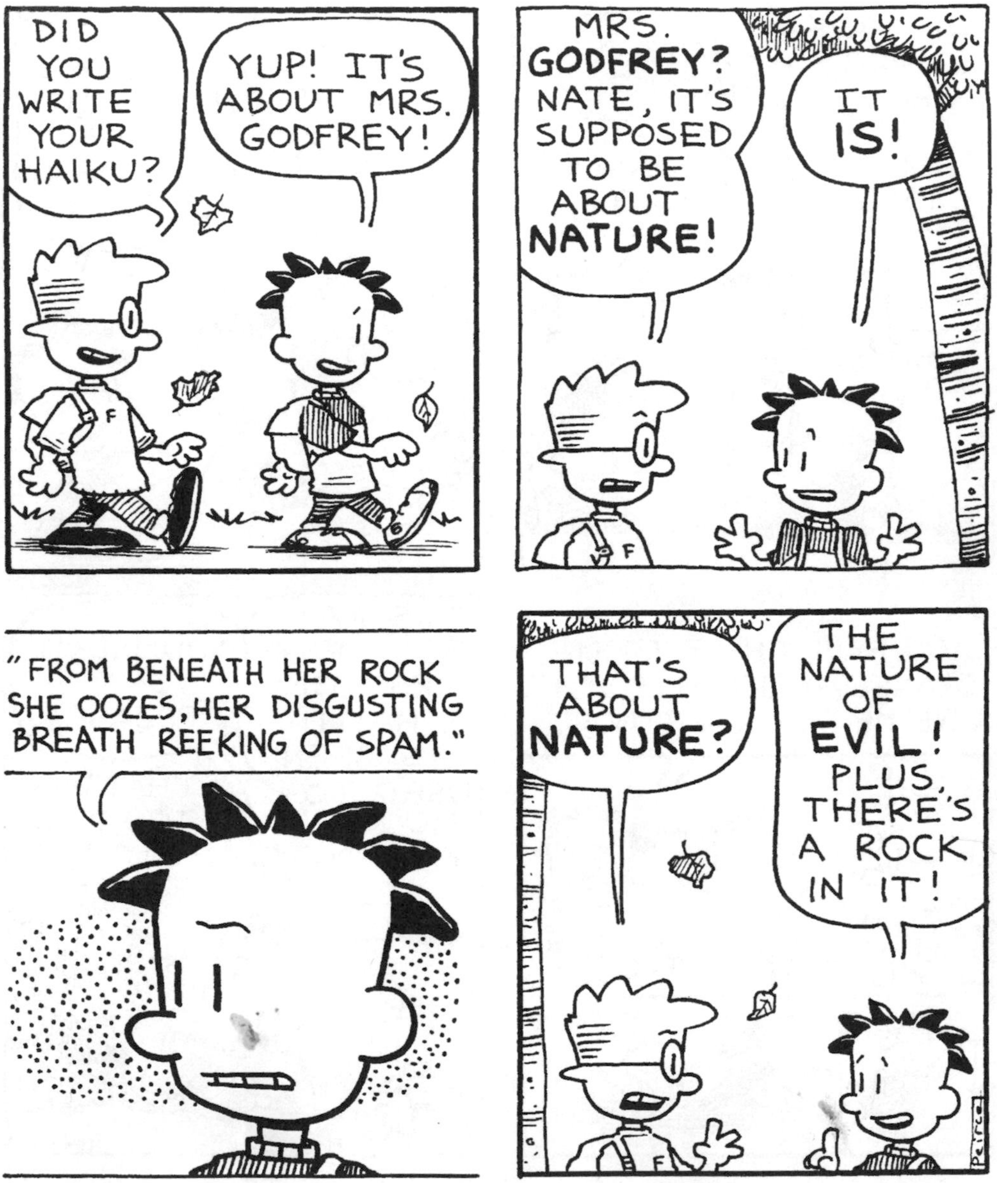
DID YOU WRITE YOUR HAIKU?
YUP! IT'S ABOUT MRS. GODFREY!
MRS. **GODFREY?** NATE, IT'S SUPPOSED TO BE ABOUT **NATURE!**
IT **IS!**
"FROM BENEATH HER ROCK SHE OOZES, HER DISGUSTING BREATH REEKING OF SPAM."
THAT'S ABOUT **NATURE?**
THE NATURE OF **EVIL!** PLUS, THERE'S A ROCK IN IT!
Peirce

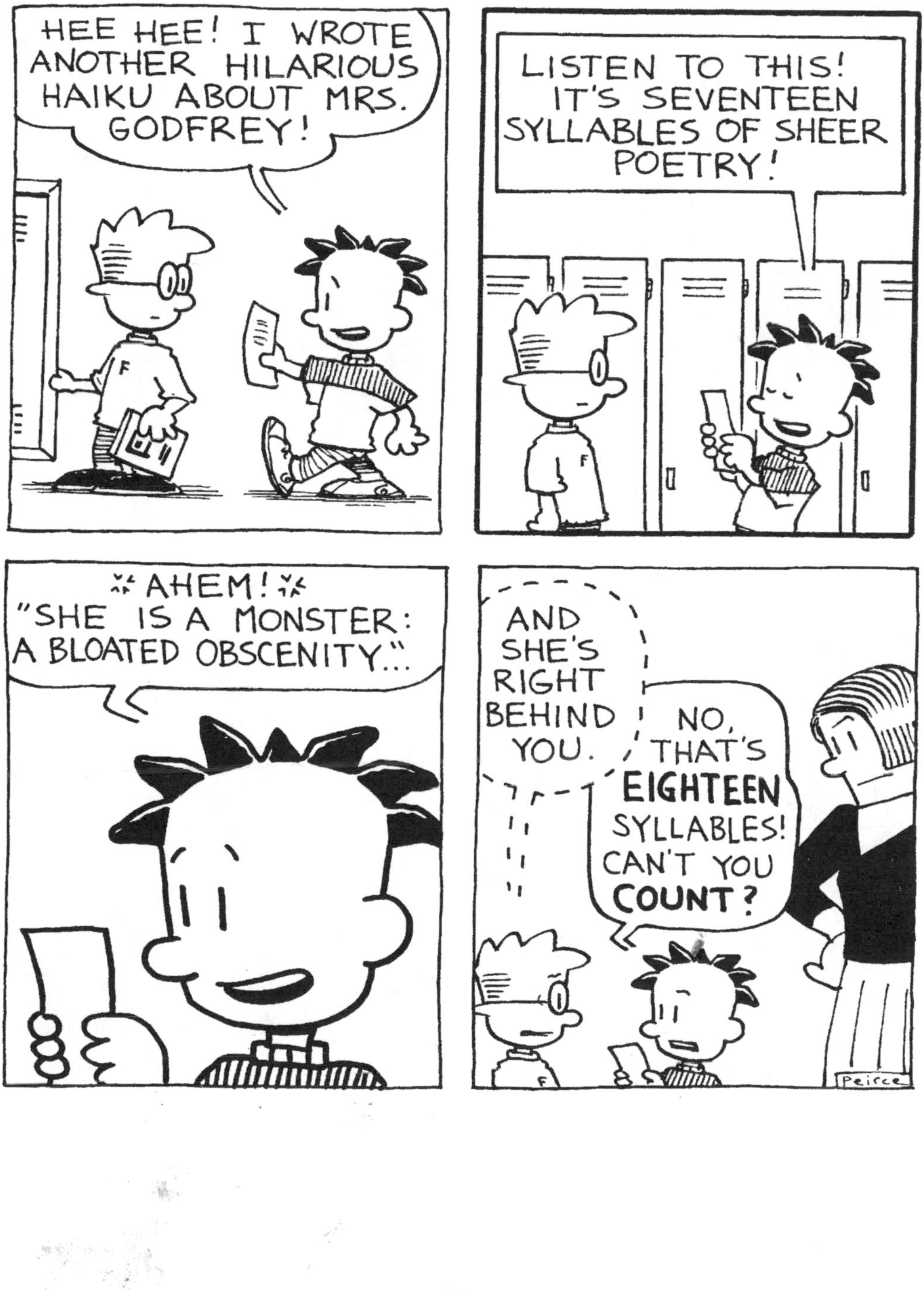
HEE HEE! I WROTE ANOTHER HILARIOUS HAIKU ABOUT MRS. GODFREY!
LISTEN TO THIS! IT'S SEVENTEEN SYLLABLES OF SHEER POETRY!
AHEM! "SHE IS A MONSTER: A BLOATED OBSCENITY."...
AND SHE'S RIGHT BEHIND YOU.
NO, THAT'S **EIGHTEEN** SYLLABLES! CAN'T YOU **COUNT**?
Peirce

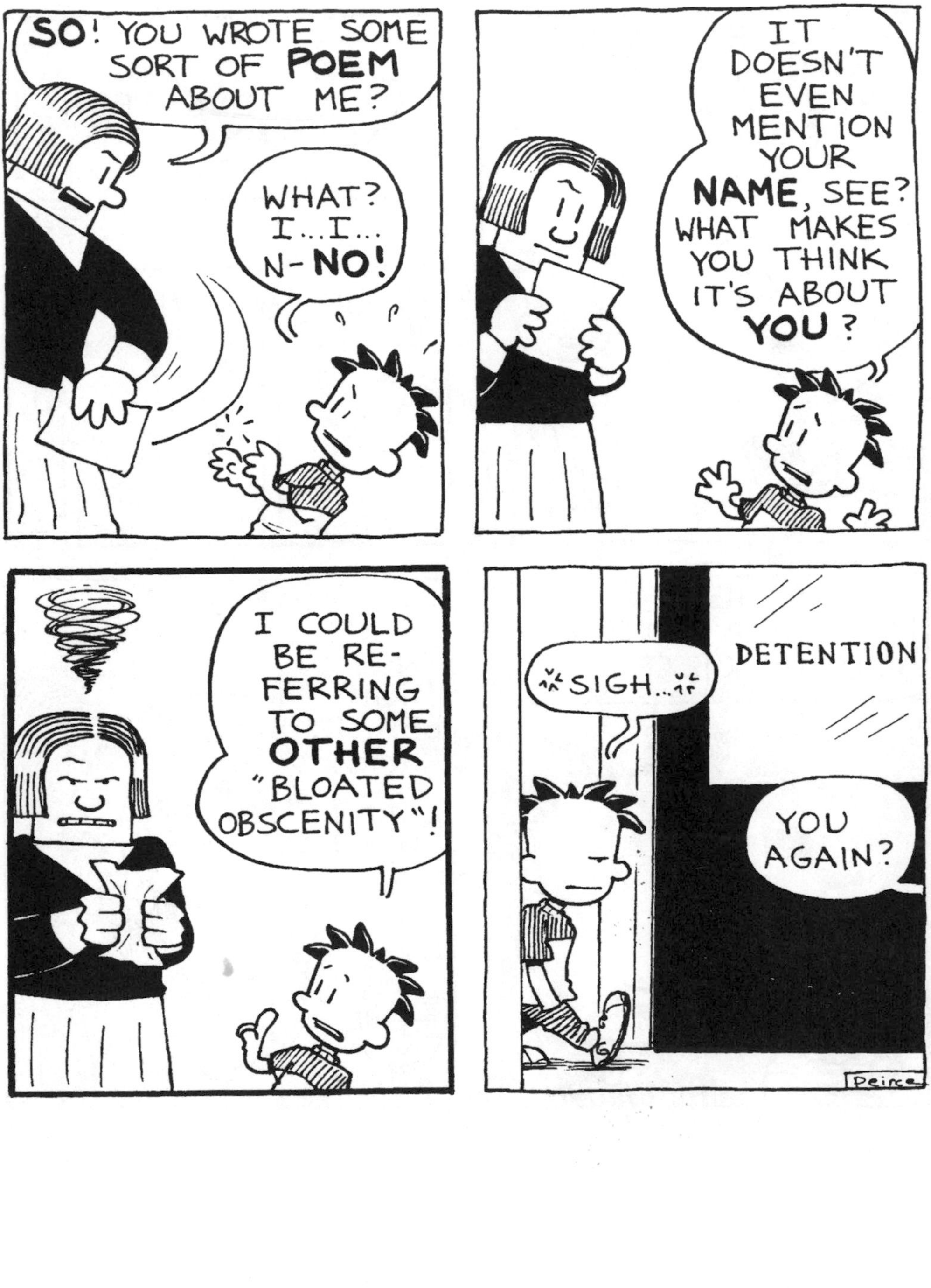

SO! YOU WROTE SOME SORT OF POEM ABOUT ME?
WHAT? I...I... N-NO!
IT DOESN'T EVEN MENTION YOUR NAME, SEE? WHAT MAKES YOU THINK IT'S ABOUT YOU?
I COULD BE RE-FERRING TO SOME OTHER "BLOATED OBSCENITY"!
SIGH...
DETENTION
YOU AGAIN?
Peirce

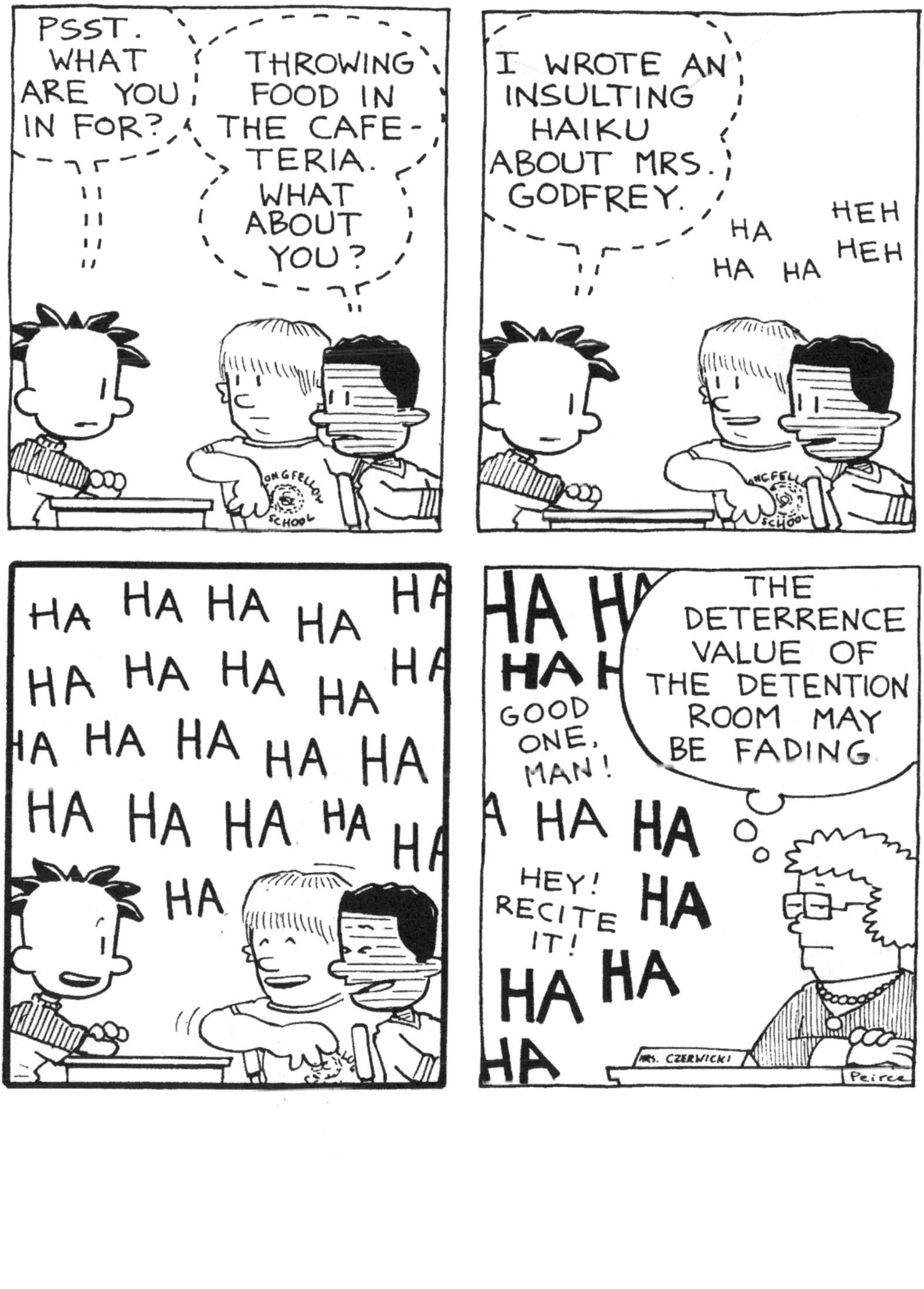
PSST. WHAT ARE YOU IN FOR?
THROWING FOOD IN THE CAFE-TERIA. WHAT ABOUT YOU?
I WROTE AN INSULTING HAIKU ABOUT MRS. GODFREY.
HA HEH HA HA HEH
HA HA HA HA HA HA HA HA HA HA HA HA HA HA HA HA HA HA HA HA HA HA HA HA
GOOD ONE, MAN!
HEY! RECITE IT!
THE DETERRENCE VALUE OF THE DETENTION ROOM MAY BE FADING.
MRS. CZERWICKI
Peirce

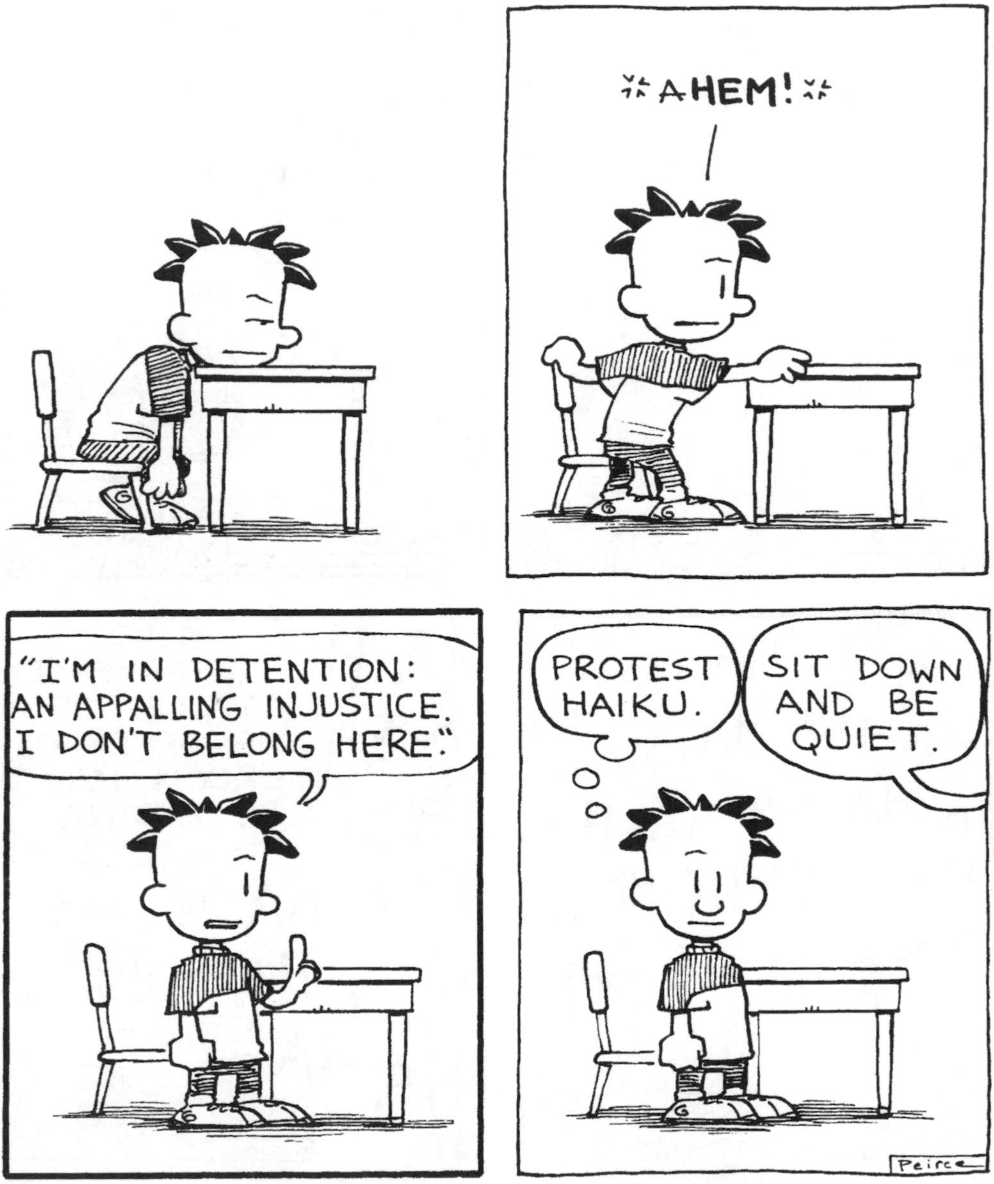
AHEM!
"I'M IN DETENTION:
AN APPALLING INJUSTICE.
I DON'T BELONG HERE."
PROTEST HAIKU.
SIT DOWN AND BE QUIET.
Peirce

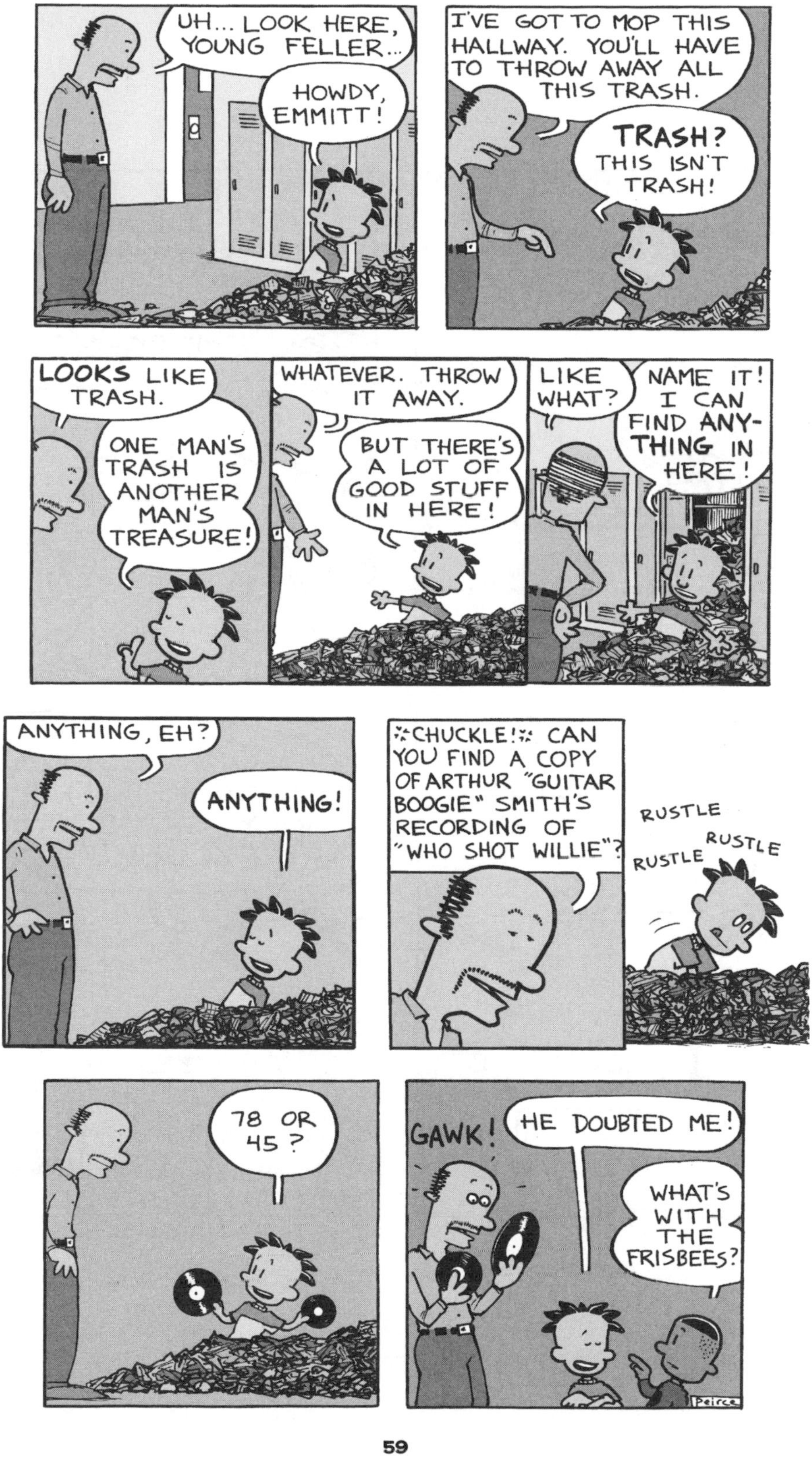
UH... LOOK HERE, YOUNG FELLER...
HOWDY, EMMITT!
I'VE GOT TO MOP THIS HALLWAY. YOU'LL HAVE TO THROW AWAY ALL THIS TRASH.
TRASH? THIS ISN'T TRASH!
LOOKS LIKE TRASH.
ONE MAN'S TRASH IS ANOTHER MAN'S TREASURE!
WHATEVER. THROW IT AWAY.
BUT THERE'S A LOT OF GOOD STUFF IN HERE!
LIKE WHAT?
NAME IT! I CAN FIND ANYTHING IN HERE!
ANYTHING, EH?
ANYTHING!
CHUCKLE! CAN YOU FIND A COPY OF ARTHUR "GUITAR BOOGIE" SMITH'S RECORDING OF "WHO SHOT WILLIE"?
RUSTLE
RUSTLE
RUSTLE
78 OR 45?
GAWK!
HE DOUBTED ME!
WHAT'S WITH THE FRISBEES?
Peirce

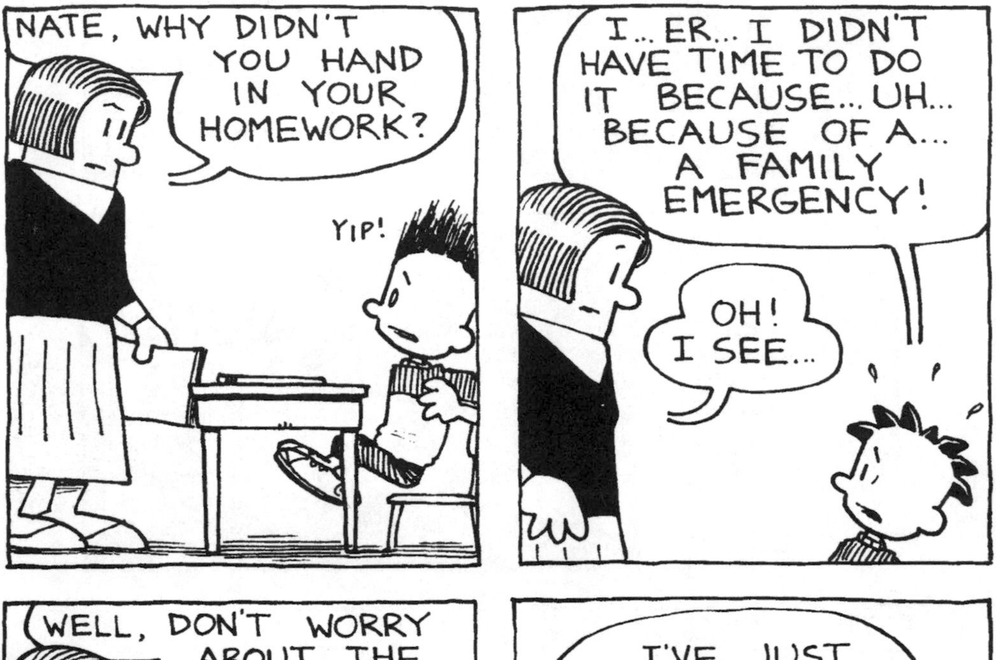
NATE, WHY DIDN'T YOU HAND IN YOUR HOMEWORK?
YIP!
I... ER... I DIDN'T HAVE TIME TO DO IT BECAUSE... UH... BECAUSE OF A... A FAMILY EMERGENCY!
OH! I SEE...
WELL, DON'T WORRY ABOUT THE HOMEWORK, NATE. I HOPE EVERYTHING WORKS OUT ALL RIGHT.
I'VE JUST DISCOVERED THE HOLY GRAIL OF EXCUSES!
PEIRCE

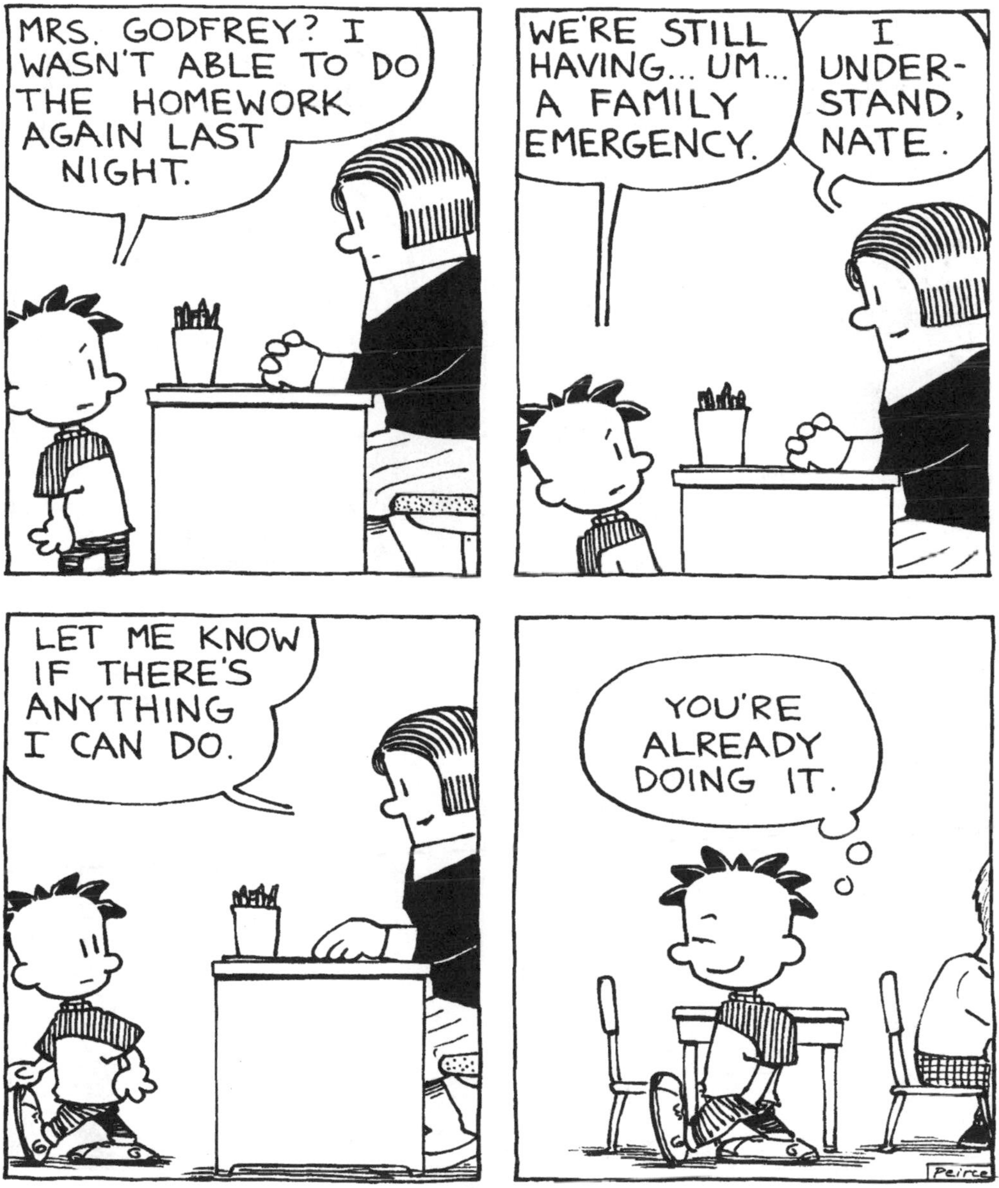
MRS. GODFREY? I WASN'T ABLE TO DO THE HOMEWORK AGAIN LAST NIGHT.
WE'RE STILL HAVING... UM... A FAMILY EMERGENCY.
I UNDERSTAND, NATE.
LET ME KNOW IF THERE'S ANYTHING I CAN DO.
YOU'RE ALREADY DOING IT.
Peirce

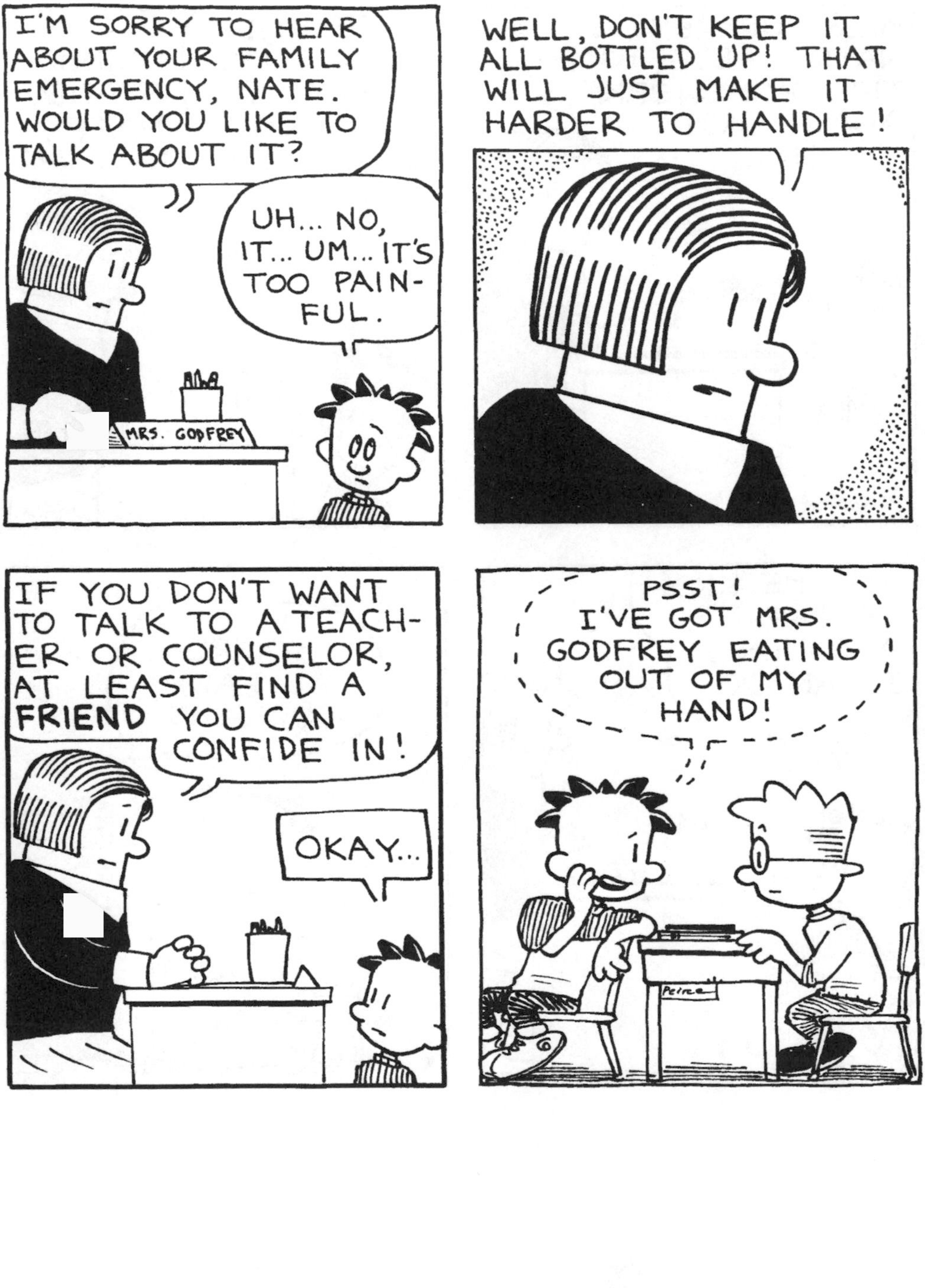
I'M SORRY TO HEAR ABOUT YOUR FAMILY EMERGENCY, NATE. WOULD YOU LIKE TO TALK ABOUT IT?
UH... NO, IT... UM... IT'S TOO PAIN-FUL.
MRS. GODFREY
WELL, DON'T KEEP IT ALL BOTTLED UP! THAT WILL JUST MAKE IT HARDER TO HANDLE!
IF YOU DON'T WANT TO TALK TO A TEACH-ER OR COUNSELOR, AT LEAST FIND A **FRIEND** YOU CAN CONFIDE IN!
OKAY...
PSST! I'VE GOT MRS. GODFREY EATING OUT OF MY HAND!
Peirce

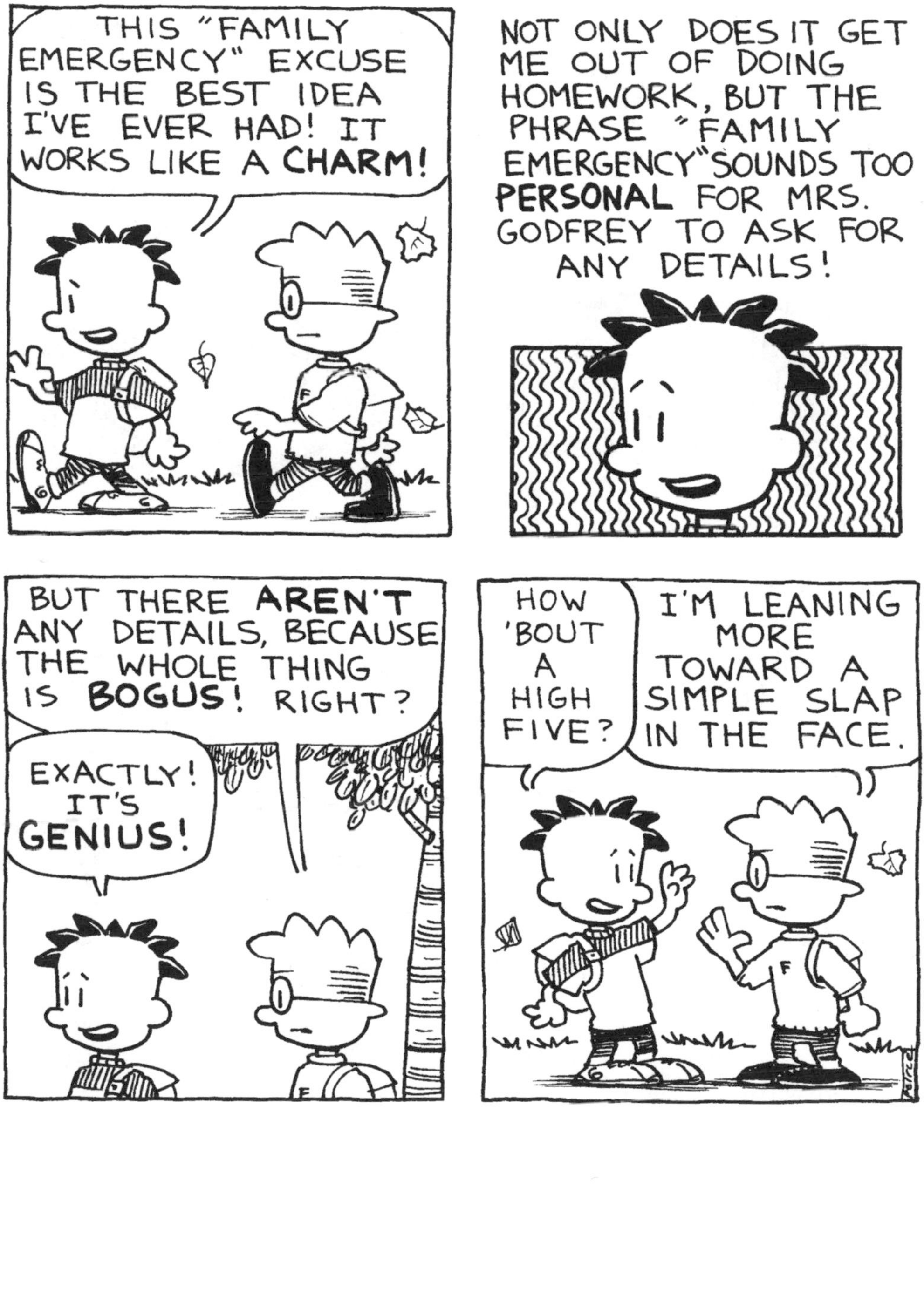
THIS "FAMILY EMERGENCY" EXCUSE IS THE BEST IDEA I'VE EVER HAD! IT WORKS LIKE A **CHARM**!
NOT ONLY DOES IT GET ME OUT OF DOING HOMEWORK, BUT THE PHRASE "FAMILY EMERGENCY" SOUNDS TOO **PERSONAL** FOR MRS. GODFREY TO ASK FOR ANY DETAILS!
BUT THERE **AREN'T** ANY DETAILS, BECAUSE THE WHOLE THING IS **BOGUS**! RIGHT?
EXACTLY! IT'S GENIUS!
HOW 'BOUT A HIGH FIVE?
I'M LEANING MORE TOWARD A SIMPLE SLAP IN THE FACE.

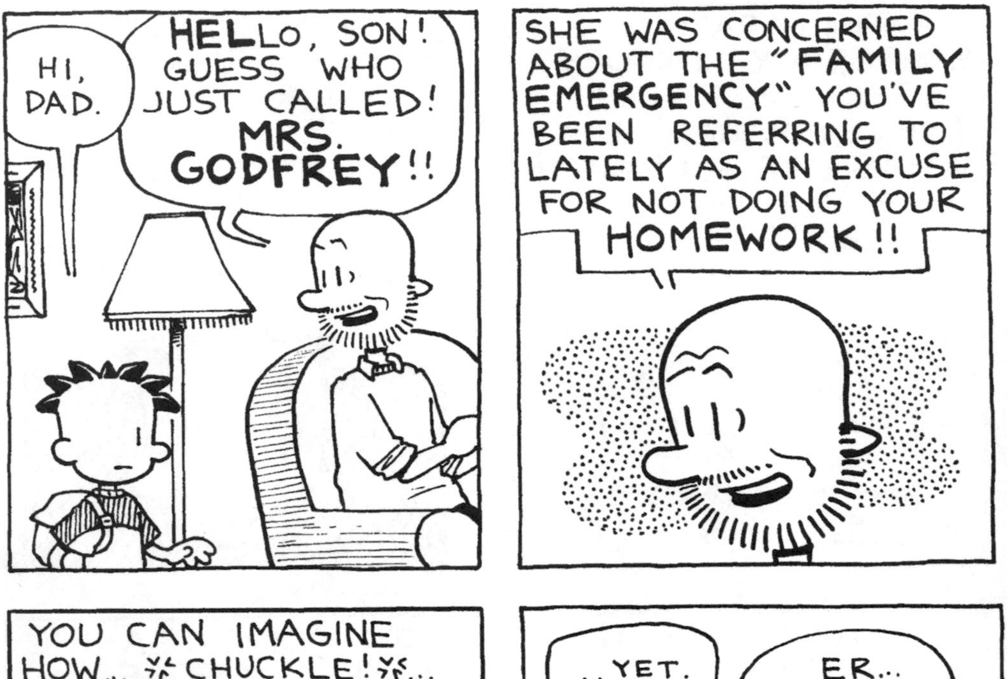
HI, DAD.
HELLO, SON! GUESS WHO JUST CALLED! MRS. GODFREY!!
SHE WAS CONCERNED ABOUT THE "FAMILY EMERGENCY" YOU'VE BEEN REFERRING TO LATELY AS AN EXCUSE FOR NOT DOING YOUR HOMEWORK!!
YOU CAN IMAGINE HOW... *CHUCKLE!*... AWKWARD IT WAS FOR ME TO TELL HER THERE IS NO FAMILY EMERGENCY!...
...YET.
ER... I'LL BE IN MY ROOM.
Peirce

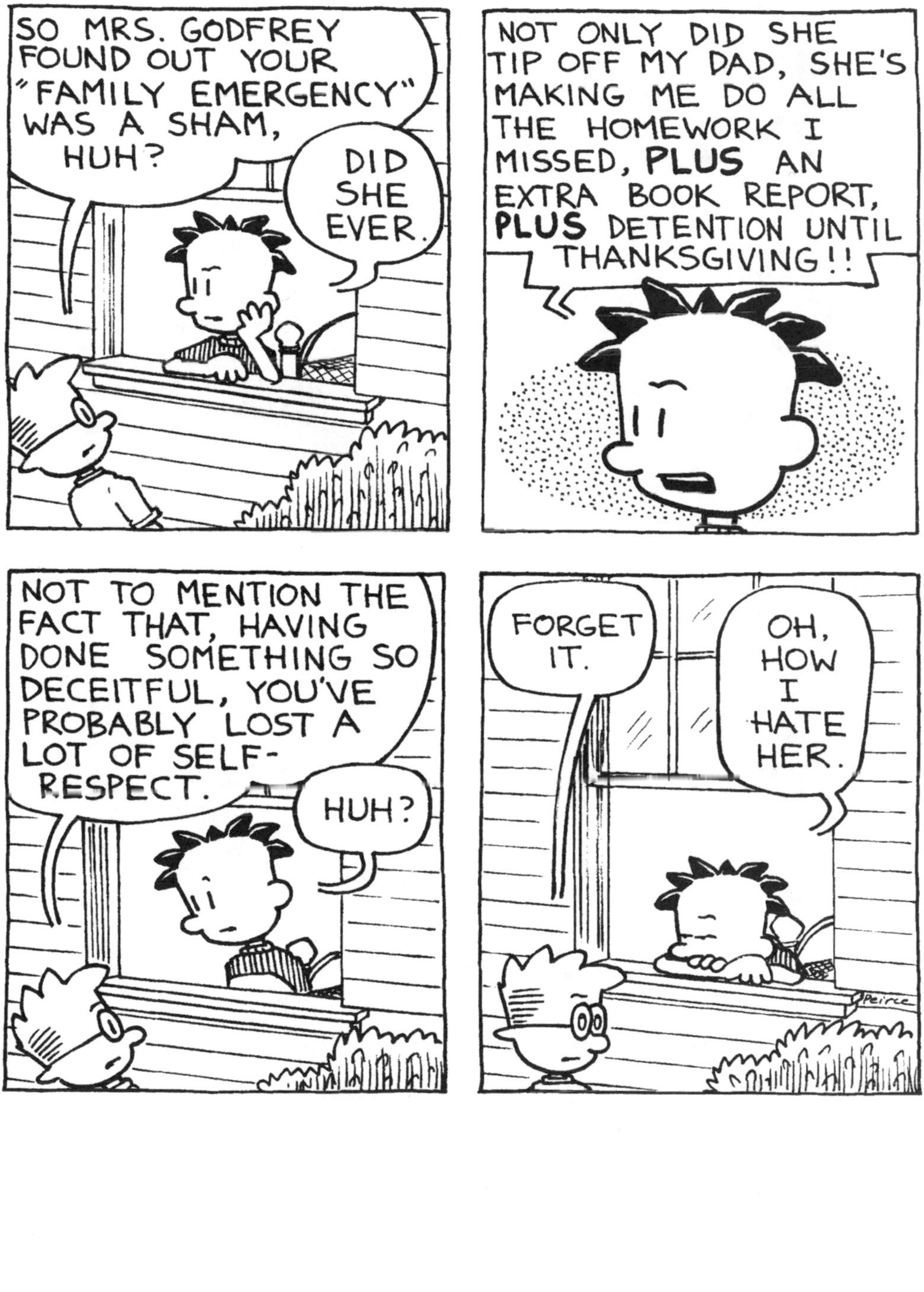
SO MRS. GODFREY FOUND OUT YOUR "FAMILY EMERGENCY" WAS A SHAM, HUH?
DID SHE EVER.
NOT ONLY DID SHE TIP OFF MY DAD, SHE'S MAKING ME DO ALL THE HOMEWORK I MISSED, **PLUS** AN EXTRA BOOK REPORT, **PLUS** DETENTION UNTIL THANKSGIVING!!
NOT TO MENTION THE FACT THAT, HAVING DONE SOMETHING SO DECEITFUL, YOU'VE PROBABLY LOST A LOT OF SELF-RESPECT.
HUH?
FORGET IT.
OH, HOW I HATE HER.
Peirce

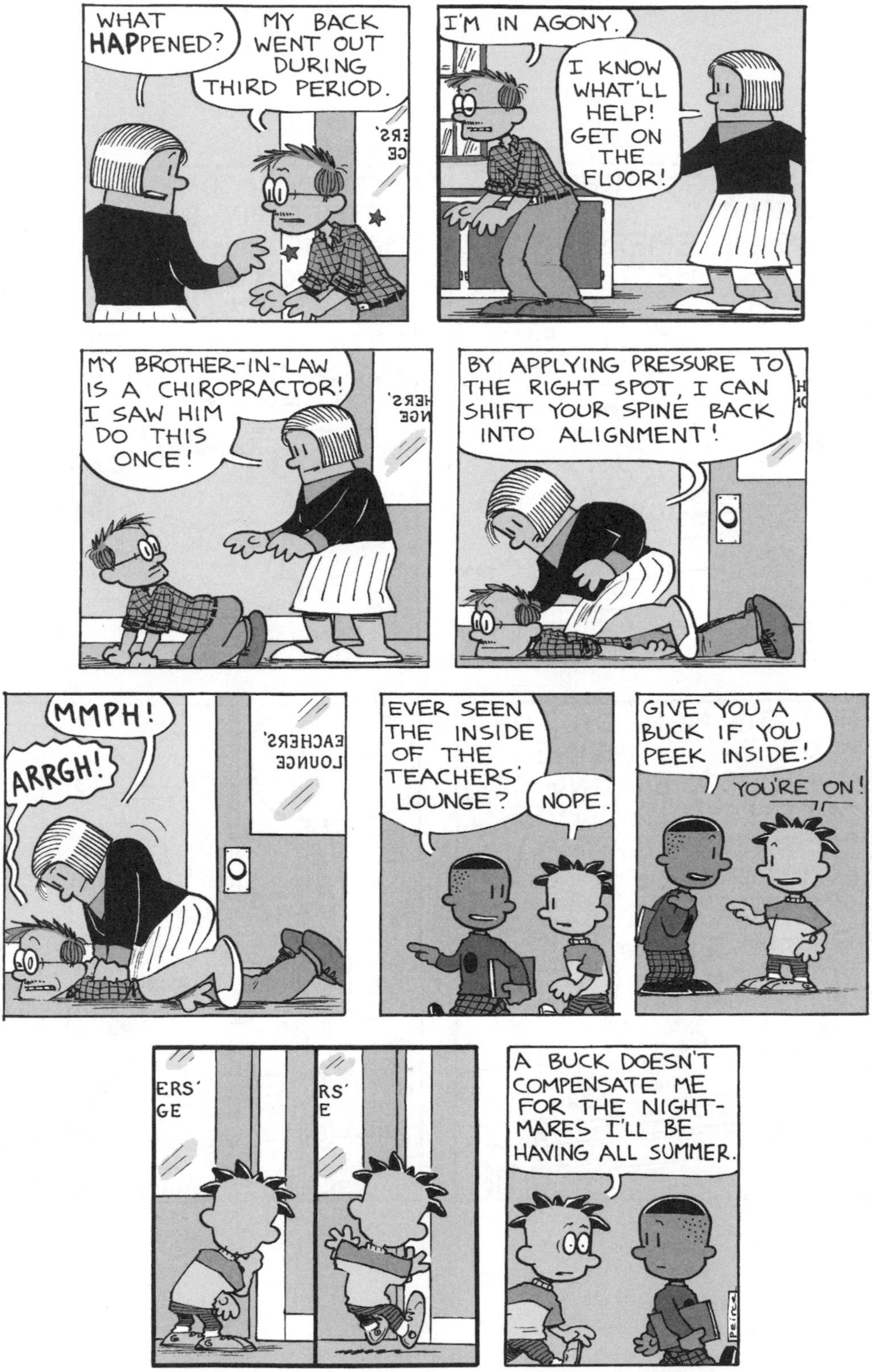
WHAT HAPPENED?
MY BACK WENT OUT DURING THIRD PERIOD.
I'M IN AGONY.
I KNOW WHAT'LL HELP! GET ON THE FLOOR!
MY BROTHER-IN-LAW IS A CHIROPRACTOR! I SAW HIM DO THIS ONCE!
BY APPLYING PRESSURE TO THE RIGHT SPOT, I CAN SHIFT YOUR SPINE BACK INTO ALIGNMENT!
MMPH!
ARRGH!
EVER SEEN THE INSIDE OF THE TEACHERS' LOUNGE?
NOPE.
GIVE YOU A BUCK IF YOU PEEK INSIDE!
YOU'RE ON!
A BUCK DOESN'T COMPENSATE ME FOR THE NIGHT-MARES I'LL BE HAVING ALL SUMMER.

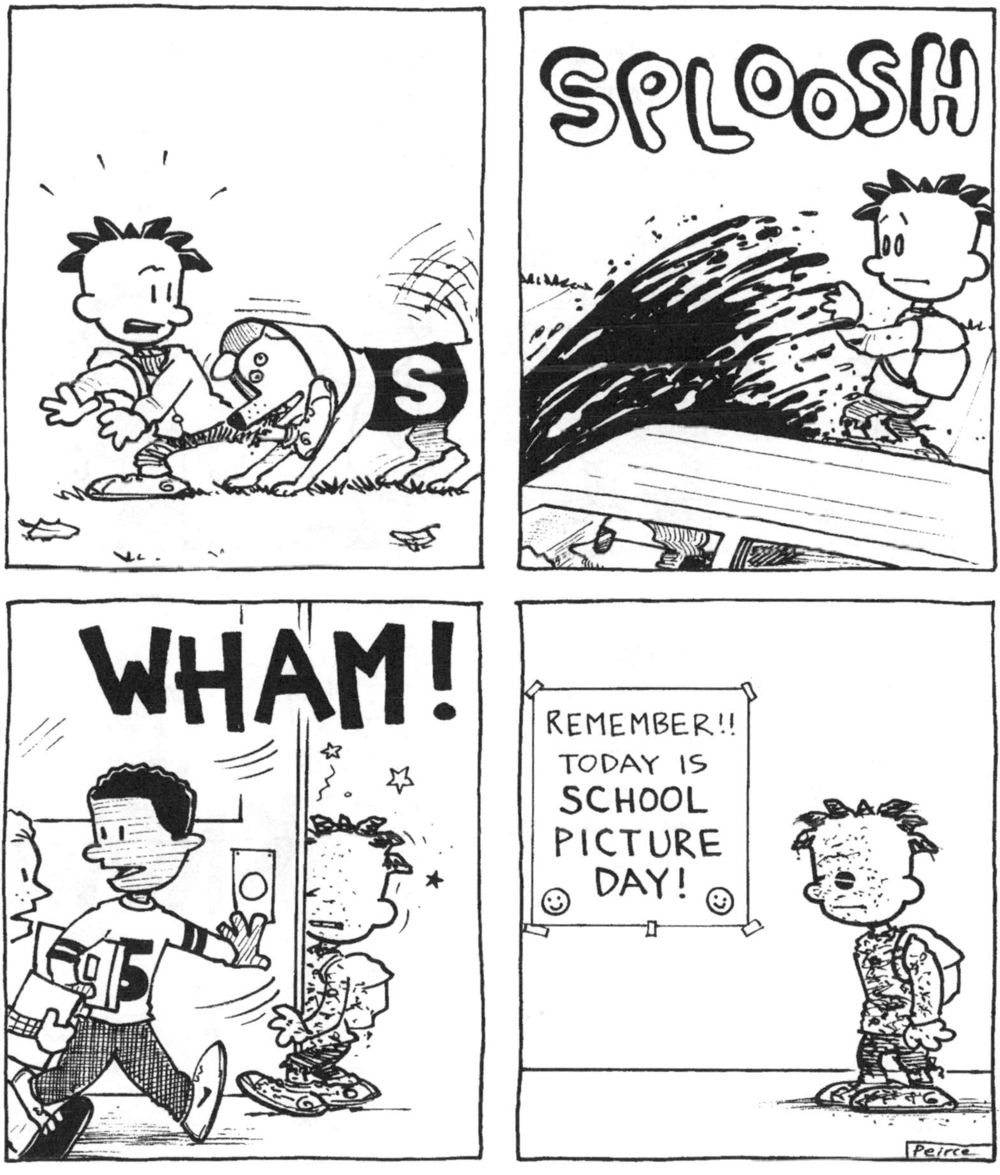
SPLOOSH
WHAM!
REMEMBER!!
TODAY IS
SCHOOL
PICTURE
DAY!
Peirce

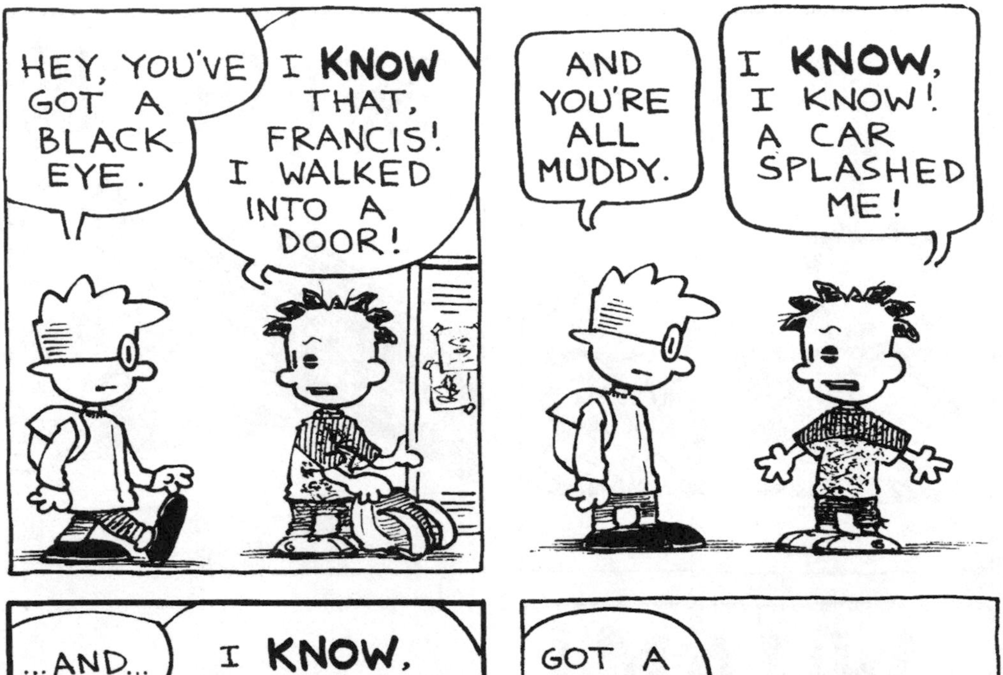
HEY, YOU'VE GOT A BLACK EYE.
I KNOW THAT, FRANCIS! I WALKED INTO A DOOR!
AND YOU'RE ALL MUDDY.
I KNOW, I KNOW! A CAR SPLASHED ME!
...AND...
I KNOW, FRANCIS! IT'S SCHOOL PICTURE DAY! YOU DON'T HAVE TO POINT THAT OUT! I KNOW THAT ALREADY!
GOT A LITTLE ZIT THERE.
I KNOW!
PEIRCE

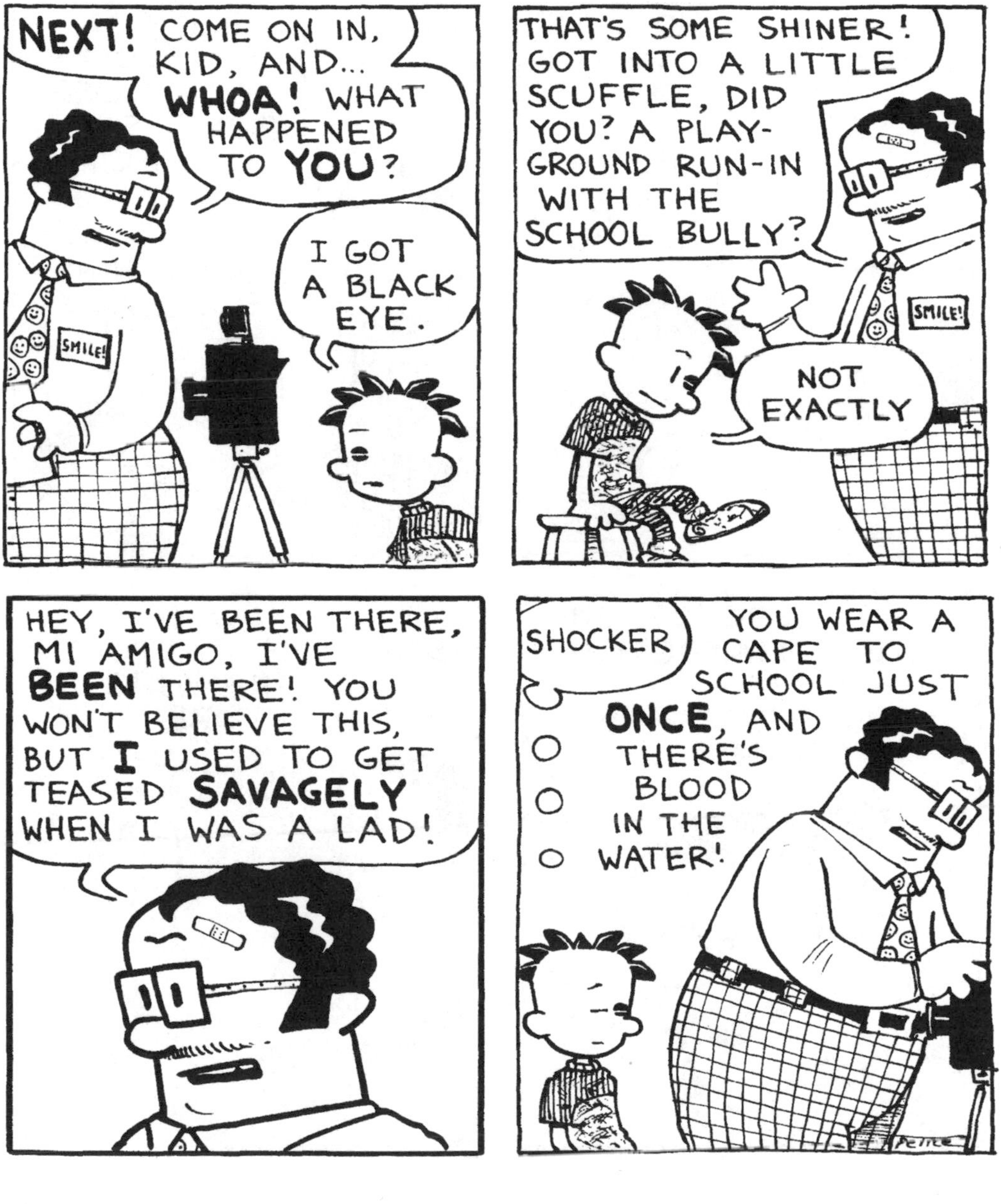
NEXT! COME ON IN, KID, AND... WHOA! WHAT HAPPENED TO YOU?
SMILE!
I GOT A BLACK EYE.
THAT'S SOME SHINER! GOT INTO A LITTLE SCUFFLE, DID YOU? A PLAY-GROUND RUN-IN WITH THE SCHOOL BULLY?
SMILE!
NOT EXACTLY
HEY, I'VE BEEN THERE, MI AMIGO, I'VE BEEN THERE! YOU WON'T BELIEVE THIS, BUT I USED TO GET TEASED SAVAGELY WHEN I WAS A LAD!
SHOCKER
YOU WEAR A CAPE TO SCHOOL JUST ONCE, AND THERE'S BLOOD IN THE WATER!

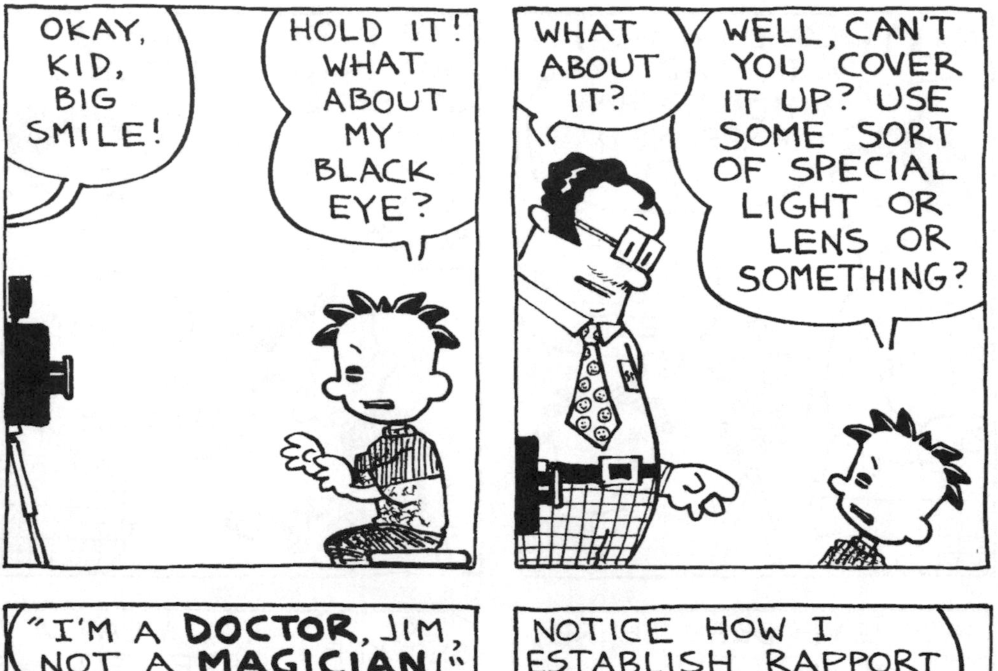
OKAY, KID, BIG SMILE!
HOLD IT! WHAT ABOUT MY BLACK EYE?
WHAT ABOUT IT?
WELL, CAN'T YOU COVER IT UP? USE SOME SORT OF SPECIAL LIGHT OR LENS OR SOMETHING?
"I'M A **DOCTOR**, JIM, NOT A **MAGICIAN**!"
STAR TREK: EPISODE 47, SCENE 32!
HA HA HA
HA HA HA
NOTICE HOW I ESTABLISH RAPPORT BY REFERENCING POP CULTURE.
WHAT A TWIT.
Peirce

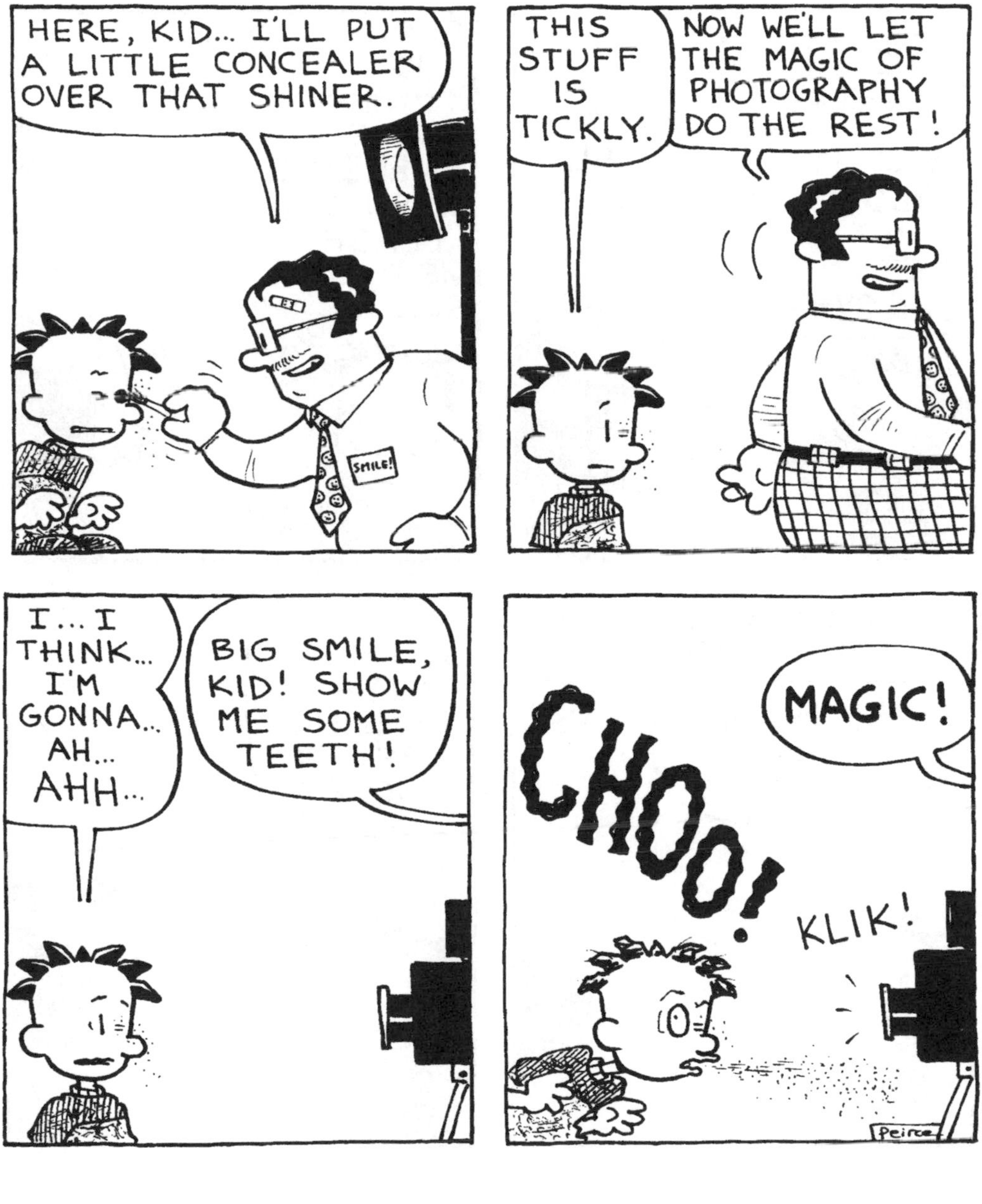
HERE, KID... I'LL PUT A LITTLE CONCEALER OVER THAT SHINER.
SMILE!
THIS STUFF IS TICKLY.
NOW WE'LL LET THE MAGIC OF PHOTOGRAPHY DO THE REST!
I... I THINK... I'M GONNA... AH... AHH...
BIG SMILE, KID! SHOW ME SOME TEETH!
CHOO!
MAGIC!
KLIK!
Peirce

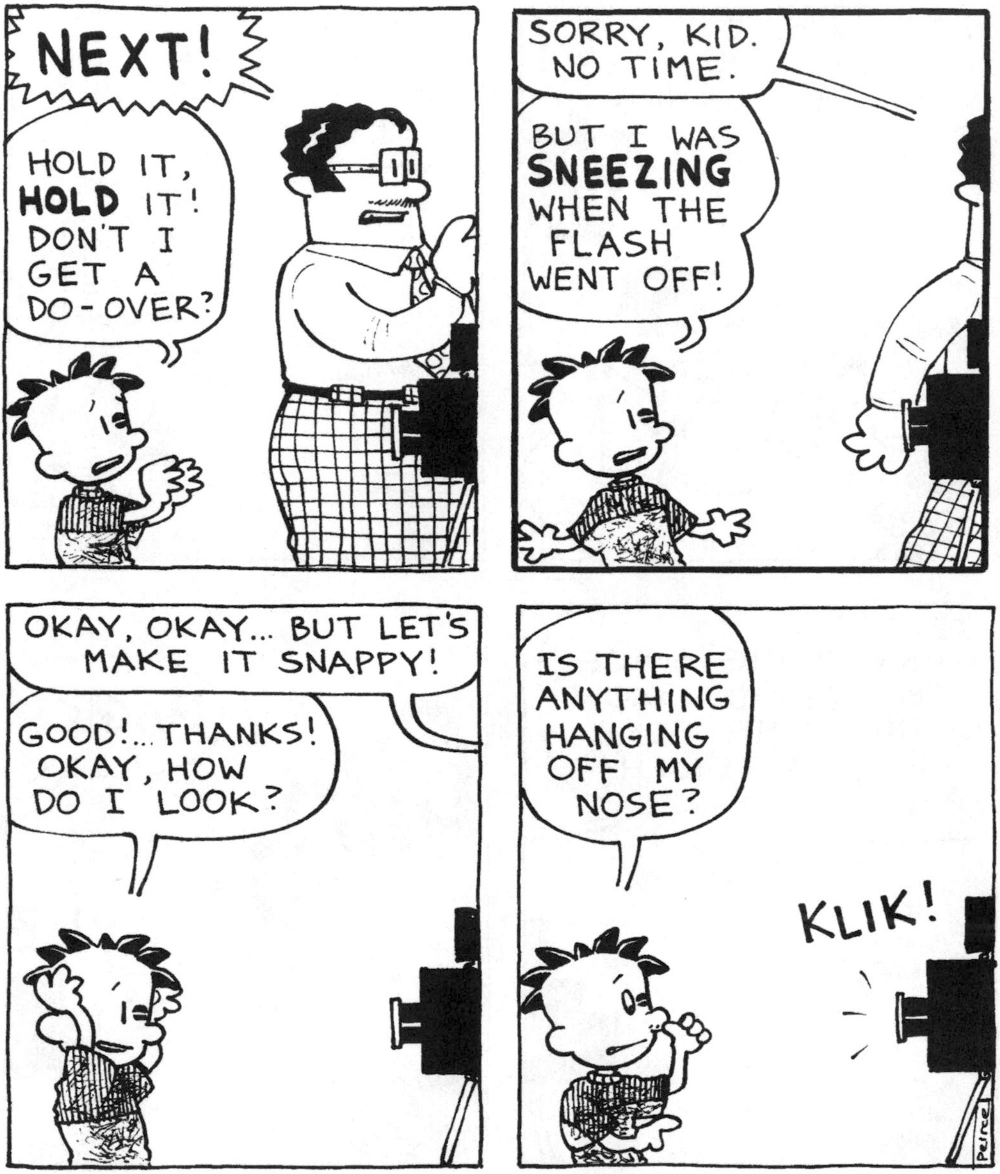
NEXT!
HOLD IT, **HOLD** IT! DON'T I GET A DO-OVER?
SORRY, KID. NO TIME.
BUT I WAS **SNEEZING** WHEN THE FLASH WENT OFF!
OKAY, OKAY... BUT LET'S MAKE IT SNAPPY!
GOOD!... THANKS! OKAY, HOW DO I LOOK?
IS THERE ANYTHING HANGING OFF MY NOSE?
KLIK!
Peirce

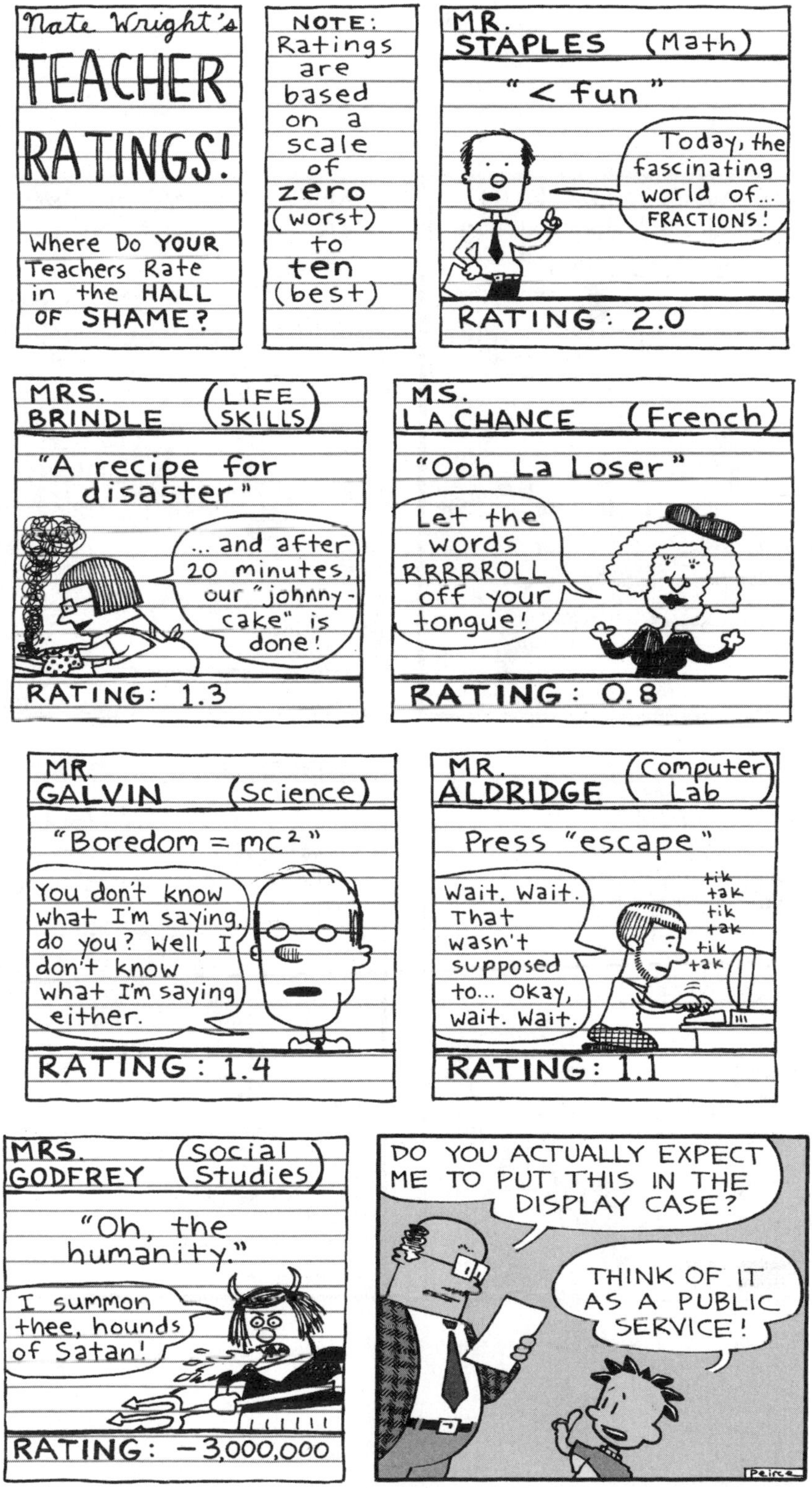
Nate Wright's
TEACHER RATINGS!
Where Do YOUR Teachers Rate in the HALL OF SHAME?
NOTE: Ratings are based on a scale of zero (worst) to ten (best)
MR. STAPLES (Math)
"< fun"
Today, the fascinating world of... FRACTIONS!
RATING: 2.0
MRS. BRINDLE (LIFE SKILLS)
"A recipe for disaster"
... and after 20 minutes, our "johnny-cake" is done!
RATING: 1.3
MS. LA CHANCE (French)
"Ooh La Loser"
Let the words RRRRROLL off your tongue!
RATING: 0.8
MR. GALVIN (Science)
"Boredom = mc²"
You don't know what I'm saying, do you? Well, I don't know what I'm saying either.
RATING: 1.4
MR. ALDRIDGE (Computer Lab)
Press "escape"
Wait. Wait. That wasn't supposed to... okay, wait. Wait.
tik tak tik tak tik tak
RATING: 1.1
MRS. GODFREY (Social Studies)
"Oh, the humanity."
I summon thee, hounds of Satan!
RATING: −3,000,000
DO YOU ACTUALLY EXPECT ME TO PUT THIS IN THE DISPLAY CASE?
THINK OF IT AS A PUBLIC SERVICE!
Peirce

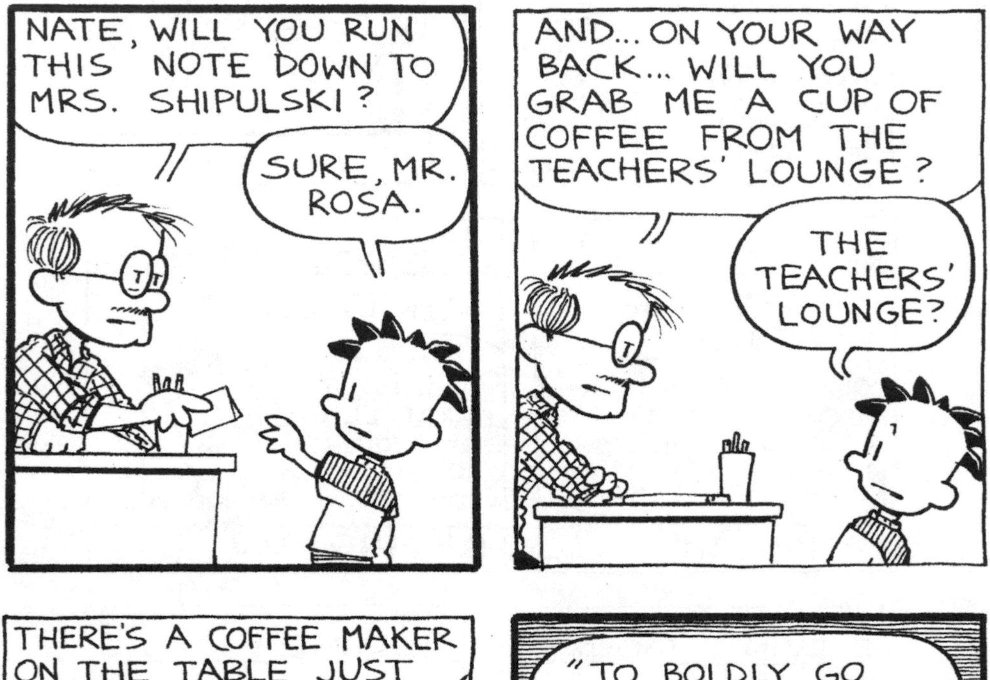
NATE, WILL YOU RUN THIS NOTE DOWN TO MRS. SHIPULSKI?
SURE, MR. ROSA.
AND... ON YOUR WAY BACK... WILL YOU GRAB ME A CUP OF COFFEE FROM THE TEACHERS' LOUNGE?
THE TEACHERS' LOUNGE?
THERE'S A COFFEE MAKER ON THE TABLE JUST INSIDE THE DOOR.
OK.
"TO BOLDLY GO WHERE NO ONE HAS GONE BEFORE."
Peirce

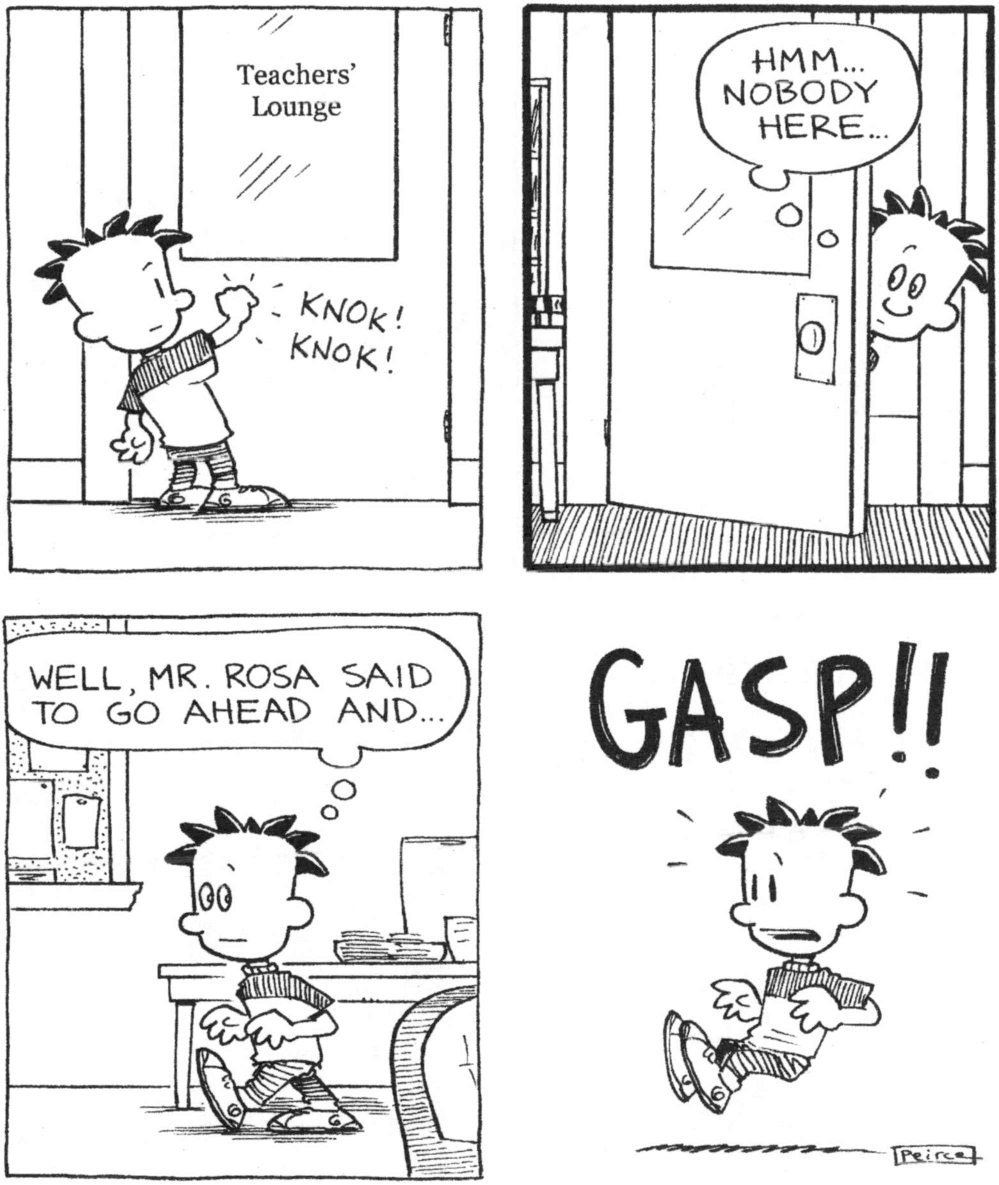
Teachers' Lounge
KNOK! KNOK!
HMM... NOBODY HERE...
WELL, MR. ROSA SAID TO GO AHEAD AND...
GASP!!
Peirce

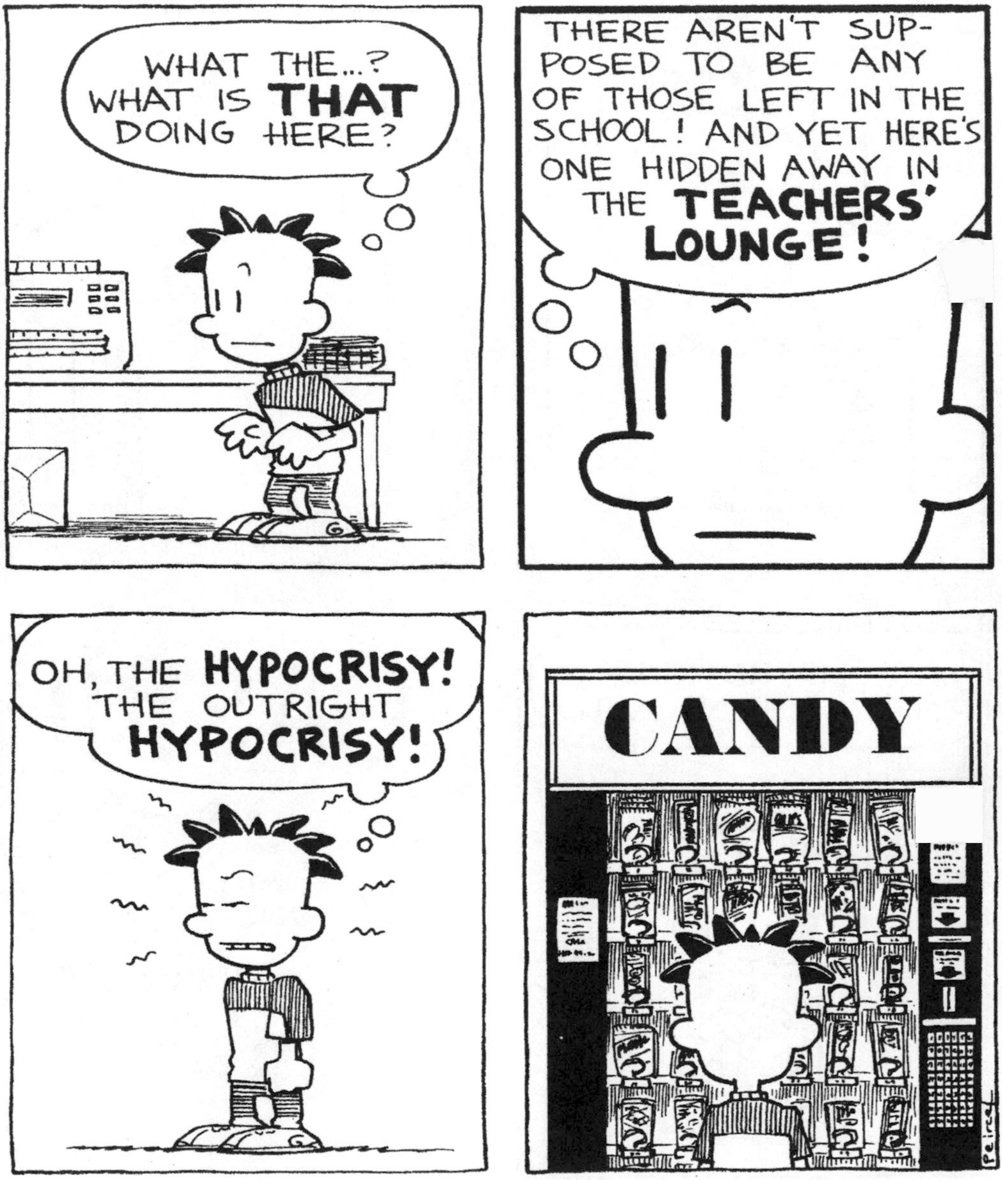
WHAT THE...? WHAT IS THAT DOING HERE?
THERE AREN'T SUPPOSED TO BE ANY OF THOSE LEFT IN THE SCHOOL! AND YET HERE'S ONE HIDDEN AWAY IN THE TEACHERS' LOUNGE!
OH, THE HYPOCRISY! THE OUTRIGHT HYPOCRISY!
CANDY
PEIRCE

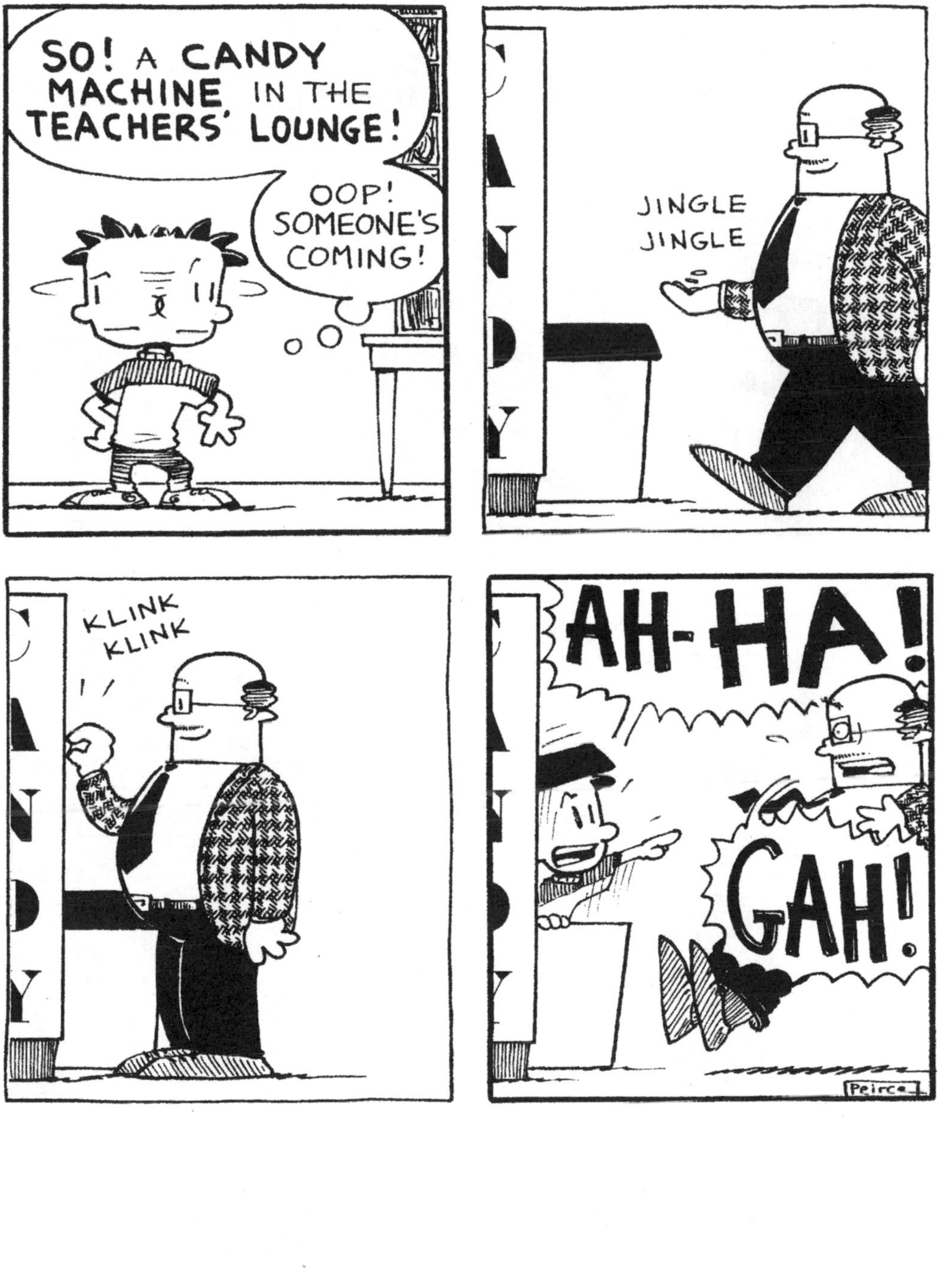
SO! A CANDY MACHINE IN THE TEACHERS' LOUNGE!
OOP! SOMEONE'S COMING!
JINGLE JINGLE
KLINK KLINK
AH-HA!
GAH!
Peirce

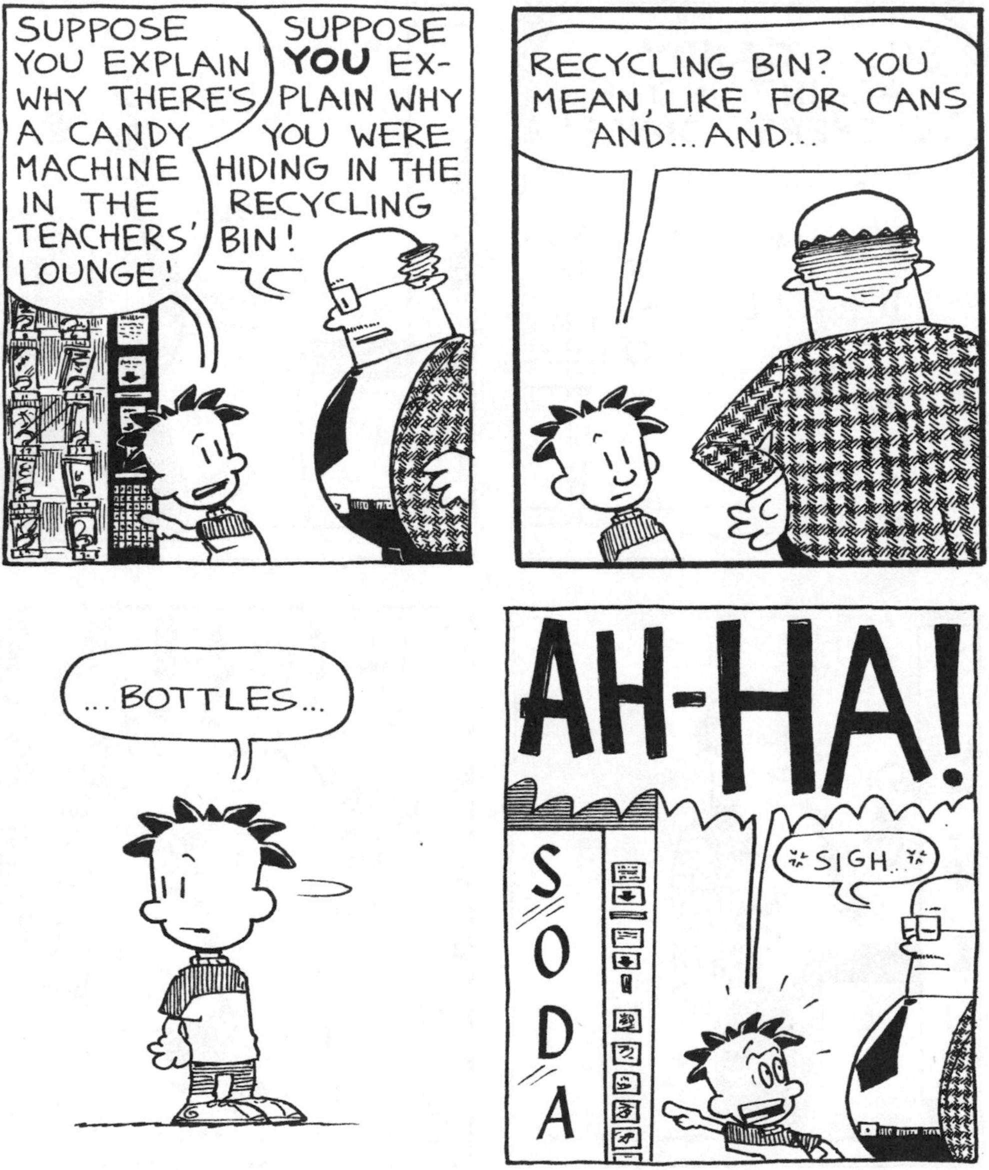
SUPPOSE YOU EXPLAIN WHY THERE'S A CANDY MACHINE IN THE TEACHERS' LOUNGE!
SUPPOSE **YOU** EXPLAIN WHY YOU WERE HIDING IN THE RECYCLING BIN!
RECYCLING BIN? YOU MEAN, LIKE, FOR CANS AND... AND...
... BOTTLES...
AH-HA!
SIGH..
SODA

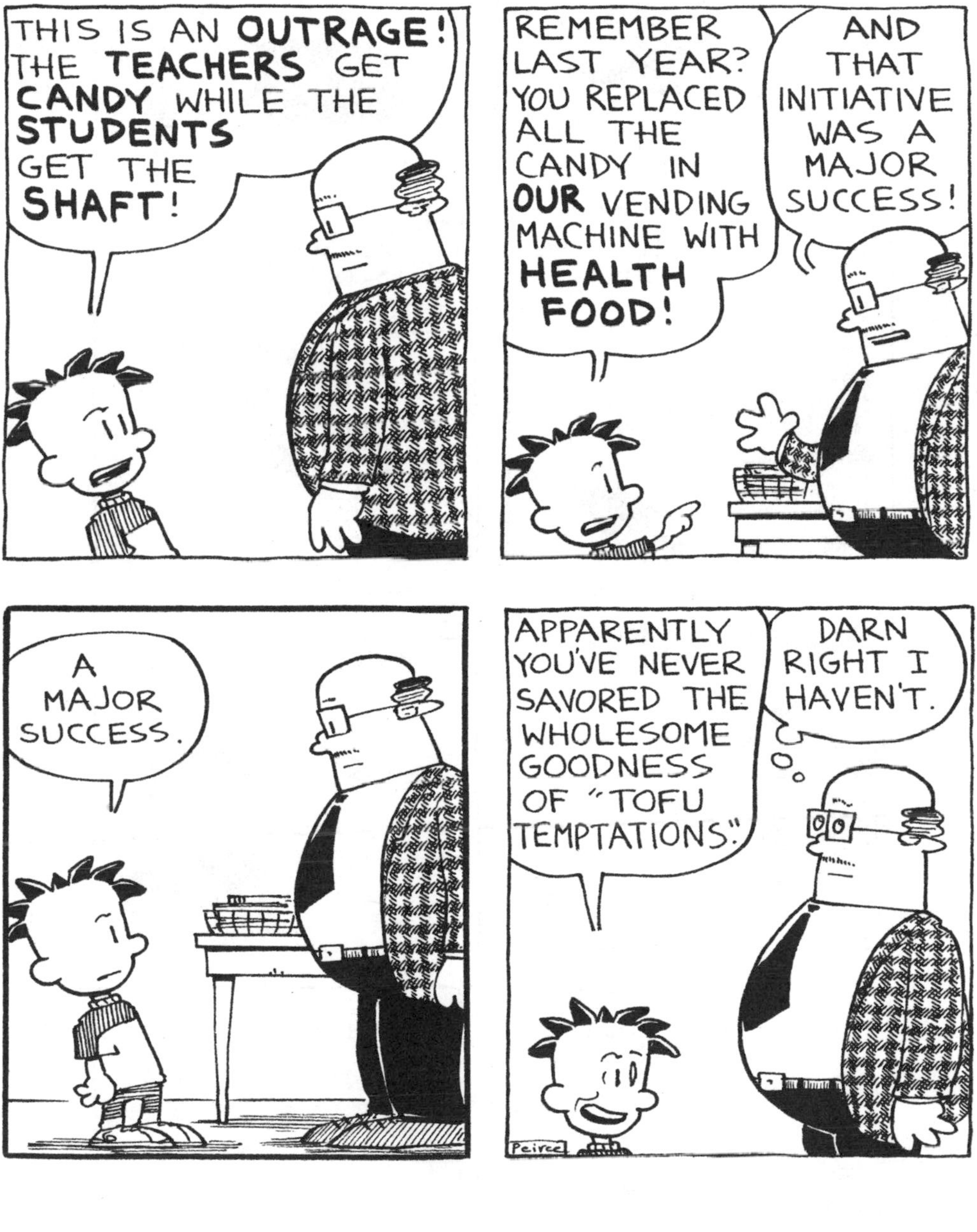
THIS IS AN **OUTRAGE**! THE **TEACHERS** GET **CANDY** WHILE THE **STUDENTS** GET THE **SHAFT**!
REMEMBER LAST YEAR? YOU REPLACED ALL THE CANDY IN **OUR** VENDING MACHINE WITH **HEALTH FOOD**!
AND THAT INITIATIVE WAS A MAJOR SUCCESS!
A MAJOR SUCCESS.
APPARENTLY YOU'VE NEVER SAVORED THE WHOLESOME GOODNESS OF "TOFU TEMPTATIONS."
DARN RIGHT I HAVEN'T.
Peirce

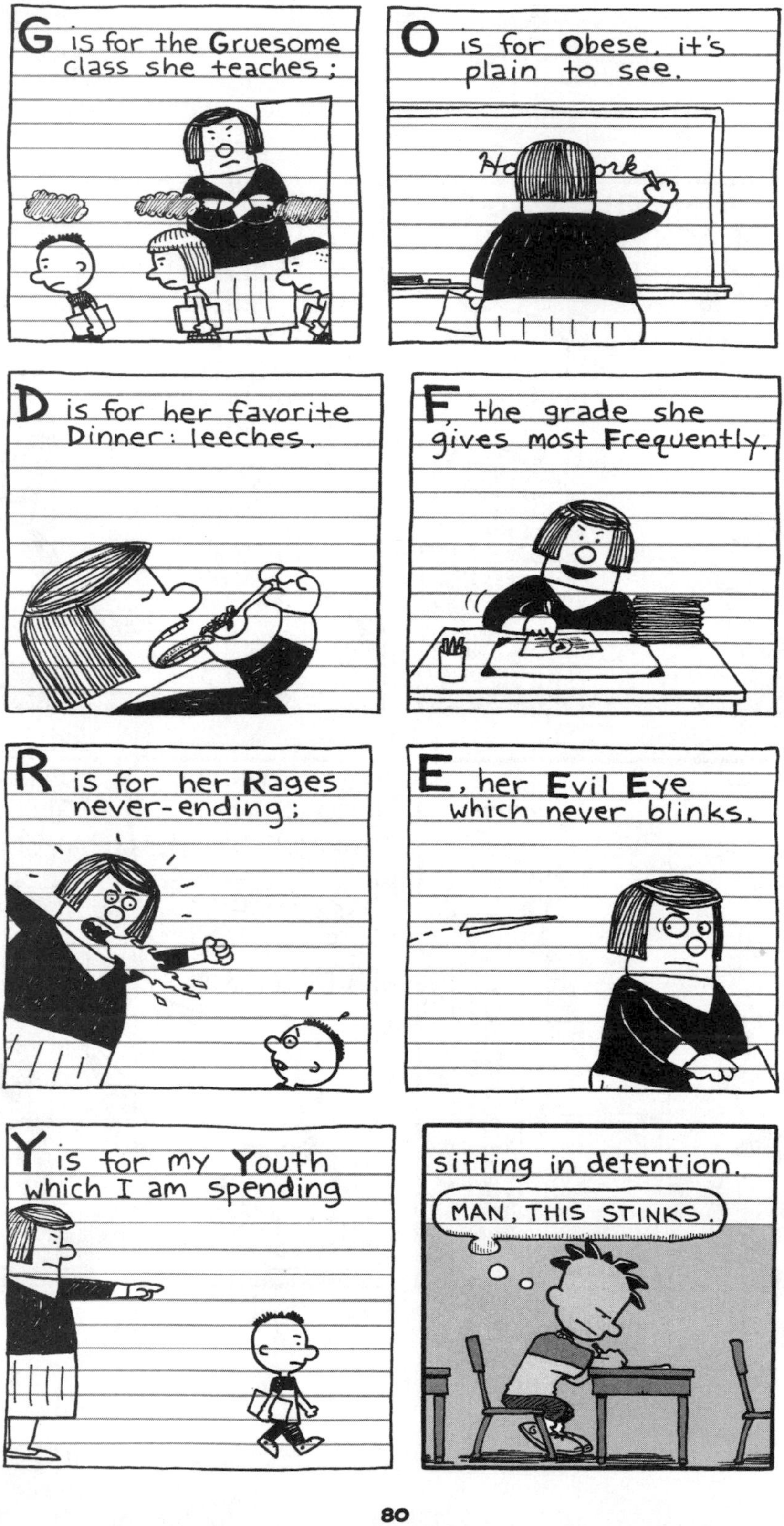
G is for the Gruesome class she teaches;
O is for Obese, it's plain to see.
D is for her favorite Dinner: leeches.
F, the grade she gives most Frequently.
R is for her Rages never-ending;
E, her Evil Eye which never blinks.
Y is for my Youth which I am spending
sitting in detention.
MAN, THIS STINKS.

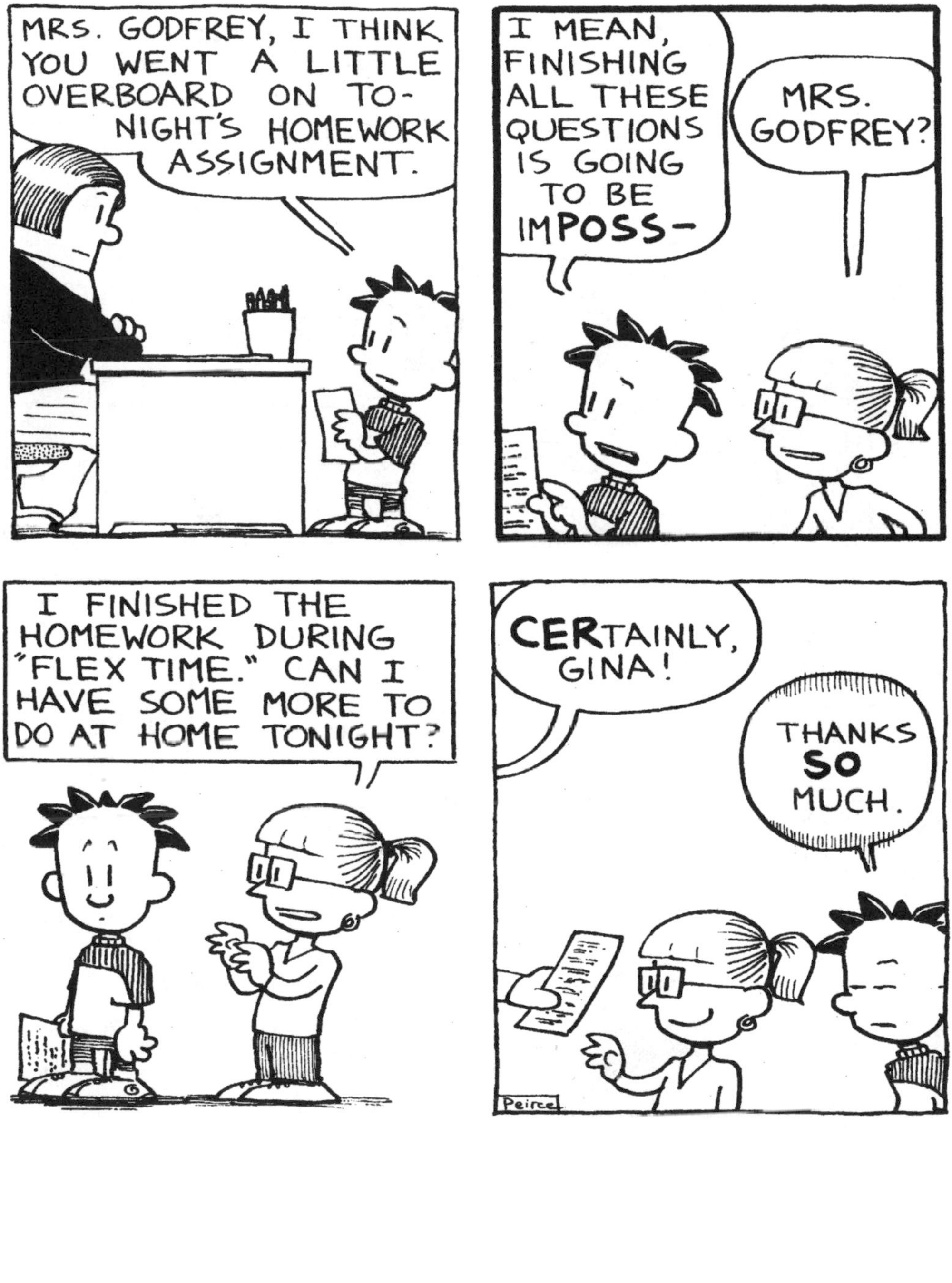
MRS. GODFREY, I THINK YOU WENT A LITTLE OVERBOARD ON TO-NIGHT'S HOMEWORK ASSIGNMENT.
I MEAN, FINISHING ALL THESE QUESTIONS IS GOING TO BE IMPOSS—
MRS. GODFREY?
I FINISHED THE HOMEWORK DURING "FLEX TIME." CAN I HAVE SOME MORE TO DO AT HOME TONIGHT?
CERTAINLY, GINA!
THANKS SO MUCH.
Peirce

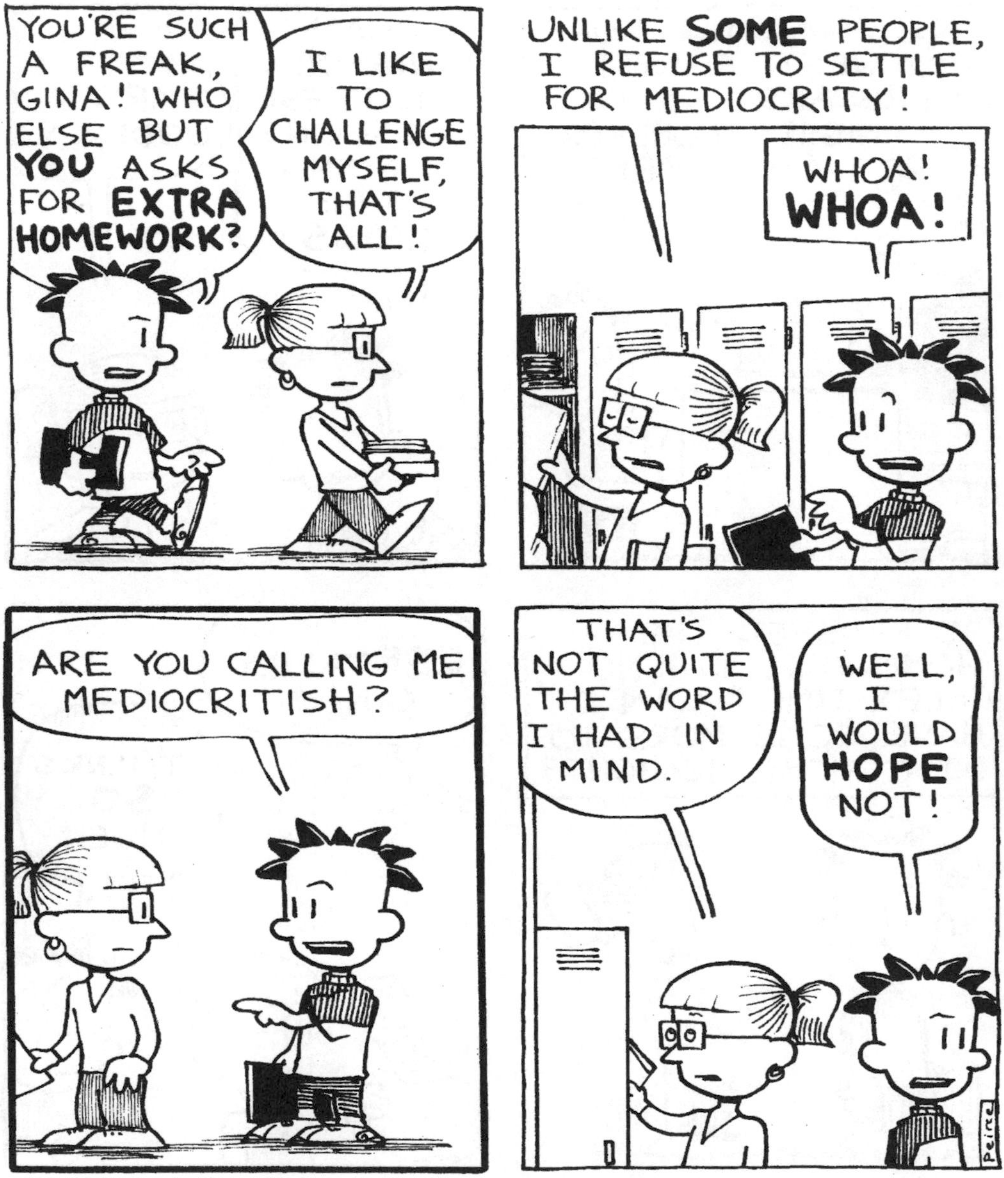
YOU'RE SUCH A FREAK, GINA! WHO ELSE BUT **YOU** ASKS FOR **EXTRA HOMEWORK?**
I LIKE TO CHALLENGE MYSELF, THAT'S ALL!
UNLIKE **SOME** PEOPLE, I REFUSE TO SETTLE FOR MEDIOCRITY!
WHOA! **WHOA!**
ARE YOU CALLING ME MEDIOCRITISH?
THAT'S NOT QUITE THE WORD I HAD IN MIND.
WELL, I WOULD **HOPE** NOT!
Peirce

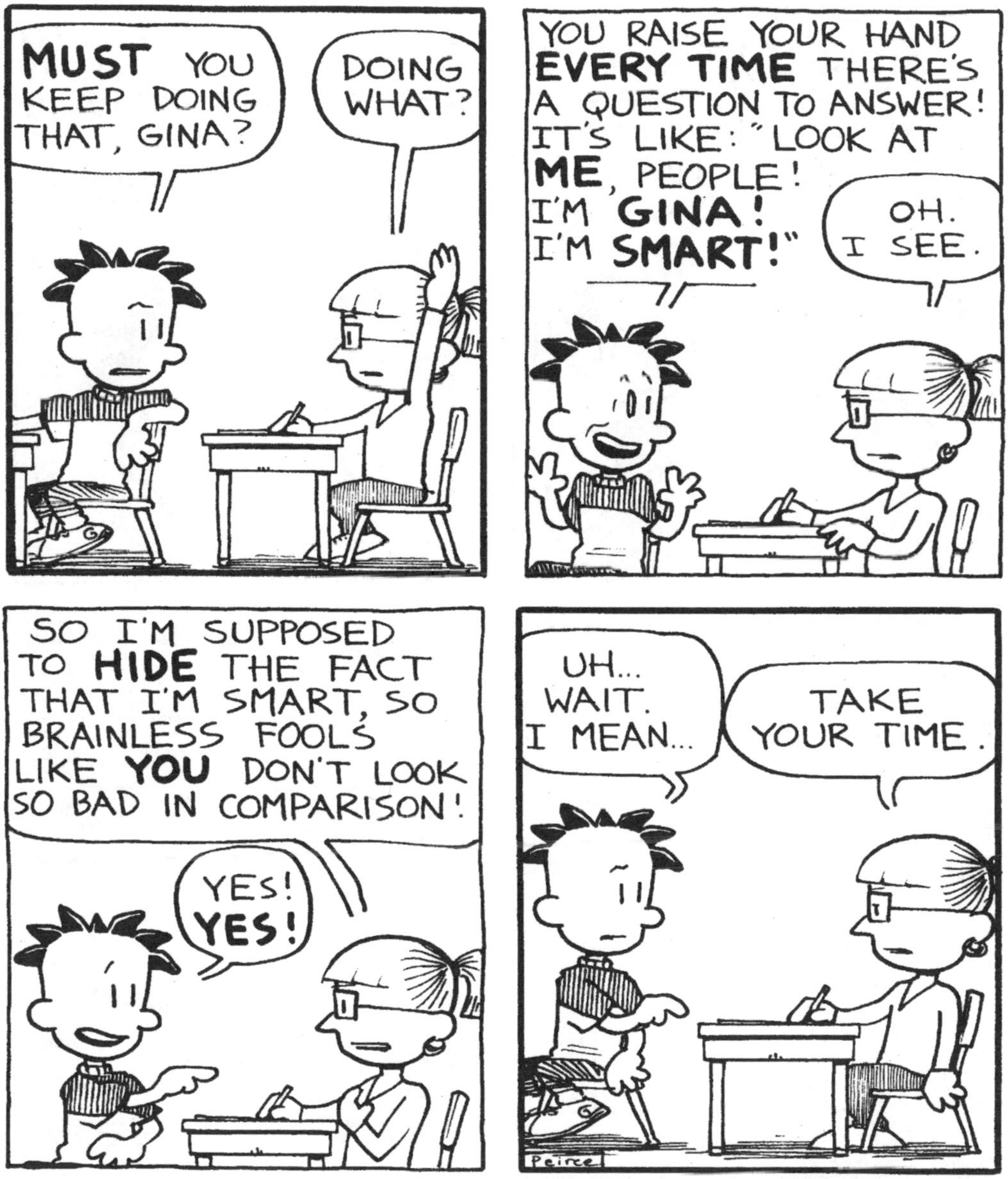
MUST YOU KEEP DOING THAT, GINA?
DOING WHAT?
YOU RAISE YOUR HAND EVERY TIME THERE'S A QUESTION TO ANSWER! IT'S LIKE: "LOOK AT ME, PEOPLE! I'M GINA! I'M SMART!"
OH. I SEE.
SO I'M SUPPOSED TO HIDE THE FACT THAT I'M SMART, SO BRAINLESS FOOLS LIKE YOU DON'T LOOK SO BAD IN COMPARISON!
YES! YES!
UH... WAIT. I MEAN...
TAKE YOUR TIME.
Peirce

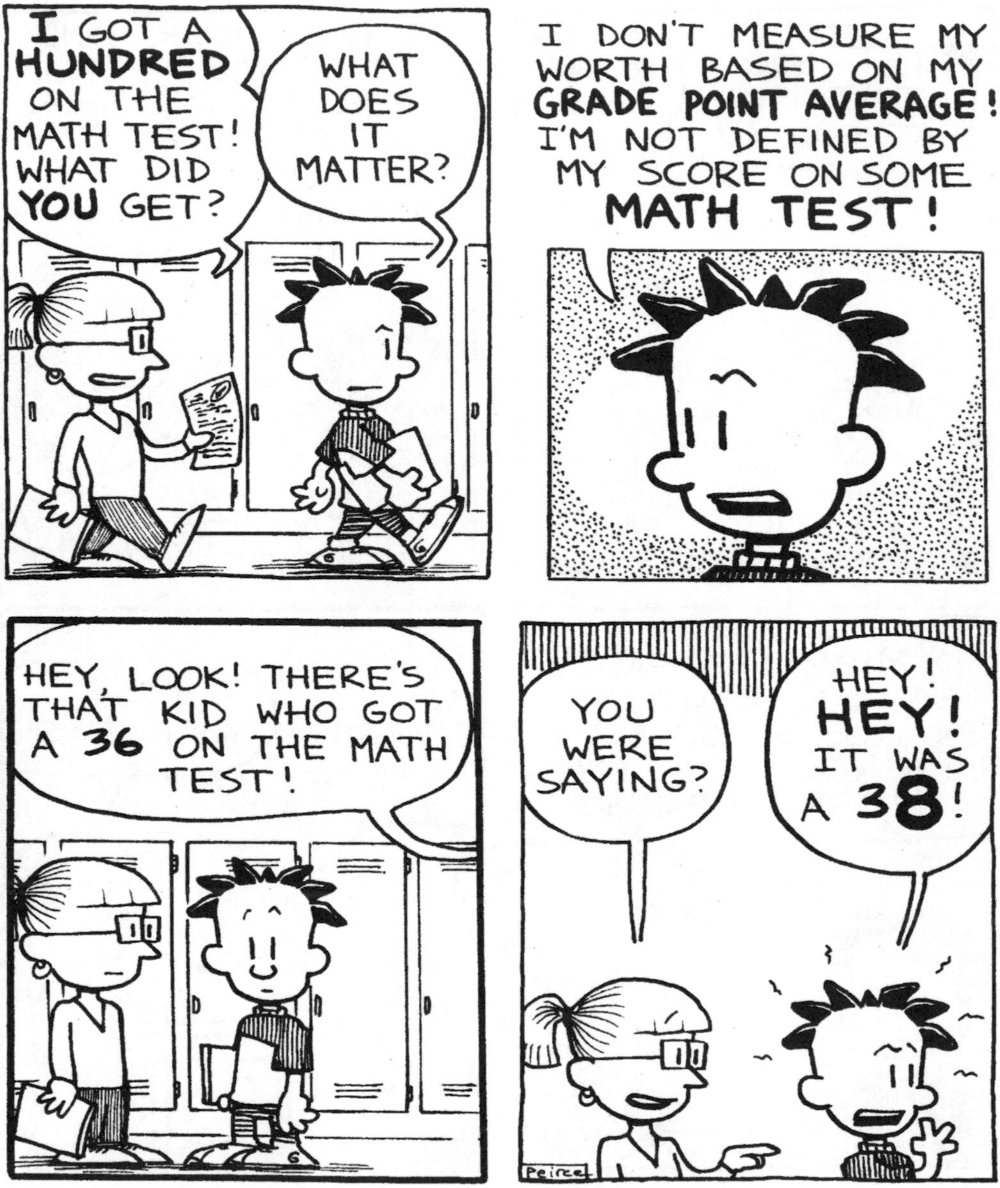
I GOT A HUNDRED ON THE MATH TEST! WHAT DID YOU GET?
WHAT DOES IT MATTER?
I DON'T MEASURE MY WORTH BASED ON MY GRADE POINT AVERAGE! I'M NOT DEFINED BY MY SCORE ON SOME MATH TEST!
HEY, LOOK! THERE'S THAT KID WHO GOT A 36 ON THE MATH TEST!
YOU WERE SAYING?
HEY! HEY! IT WAS A 38!
Peirce

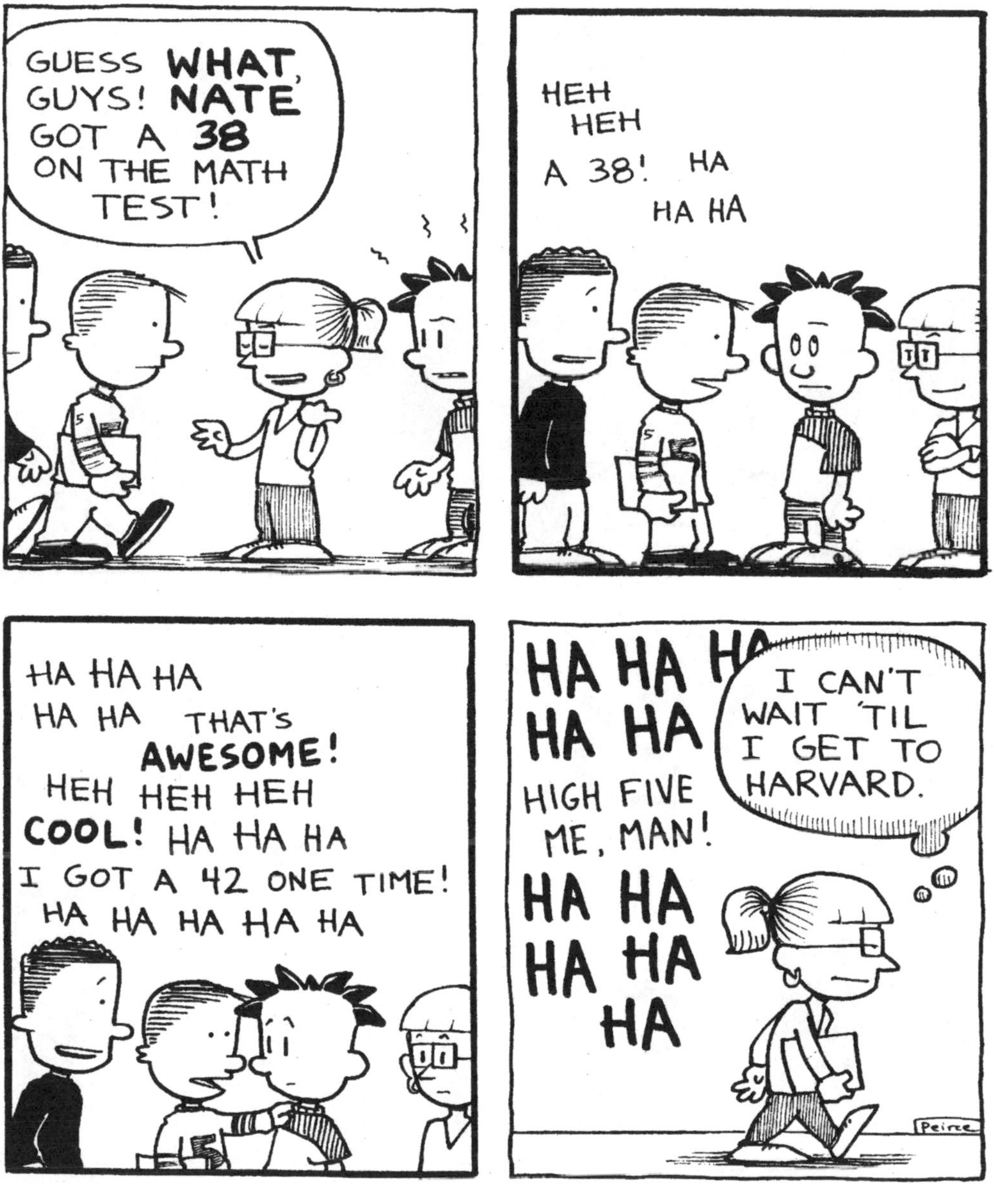
GUESS WHAT, GUYS! NATE GOT A 38 ON THE MATH TEST!
HEH HEH
A 38! HA
HA HA
HA HA HA
HA HA THAT'S AWESOME!
HEH HEH HEH
COOL! HA HA HA
I GOT A 42 ONE TIME!
HA HA HA HA HA
HA HA HA
HA HA
HIGH FIVE ME, MAN!
HA HA
HA HA
HA
I CAN'T WAIT 'TIL I GET TO HARVARD.
Peirce

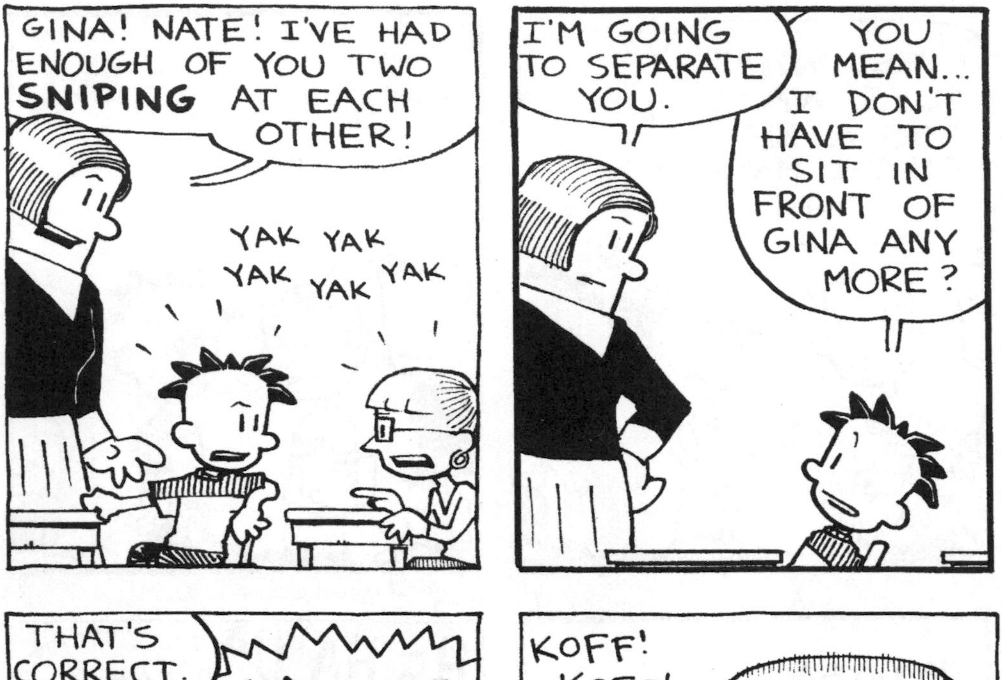
GINA! NATE! I'VE HAD ENOUGH OF YOU TWO **SNIPING** AT EACH OTHER!
YAK YAK YAK YAK YAK
I'M GOING TO SEPARATE YOU.
YOU MEAN... I DON'T HAVE TO SIT IN FRONT OF GINA ANY MORE?
THAT'S CORRECT.
YES!
KOFF! KOFF! KOFF! HACK! ACCK! KOFF!
CAREFUL WHAT YOU WISH FOR.
TISSUES
Peirce

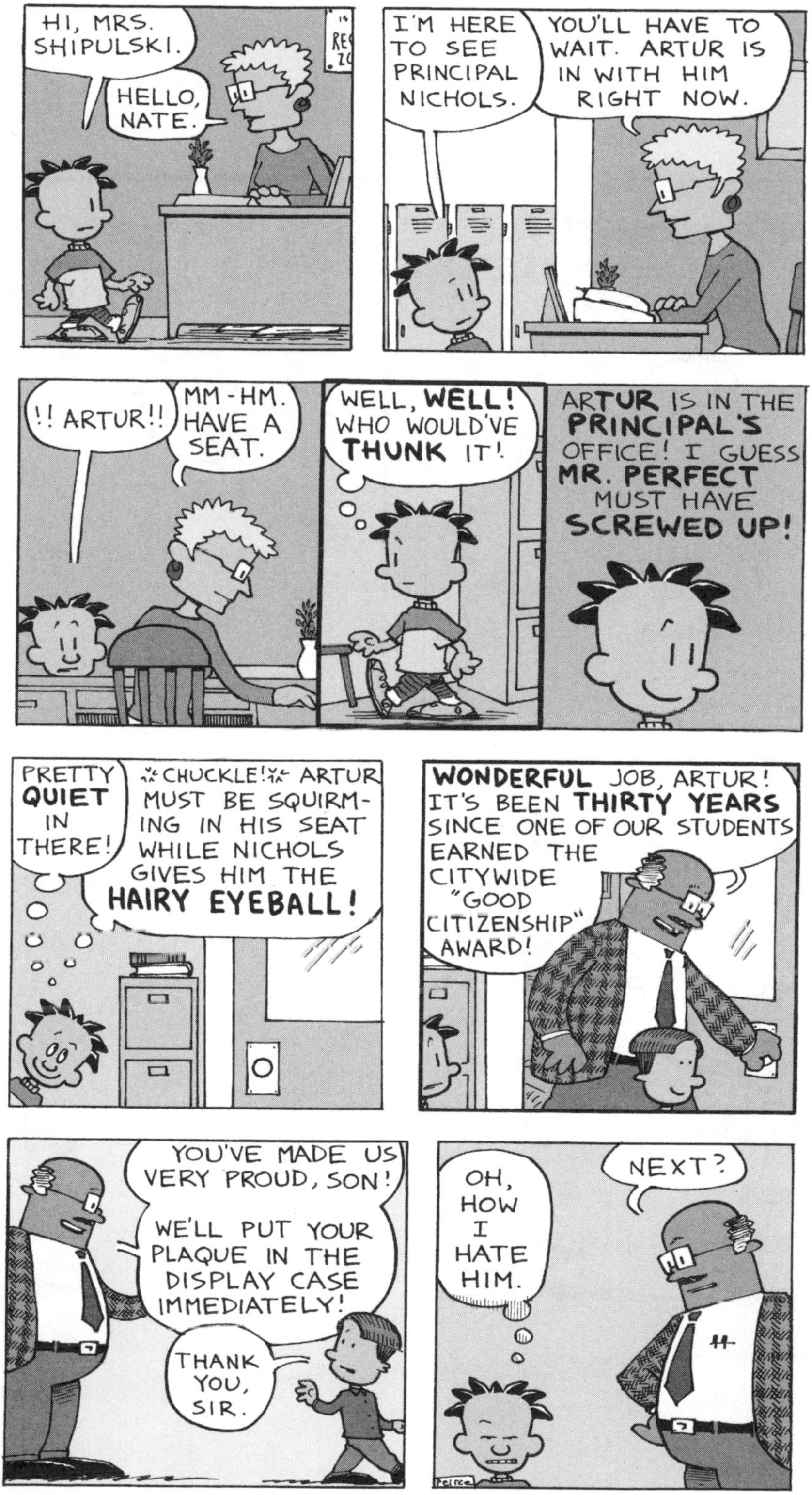
HI, MRS. SHIPULSKI.
HELLO, NATE.
I'M HERE TO SEE PRINCIPAL NICHOLS.
YOU'LL HAVE TO WAIT. ARTUR IS IN WITH HIM RIGHT NOW.
!! ARTUR!!
MM-HM. HAVE A SEAT.
WELL, WELL! WHO WOULD'VE THUNK IT!
ARTUR IS IN THE PRINCIPAL'S OFFICE! I GUESS MR. PERFECT MUST HAVE SCREWED UP!
PRETTY QUIET IN THERE!
CHUCKLE! ARTUR MUST BE SQUIRMING IN HIS SEAT WHILE NICHOLS GIVES HIM THE HAIRY EYEBALL!
WONDERFUL JOB, ARTUR! IT'S BEEN THIRTY YEARS SINCE ONE OF OUR STUDENTS EARNED THE CITYWIDE "GOOD CITIZENSHIP" AWARD!
YOU'VE MADE US VERY PROUD, SON!
WE'LL PUT YOUR PLAQUE IN THE DISPLAY CASE IMMEDIATELY!
THANK YOU, SIR.
OH, HOW I HATE HIM.
NEXT?

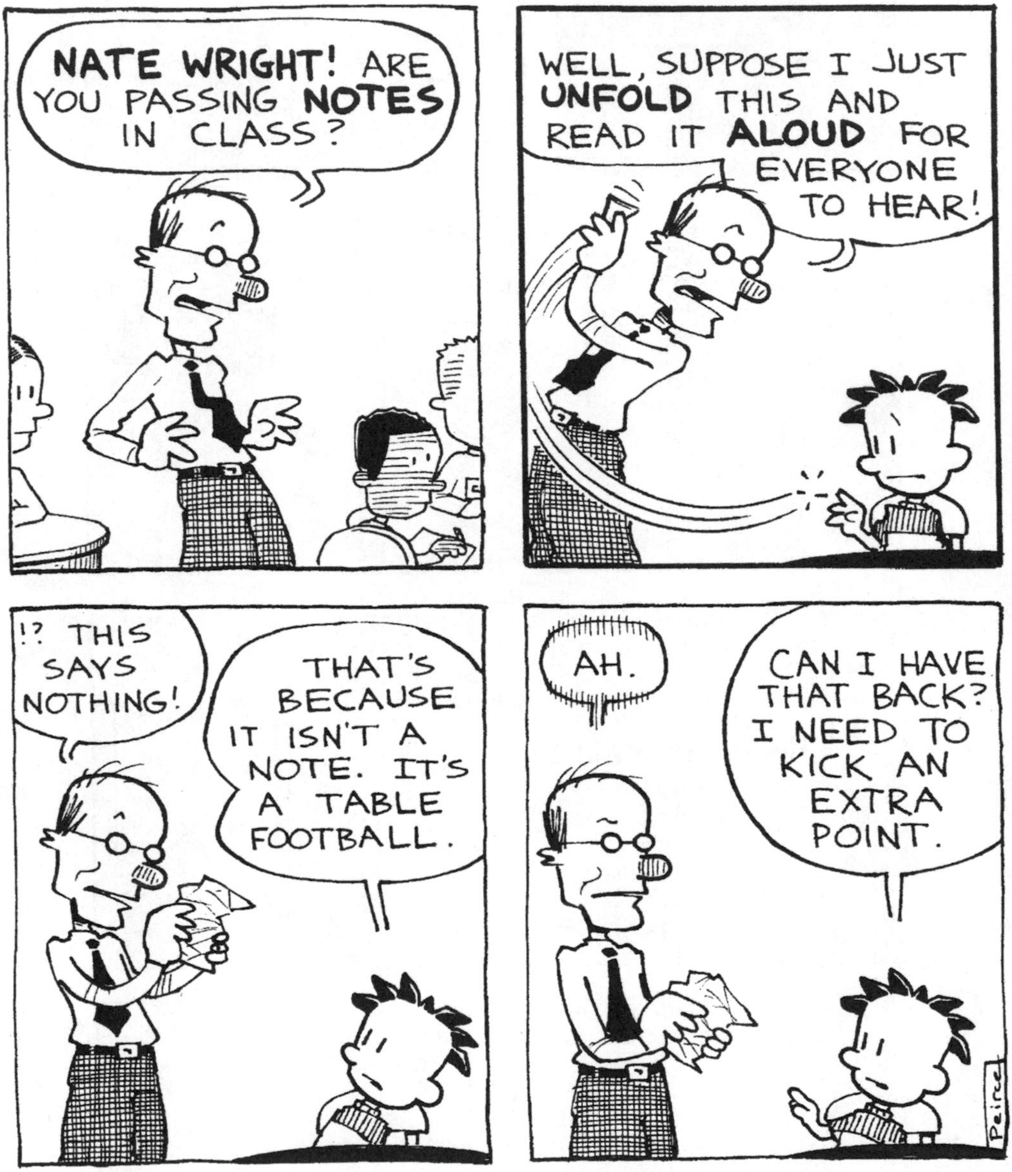
NATE WRIGHT! ARE YOU PASSING NOTES IN CLASS?
WELL, SUPPOSE I JUST UNFOLD THIS AND READ IT ALOUD FOR EVERYONE TO HEAR!
!? THIS SAYS NOTHING!
THAT'S BECAUSE IT ISN'T A NOTE. IT'S A TABLE FOOTBALL.
AH.
CAN I HAVE THAT BACK? I NEED TO KICK AN EXTRA POINT.
Peirce

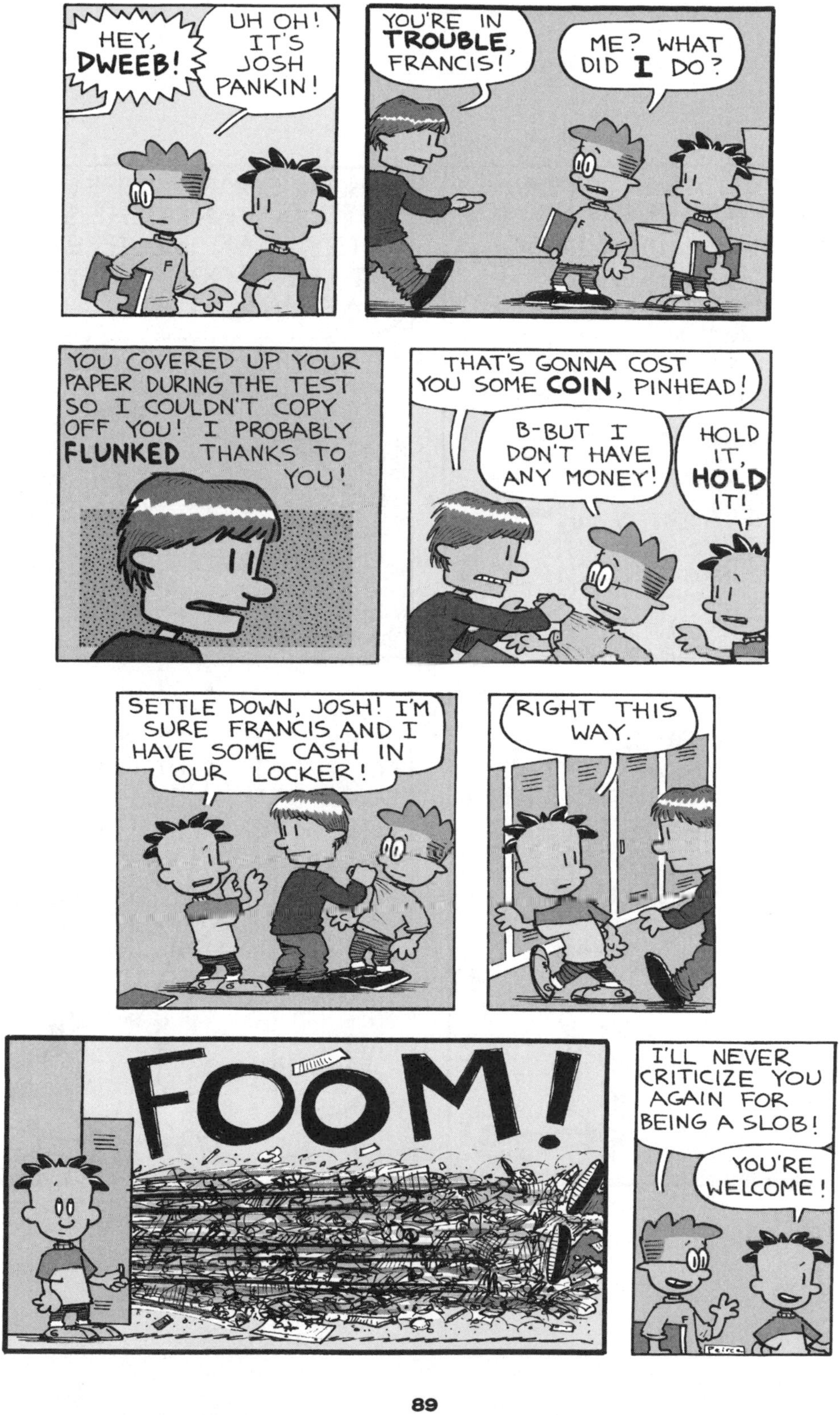
HEY, DWEEB!
UH OH! IT'S JOSH PANKIN!
YOU'RE IN TROUBLE, FRANCIS!
ME? WHAT DID I DO?
YOU COVERED UP YOUR PAPER DURING THE TEST SO I COULDN'T COPY OFF YOU! I PROBABLY FLUNKED THANKS TO YOU!
THAT'S GONNA COST YOU SOME COIN, PINHEAD!
B-BUT I DON'T HAVE ANY MONEY!
HOLD IT, HOLD IT!
SETTLE DOWN, JOSH! I'M SURE FRANCIS AND I HAVE SOME CASH IN OUR LOCKER!
RIGHT THIS WAY.
FOOM!
I'LL NEVER CRITICIZE YOU AGAIN FOR BEING A SLOB!
YOU'RE WELCOME!
Peirce

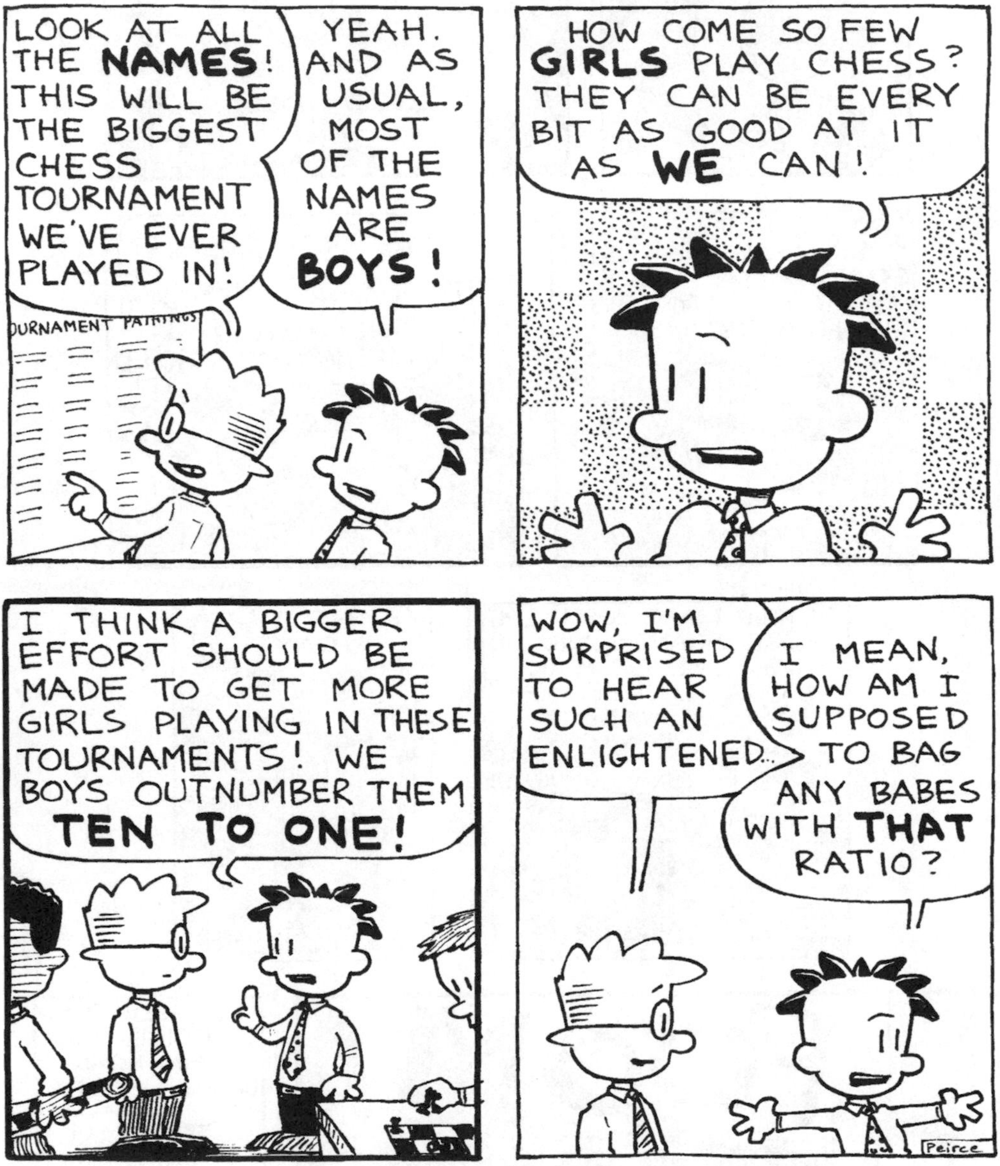
LOOK AT ALL THE **NAMES**! THIS WILL BE THE BIGGEST CHESS TOURNAMENT WE'VE EVER PLAYED IN!
YEAH. AND AS USUAL, MOST OF THE NAMES ARE **BOYS**!
OURNAMENT PAIRINGS
HOW COME SO FEW **GIRLS** PLAY CHESS? THEY CAN BE EVERY BIT AS GOOD AT IT AS **WE** CAN!
I THINK A BIGGER EFFORT SHOULD BE MADE TO GET MORE GIRLS PLAYING IN THESE TOURNAMENTS! WE BOYS OUTNUMBER THEM **TEN TO ONE**!
WOW, I'M SURPRISED TO HEAR SUCH AN ENLIGHTENED...
I MEAN, HOW AM I SUPPOSED TO BAG ANY BABES WITH **THAT** RATIO?
Peirce

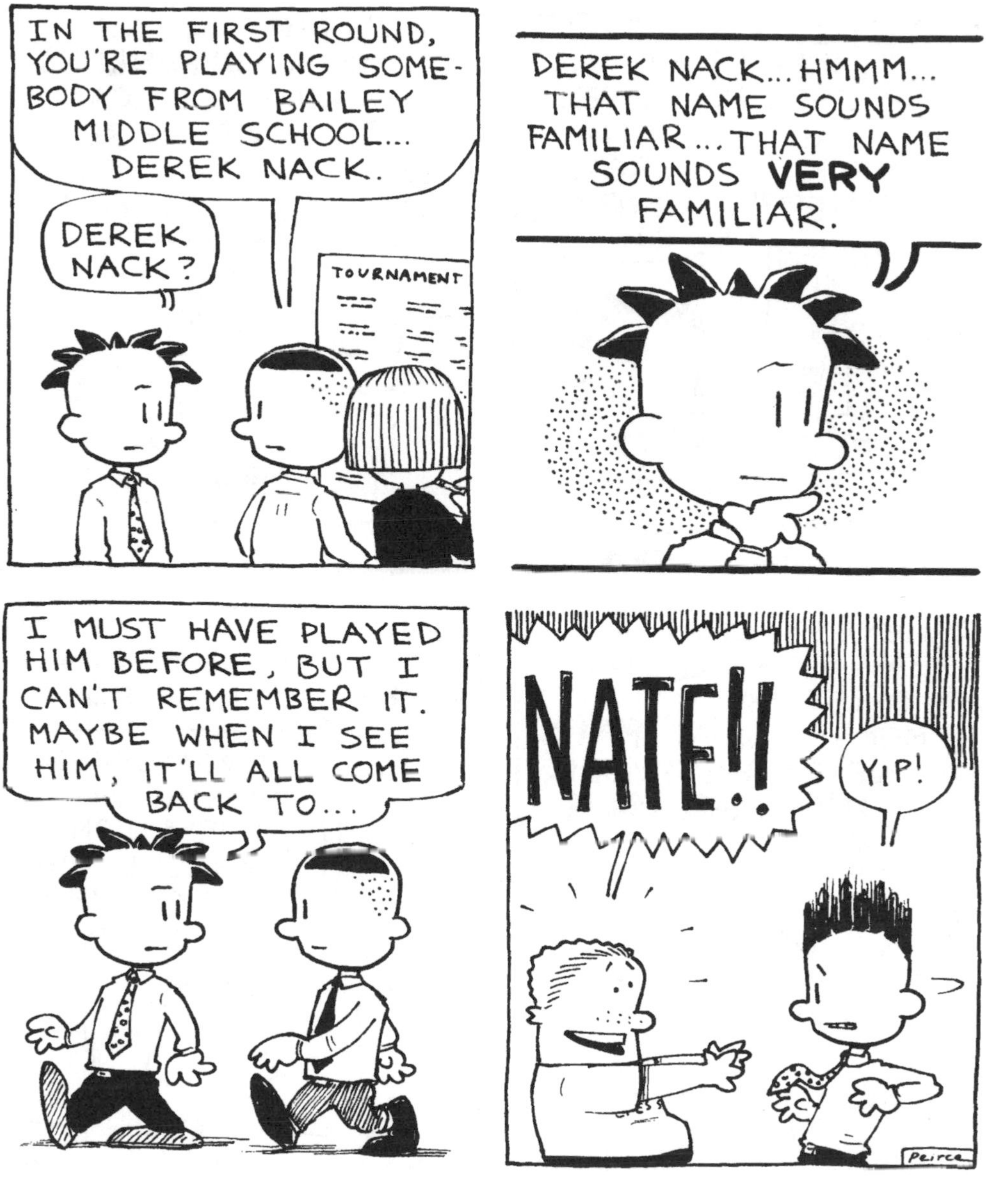
IN THE FIRST ROUND, YOU'RE PLAYING SOMEBODY FROM BAILEY MIDDLE SCHOOL... DEREK NACK.
DEREK NACK?
TOURNAMENT
DEREK NACK... HMMM... THAT NAME SOUNDS FAMILIAR... THAT NAME SOUNDS **VERY** FAMILIAR.
I MUST HAVE PLAYED HIM BEFORE, BUT I CAN'T REMEMBER IT. MAYBE WHEN I SEE HIM, IT'LL ALL COME BACK TO...
NATE!!
YIP!
Peirce

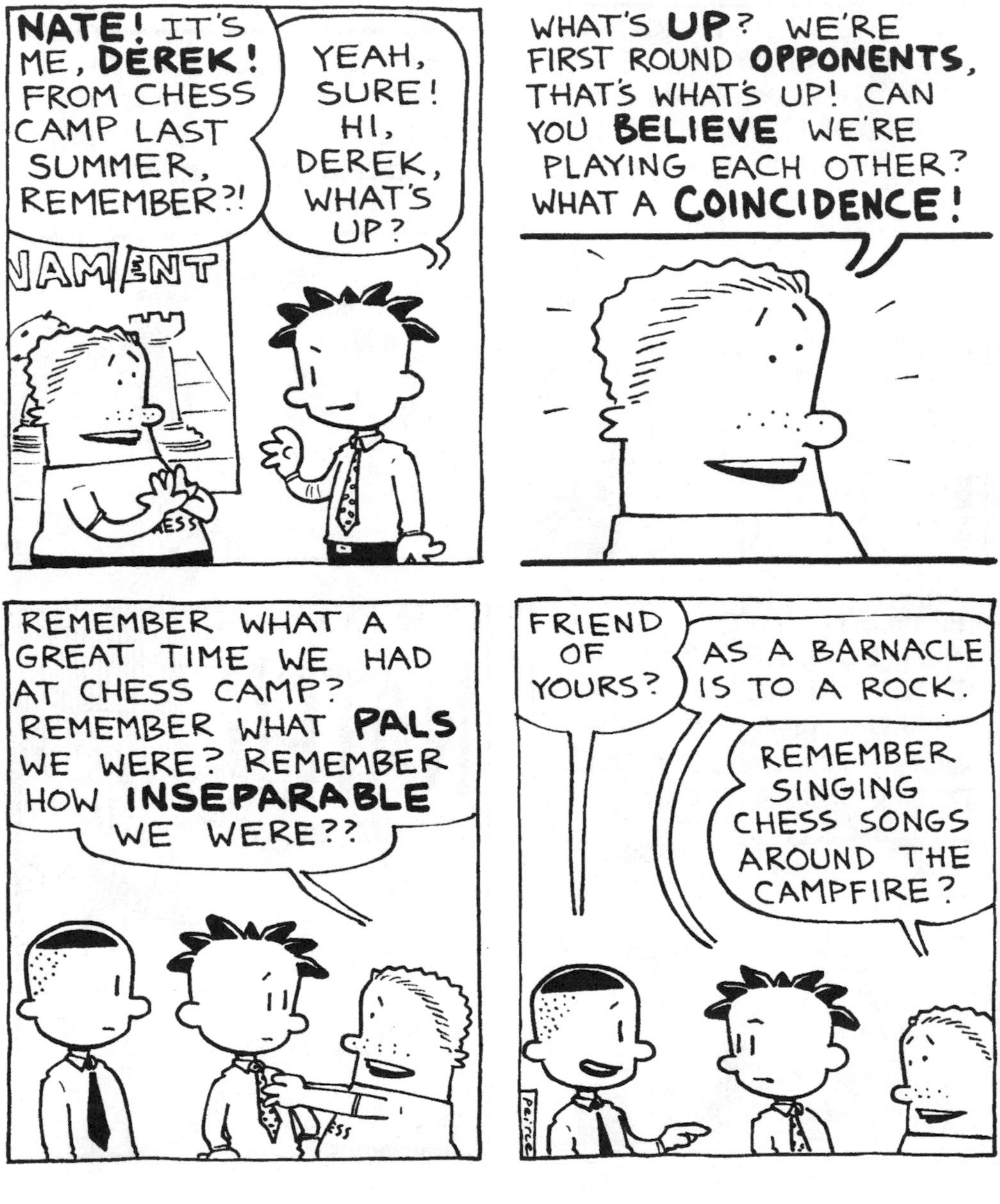
NATE! IT'S ME, DEREK! FROM CHESS CAMP LAST SUMMER, REMEMBER?!
YEAH, SURE! HI, DEREK, WHAT'S UP?
WHAT'S UP? WE'RE FIRST ROUND OPPONENTS, THAT'S WHAT'S UP! CAN YOU BELIEVE WE'RE PLAYING EACH OTHER? WHAT A COINCIDENCE!
REMEMBER WHAT A GREAT TIME WE HAD AT CHESS CAMP? REMEMBER WHAT PALS WE WERE? REMEMBER HOW INSEPARABLE WE WERE??
FRIEND OF YOURS?
AS A BARNACLE IS TO A ROCK.
REMEMBER SINGING CHESS SONGS AROUND THE CAMPFIRE?
PEIRCE

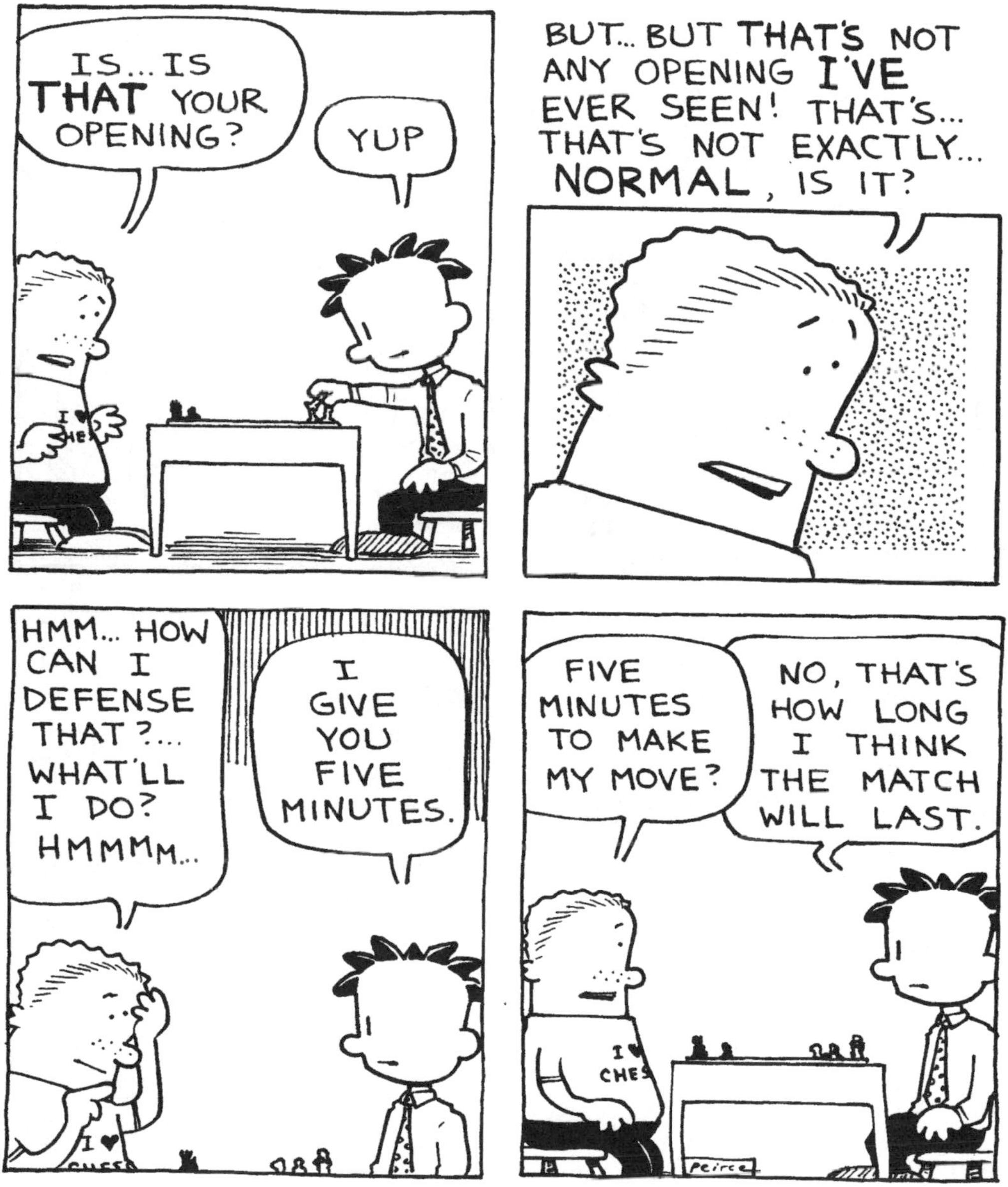
IS... IS THAT YOUR OPENING?
YUP
I ♥ CHESS
BUT... BUT THAT'S NOT ANY OPENING I'VE EVER SEEN! THAT'S... THAT'S NOT EXACTLY... NORMAL, IS IT?
HMM... HOW CAN I DEFENSE THAT?... WHAT'LL I DO? HMMMM...
I GIVE YOU FIVE MINUTES.
I ♥
FIVE MINUTES TO MAKE MY MOVE?
NO, THAT'S HOW LONG I THINK THE MATCH WILL LAST.
Peirce

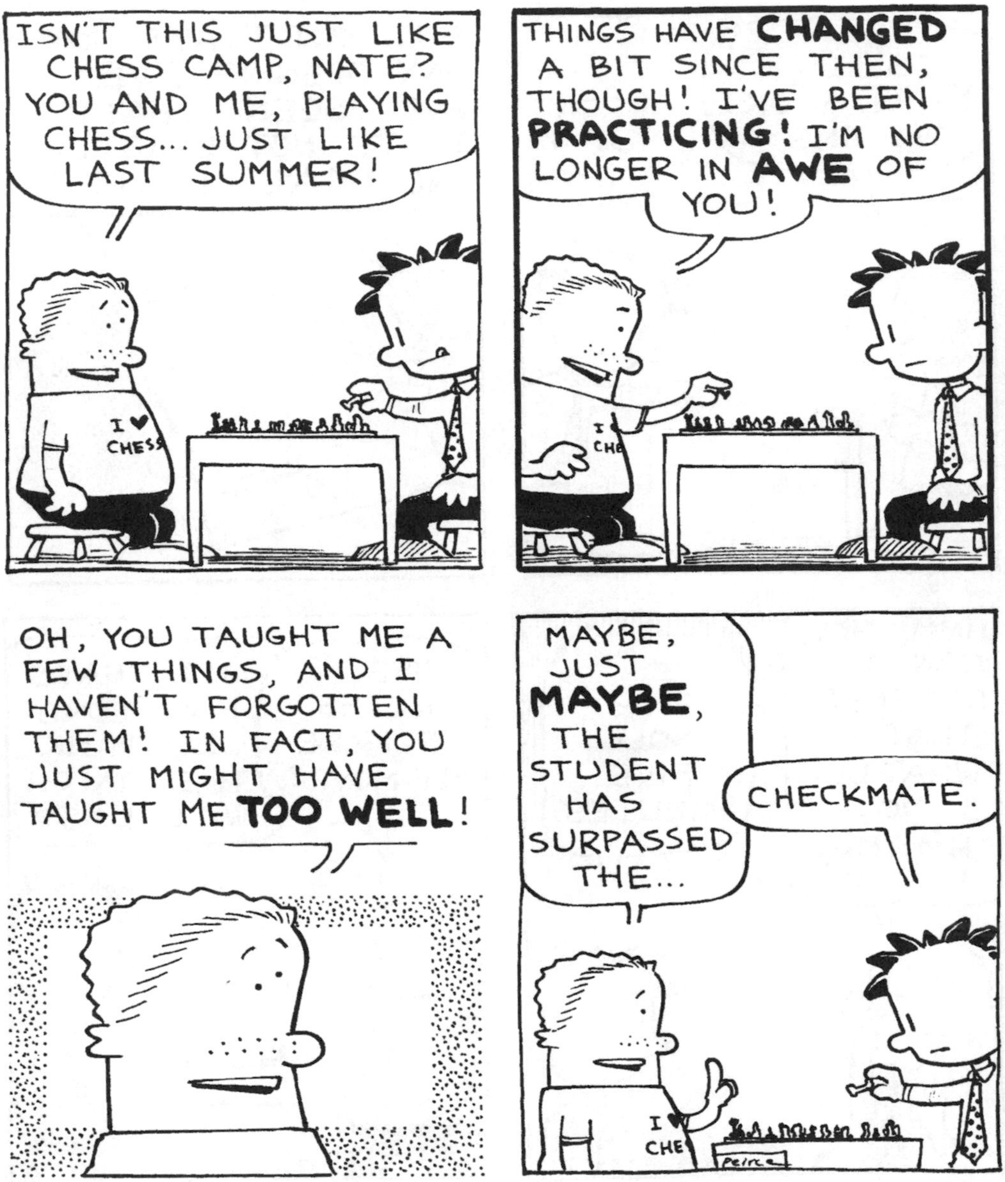

ISN'T THIS JUST LIKE CHESS CAMP, NATE? YOU AND ME, PLAYING CHESS... JUST LIKE LAST SUMMER!
I ♥ CHESS
THINGS HAVE CHANGED A BIT SINCE THEN, THOUGH! I'VE BEEN PRACTICING! I'M NO LONGER IN AWE OF YOU!
OH, YOU TAUGHT ME A FEW THINGS, AND I HAVEN'T FORGOTTEN THEM! IN FACT, YOU JUST MIGHT HAVE TAUGHT ME TOO WELL!
MAYBE, JUST MAYBE, THE STUDENT HAS SURPASSED THE...
CHECKMATE.
Peirce

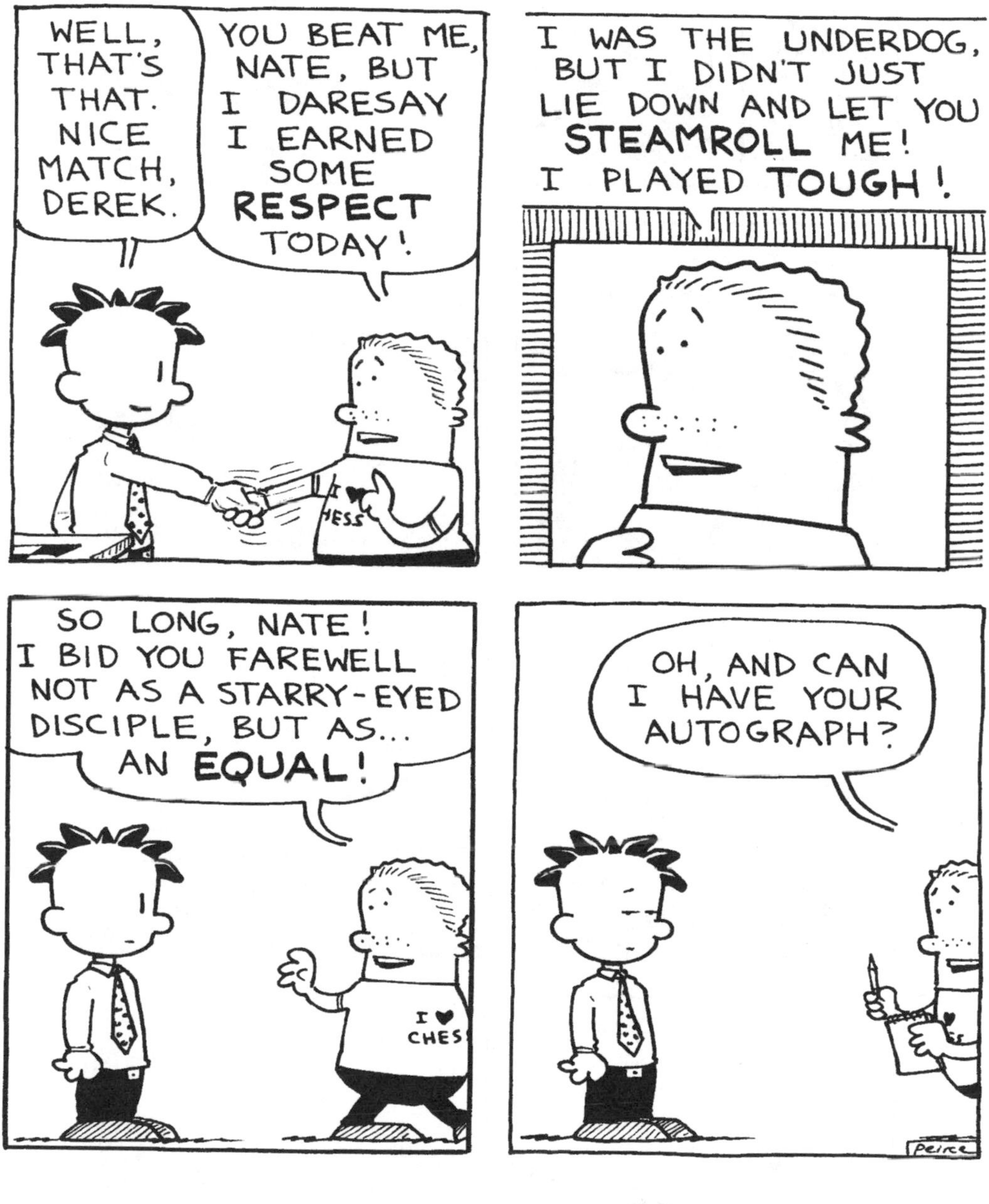
WELL, THAT'S THAT. NICE MATCH, DEREK.
YOU BEAT ME, NATE, BUT I DARESAY I EARNED SOME **RESPECT** TODAY!
I WAS THE UNDERDOG, BUT I DIDN'T JUST LIE DOWN AND LET YOU **STEAMROLL** ME! I PLAYED **TOUGH**!
SO LONG, NATE! I BID YOU FAREWELL NOT AS A STARRY-EYED DISCIPLE, BUT AS... AN **EQUAL**!
OH, AND CAN I HAVE YOUR AUTOGRAPH?
PEIRCE

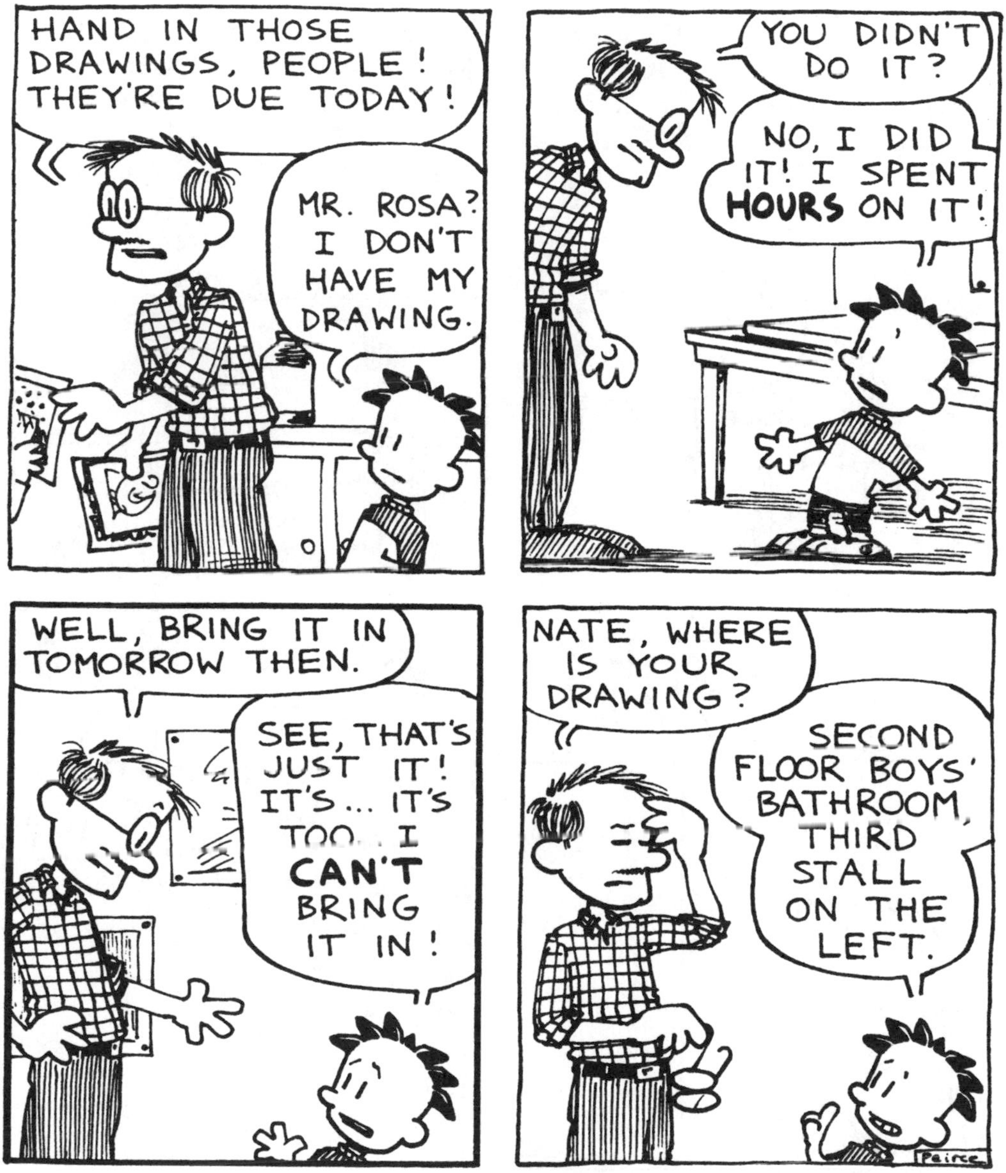
HAND IN THOSE DRAWINGS, PEOPLE! THEY'RE DUE TODAY!
MR. ROSA? I DON'T HAVE MY DRAWING.
YOU DIDN'T DO IT?
NO, I DID IT! I SPENT HOURS ON IT!
WELL, BRING IT IN TOMORROW THEN.
SEE, THAT'S JUST IT! IT'S... IT'S TOO... I CAN'T BRING IT IN!
NATE, WHERE IS YOUR DRAWING?
SECOND FLOOR BOYS' BATHROOM, THIRD STALL ON THE LEFT.
Peirce

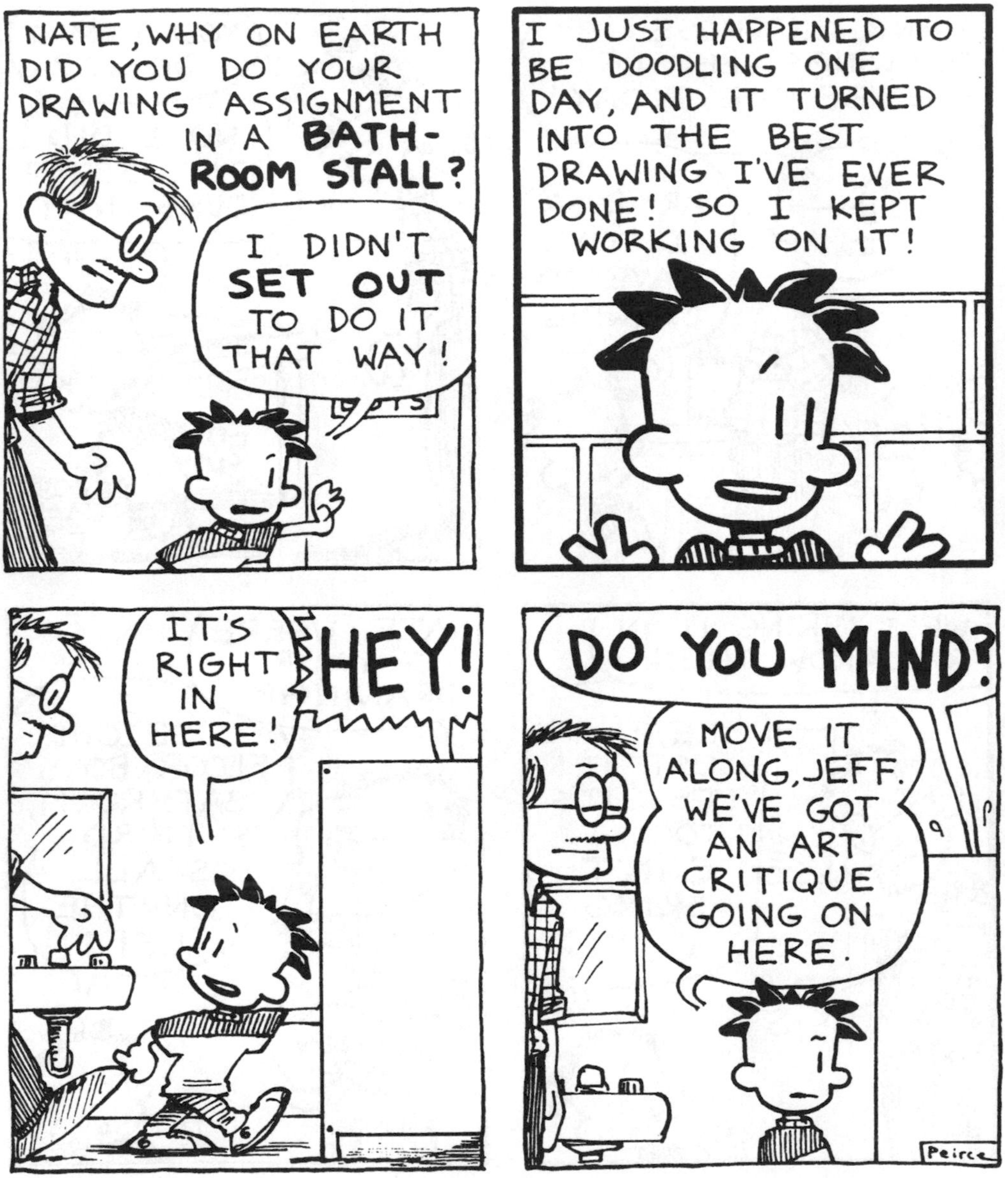
NATE, WHY ON EARTH DID YOU DO YOUR DRAWING ASSIGNMENT IN A BATH-ROOM STALL?
I DIDN'T SET OUT TO DO IT THAT WAY!
I JUST HAPPENED TO BE DOODLING ONE DAY, AND IT TURNED INTO THE BEST DRAWING I'VE EVER DONE! SO I KEPT WORKING ON IT!
IT'S RIGHT IN HERE!
HEY!
DO YOU MIND?
MOVE IT ALONG, JEFF. WE'VE GOT AN ART CRITIQUE GOING ON HERE.
Peirce

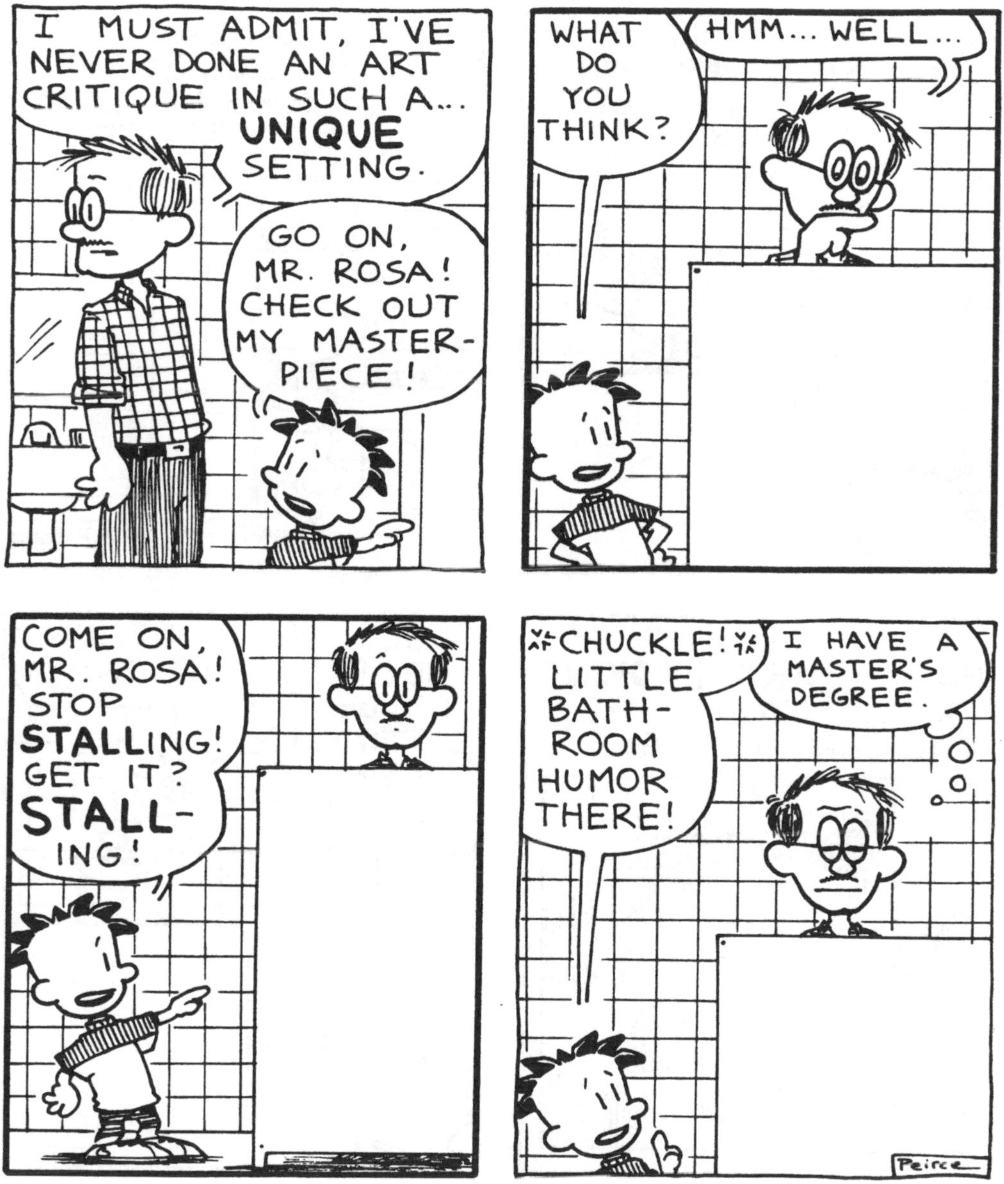
I MUST ADMIT, I'VE NEVER DONE AN ART CRITIQUE IN SUCH A... **UNIQUE** SETTING.
GO ON, MR. ROSA! CHECK OUT MY MASTER-PIECE!
WHAT DO YOU THINK?
HMM... WELL...
COME ON, MR. ROSA! STOP **STALL**ING! GET IT? **STALL**-ING!
CHUCKLE! LITTLE BATH-ROOM HUMOR THERE!
I HAVE A MASTER'S DEGREE.
Peirce

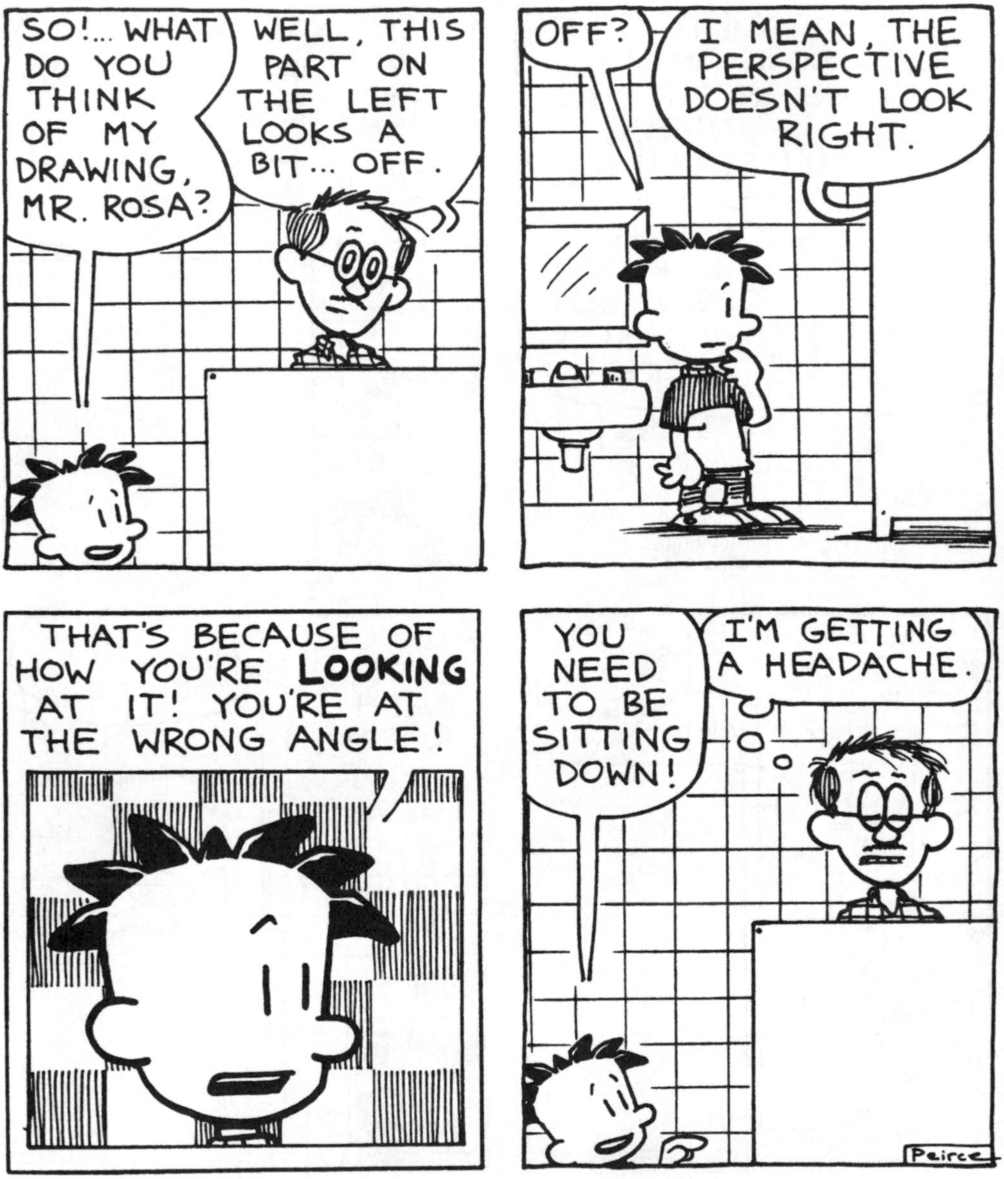
SO!... WHAT DO YOU THINK OF MY DRAWING, MR. ROSA?
WELL, THIS PART ON THE LEFT LOOKS A BIT... OFF.
OFF?
I MEAN, THE PERSPECTIVE DOESN'T LOOK RIGHT.
THAT'S BECAUSE OF HOW YOU'RE **LOOKING** AT IT! YOU'RE AT THE WRONG ANGLE!
YOU NEED TO BE SITTING DOWN!
I'M GETTING A HEADACHE.
Peirce

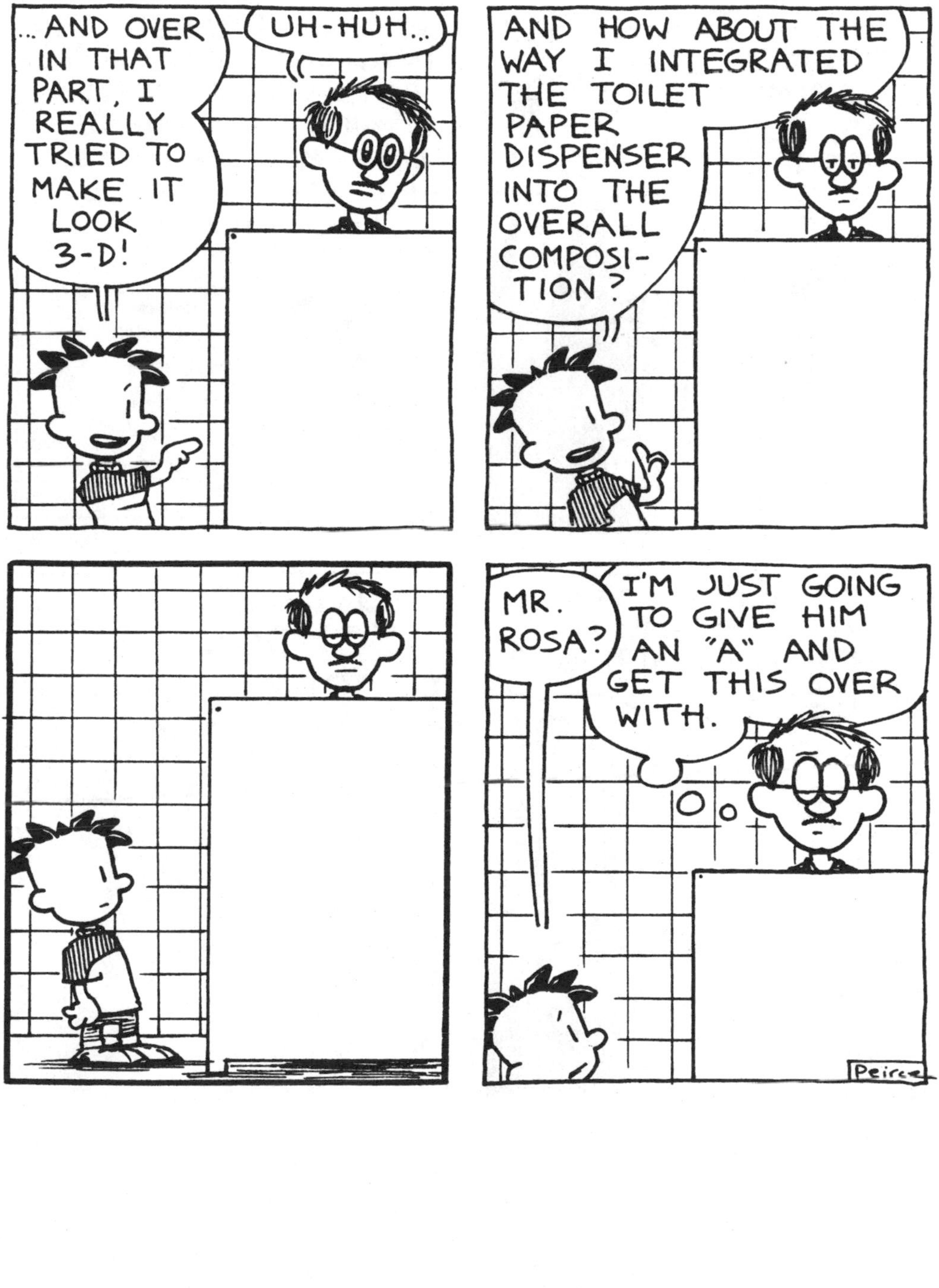
...AND OVER IN THAT PART, I REALLY TRIED TO MAKE IT LOOK 3-D!
UH-HUH...
AND HOW ABOUT THE WAY I INTEGRATED THE TOILET PAPER DISPENSER INTO THE OVERALL COMPOSITION?
MR. ROSA?
I'M JUST GOING TO GIVE HIM AN "A" AND GET THIS OVER WITH.
Peirce

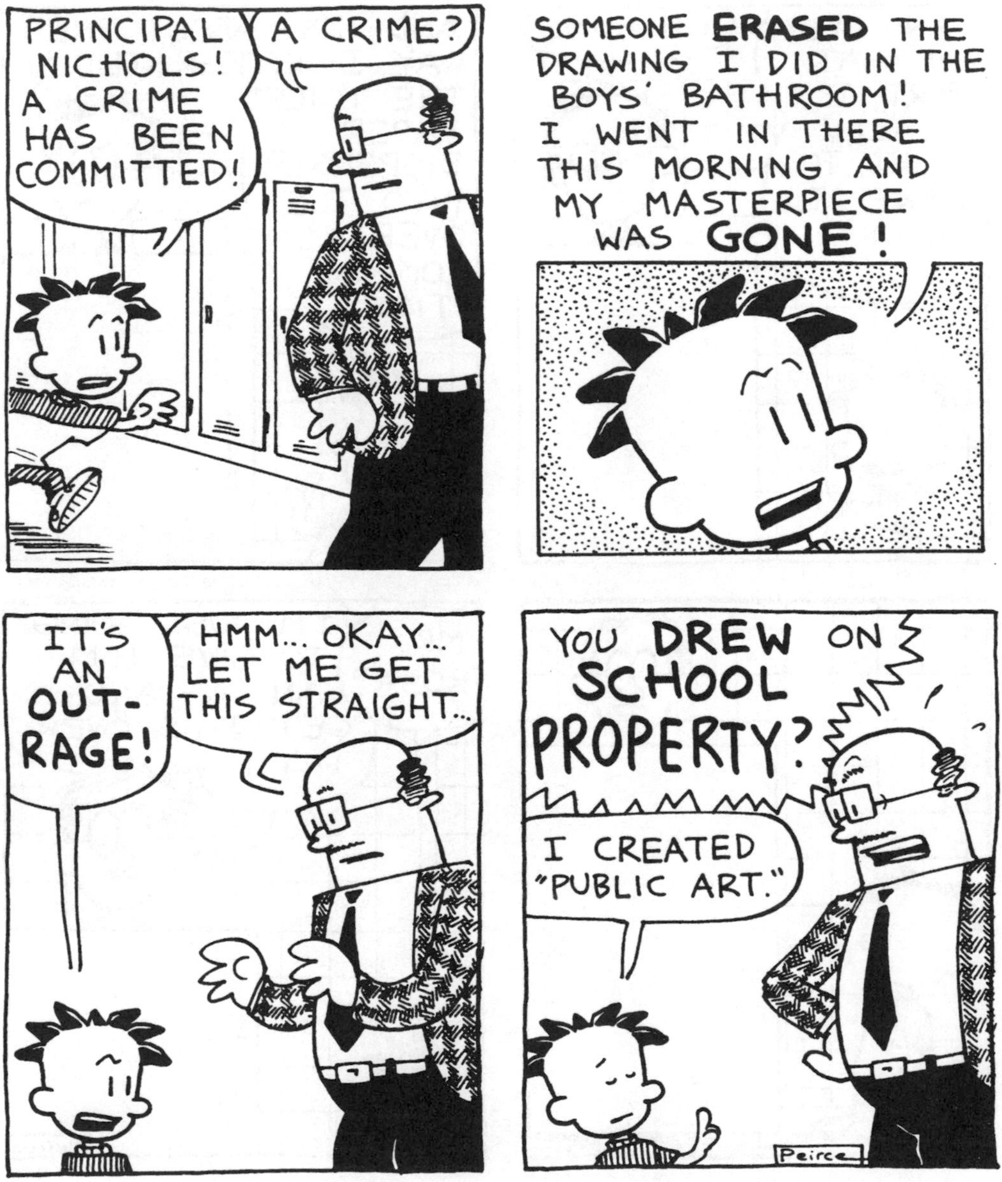
PRINCIPAL NICHOLS! A CRIME HAS BEEN COMMITTED!
A CRIME?
SOMEONE ERASED THE DRAWING I DID IN THE BOYS' BATHROOM! I WENT IN THERE THIS MORNING AND MY MASTERPIECE WAS GONE!
IT'S AN OUT-RAGE!
HMM... OKAY... LET ME GET THIS STRAIGHT...
YOU DREW ON SCHOOL PROPERTY?
I CREATED "PUBLIC ART."
Peirce

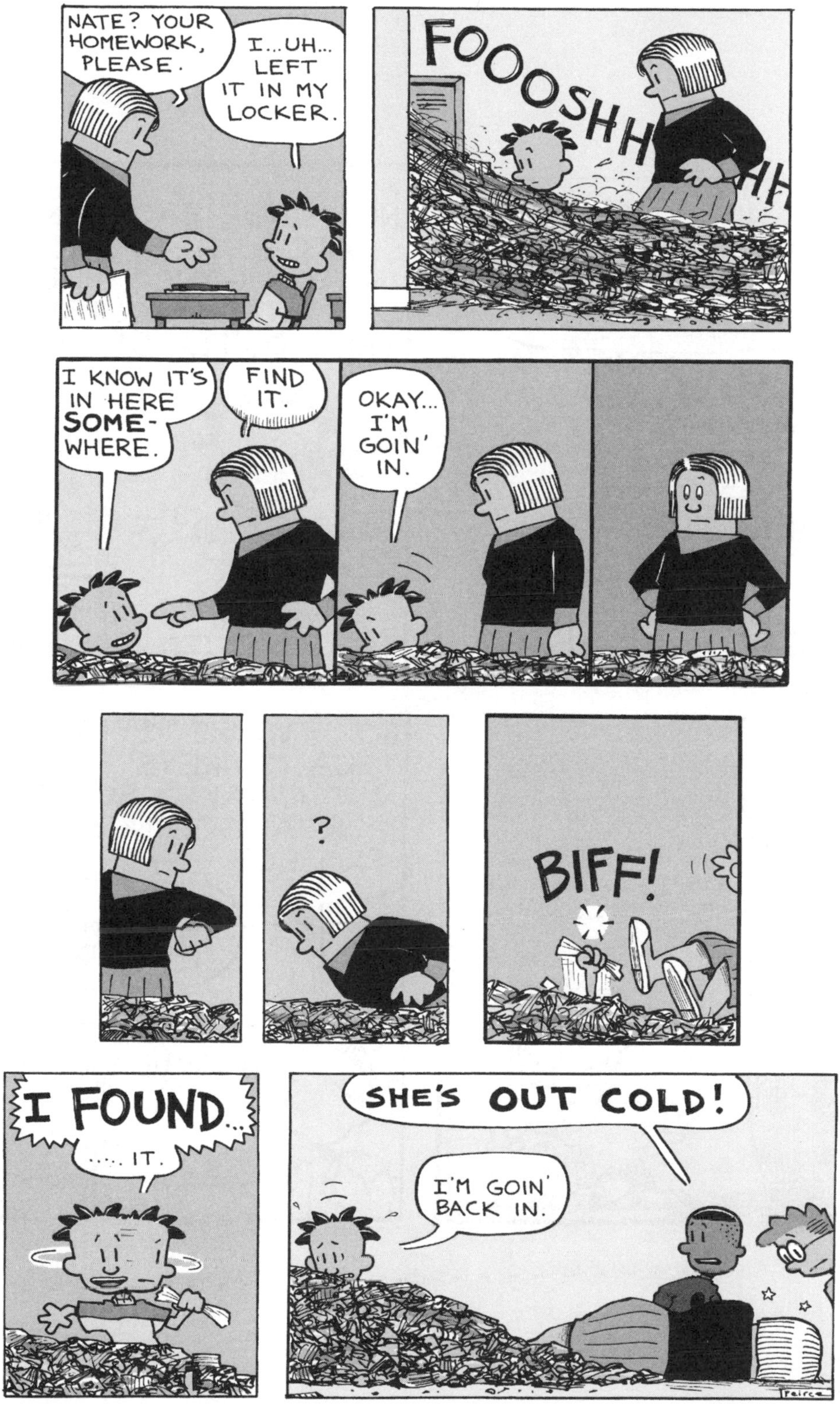
NATE? YOUR HOMEWORK, PLEASE.
I... UH... LEFT IT IN MY LOCKER.
FOOOSHHHH
I KNOW IT'S IN HERE **SOME**-WHERE.
FIND IT.
OKAY... I'M GOIN' IN.
?
BIFF!
I FOUND...
..... IT.
SHE'S OUT COLD!
I'M GOIN' BACK IN.
Peirce

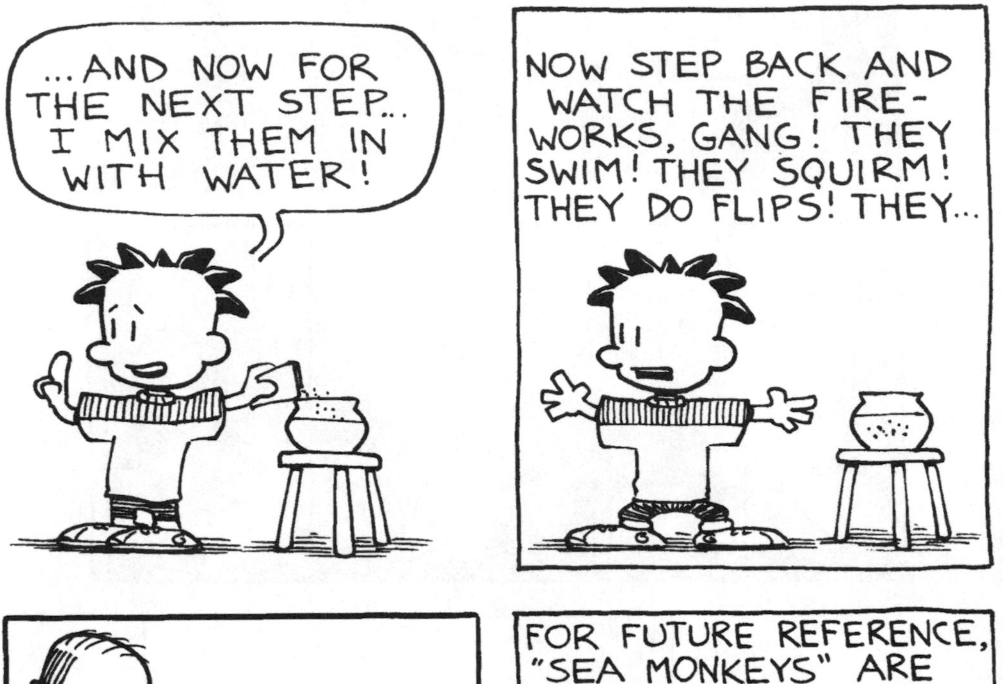
...AND NOW FOR THE NEXT STEP... I MIX THEM IN WITH WATER!
NOW STEP BACK AND WATCH THE FIRE-WORKS, GANG! THEY SWIM! THEY SQUIRM! THEY DO FLIPS! THEY...
FOR FUTURE REFERENCE, "SEA MONKEYS" ARE NOT A VALID SUBJECT FOR A SCIENCE PROJECT.
I'LL WRITE THAT DOWN.

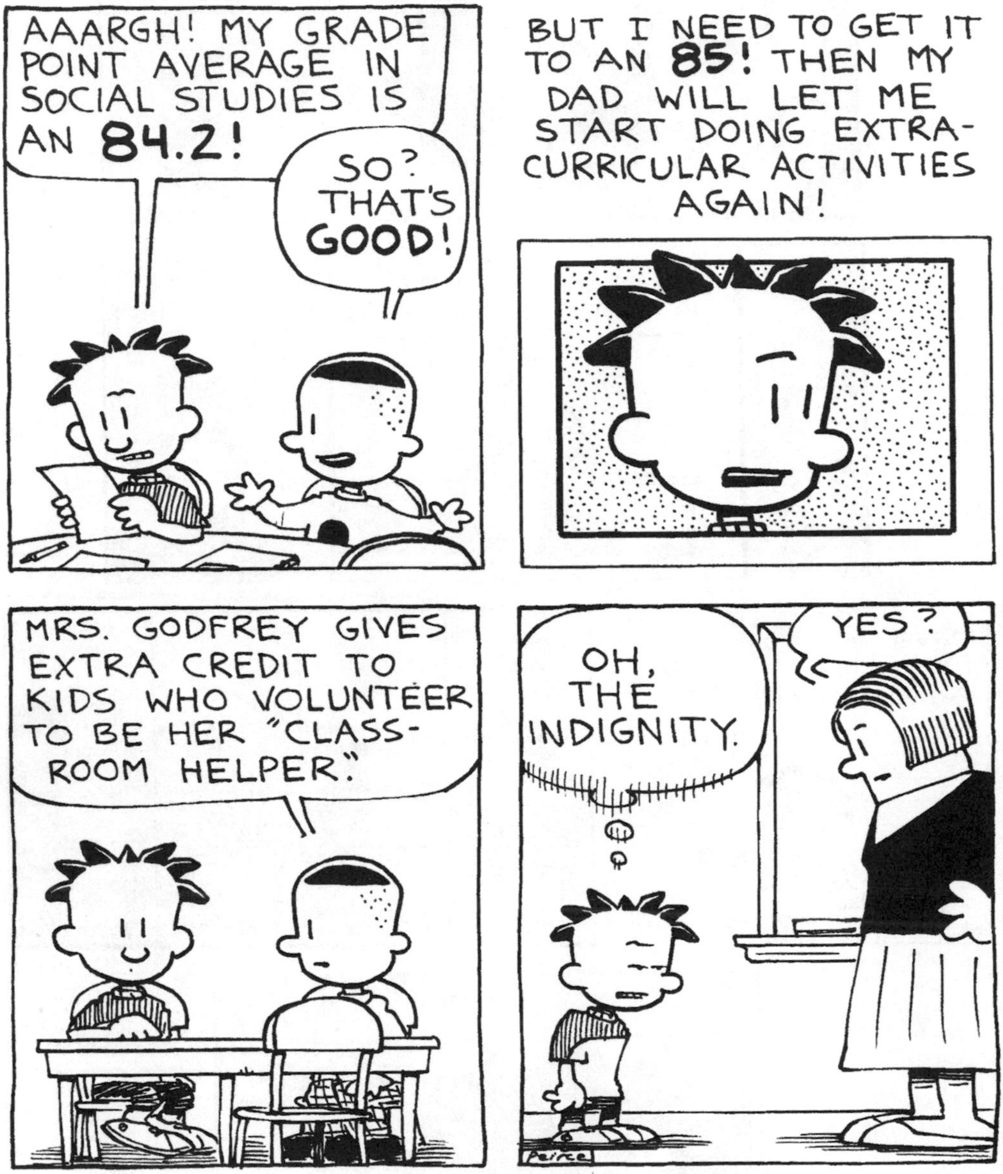
AAARGH! MY GRADE POINT AVERAGE IN SOCIAL STUDIES IS AN 84.2!
SO? THAT'S GOOD!
BUT I NEED TO GET IT TO AN 85! THEN MY DAD WILL LET ME START DOING EXTRA-CURRICULAR ACTIVITIES AGAIN!
MRS. GODFREY GIVES EXTRA CREDIT TO KIDS WHO VOLUNTEER TO BE HER "CLASS-ROOM HELPER."
YES?
OH, THE INDIGNITY.
Peirce

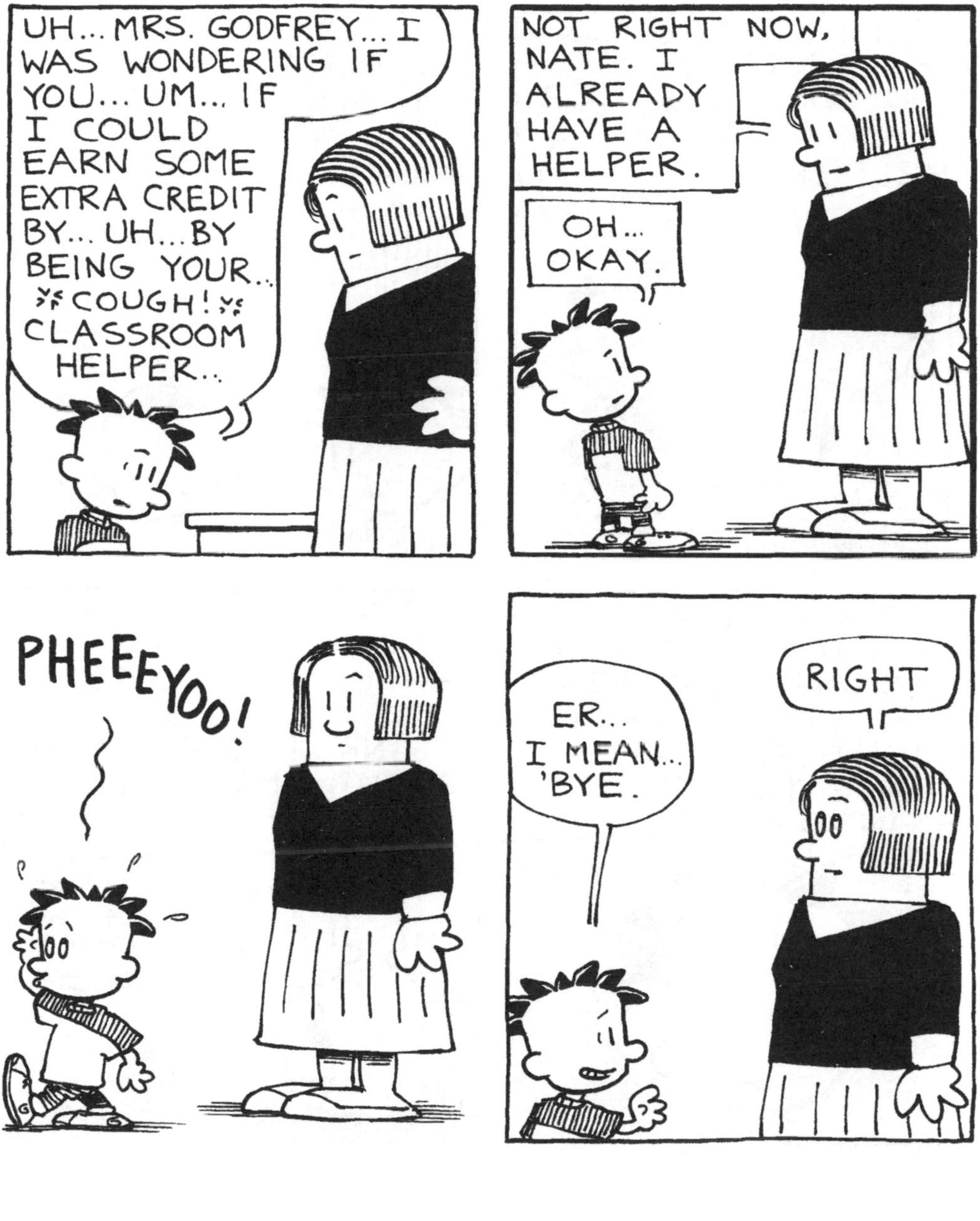
UH... MRS. GODFREY... I WAS WONDERING IF YOU... UM... IF I COULD EARN SOME EXTRA CREDIT BY... UH... BY BEING YOUR... *COUGH!* CLASSROOM HELPER...
NOT RIGHT NOW, NATE. I ALREADY HAVE A HELPER.
OH... OKAY.
PHEEEEYOO!
ER... I MEAN... 'BYE.
RIGHT

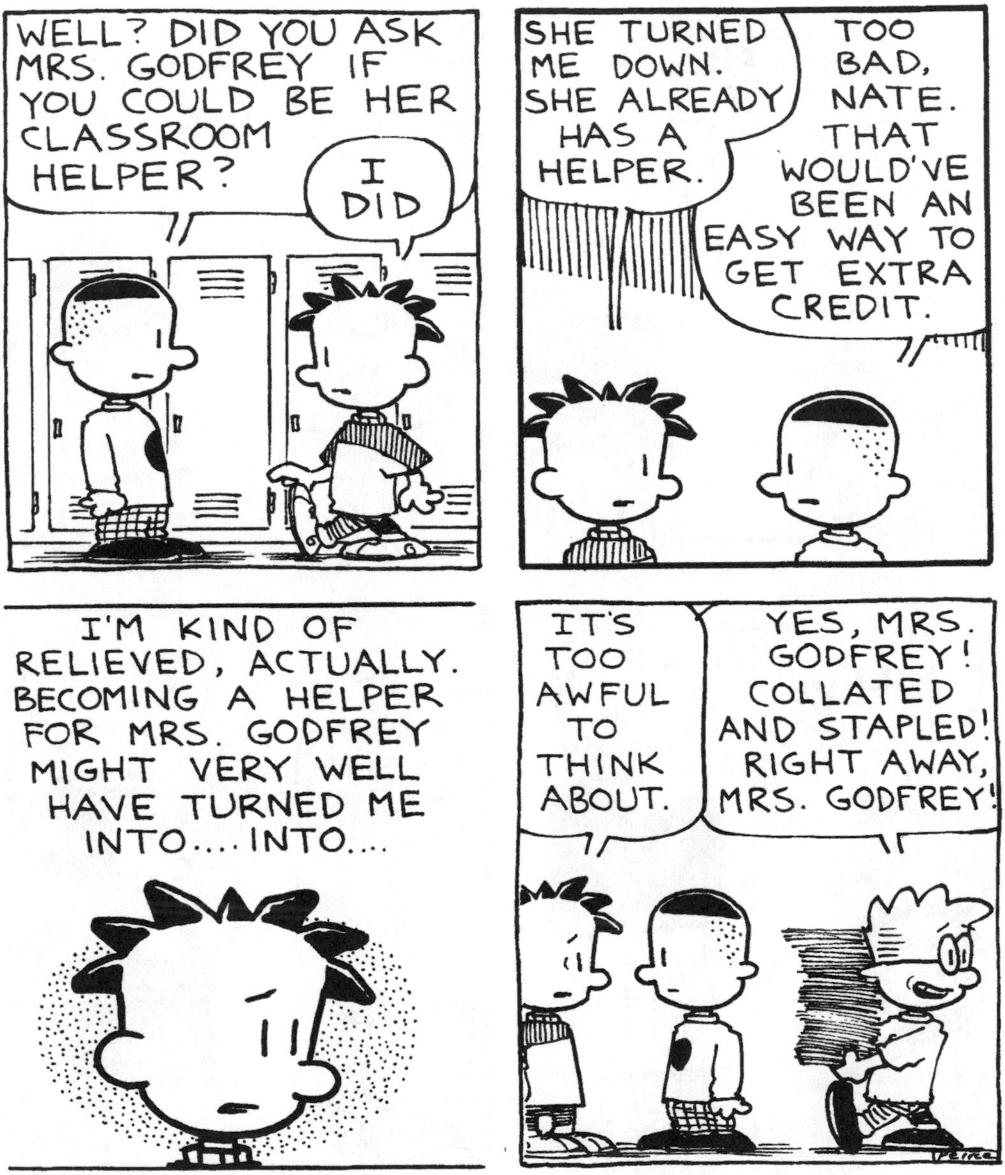
WELL? DID YOU ASK MRS. GODFREY IF YOU COULD BE HER CLASSROOM HELPER?
I DID
SHE TURNED ME DOWN. SHE ALREADY HAS A HELPER.
TOO BAD, NATE. THAT WOULD'VE BEEN AN EASY WAY TO GET EXTRA CREDIT.
I'M KIND OF RELIEVED, ACTUALLY. BECOMING A HELPER FOR MRS. GODFREY MIGHT VERY WELL HAVE TURNED ME INTO.... INTO....
IT'S TOO AWFUL TO THINK ABOUT.
YES, MRS. GODFREY! COLLATED AND STAPLED! RIGHT AWAY, MRS. GODFREY!

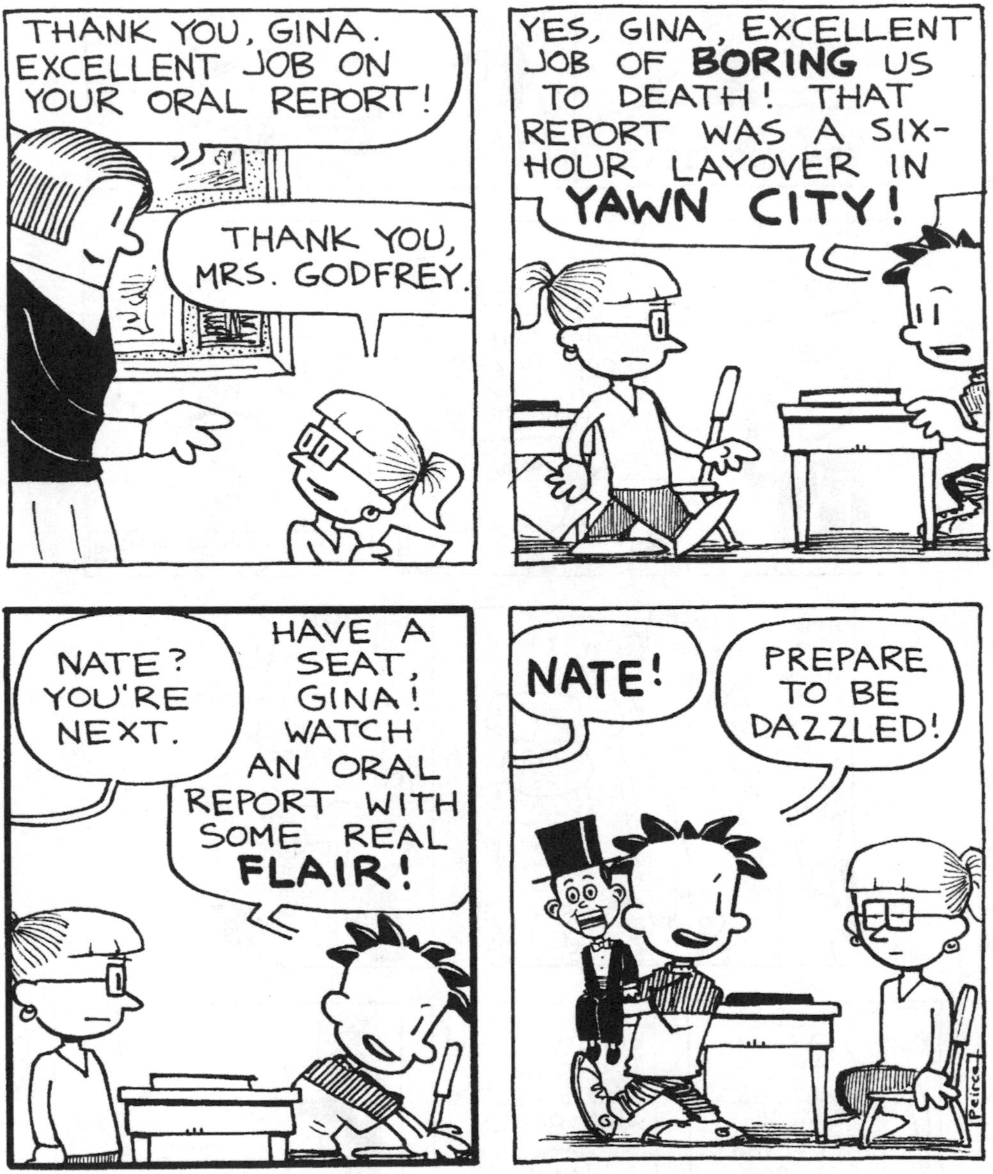
THANK YOU, GINA. EXCELLENT JOB ON YOUR ORAL REPORT!
THANK YOU, MRS. GODFREY.
YES, GINA, EXCELLENT JOB OF BORING US TO DEATH! THAT REPORT WAS A SIX-HOUR LAYOVER IN YAWN CITY!
NATE? YOU'RE NEXT.
HAVE A SEAT, GINA! WATCH AN ORAL REPORT WITH SOME REAL FLAIR!
NATE!
PREPARE TO BE DAZZLED!
Peirce

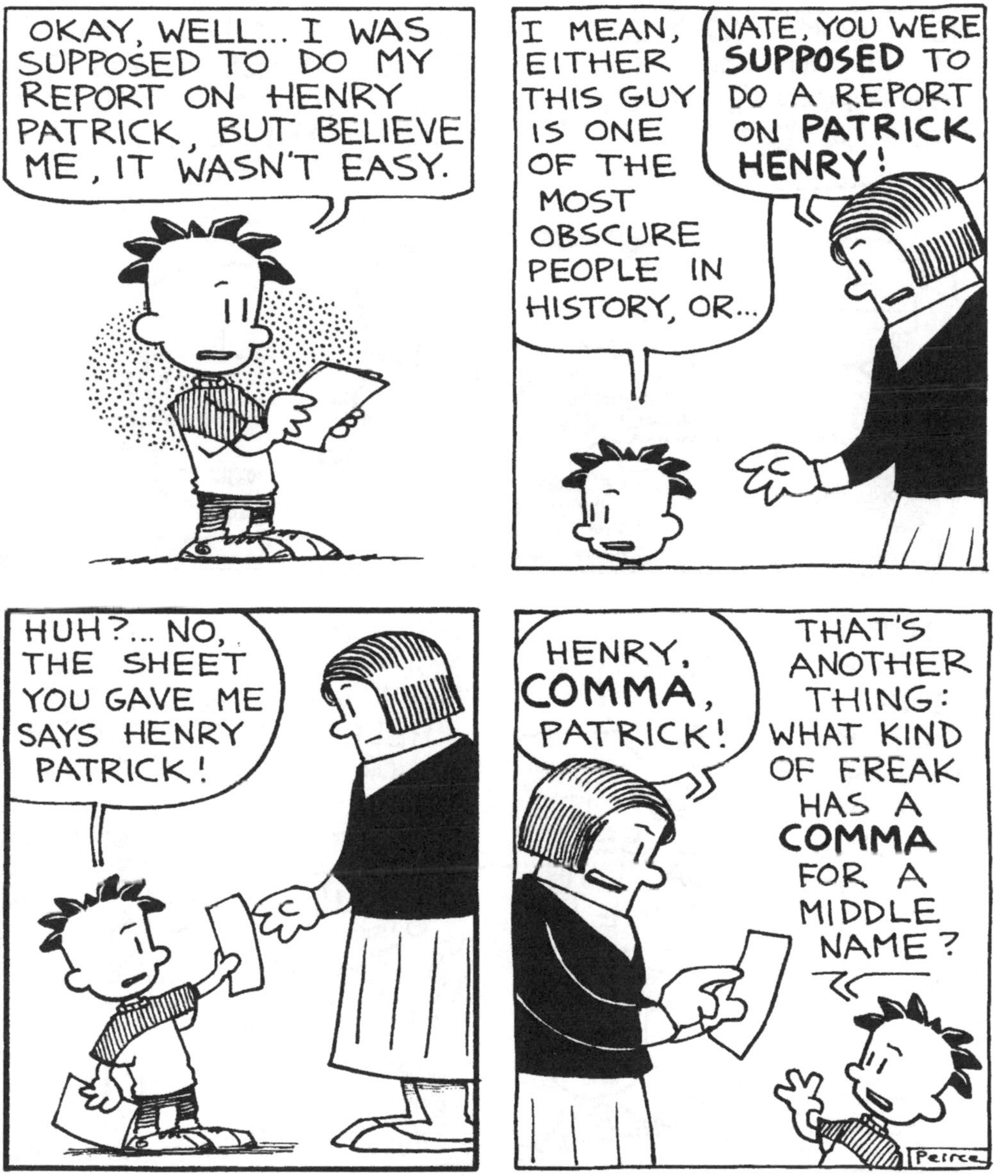

OKAY, WELL... I WAS SUPPOSED TO DO MY REPORT ON HENRY PATRICK, BUT BELIEVE ME, IT WASN'T EASY.
I MEAN, EITHER THIS GUY IS ONE OF THE MOST OBSCURE PEOPLE IN HISTORY, OR...
NATE, YOU WERE **SUPPOSED** TO DO A REPORT ON **PATRICK HENRY**!
HUH?... NO, THE SHEET YOU GAVE ME SAYS HENRY PATRICK!
HENRY, **COMMA**, PATRICK!
THAT'S ANOTHER THING: WHAT KIND OF FREAK HAS A **COMMA** FOR A MIDDLE NAME?
Peirce

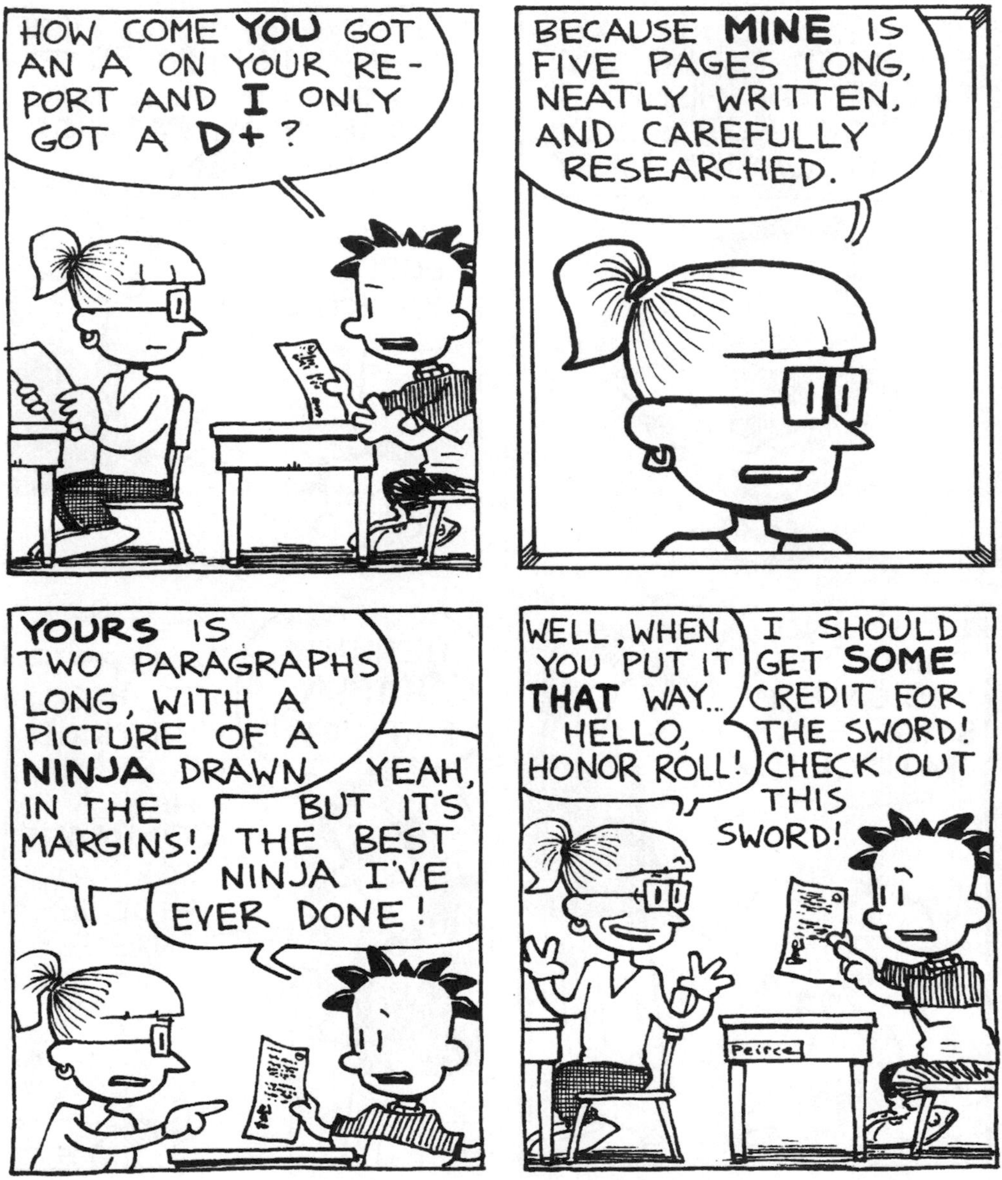
HOW COME YOU GOT AN A ON YOUR RE-PORT AND I ONLY GOT A D+?
BECAUSE MINE IS FIVE PAGES LONG, NEATLY WRITTEN, AND CAREFULLY RESEARCHED.
YOURS IS TWO PARAGRAPHS LONG, WITH A PICTURE OF A NINJA DRAWN IN THE MARGINS!
YEAH, BUT IT'S THE BEST NINJA I'VE EVER DONE!
WELL, WHEN YOU PUT IT THAT WAY... HELLO, HONOR ROLL!
I SHOULD GET SOME CREDIT FOR THE SWORD! CHECK OUT THIS SWORD!
Peirce

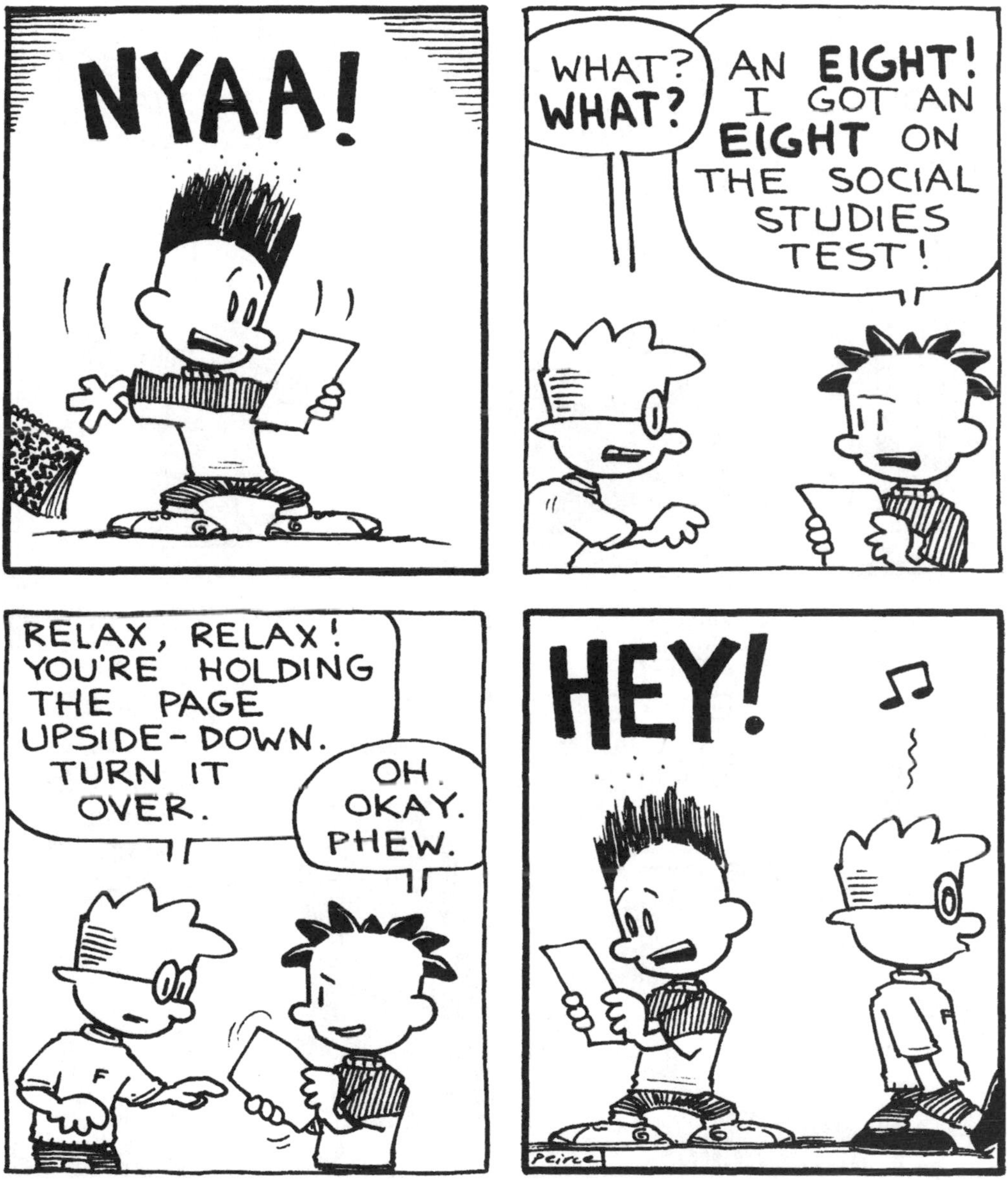
NYAA!
WHAT? WHAT?
AN EIGHT! I GOT AN EIGHT ON THE SOCIAL STUDIES TEST!
RELAX, RELAX! YOU'RE HOLDING THE PAGE UPSIDE-DOWN. TURN IT OVER.
OH. OKAY. PHEW.
HEY!
Peirce

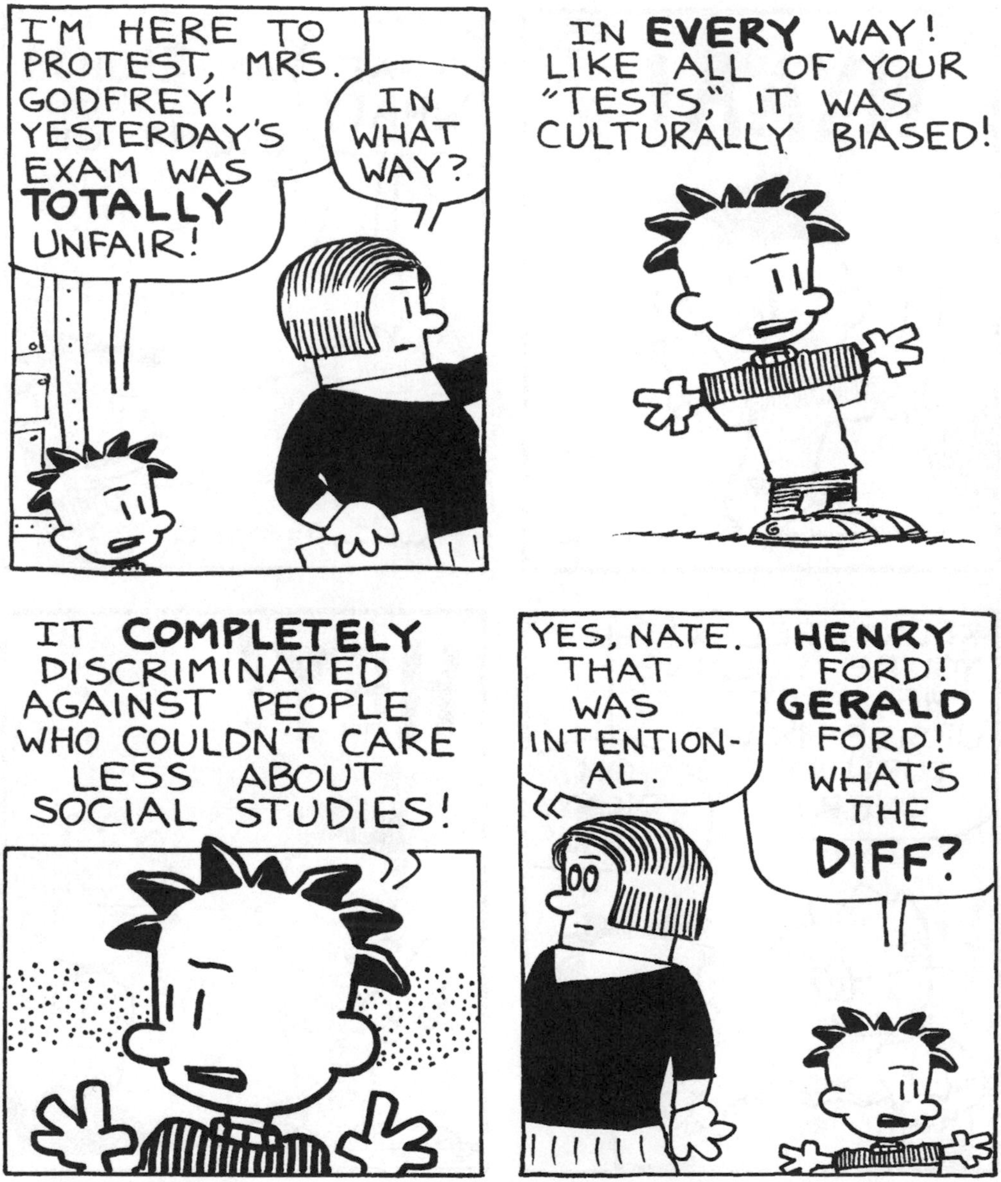

I'M HERE TO PROTEST, MRS. GODFREY! YESTERDAY'S EXAM WAS **TOTALLY** UNFAIR!
IN WHAT WAY?
IN **EVERY** WAY! LIKE ALL OF YOUR "TESTS," IT WAS CULTURALLY BIASED!
IT **COMPLETELY** DISCRIMINATED AGAINST PEOPLE WHO COULDN'T CARE LESS ABOUT SOCIAL STUDIES!
YES, NATE. THAT WAS INTENTION-AL.
HENRY FORD! **GERALD** FORD! WHAT'S THE **DIFF?**

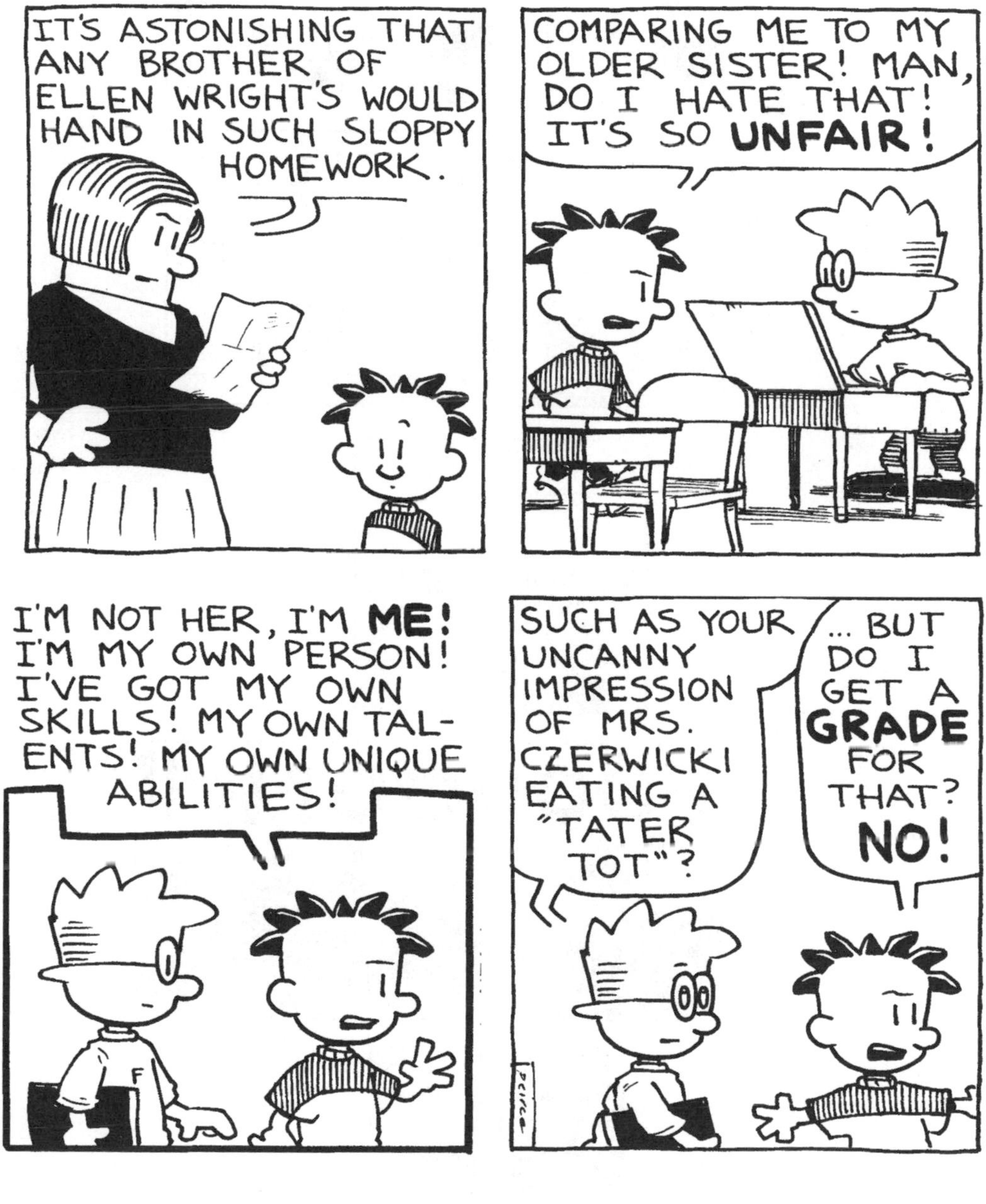
IT'S ASTONISHING THAT ANY BROTHER OF ELLEN WRIGHT'S WOULD HAND IN SUCH SLOPPY HOMEWORK.
COMPARING ME TO MY OLDER SISTER! MAN, DO I HATE THAT! IT'S SO UNFAIR!
I'M NOT HER, I'M ME! I'M MY OWN PERSON! I'VE GOT MY OWN SKILLS! MY OWN TAL-ENTS! MY OWN UNIQUE ABILITIES!
SUCH AS YOUR UNCANNY IMPRESSION OF MRS. CZERWICKI EATING A "TATER TOT"?
... BUT DO I GET A GRADE FOR THAT? NO!
F
PEIRCE

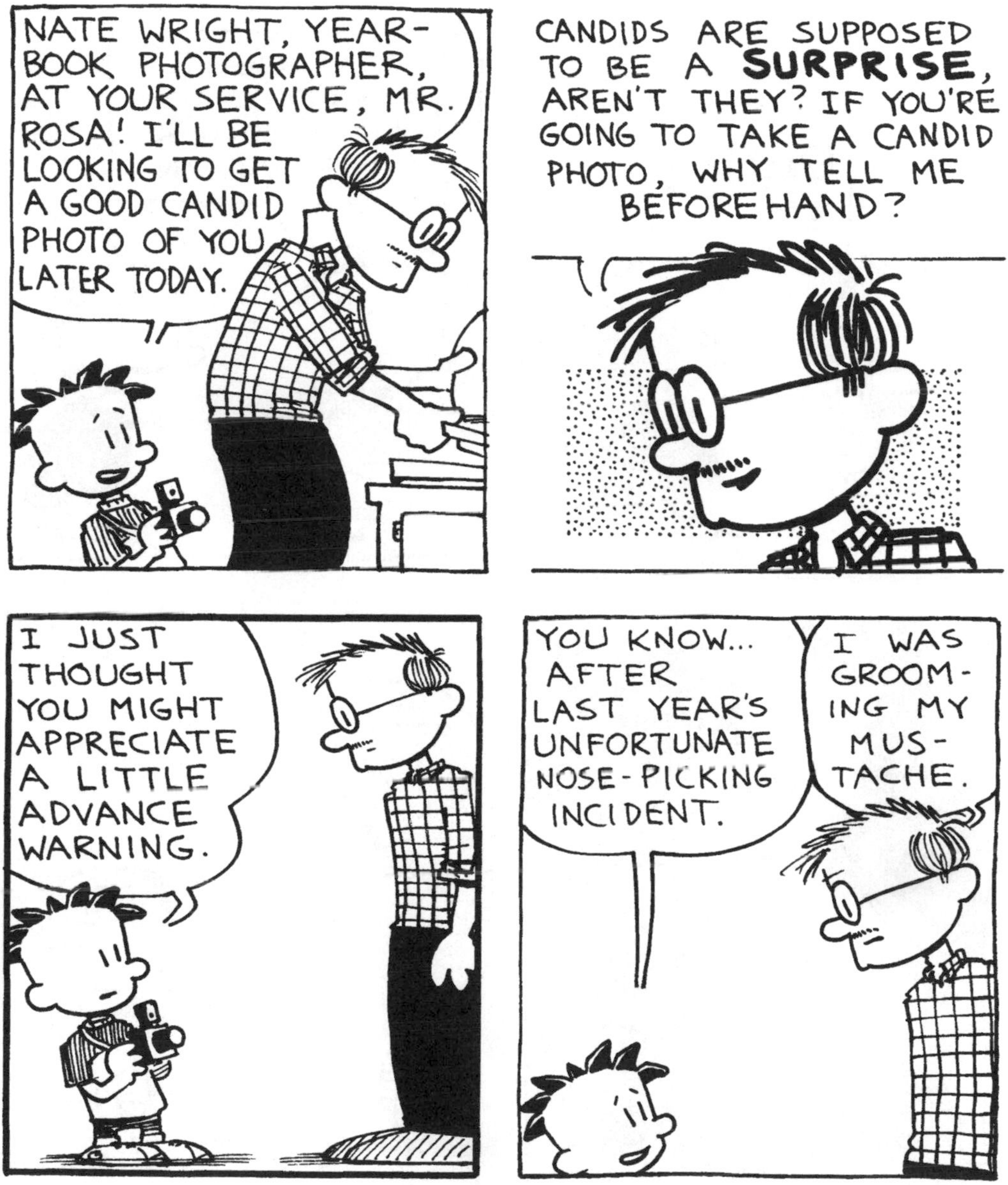
NATE WRIGHT, YEARBOOK PHOTOGRAPHER, AT YOUR SERVICE, MR. ROSA! I'LL BE LOOKING TO GET A GOOD CANDID PHOTO OF YOU LATER TODAY.
CANDIDS ARE SUPPOSED TO BE A **SURPRISE**, AREN'T THEY? IF YOU'RE GOING TO TAKE A CANDID PHOTO, WHY TELL ME BEFOREHAND?
I JUST THOUGHT YOU MIGHT APPRECIATE A LITTLE ADVANCE WARNING.
YOU KNOW... AFTER LAST YEAR'S UNFORTUNATE NOSE-PICKING INCIDENT.
I WAS GROOMING MY MUSTACHE.

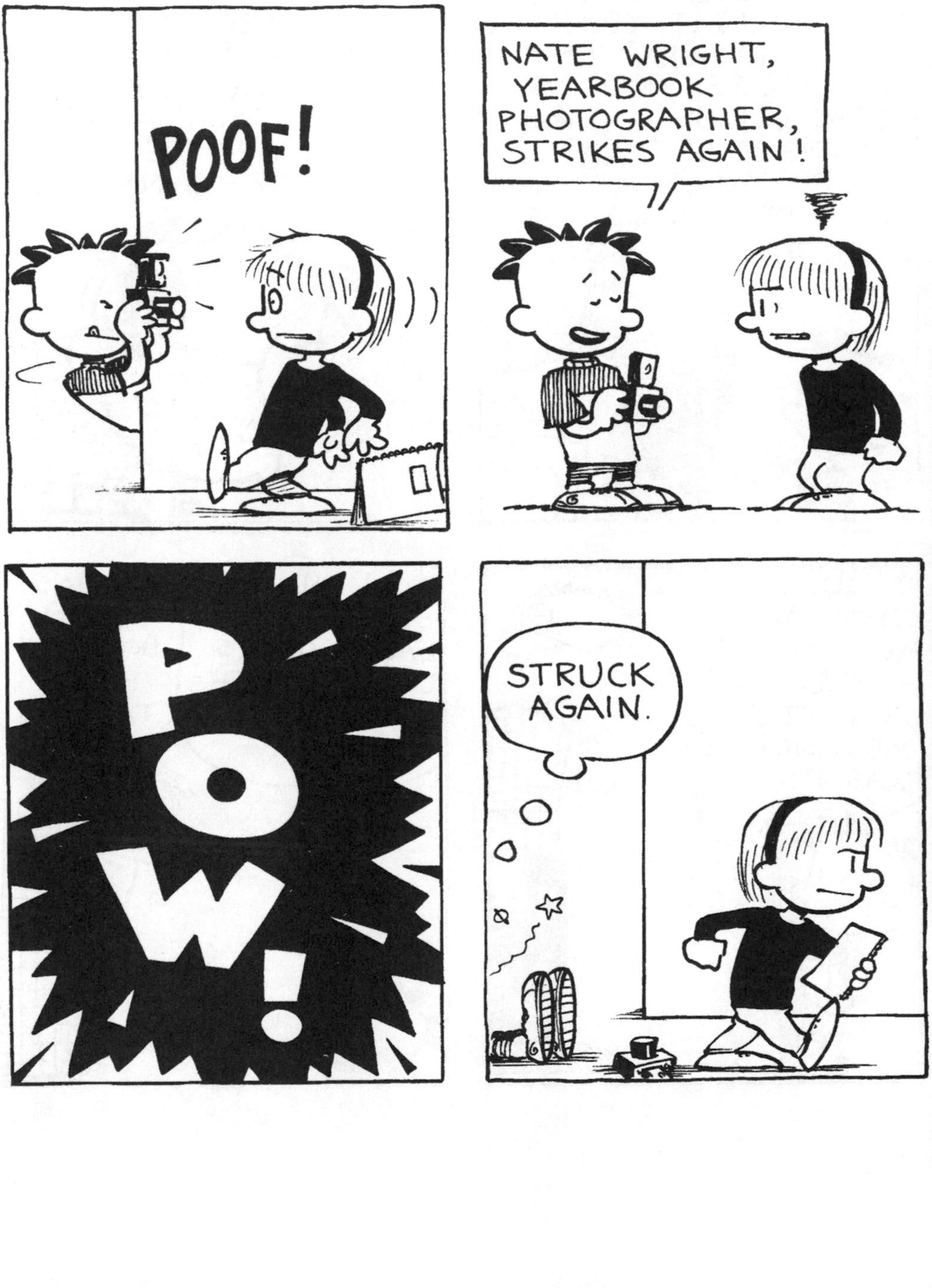
POOF!
NATE WRIGHT, YEARBOOK PHOTOGRAPHER, STRIKES AGAIN!
POW!
STRUCK AGAIN.

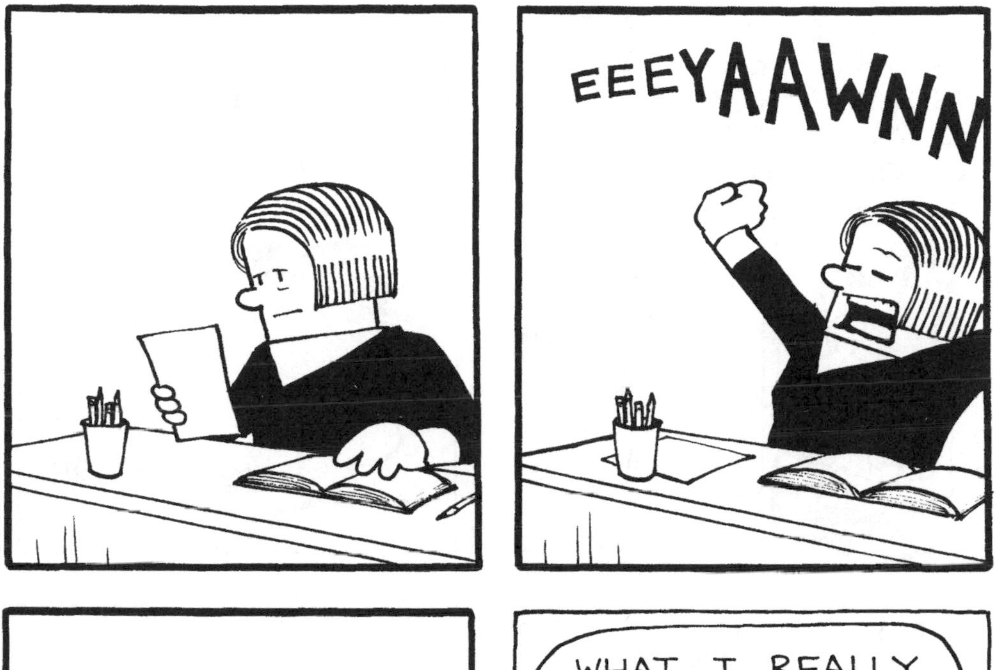
EEEYAAWNN
CLICK!
WHAT I REALLY, REALLY NEED IS A CAMERA WITH A SILENCER.

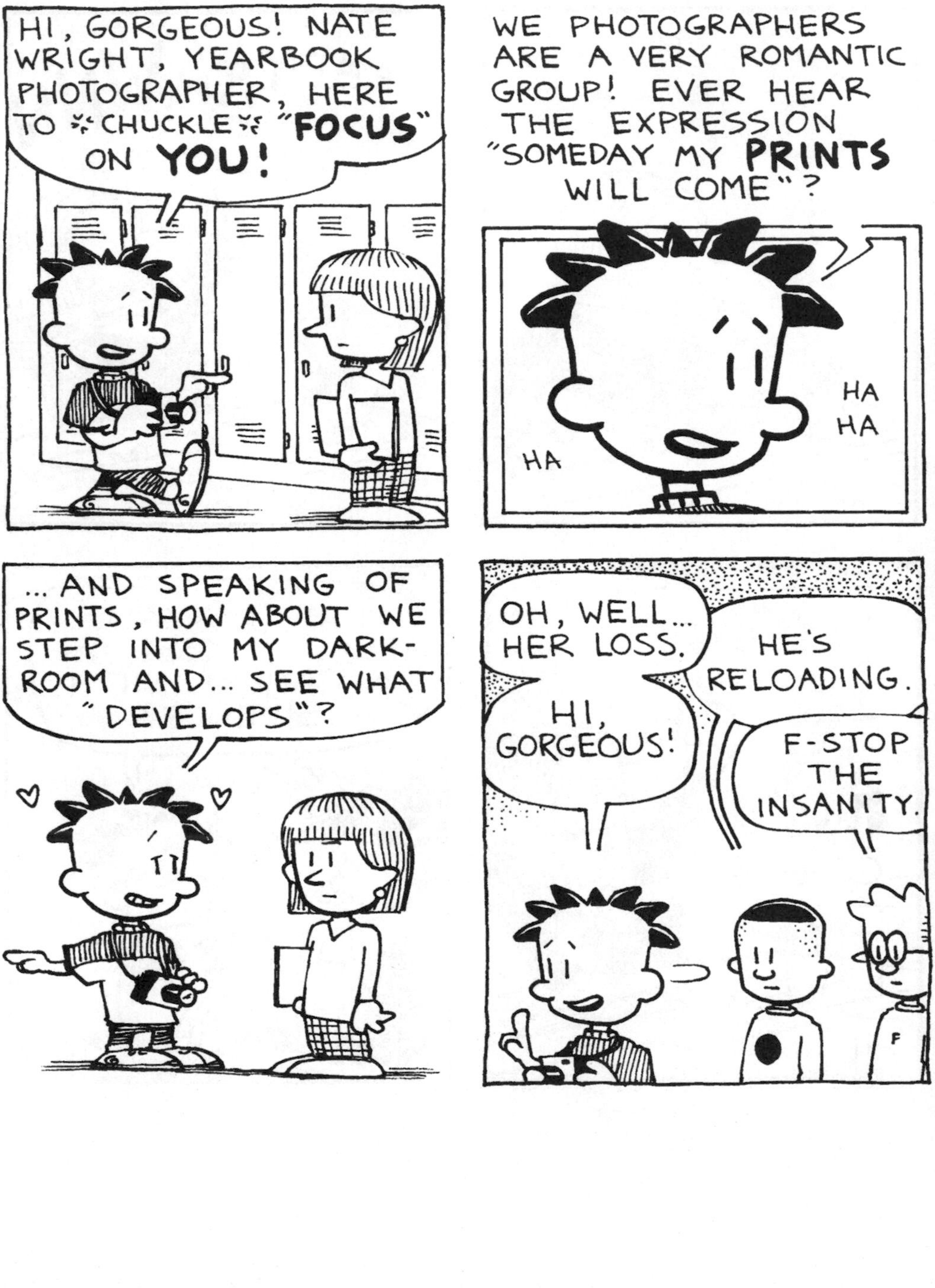
HI, GORGEOUS! NATE WRIGHT, YEARBOOK PHOTOGRAPHER, HERE TO *CHUCKLE* "FOCUS" ON YOU!
WE PHOTOGRAPHERS ARE A VERY ROMANTIC GROUP! EVER HEAR THE EXPRESSION "SOMEDAY MY PRINTS WILL COME"?
HA HA
HA
... AND SPEAKING OF PRINTS, HOW ABOUT WE STEP INTO MY DARK-ROOM AND... SEE WHAT "DEVELOPS"?
OH, WELL... HER LOSS.
HI, GORGEOUS!
HE'S RELOADING.
F-STOP THE INSANITY.

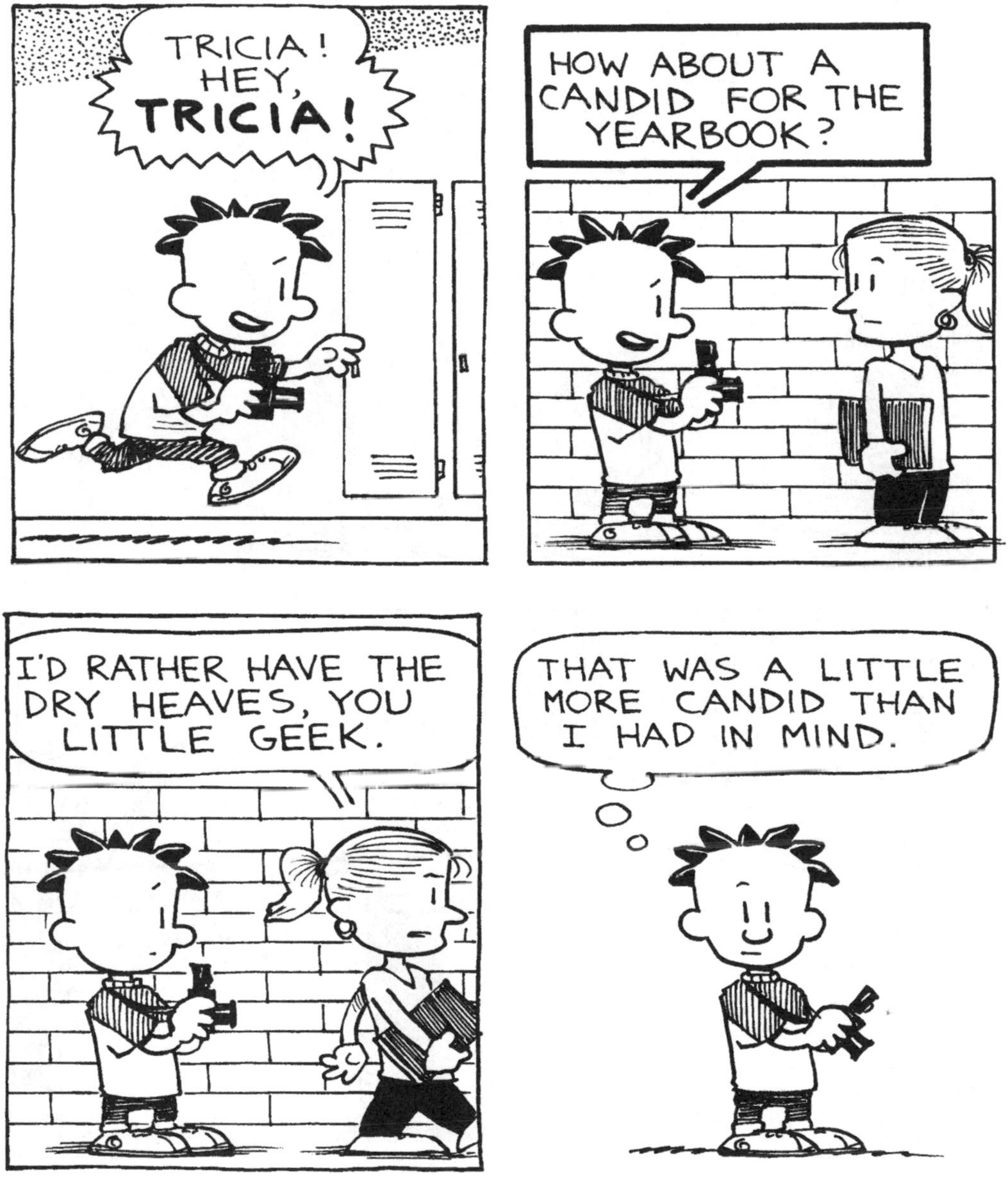
TRICIA! HEY, TRICIA!
HOW ABOUT A CANDID FOR THE YEARBOOK?
I'D RATHER HAVE THE DRY HEAVES, YOU LITTLE GEEK.
THAT WAS A LITTLE MORE CANDID THAN I HAD IN MIND.

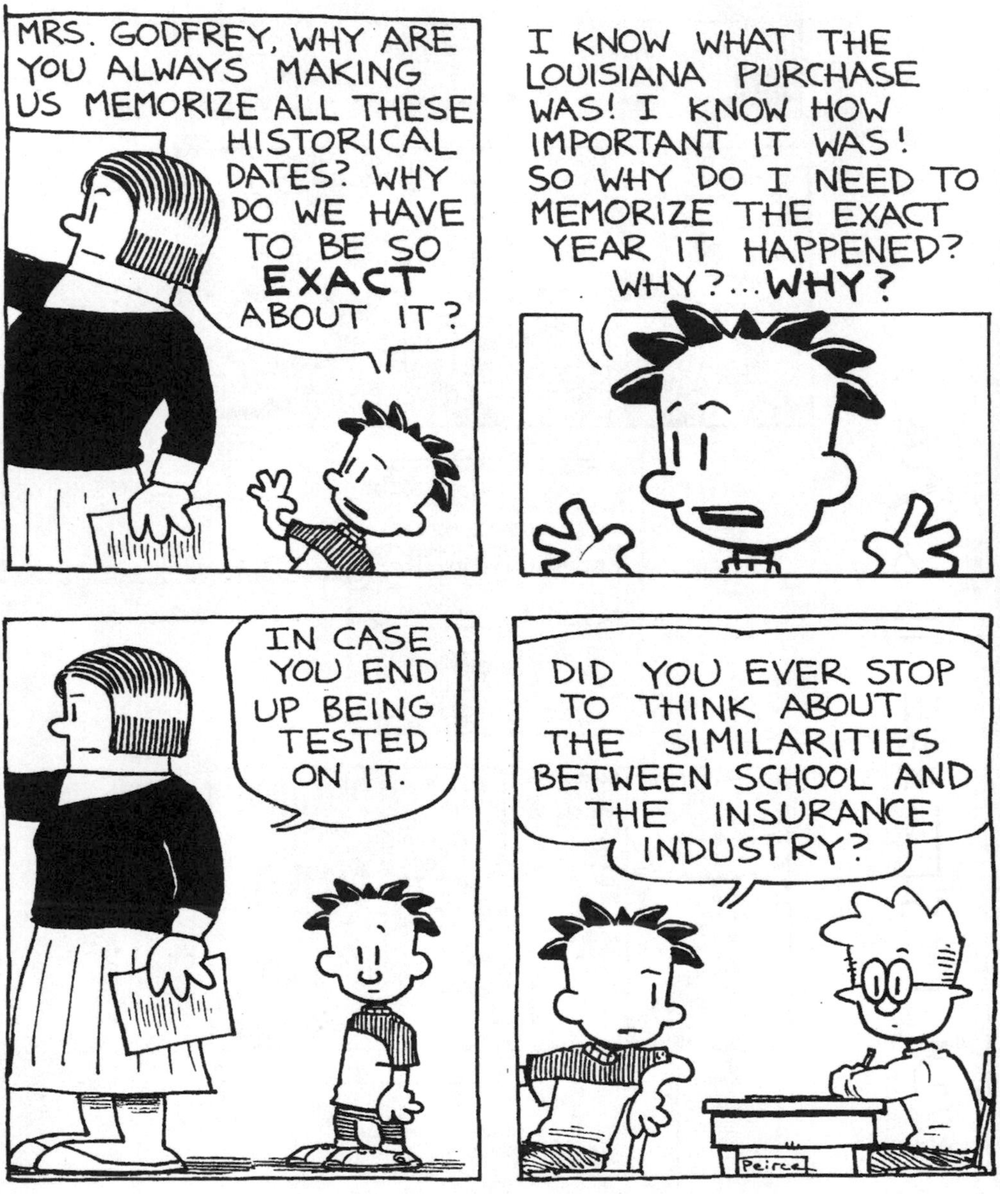
MRS. GODFREY, WHY ARE YOU ALWAYS MAKING US MEMORIZE ALL THESE HISTORICAL DATES? WHY DO WE HAVE TO BE SO **EXACT** ABOUT IT?
I KNOW WHAT THE LOUISIANA PURCHASE WAS! I KNOW HOW IMPORTANT IT WAS! SO WHY DO I NEED TO MEMORIZE THE EXACT YEAR IT HAPPENED? WHY?... **WHY?**
IN CASE YOU END UP BEING TESTED ON IT.
DID YOU EVER STOP TO THINK ABOUT THE SIMILARITIES BETWEEN SCHOOL AND THE INSURANCE INDUSTRY?
Peirce

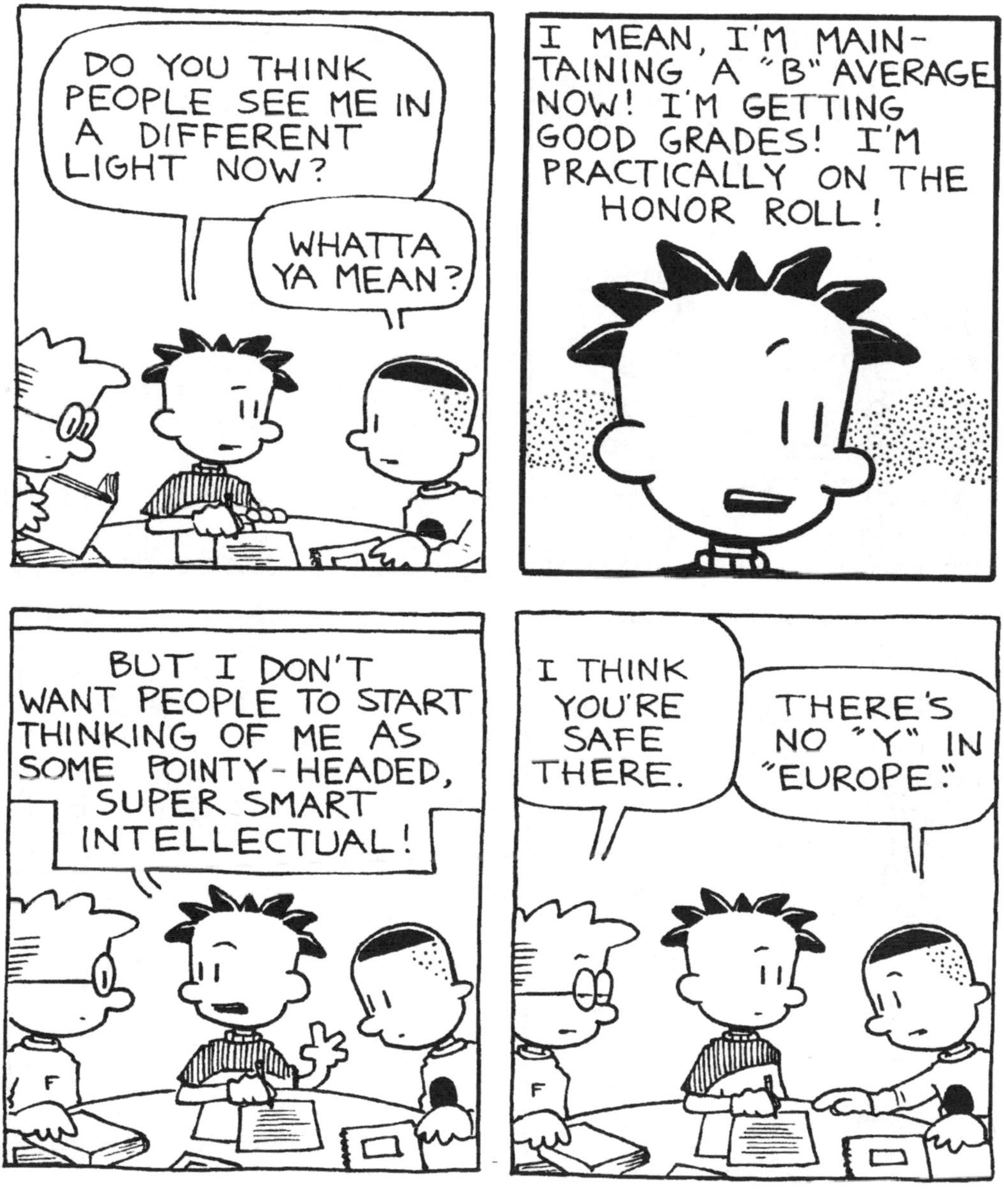
DO YOU THINK PEOPLE SEE ME IN A DIFFERENT LIGHT NOW?
WHATTA YA MEAN?
I MEAN, I'M MAINTAINING A "B" AVERAGE NOW! I'M GETTING GOOD GRADES! I'M PRACTICALLY ON THE HONOR ROLL!
BUT I DON'T WANT PEOPLE TO START THINKING OF ME AS SOME POINTY-HEADED, SUPER SMART INTELLECTUAL!
I THINK YOU'RE SAFE THERE.
THERE'S NO "Y" IN "EUROPE."

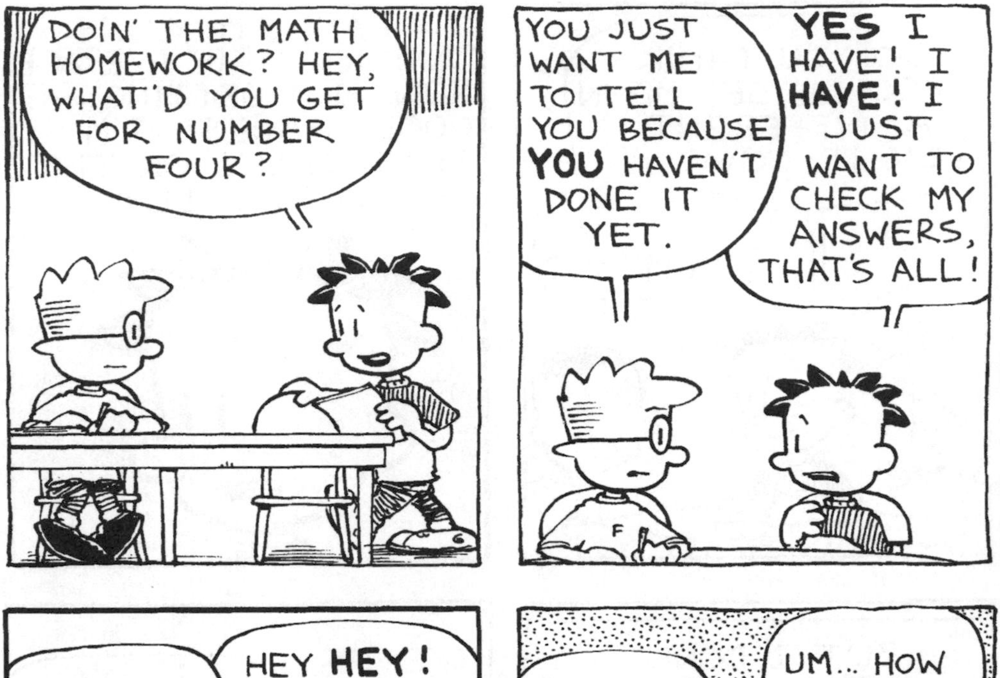
DOIN' THE MATH HOMEWORK? HEY, WHAT'D YOU GET FOR NUMBER FOUR?
YOU JUST WANT ME TO TELL YOU BECAUSE YOU HAVEN'T DONE IT YET.
YES I HAVE! I HAVE! I JUST WANT TO CHECK MY ANSWERS, THAT'S ALL!
I GOT 33 JILLION.
HEY HEY! I GOT THE VERY SAME ANSWER!
YOU WOULD.
UM... HOW MANY ZEROS IN A JILLION AGAIN?
PEIRCE

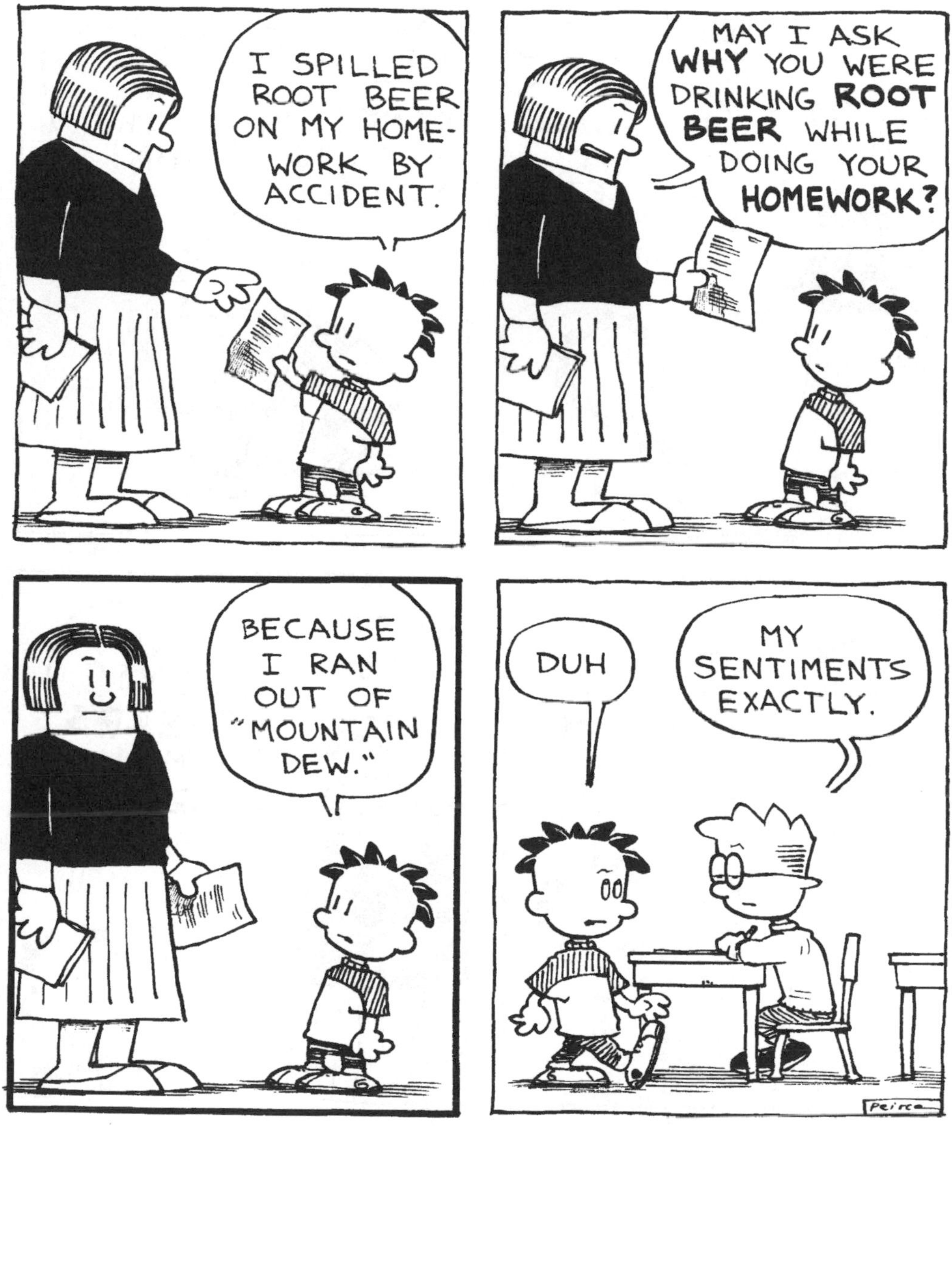
I SPILLED ROOT BEER ON MY HOME-WORK BY ACCIDENT.
MAY I ASK **WHY** YOU WERE DRINKING **ROOT BEER** WHILE DOING YOUR **HOMEWORK?**
BECAUSE I RAN OUT OF "MOUNTAIN DEW."
DUH
MY SENTIMENTS EXACTLY.
Peirce

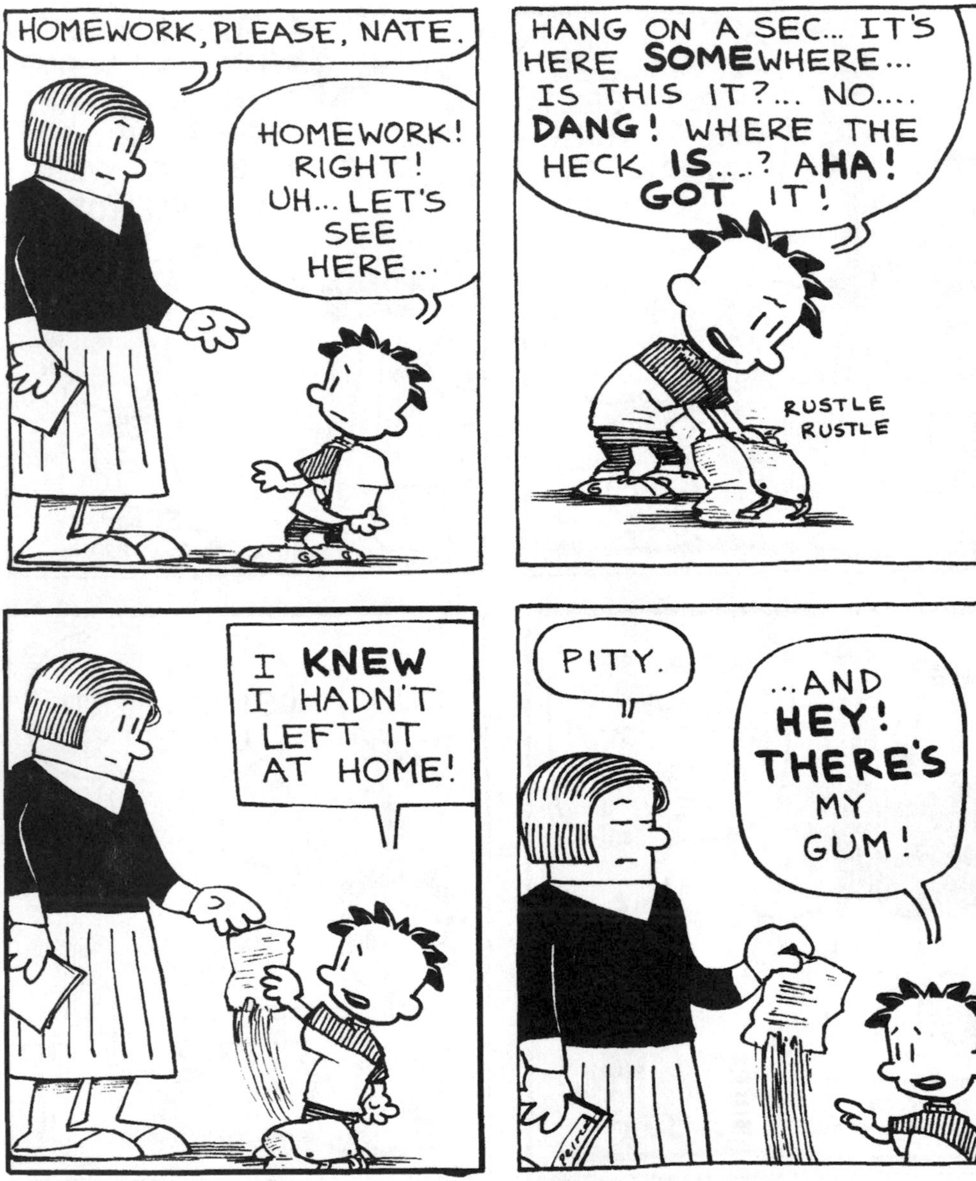
HOMEWORK, PLEASE, NATE.
HOMEWORK! RIGHT! UH... LET'S SEE HERE...
HANG ON A SEC... IT'S HERE SOMEWHERE... IS THIS IT?... NO.... DANG! WHERE THE HECK IS....? AHA! GOT IT!
RUSTLE RUSTLE
I KNEW I HADN'T LEFT IT AT HOME!
PITY.
...AND HEY! THERE'S MY GUM!

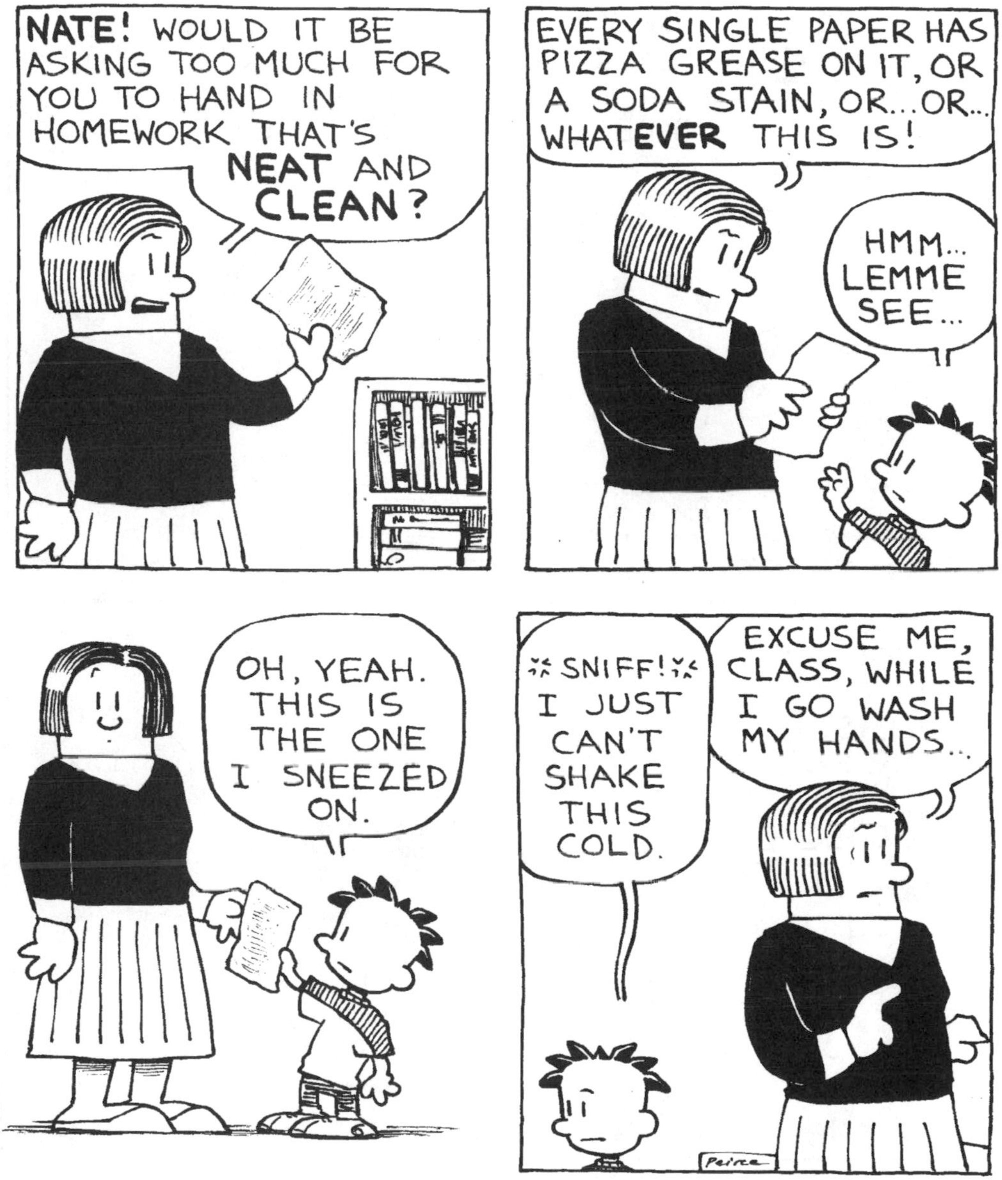
NATE! WOULD IT BE ASKING TOO MUCH FOR YOU TO HAND IN HOMEWORK THAT'S NEAT AND CLEAN?
EVERY SINGLE PAPER HAS PIZZA GREASE ON IT, OR A SODA STAIN, OR... OR... WHATEVER THIS IS!
HMM... LEMME SEE...
OH, YEAH. THIS IS THE ONE I SNEEZED ON.
SNIFF! I JUST CAN'T SHAKE THIS COLD.
EXCUSE ME, CLASS, WHILE I GO WASH MY HANDS...
Peirce

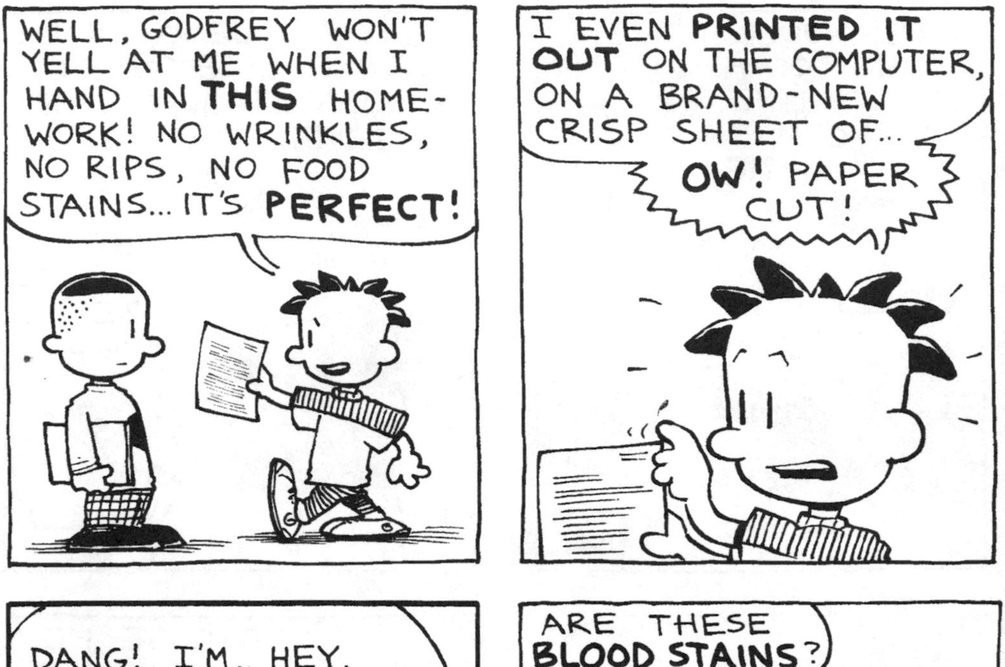
WELL, GODFREY WON'T YELL AT ME WHEN I HAND IN **THIS** HOME-WORK! NO WRINKLES, NO RIPS, NO FOOD STAINS... IT'S **PERFECT**!
I EVEN **PRINTED IT OUT** ON THE COMPUTER, ON A BRAND-NEW CRISP SHEET OF...
OW! PAPER CUT!
DANG!... I'M... HEY, TEDDY, DO YOU HAVE A TISSUE?... HEY, SOMEBODY GET ME A "BAND-AID"! OW! OWOWOW!
ARE THESE **BLOOD STAINS**?
I'M JINXED.
Peirce

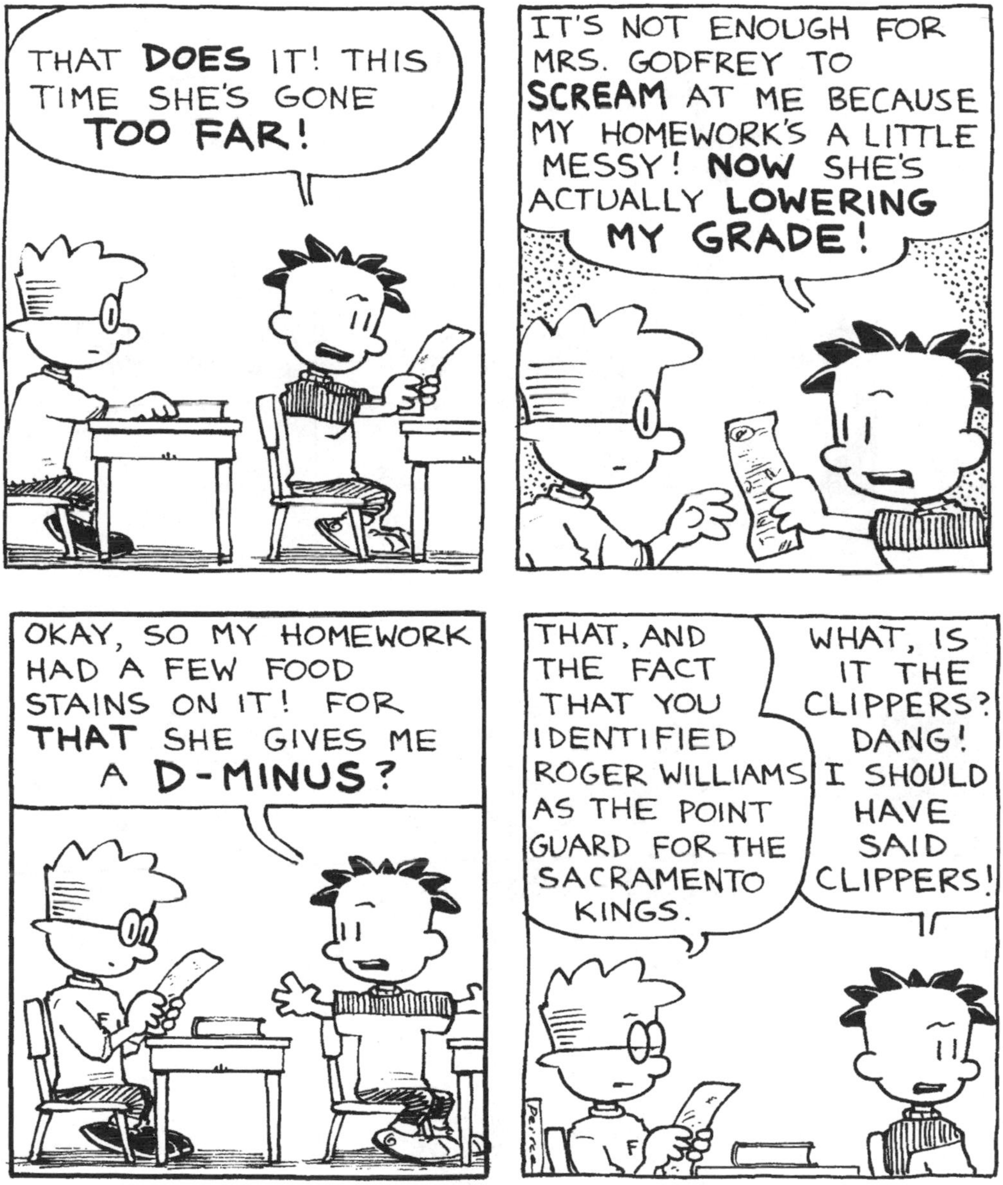
THAT DOES IT! THIS TIME SHE'S GONE TOO FAR!
IT'S NOT ENOUGH FOR MRS. GODFREY TO SCREAM AT ME BECAUSE MY HOMEWORK'S A LITTLE MESSY! NOW SHE'S ACTUALLY LOWERING MY GRADE!
OKAY, SO MY HOMEWORK HAD A FEW FOOD STAINS ON IT! FOR THAT SHE GIVES ME A D-MINUS?
THAT, AND THE FACT THAT YOU IDENTIFIED ROGER WILLIAMS AS THE POINT GUARD FOR THE SACRAMENTO KINGS.
WHAT, IS IT THE CLIPPERS? DANG! I SHOULD HAVE SAID CLIPPERS!

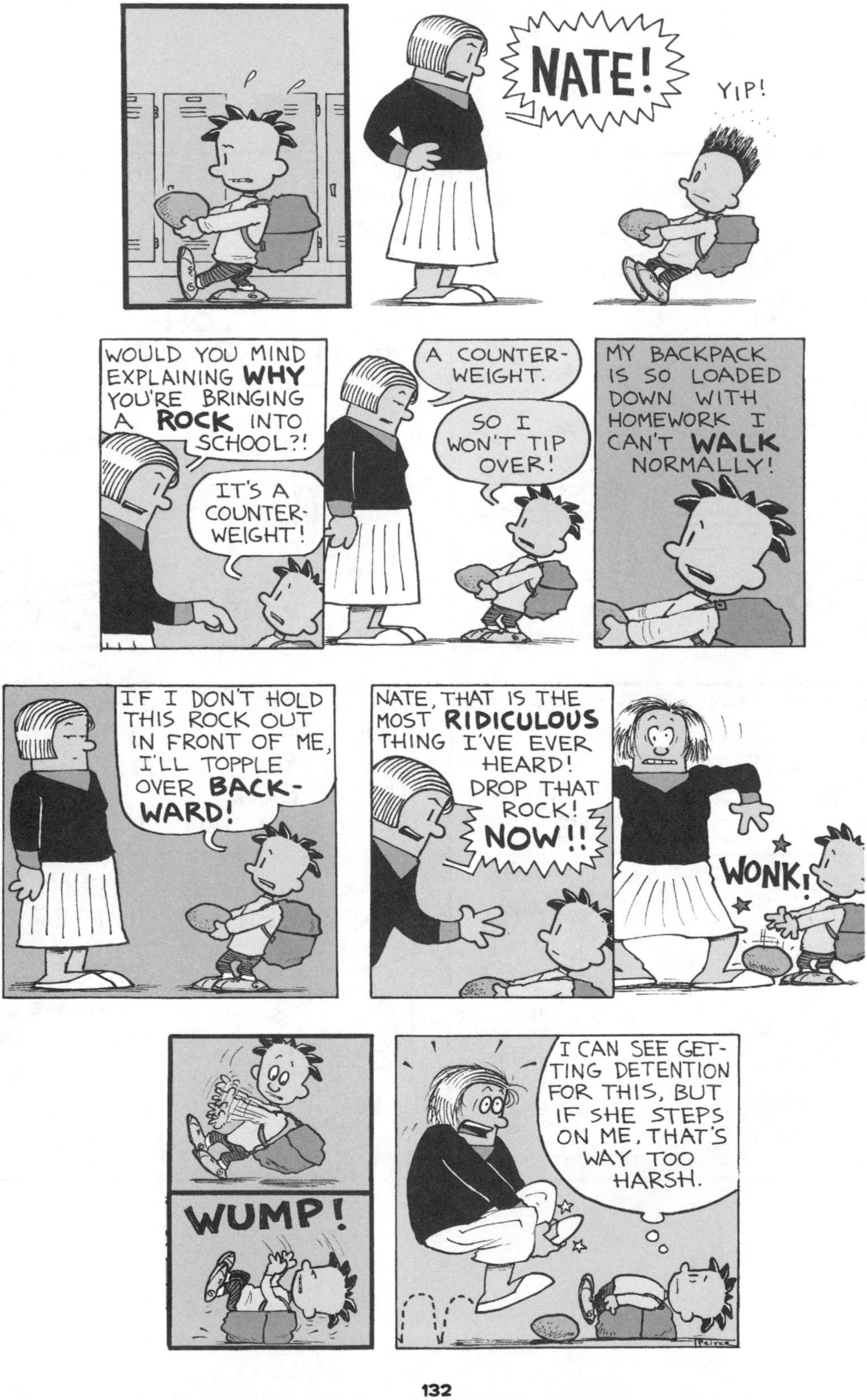
NATE!
YIP!
WOULD YOU MIND EXPLAINING **WHY** YOU'RE BRINGING A **ROCK** INTO SCHOOL?!
IT'S A COUNTER-WEIGHT!
A COUNTER-WEIGHT.
SO I WON'T TIP OVER!
MY BACKPACK IS SO LOADED DOWN WITH HOMEWORK I CAN'T **WALK** NORMALLY!
IF I DON'T HOLD THIS ROCK OUT IN FRONT OF ME, I'LL TOPPLE OVER **BACK-WARD!**
NATE, THAT IS THE MOST **RIDICULOUS** THING I'VE EVER HEARD! DROP THAT ROCK! **NOW!!**
WONK!
WUMP!
I CAN SEE GET-TING DETENTION FOR THIS, BUT IF SHE STEPS ON ME, THAT'S WAY TOO HARSH.
Peirce

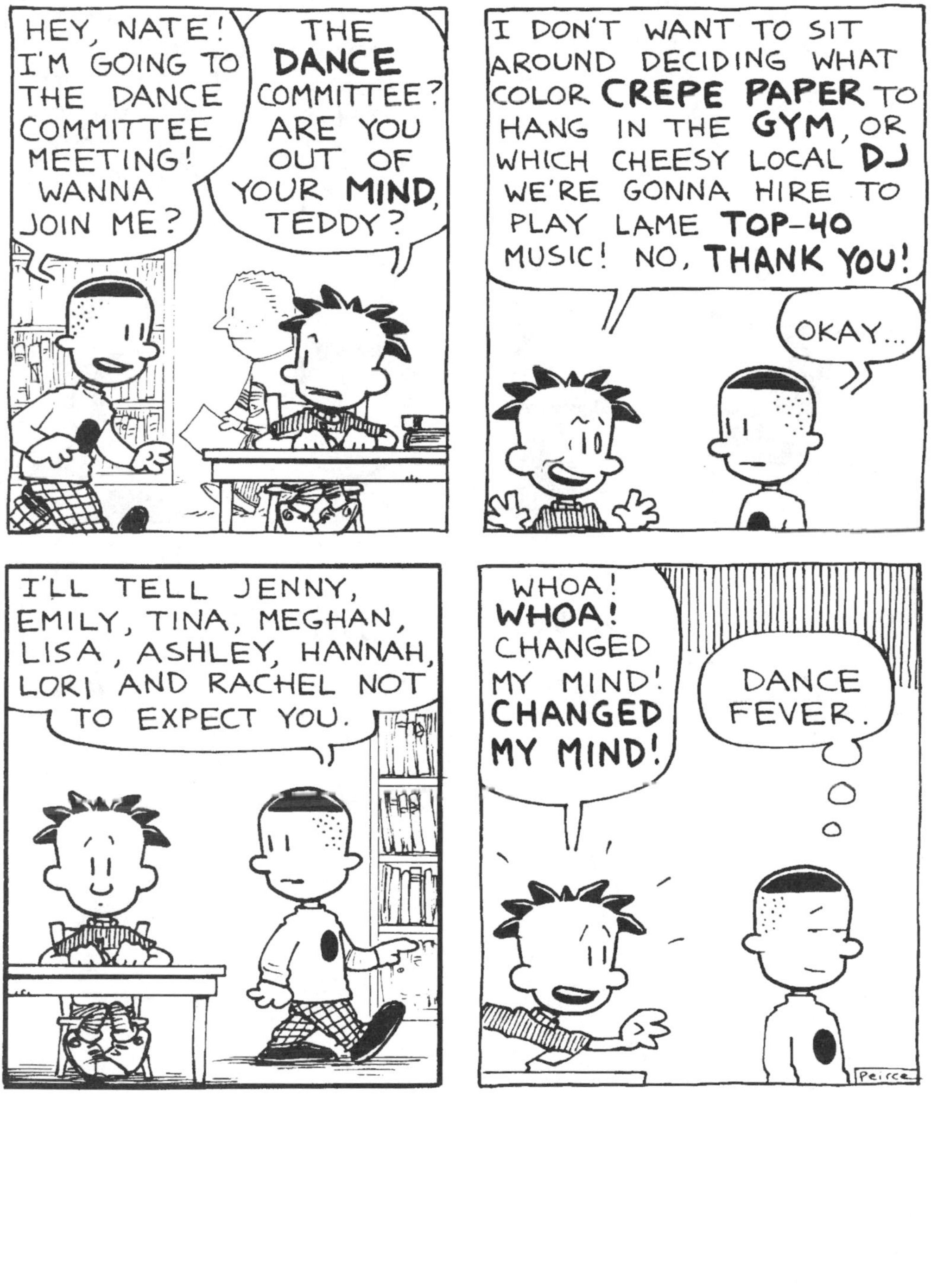
HEY, NATE! I'M GOING TO THE DANCE COMMITTEE MEETING! WANNA JOIN ME?
THE **DANCE** COMMITTEE? ARE YOU OUT OF YOUR **MIND**, TEDDY?
I DON'T WANT TO SIT AROUND DECIDING WHAT COLOR **CREPE PAPER** TO HANG IN THE **GYM**, OR WHICH CHEESY LOCAL **DJ** WE'RE GONNA HIRE TO PLAY LAME **TOP-40** MUSIC! NO, **THANK YOU**!
OKAY...
I'LL TELL JENNY, EMILY, TINA, MEGHAN, LISA, ASHLEY, HANNAH, LORI AND RACHEL NOT TO EXPECT YOU.
WHOA! **WHOA!** CHANGED MY MIND! **CHANGED MY MIND!**
DANCE FEVER.
Peirce

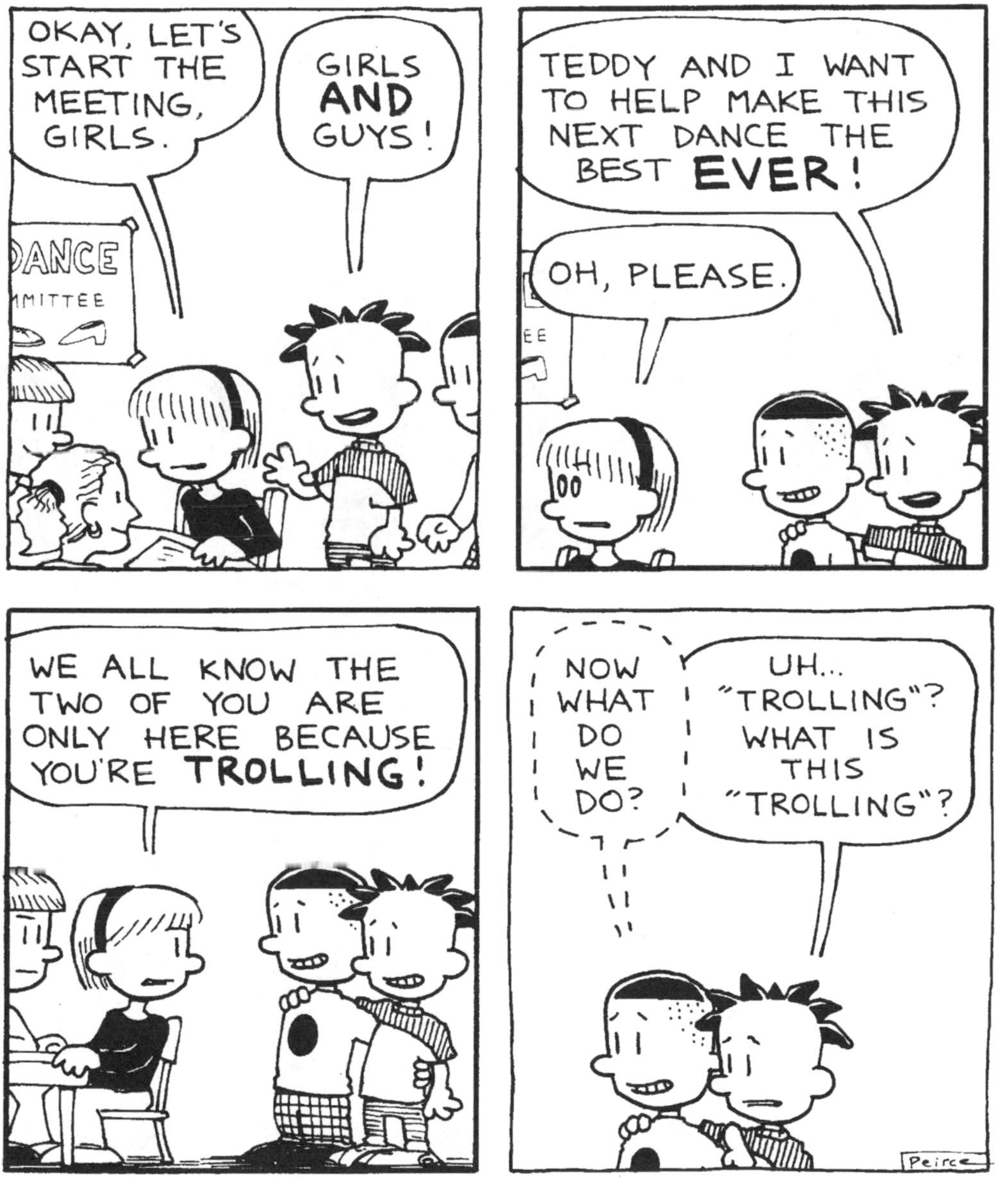
OKAY, LET'S START THE MEETING, GIRLS.
GIRLS **AND** GUYS!
DANCE
MMITTEE
TEDDY AND I WANT TO HELP MAKE THIS NEXT DANCE THE BEST **EVER**!
OH, PLEASE.
WE ALL KNOW THE TWO OF YOU ARE ONLY HERE BECAUSE YOU'RE **TROLLING**!
NOW WHAT DO WE DO?
UH... "TROLLING"? WHAT IS THIS "TROLLING"?
Peirce

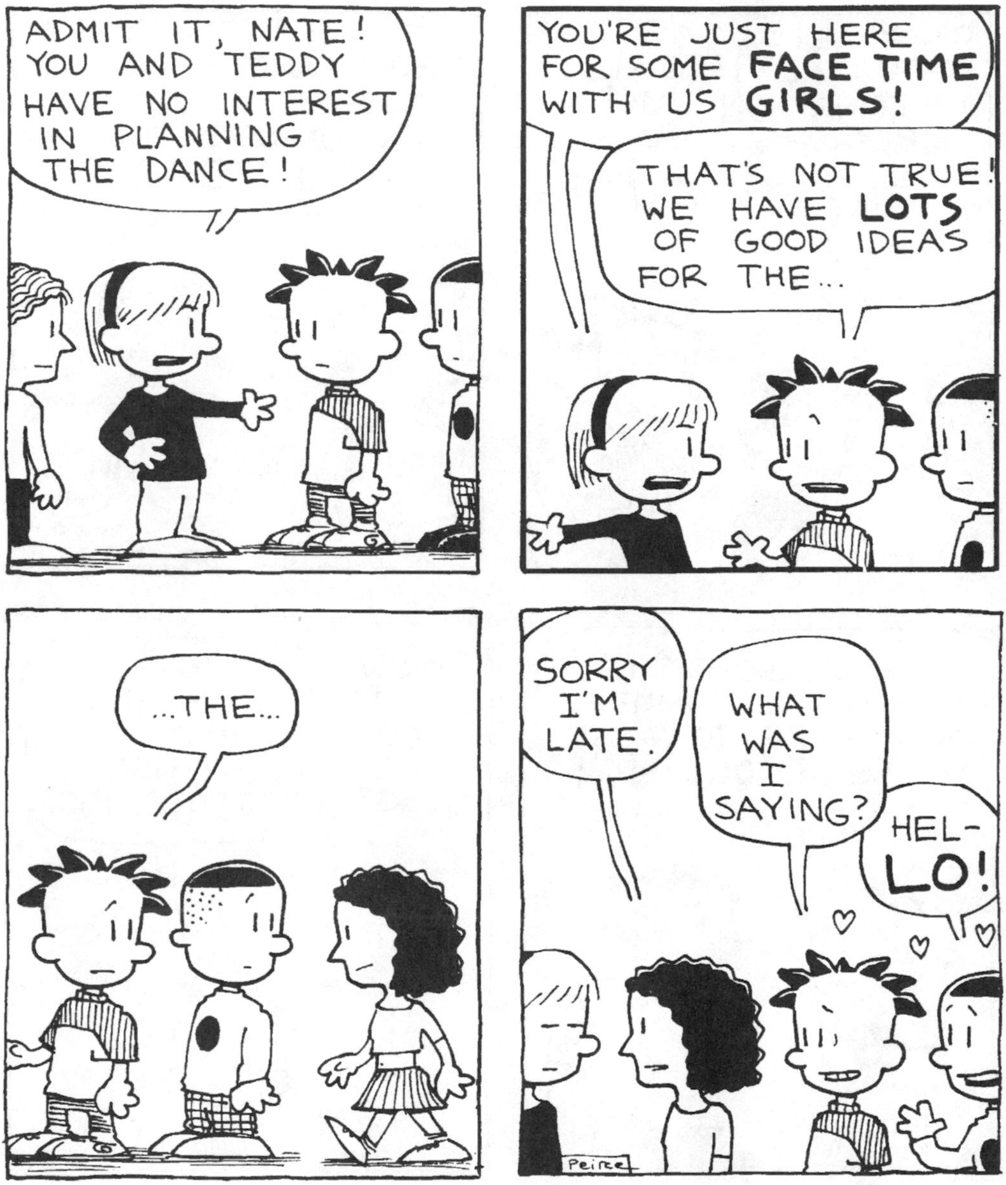
ADMIT IT, NATE! YOU AND TEDDY HAVE NO INTEREST IN PLANNING THE DANCE!
YOU'RE JUST HERE FOR SOME **FACE TIME** WITH US **GIRLS**!
THAT'S NOT TRUE! WE HAVE **LOTS** OF GOOD IDEAS FOR THE...
...THE...
SORRY I'M LATE.
WHAT WAS I SAYING?
HEL-**LO**!
Peirce

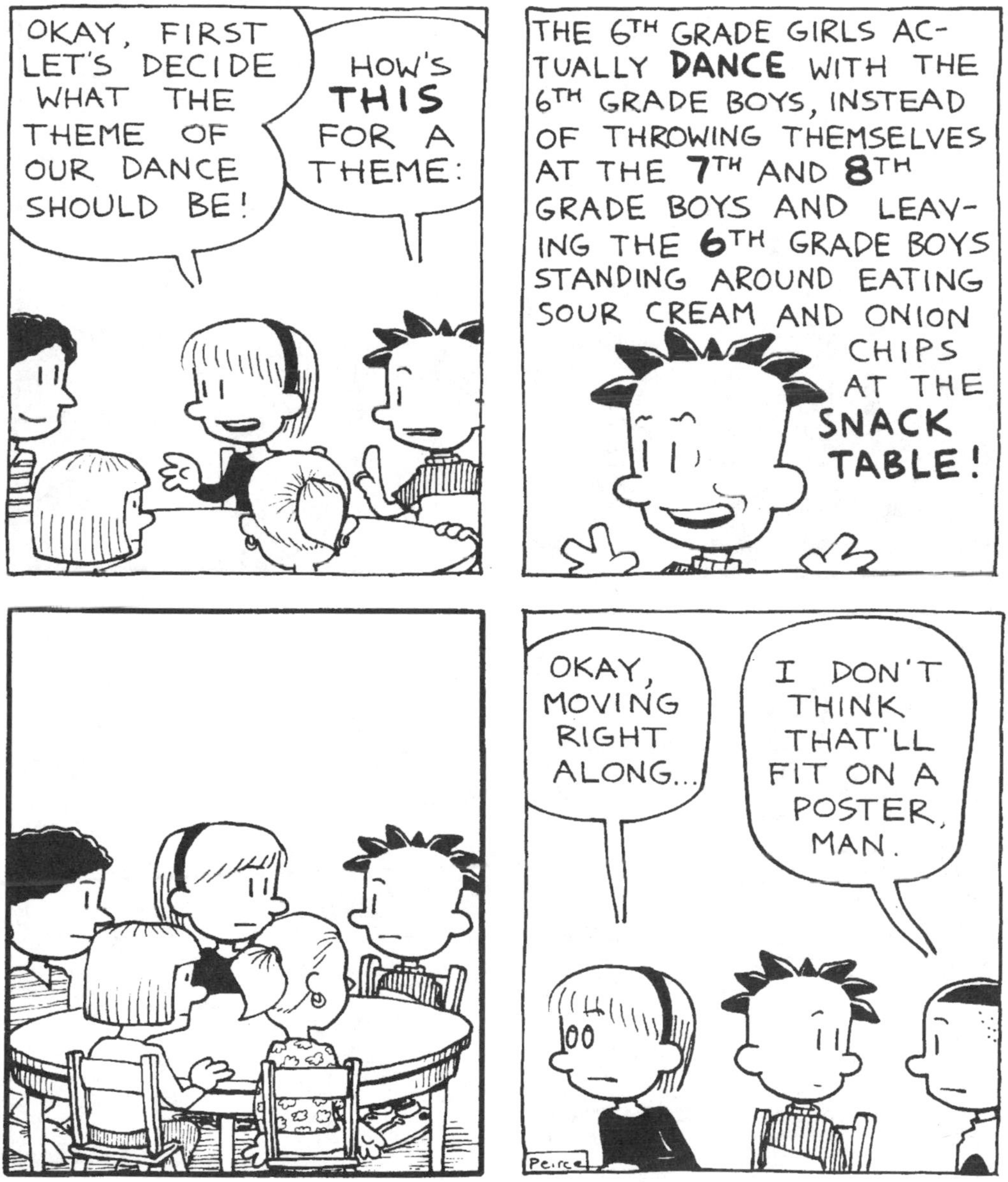
OKAY, FIRST LET'S DECIDE WHAT THE THEME OF OUR DANCE SHOULD BE!
HOW'S THIS FOR A THEME:
THE 6TH GRADE GIRLS ACTUALLY DANCE WITH THE 6TH GRADE BOYS, INSTEAD OF THROWING THEMSELVES AT THE 7TH AND 8TH GRADE BOYS AND LEAVING THE 6TH GRADE BOYS STANDING AROUND EATING SOUR CREAM AND ONION CHIPS AT THE SNACK TABLE!
OKAY, MOVING RIGHT ALONG...
I DON'T THINK THAT'LL FIT ON A POSTER, MAN.
Peirce

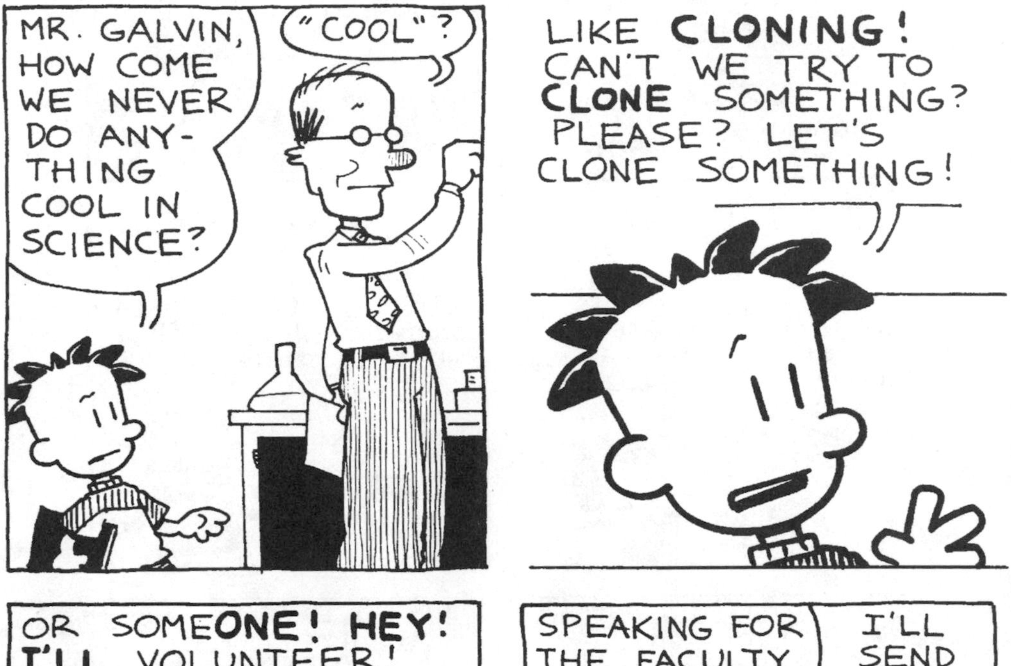
MR. GALVIN, HOW COME WE NEVER DO ANY-THING COOL IN SCIENCE?
"COOL"?
LIKE **CLONING**! CAN'T WE TRY TO **CLONE** SOMETHING? PLEASE? LET'S CLONE SOMETHING!
OR SOME**ONE**! **HEY**! **I'LL** VOLUNTEER! **I'D** GET CLONED IN A **HEART**BEAT! LET'S CLONE **ME**!
SPEAKING FOR THE FACULTY, NATE, ONE OF YOU IS QUITE ENOUGH.
I'LL SEND MY **CLONE** TO SOCIAL STUDIES, WHILE **I** WATCH CARTOONS IN THE A.V. ROOM!
Peirce

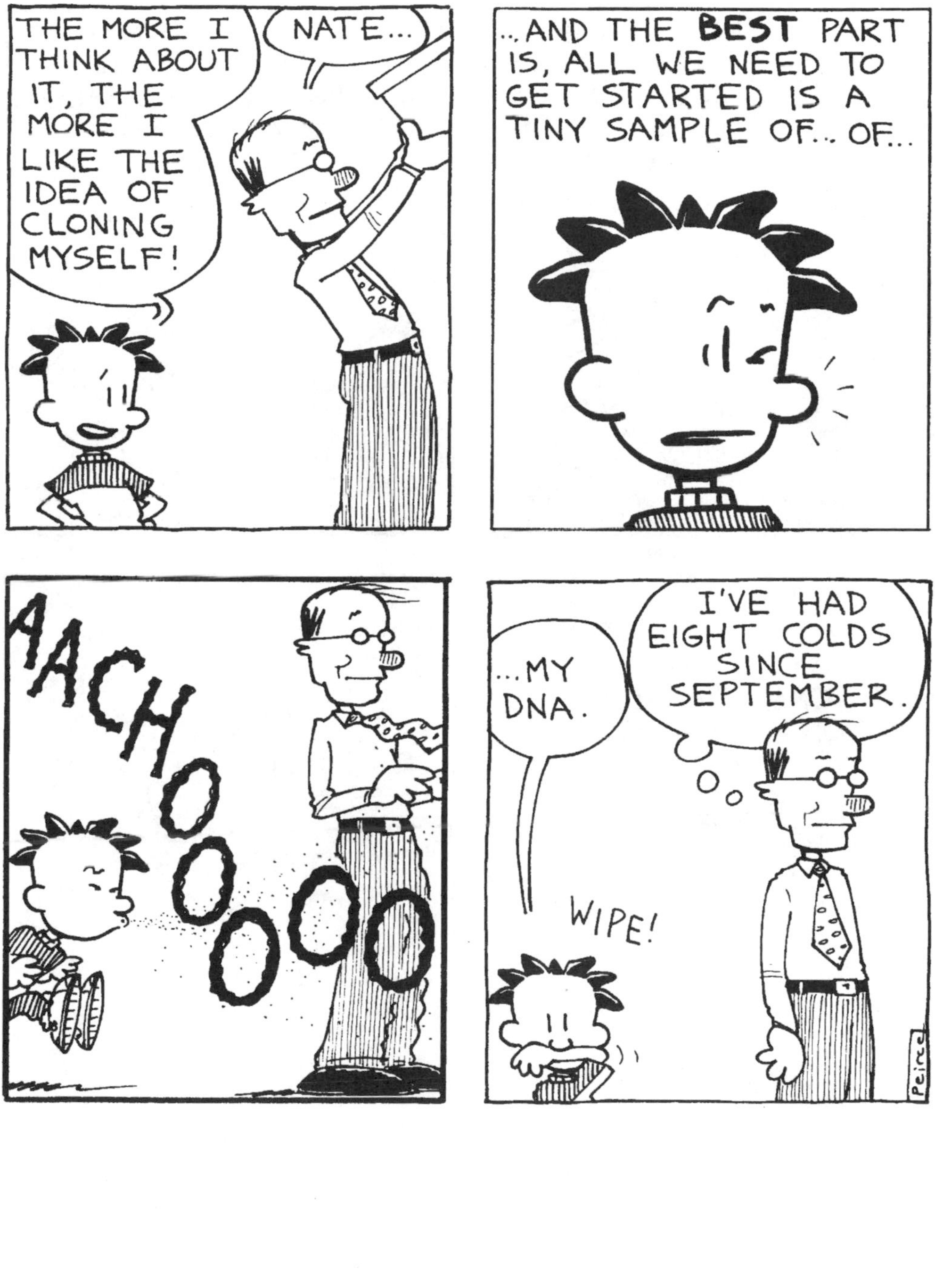
THE MORE I THINK ABOUT IT, THE MORE I LIKE THE IDEA OF CLONING MYSELF!
NATE...
...AND THE **BEST** PART IS, ALL WE NEED TO GET STARTED IS A TINY SAMPLE OF... OF...
AACHOOOOOO
...MY DNA.
I'VE HAD EIGHT COLDS SINCE SEPTEMBER.
WIPE!
Peirce

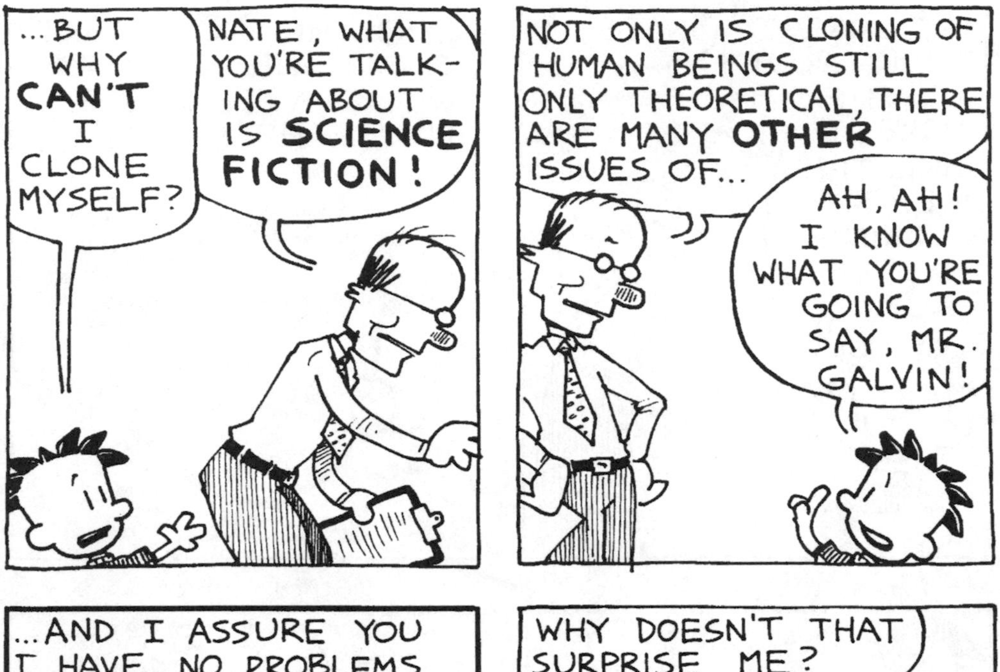
...BUT WHY **CAN'T** I CLONE MYSELF?
NATE, WHAT YOU'RE TALKING ABOUT IS **SCIENCE FICTION**!
NOT ONLY IS CLONING OF HUMAN BEINGS STILL ONLY THEORETICAL, THERE ARE MANY **OTHER** ISSUES OF...
AH, AH! I KNOW WHAT YOU'RE GOING TO SAY, MR. GALVIN!
...AND I ASSURE YOU I HAVE NO PROBLEMS AT ALL WITH THE **ETHICAL RAMIFICATIONS** OF CLONING MYSELF!
WHY DOESN'T THAT SURPRISE ME?
NOW IF **MRS. GODFREY** WANTED TO GET CLONED!... **THEN** WE'D HAVE A PROBLEM!
Peirce

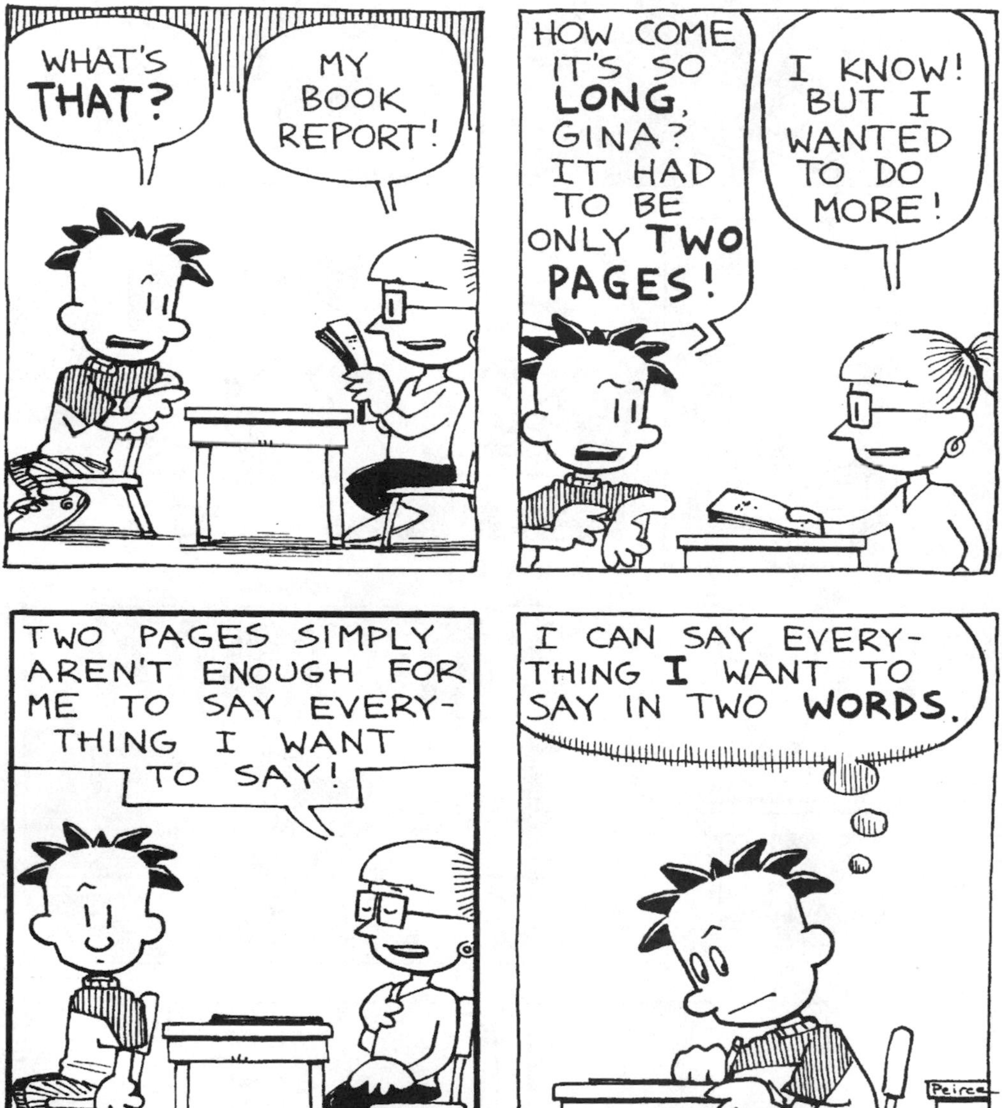
WHAT'S THAT?
MY BOOK REPORT!
HOW COME IT'S SO LONG, GINA? IT HAD TO BE ONLY TWO PAGES!
I KNOW! BUT I WANTED TO DO MORE!
TWO PAGES SIMPLY AREN'T ENOUGH FOR ME TO SAY EVERY-THING I WANT TO SAY!
I CAN SAY EVERY-THING I WANT TO SAY IN TWO WORDS.
Peirce

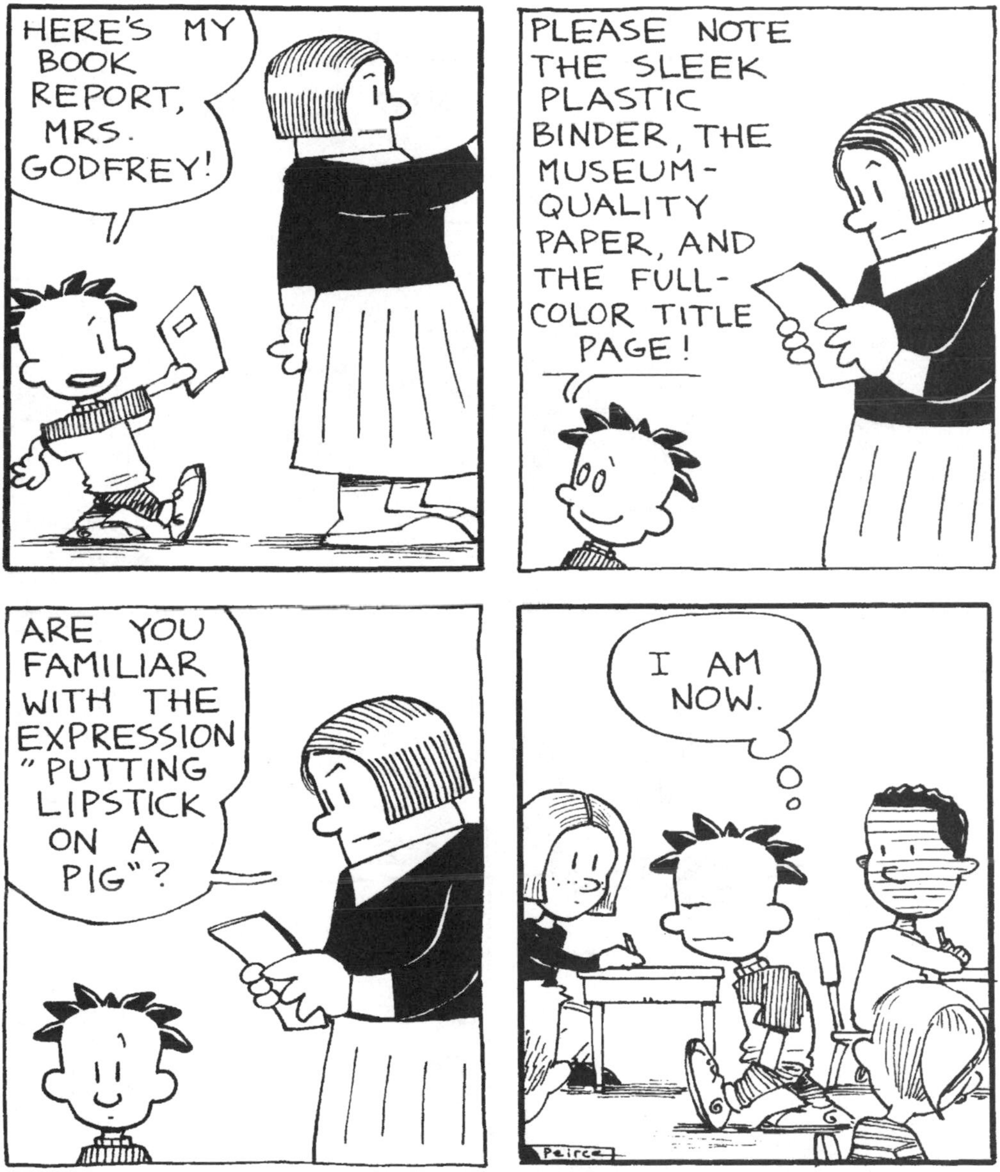
HERE'S MY BOOK REPORT, MRS. GODFREY!
PLEASE NOTE THE SLEEK PLASTIC BINDER, THE MUSEUM-QUALITY PAPER, AND THE FULL-COLOR TITLE PAGE!
ARE YOU FAMILIAR WITH THE EXPRESSION "PUTTING LIPSTICK ON A PIG"?
I AM NOW.
Peirce

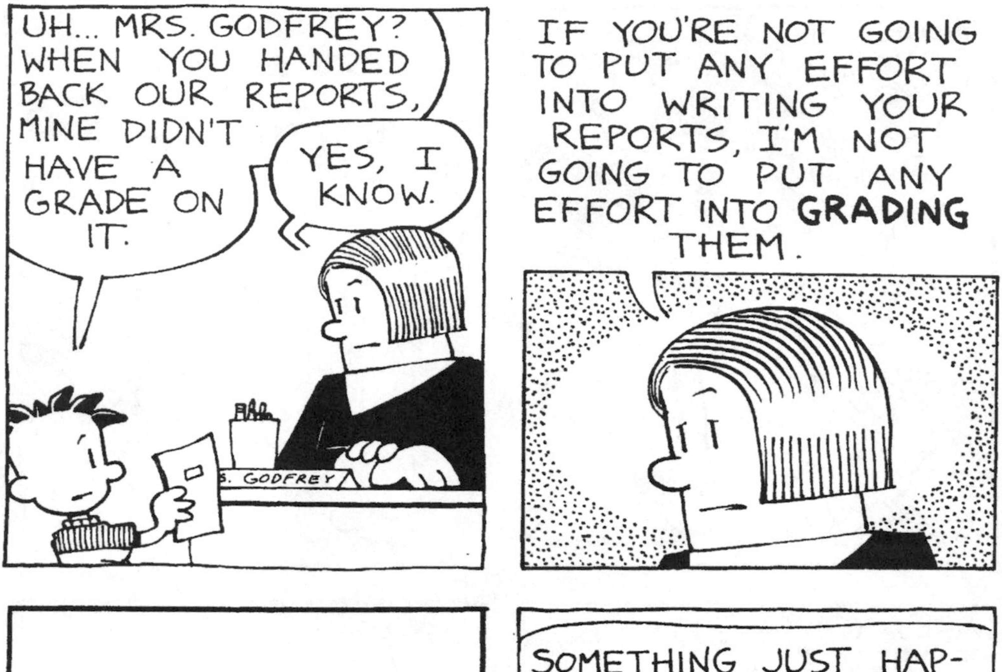
UH... MRS. GODFREY? WHEN YOU HANDED BACK OUR REPORTS, MINE DIDN'T HAVE A GRADE ON IT.
YES, I KNOW.
S. GODFREY
IF YOU'RE NOT GOING TO PUT ANY EFFORT INTO WRITING YOUR REPORTS, I'M NOT GOING TO PUT ANY EFFORT INTO **GRADING** THEM.
MRS. GODFREY
SOMETHING JUST HAPPENED THAT'S EITHER VERY, VERY GOOD OR VERY, VERY BAD.
Peirce

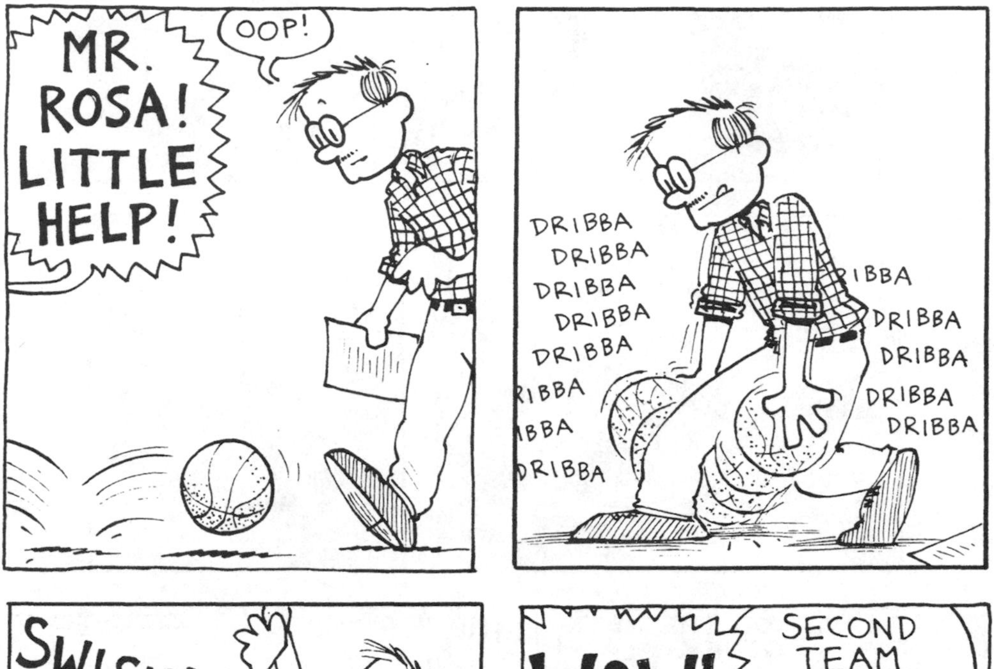
MR. ROSA! LITTLE HELP!
OOP!
DRIBBA DRIBBA DRIBBA DRIBBA DRIBBA
SWISH!
WOW!
SECOND TEAM ALL-STATE, 1974.
Peirce

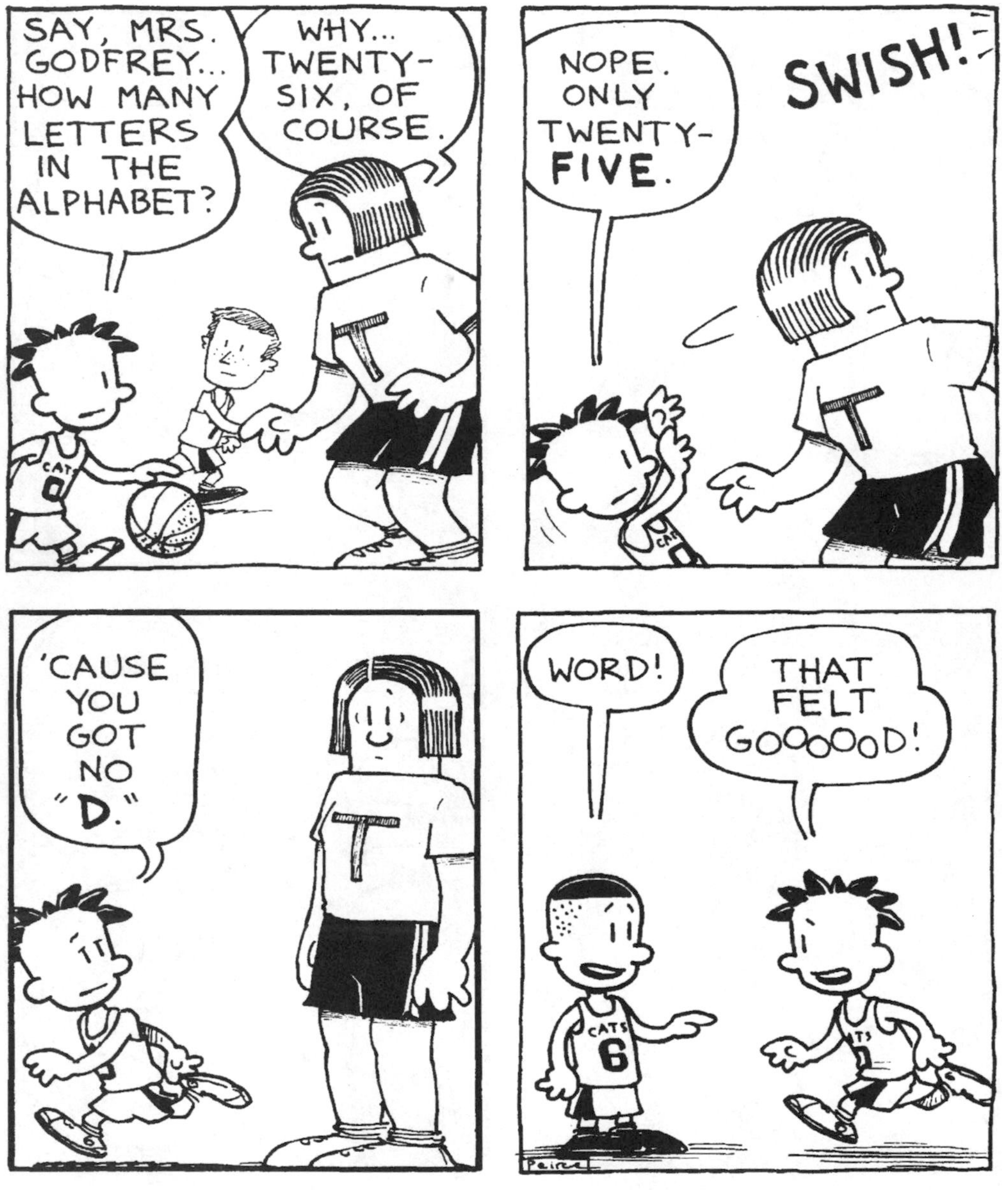
SAY, MRS. GODFREY... HOW MANY LETTERS IN THE ALPHABET?
WHY... TWENTY-SIX, OF COURSE.
NOPE. ONLY TWENTY-FIVE.
SWISH!
'CAUSE YOU GOT NO "D."
WORD!
THAT FELT GOOOOOOD!
CATS
6
Peirce

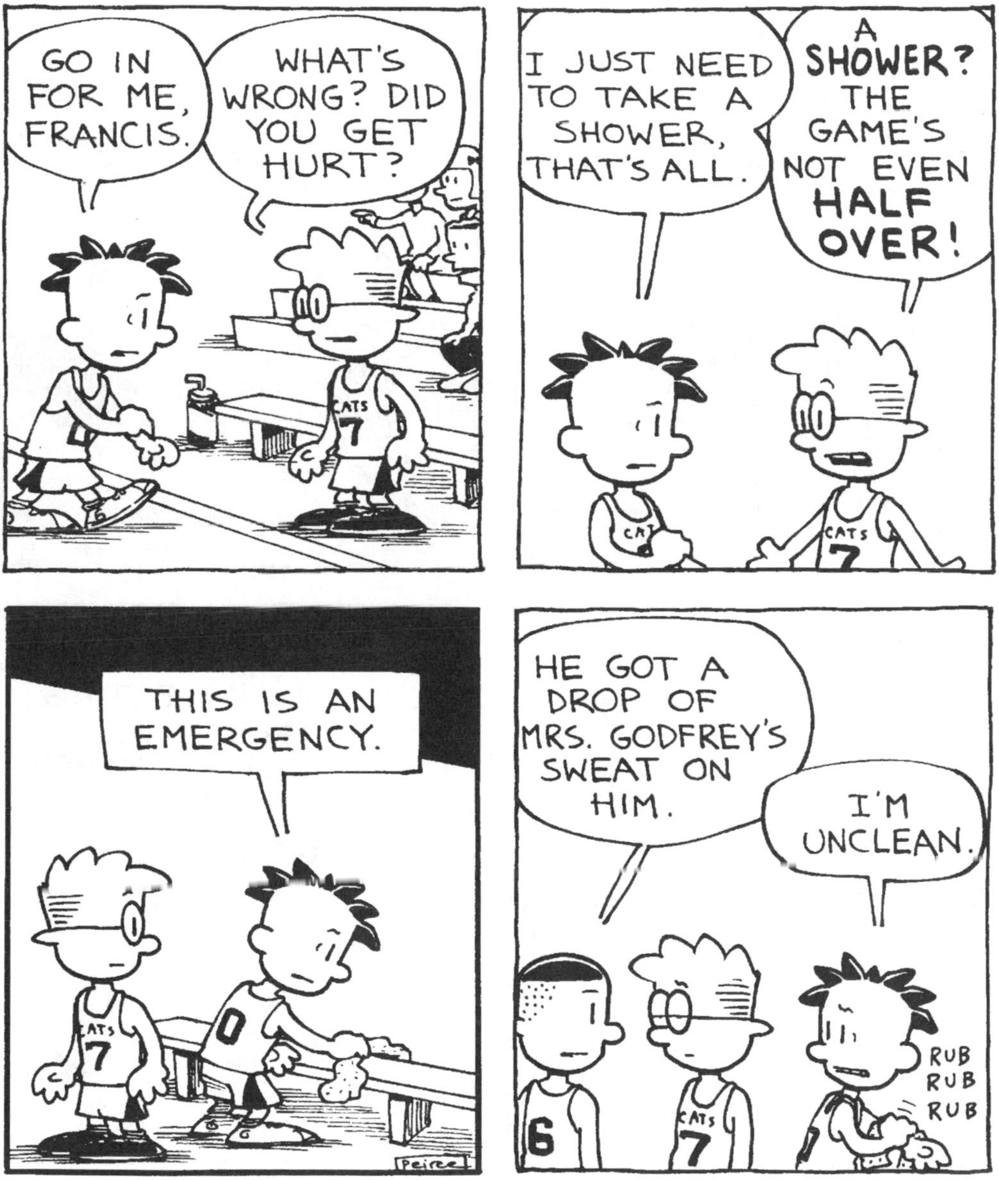
GO IN FOR ME, FRANCIS.
WHAT'S WRONG? DID YOU GET HURT?
CATS 7
I JUST NEED TO TAKE A SHOWER, THAT'S ALL.
A **SHOWER**? THE GAME'S NOT EVEN **HALF OVER**!
THIS IS AN EMERGENCY.
HE GOT A DROP OF MRS. GODFREY'S SWEAT ON HIM.
I'M UNCLEAN.
RUB RUB RUB
Peirce

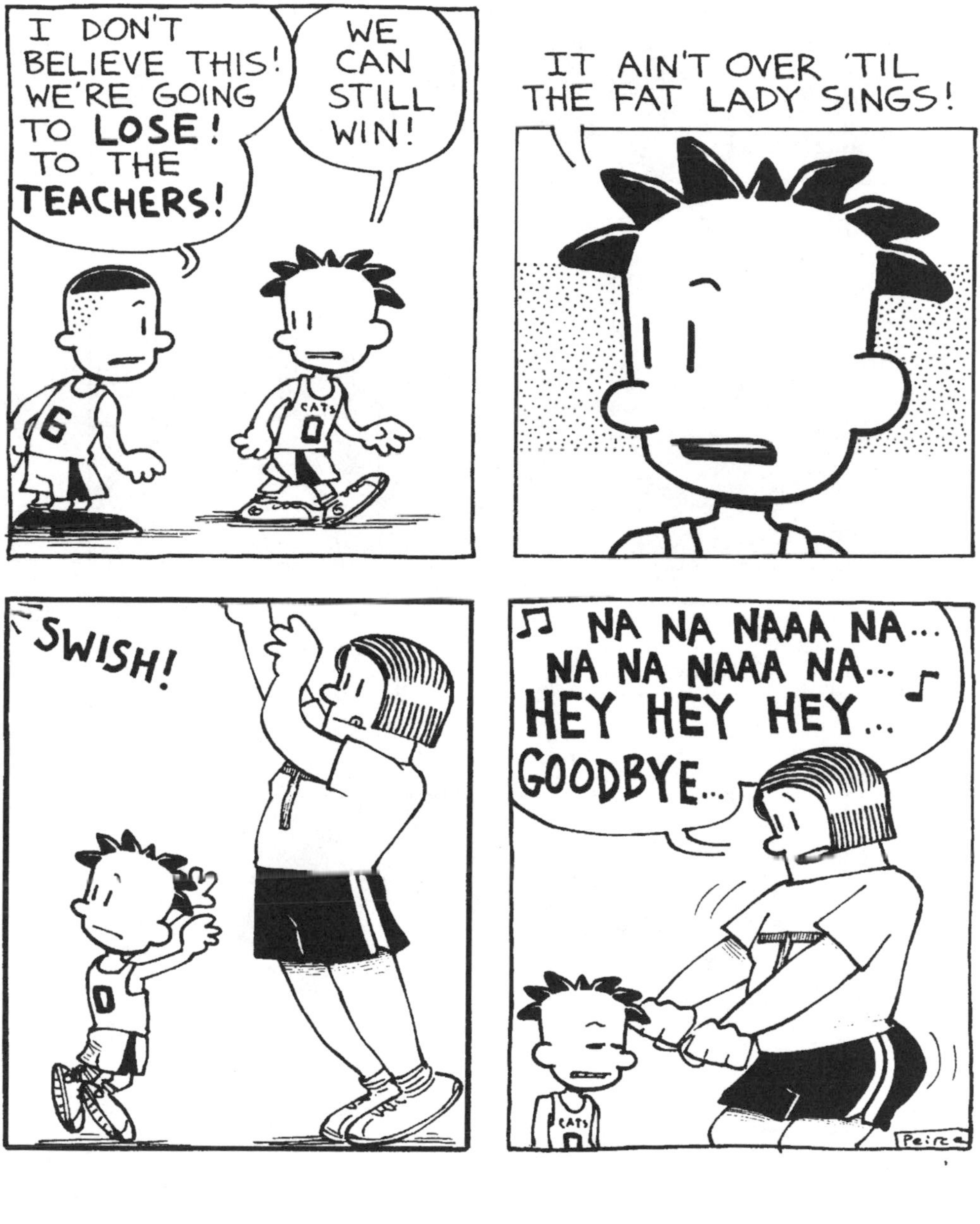
I DON'T BELIEVE THIS! WE'RE GOING TO **LOSE**! TO THE **TEACHERS**!
WE CAN STILL WIN!
IT AIN'T OVER 'TIL THE FAT LADY SINGS!
SWISH!
NA NA NAAA NA... NA NA NAAA NA... HEY HEY HEY... GOODBYE...
Peirce

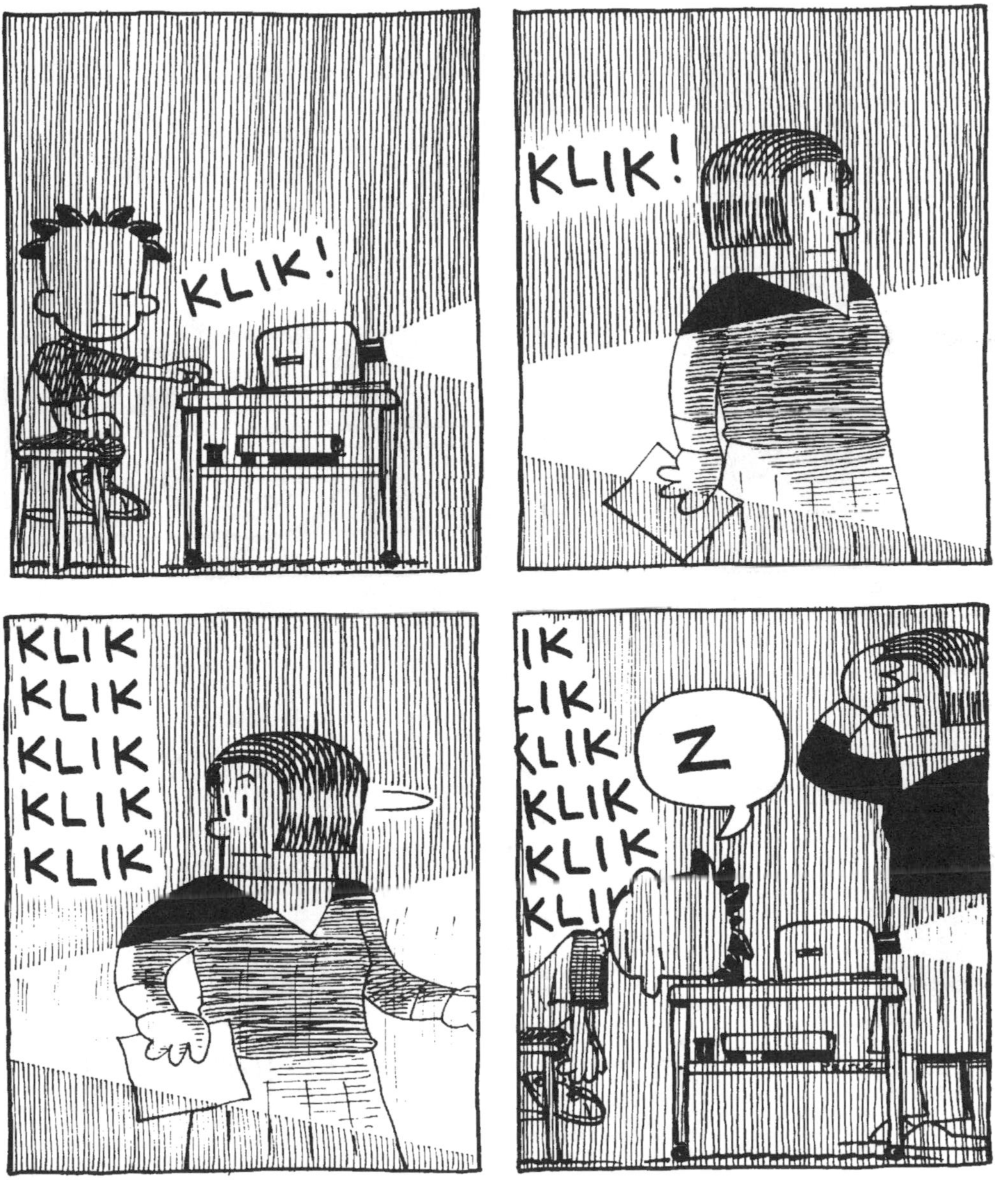
KLIK!
KLIK!
KLIK
KLIK
KLIK
KLIK
KLIK
IK
LIK
KLIK
KLIK
KLIK
KLI
Z

ARTUR IS HOPELESS! I'M GOING TO TUTOR HIM.

TUTOR HIM? IN **WHAT**?

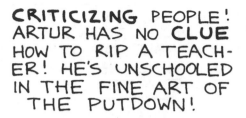

CRITICIZING PEOPLE! ARTUR HAS NO **CLUE** HOW TO RIP A TEACHER! HE'S UNSCHOOLED IN THE FINE ART OF THE PUTDOWN!

SO YOU'RE GOING TO TEACH ARTUR HOW TO SAY INSULTING THINGS ABOUT OTHER PEOPLE.

EXACTLY!

YOU'RE SUCH AN IDIOT.

RIGHT, STUFF LIKE THAT. ONLY MORE IMAGINATIVE.

176

183

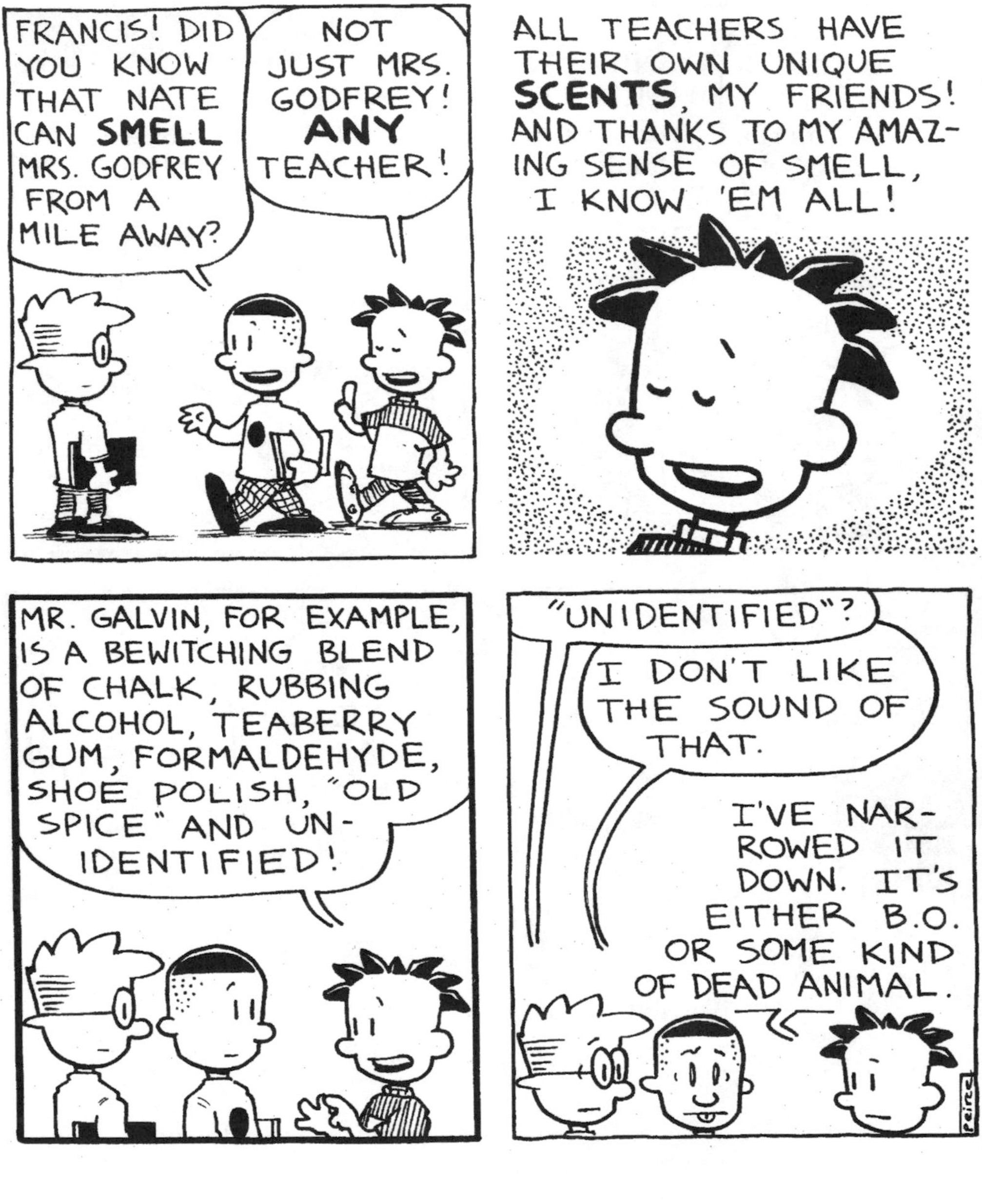

FRANCIS! DID YOU KNOW THAT NATE CAN **SMELL** MRS. GODFREY FROM A MILE AWAY?
NOT JUST MRS. GODFREY! **ANY** TEACHER!
ALL TEACHERS HAVE THEIR OWN UNIQUE **SCENTS**, MY FRIENDS! AND THANKS TO MY AMAZING SENSE OF SMELL, I KNOW 'EM ALL!
MR. GALVIN, FOR EXAMPLE, IS A BEWITCHING BLEND OF CHALK, RUBBING ALCOHOL, TEABERRY GUM, FORMALDEHYDE, SHOE POLISH, "OLD SPICE" AND UNIDENTIFIED!
"UNIDENTIFIED"?
I DON'T LIKE THE SOUND OF THAT.
I'VE NARROWED IT DOWN. IT'S EITHER B.O. OR SOME KIND OF DEAD ANIMAL.
PEIRCE

189

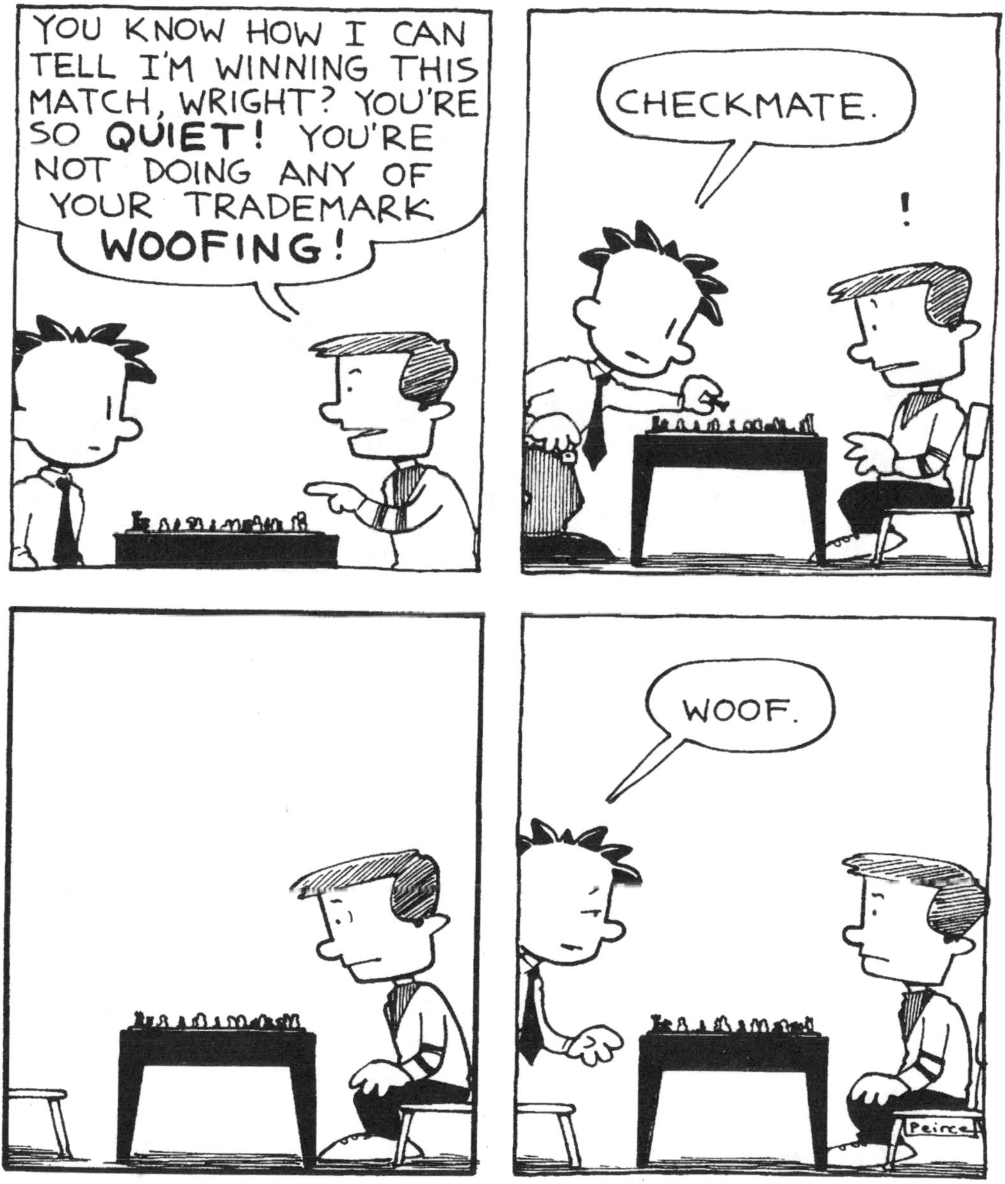
YOU KNOW HOW I CAN TELL I'M WINNING THIS MATCH, WRIGHT? YOU'RE SO **QUIET**! YOU'RE NOT DOING ANY OF YOUR TRADEMARK **WOOFING**!
CHECKMATE.
!
WOOF.
Peirce

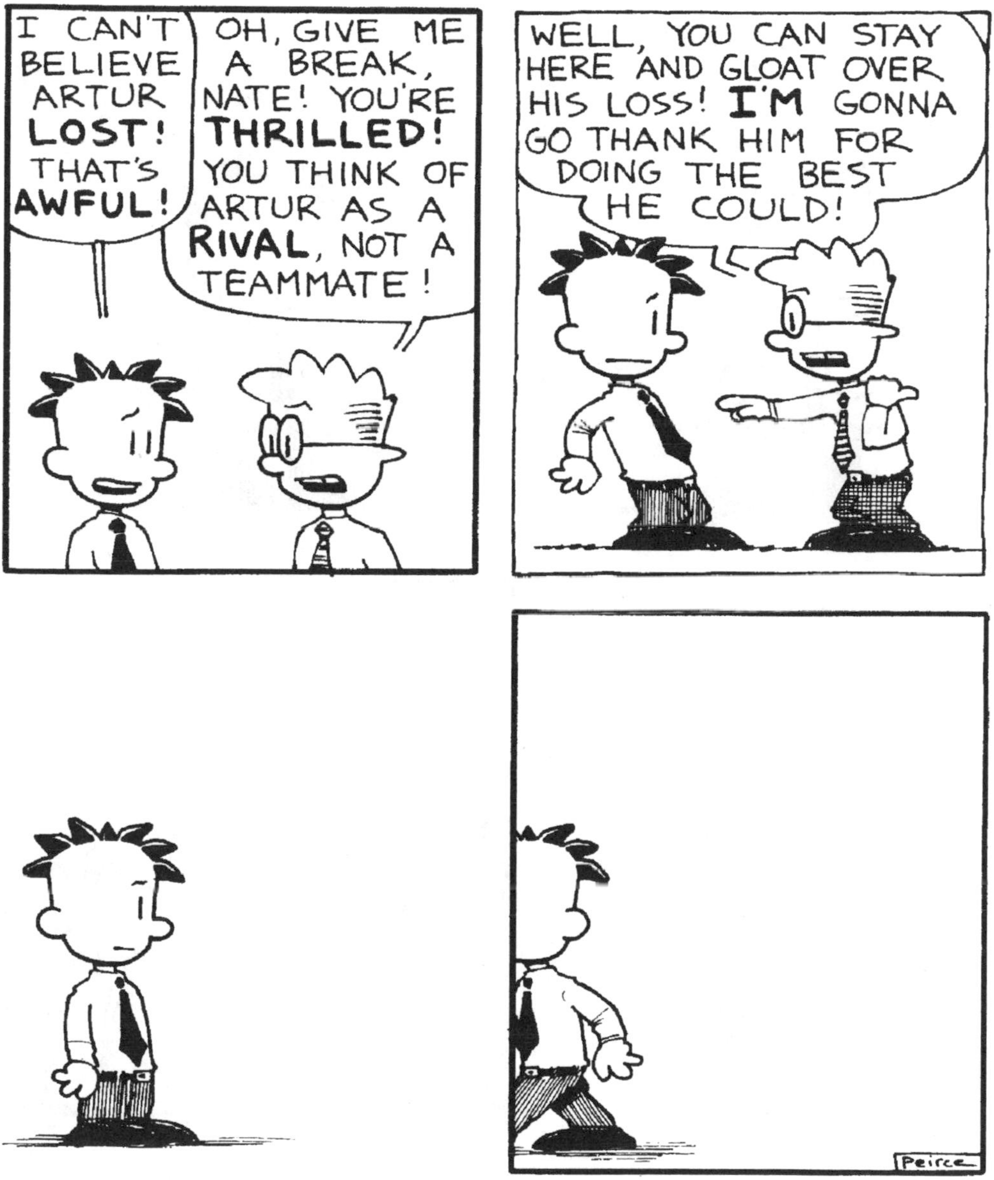
I CAN'T BELIEVE ARTUR LOST! THAT'S AWFUL!
OH, GIVE ME A BREAK, NATE! YOU'RE THRILLED! YOU THINK OF ARTUR AS A RIVAL, NOT A TEAMMATE!
WELL, YOU CAN STAY HERE AND GLOAT OVER HIS LOSS! I'M GONNA GO THANK HIM FOR DOING THE BEST HE COULD!
Peirce

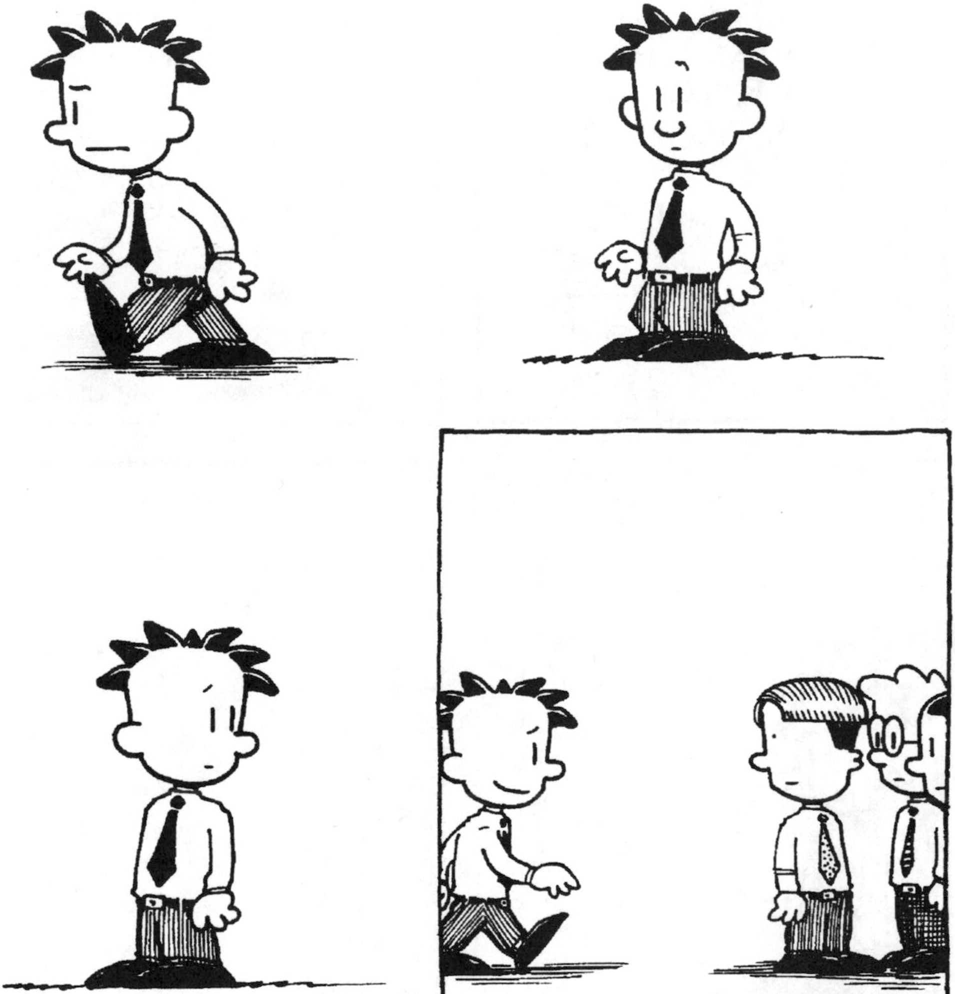
Peirce

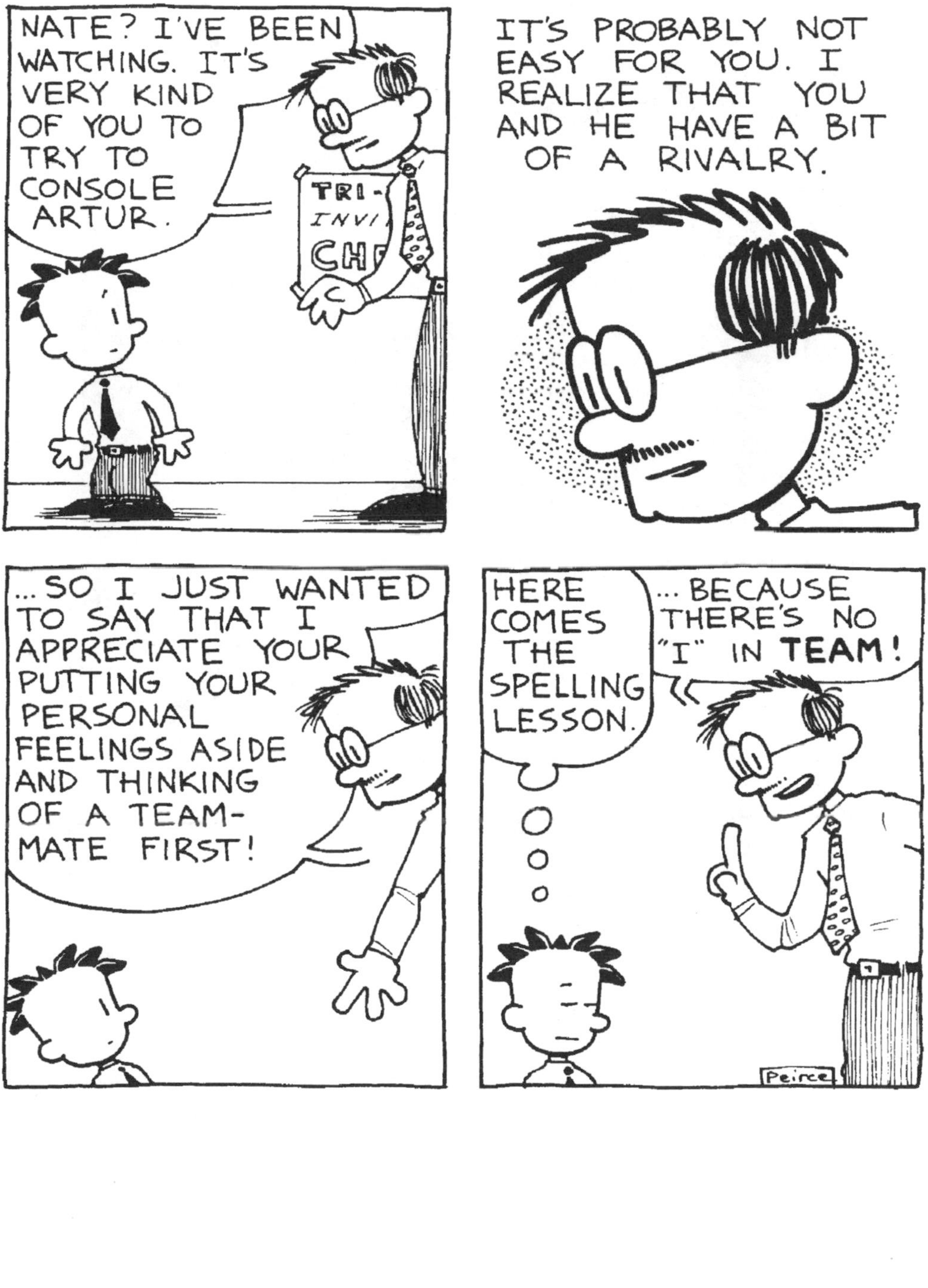
NATE? I'VE BEEN WATCHING. IT'S VERY KIND OF YOU TO TRY TO CONSOLE ARTUR.
TRI-
INVI
CH
IT'S PROBABLY NOT EASY FOR YOU. I REALIZE THAT YOU AND HE HAVE A BIT OF A RIVALRY.
...SO I JUST WANTED TO SAY THAT I APPRECIATE YOUR PUTTING YOUR PERSONAL FEELINGS ASIDE AND THINKING OF A TEAM-MATE FIRST!
HERE COMES THE SPELLING LESSON.
...BECAUSE THERE'S NO "I" IN **TEAM**!
Peirce